CUT FROM STRONG CLOTH
Linda Harris Sittig

Bee.

Merry Christmas, December 25. 2014
We personally know the
author
C.M.

Freedom Forge Press, LLC
www.FreedomForgePress.com

Cut From Strong Cloth

by Linda Harris Sittig

Published by Freedom Forge Press, LLC

www.FreedomForgePress.com

ISBN: 978-1-940553-02-3

This book is dedicated to—

My mother Mildred, who shared the stories ~
My husband Jim, who encouraged me to write them down ~
My ancestor Ellen Canavan, who inspired this novel ~

Cut From Strong Cloth

TABLE OF CONTENTS

Well-behaved women make history when they do the unexpected, when they create and preserve records, and when later generations care.

Well-Behaved Women Seldom Make History
By Laurel Thatcher Ulrich

CHAPTER 1

April 1855

The lifeless body slid down the tilted plank and splashed into the frigid waters of the Atlantic.

Fourteen-year-old Ellen Canavan riveted her gaze on the ocean's surface and held her breath. Her father's shrouded corpse bobbled for a moment. *Please, God, don't let the fish eat him.* Then the stones inside the burial cloth pulled his feet down.

Unaware of the damp wind whipping her hair or the sun slipping behind grey clouds, she averted her eyes at the last moment as the ocean current sucked him under. Then she exhaled.

A man standing behind her coughed and hawked up a gob of phlegm. He walked to the railing and proceeded to spit the wad off into the sea. How dare him! She turned away in agony and disbelief. Her legs wobbled a bit, and she started to crumple when her brother Patrick brought his hand under her arm and helped her to remain upright.

"Patrick," she whispered.

"Be strong, Ellen. 'Tis what Da would have expected of us." Ten years her senior, Patrick towered above her and stood with jaw squared and shoulders rigid.

The ship's timbers groaned as a strong wave rammed the ship, and the passengers grasped each other. Ellen's eyes opened wide as she peered up at the masts, fearful that one might break and come crashing down on the deck. She pressed herself into her brother and clasped her woolen shawl tighter across her chest. *Da wove this shawl for me. I hope it can protect me. St. Brigid, give me courage. Holy Mary, forgive me my sins.* Ellen whispered the prayer learned from Da, but her thin frame trembled with the knowledge that she had been the cause of her father's death.

She gazed at her brother, whose normal rosy-cheeked complexion, like hers, had paled from all the hours spent below deck; but he remained stoic. Then she turned to look at the wailing women who, in the Irish tradition, were sending Da off to meet the angels in heaven. *None of them know I'm responsible for this.*

"Patrick," she murmured. "How will we ever get on without him?"

Patrick shrugged. "We have to survive."

Ellen peered over at her mother, usually in full command of all situations, but who now stood shaken and forlorn, clothed in a borrowed mourning dress. An unexpected feeling of tenderness for her mother thumped in Ellen's chest, but she did not act upon it. *Mam doesn't want me near her right now. If she knew the truth, she would hate me forever.*

As the priest led the group in one final prayer, Ellen heard keening wails drifting out over the greedy sea.

The wind shifted again. In the far distance, thunder crashed. Menacing clouds raced along the horizon. She steeled herself not to be afraid, but to remember how Da had taught her to conquer fear.

"When you're scared of something, Ellen, just ask St. Brigid to give you courage. That way you'll never be afraid of what's to come. Look fear right in the face and then spit in its eye. 'Tis the Canavan motto. That, and family sticks together. No matter what."

It was as if she could still hear his voice.

She tried to be courageous about his death, but guilt took over. The image of the whiskey bottle she had given Da would not disappear. Wedged behind a pile of broken timbers, she had stolen it hoping to ease his raucous coughing. He had winked and said, "No use telling Mam about this. We don't need her getting all riled up."

Ellen had told no one. Not even after Da started vomiting blood

into the chamber pot. Two days later, he was dead. How could she tell anyone about the rot-gut whiskey now?

The funeral bell tolled three times in conclusion, and the *S.S. Eleanora* continued to plow through the choppy waves. The funeral crowd scattered. Ellen's mother broke down sobbing, and Ellen found it hard to breathe. Grief too deep and pain too raw held her captive. Anguish rose from her stomach as bile in her throat.

She turned and vomited her breakfast tea on the deck. Neither Patrick nor her mother seemed to notice. She wiped her mouth on her sleeve and watched as Patrick turned from the priest and led his mother away. Not knowing what else to do, she sat down on a nearby coil of rope, burying her head in her arms. *Who will love me now? I was Da's favorite, and both Mam and Patrick know that.*

The tears finally came.

***

She stayed curled on the rope until rain soaked her shoulders. No one came looking for her, so she climbed back down the wooden ladder into steerage. The darkness of the hold with its putrid smells of stale urine and unwashed, sweat-stained bodies assaulted her. She maneuvered past the other passengers crammed together in berths until she arrived at her family's allotted space. Finding her mother asleep was a relief. Ellen could not face her just yet. Patrick was nowhere in sight.

Someone had prepared a meager funeral meal of stirabout. The mixture of thinned oatmeal with watery milk and a splash of molasses held no appeal. She climbed to the top berth, pulled off her rain-caked dress, wrapped herself in an old quilt, and reached for the rag doll of her cradle days. She had retrieved it from her valise the day Da died. A homemade gift from his hands, it was now a connection back to him. She lie down on the dingy straw-filled mattress and quickly plunged into the stupor of grief sleep.

All night, images of Da's shroud and the hilly pastures of back home kept appearing in her mind until everything blended together. In the dream she wandered as a child through the green fields dotted with

Cut From Strong Cloth

stones and sheep that punctuated the landscape of County Tyrone. She saw tufts of Da's sandy-colored hair jutting out from under his rough tweed cap and his big calloused hand cradling her small one. But then the stones changed into whiskey bottles, and Da was trying to drink each one. She struggled to pull the bottles away, but new ones kept appearing. She screamed. "No!"

Bolting upright in the bunk, her face soaked with tears, she looked around the berth. The commotion woke Patrick, sleeping in the other lower bunk, and he got up.

"Ellen, what's a matter? Did you have a bad dream? Come here."

She climbed down. "Oh God, I miss Da so!" She sought solace in Patrick's arms, burying her face in his rough woolen shirt. He offered no words of comfort, but just held her. Da had always been her real protector and it would be just three of them now—Mam, Patrick, and Ellen.

"Ellen, I think 'tis early morning. We can go up on deck for some fresh air before the sailors start their rounds."

They emerged on deck, and she shielded her eyes from the unaccustomed light of dawn. No matter which way she looked, an unending seascape of dull gray-green water met her view.

"Look, see over there? In just another three weeks we'll spy the coastline of Philadelphia. Just think, Ellen, soon we'll become Americans."

Where Philadelphia is, I no longer care. It will never be special. Da promised to let me be his weaving assistant there, and that willna happen now. She shivered.

"Are you cold? You should've brought a cover. I'll go back and get a wrap and check on Mam."

She watched Patrick retreat back into the hold and then turned her gaze to the continuous undulation of the waves.

The quiet of morning dissolved when a rowdy gang of four boys burst forth from the other side of the hold. Barefoot, dressed in patched pants and ragged shirts, they sauntered over to an area of the deck where two young girls were playing with a doll.

"Looky here! What do we have?"

"Hey, Seamus, it's just some scrawny girls."

"That's right; scrawny little runts, ain't ya?"

Ellen watched as the boys taunted the two younger children.

The leader of the gang, the boy they had called Seamus, darted between the two girls and snatched the doll away from them. He threw it to another boy and soon they began to toss the plaything back and forth, always keeping it above the girls' reach.

Da wouldn't let them get away with that. "Stand up for what's right, Ellen. Look fear right in the face and spit in its eye."

Ellen walked over to the gang. "Give them back the doll."

The boys looked at one another and then burst out with loud guffaws. "You gonna make us?"

"If necessary. I'm older than you and I know the captain. I'll report you as thieves. You know what they do to thieves on board a ship, don't you?"

The boys looked around. "Aw, forget it; just a dumb toy." They retreated with less bravado than before.

"Thank you, Miss. You was awful brave."

Ellen smiled at the girls. "You have to learn to look fear in the face and spit in its eye. That way other people won't bother you. And I know how special a doll can be."

She heard someone give a low whistle and turned to see a man grinning at her. She was close enough to see a scar that ran the entire length of his right jaw.

"Pretty impressive, I would say. Dinna realize you knew the captain." He smiled, then peered at her more closely. "Was it your Da that died yesterday?"

She stared at him for a few silent moments. "Yes."

He removed his cap. "I'm sorry for your loss."

"Thank you." She hesitated. "I should go back and meet my brother."

The stranger looked at her, watching as she squared her shoulders, held her head up high, and walked back towards the hold.

"Pretty independent," he commented to no one in particular.

Ellen climbed back down the steep ladder, threading her way

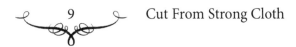

Cut From Strong Cloth

past piles of belongings spilling out from under berths, and then skirted the group of women praying the rosary, each one bent over counting her beads. Finally arriving back at their family's bunks, she found Patrick fiddling with some clothes.

"Why did you come back? I was just about to come up."

"I'm hungry."

"Leave it alone, Ellen. You'll have to wait until another family offers us some food. You should have eaten last night. Then you wouldn't be hungry now."

Ellen retreated to her bunk to sleep, but she woke with sharp hunger pains. Patrick stood by his bunk, shuffling a deck of cards and enjoying some game that didn't require another player.

"Patrick, did anyone bring food?" She felt nauseous and the beginnings of a headache as she sat up.

"Not yet. Look, tomorrow's ration day again. We can last one more day."

Ellen looked over at their mother, lying motionless in the bed.

"What if Mam doesn't go tomorrow and get the rations? Then we'll have to wait another three days. Patrick, can't you go up and talk to the cook? You could explain about Da."

"Are you daft? Mam would be furious if she found out. How would that look, Cecilia Canavan's family begging for food?"

"We wouldn't be begging. Those rations are due our family. Da wouldn't let us go hungry."

"No, Ellen. Stop asking, and stop thinking about it."

Why was Patrick so often irritated with her? He left their assigned twelve cubic feet and wound his way past the other steerage passengers packed as tight as fish ready for market. With a silhouette reminiscent of Da, his square frame supported a slight, peculiar gait as he walked away.

She climbed down to the floor and peered at her mother still hunched towards the coarse plank wall of the bunk. Hesitating for a moment, Ellen remembered the time when a bully had tried to steal her lunch pail. Da had said, "I hope you tackled him right in the road. Whatever belongs to you is rightfully yours."

She quietly retrieved the family's three-legged cooking pot stashed next to their sea store of tin plates, cups, and tea boiler. Their chamber pot was stowed under a different bunk. The food guarantee was oatmeal, rice, sugar, molasses, and tea, along with six pints of water. *I canna buy any of the shriveled vegetables or salted fish for sale, but the cook should give me the other food we're entitled to.*

Lugging the cooking pot, she trudged up on deck and found a queue of people already waiting for their turn at the cook stove. Ellen kept her balance against the constant, uneven movement of the ship as she joined the line.

Ellen did not like the cook, but she knew she had little choice. Mahoney, known only by his last name, was in charge of the entire process and feared by all. She looked at the grease-stained apron that covered his filthy clothes and saw some ashes blow out of his clay pipe and land in someone's stew. She was too hungry to care.

"Hey! What do ya think yer doing?" quizzed an old hag with broken teeth and sour breath. Ellen looked up. A stubble of white whiskers protruded from the woman's chin.

"I've come to get our family's rations. Our Da's been sick."

"Your troubles ain't our troubles. I know you, and yer family turn ain't today. Mahoney don't give out early rations. So go back to the hold and wait for your given time."

Ellen made no reply, but shifted her pot from one hand to the other. She also made no effort at leaving the queue.

"Go on back, I tell ya."

"Wait. Maybe I can help you."

Ellen turned to face the new voice. It belonged to the same man she had met briefly on deck that morning.

"You haven't eaten, have you?"

Ellen shook her head.

"Here, give me your pot. Stay in line."

As Ellen watched, the man maneuvered his way up and down the queue cajoling people to add just part of a carrot, a thin wedge of potato, or even half a slice of turnip to the pot. He returned with an odd assortment of food bits in the bottom of the container.

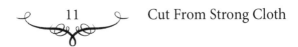

11   Cut From Strong Cloth

"There, I bought a salted herring to throw in. 'Tis not much, but together the food will give you some nourishment."

Ellen's detached attitude softened a bit as she smiled. "Thank you."

The man ushered Ellen beside him and announced to Mahoney, "This young girl needs some water for her cooking."

"Ain't my business what she needs. She missed water being handed out, that's her problem not mine."

"They buried her Da yesterday. The family hasn't eaten."

"Again, not my concern."

"Oh for the love of Christ, can't you just once act with some compassion? Haven't you ever lost someone? She's only asking for two pints of water!"

The rest of the passengers in the queue stood in shocked silence, watching to see how Mahoney would react.

He stared hard at the man. "What'll you give me?"

The stranger reached into a deep pocket and retrieved a thumb length of tobacco, offering it for the exchange.

"All right, two pints it is. But I still deduct it from them's rations tomorrow. I'll remember her."

The man turned from Mahoney and addressed Ellen. "Here, you have enough to make some soup. Is there anyone else in your family to come claim the rations tomorrow if your mother's not up to cooking?"

"I'll come back again if I have to. You have been very kind."

Half an hour later, Ellen returned to steerage with the watery meal.

"Where did you get this soup?"

"I made it myself. A man offered to give us some vegetables and threw in a herring as a gift—I think he had been at Da's funeral."

"Well don't let Mam know you accepted charity. Keep that to yourself." They devoured the soup and left a full cup for their mother. When they finished, Patrick went over to Mam's bunk and climbed in, angling himself next to her.

"Mam, Ellen's made some soup. Here, you need this to begin to

get your strength back. We all miss Da, but you have to survive for us, Mam."

With Patrick's help, Cecilia Canavan managed to raise herself to a sitting position. She accepted the cup, sipping until she finished all the broth and vegetables. Then she reclined and fell asleep once more.

Ellen felt relief that she did not have to account to Mam how she had gotten the food. Mam had rigid standards that Ellen often fought against, and mother-daughter arguments had been a part of Ellen's life ever since she could remember. She did not have the energy to fight with Mam over anything right now.

***

The next morning Ellen tapped her mother's shoulder. "Mam, 'tis rations day. You have to go up on deck to get our share." Her mother turned and peered at Ellen. Cecilia's porcelain skin was now pallid with dark circles underscoring both eyes. "Mam, if you don't feel strong enough, then Patrick or I can go get our rations."

"Rations day is it? How long have I been in the bunk?"

Ellen held up two fingers, and her mother let out a long, sad sigh.

"Go get Patrick. He can help me. I'm sorry I haven't been able to. . . ." Her voice trailed off.

Ellen helped Mam to stand and tried to smooth the wrinkles from the borrowed dress. Then she hugged her mother in a short, but caring, embrace.

"I love you, Mam. I'm so very sorry about Da." She held back a sob. If she started crying, she was afraid she wouldn't be able to stop.

Not one to show a lot of emotion, her mother parroted back, "I love you, too."

Patrick returned, his whole demeanor brightening when he saw his mother standing by the bunk, rather than asleep in it.

"I'll go with you, Mam, to get the food rations."

Their mother began to move toward the steerage ladder. Then she turned back toward Patrick with the beginning of a scowl.

"Are you coming or not? And where did Ellen get those vegeta-

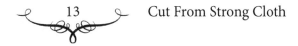

Cut From Strong Cloth

bles for the soup last night?"

Ellen stood still, wondering what Patrick would say.

"She met a man who had been at Da's funeral, and he helped her. I think the vegetables were a gift."

Ellen didn't even realize she'd been holding her breath again, but now let it out. Whether Mam believed the story or not, at least they'd been fed, and Ellen had avoided an unpleasant confrontation. Obviously Mam still knew nothing about the whiskey and Da, or blame would have already occurred.

***

No one spoke of Da, whose dream to immigrate to the United States and become a successful weaver, died with him on the voyage. Fate had delivered a cruel trick by denying him the privilege of setting foot on American soil, while forcing his family to plan for a new life there without him. Ellen went to sleep each night reciting the different names of the weaving patterns he had taught her. It was her way of keeping him near, and the beginning of a plan on how she might honor his memory.

A few weeks later, the rim of the North American coast rose right out of the morning mist as if summoned by the fairies. When the actual shoreline became visible, jubilant cheers filled the air, and all the passengers clamored on deck to catch the first glimpse of their new country. As the ship finally pulled into the Delaware River, men threw their caps in the air, women danced a jig with one another, and children left unsupervised tried to climb the railings in order to get a better view of America.

Mam, arriving now as a widow, became all business.

"Patrick, you pack up the storage trunk. Ellen, you go get the two valises. Don't stand there gawking, get moving."

Patrick hoisted the trunk holding their treasured possessions, including Mam's sewing basket and Da's weaving shuttles. When Ellen picked up her parents' suitcase, it was much lighter than when they had boarded. Ellen knew Da's clothes and bed linens had been discard-

ed overboard after his funeral by order of the captain, fearful that any evidence of disease could cause the ship to be quarantined. Still, she wished she had saved his old sweater, which held the smell of sweet tobacco mixed with his familiar body scent.

"Let's be quick, we dinna want to be the last ones off," Mam ordered.

The trio made their way through the tumultuous crowd on deck and waited to show their exit papers. Once they were cleared, they stepped onto the gangplank and headed toward the land. As their feet touched the shore, their knees buckled, but Cecilia quickly steadied herself to retain decorum. Ellen's heart raced with excitement as she spied screaming gulls swooping down from the sky and carriage traffic clogging the street near the docks.

She turned to Patrick. "Do you think we can find success here in America?"

"Don't go getting your hopes up, little sister. You're only an Irish weaver's daughter. Not likely to get rich here."

Ellen looked at him but did not reply. *You're wrong. I don't know how, but I will become a success here one day. I'll do it for Da.* She squared her shoulders, held her head up, and followed Mam and Patrick into the streets of Philadelphia.

Cut From Strong Cloth

CHAPTER 2

June 1860

"Ellen, get up! 'Tis late."

The pitch of her mother's voice, combined with the incessant banging of a wooden spoon on the staircase, let Ellen know in no uncertain terms that she had once again overslept. At least her mother no longer barged into her bedroom to waken her.

She took one luxurious stretch and caught sight of the shelf across the room where her old doll rested. A smile turned up the corners of her mouth.

Tucked away under the doll's dress lay a piece of inexpensive jewelry. Ellen kept it hidden because Mam would not approve of the giver, a poor boy Ellen had known in school. She knew her mother's dream—Ellen would "marry up" and therefore raise the family status to a higher rung in Kensington society. But no one ever asked Ellen what she wanted.

Ellen smiled to think that in five years she had matured from a spindly girl into a young woman. She looked in the mirror, picturing the way she must appear to others: a pretty nineteen-year-old with pristine Irish skin, soft mahogany hair framing her face, and moss green eyes reflecting some of the spunk she'd inherited from Da.

She smiled at her reflection, trying to remember whether it

matched the warmth of Da's countenance. *Will I ever be the success that I promised him I would be?* She flicked her fingers to scatter dust from her bureau. Damn, Mrs. Cleary. If she hadn't gone and given my job to her niece, I'd at least still be employed where I could learn more about textile sales.

Mam's insistent banging on the staircase brought Ellen out of her reverie. "Be right down," Ellen yelled. It would be pan fried potatoes and hot toast, with the sizzle of a few bangers and eggs in the old iron skillet; just like every morning.

Breakfast was the harbinger for Mam's daily mood, and one more manifestation of her control over the family. If she was already sour at breakfast, the whole day would be filled with arguments.

Ellen could not control the orchestration of the meals or Mam's moods, but she could choose what to wear—giving her a small taste of the independence she craved. She quickly washed up in the basin and then selected the new green cotton floral dress. The color complemented her eyes, and the belted waist accented her slim figure. Tiny pearl-sized black buttons cascaded down the front of the bodice, and a thin trim of ebony ribbon ran down the length of each sleeve, ending at short, modest cuffs of real lace. She smoothed the cotton fabric, enjoying the feel of its softness and then finished by attaching her grandmother's lace collar.

Turning to look in the mirror once again, she decided the dress looked good on her. Then she parted her hair in the center, combed the rest of her thick tresses into a coif at the back of her neck, and secured it with hairpins and a black grosgrain ribbon. Then she started down the stairs that lead to the ground floor and kitchen.

The Canavans lived in a Double Trinity, a narrow row house of three floors. The top floor included one wide room where Mam housed her sewing machine, dress maker's form, and all her fabrics. The room also functioned as her bedroom. The next level divided itself into two smaller bedrooms, one for Ellen and the other for Patrick. The ground floor contained a kitchen in back and a larger space out front where the Canavans had arranged the furniture to double as both a social area for the family and an office for Patrick's business, *Canavan Wool.* The back

Cut From Strong Cloth

yard housed the storage sheds for the wool, as well as the family out-house.

"Morning, Mam."

Cecilia glanced over her shoulder while continuing to cook. "My, aren't we looking stylish. Your dress doesn't seem very full, though. I fashioned it to fit over at least two petticoats."

"Well, I'm not going to wear a corset and two petticoats just to suffer with the latest drawing in *Godey's Magazine.*"

"Ellen, don't be a fool. Men love women who keep up with fashion."

"Really, Mam? I thought men love women who keep up their virtue."

"Ellen, if you are ever going to make something of yourself, you'll need to play up your womanly attributes. That's what smart women do."

"Well, I'd like to think that smart women don't need to give in to fashion trends. I'll save the corset and double petticoats for a special occasion, but in this warm weather I'll just wear a chemise and one petticoat under my dress. I do intend to make something of myself, but not with my clothes." Ellen reached up to the old cupboard for the plates and cups and glanced aside to see Mam pursing her lips—the typical reaction to Ellen's pronounced stubborn streak.

"I don't see what's wrong in using what God gave you. Hurry up, then, and eat some breakfast. There's an errand that needs to be run. This fresh loaf of barmbrack has to be delivered to Father Reilly before nine o'clock."

"Am I supposed to be using my womanly charms on Father Reilly, then?"

"I don't accept that kind of talk in this house. So stop it right now. Just be quick about your breakfast and do as I say."

But before she could say anything else, Patrick came bounding down the stairs, waltzed into the kitchen, and gave each of them a kiss on the cheek.

"How are my favorite ladies this grand and glorious morning?"

So typical. Patrick played the role of favored child well, melting

the tension in their mother's shoulders just by walking into the room.

Studying him for a moment, Ellen mused once again how different they looked from one another. Patrick's chestnut hair was shades lighter than hers, and his languid blue eyes matched Mam's. Both siblings exhibited outgoing personalities, but neither carried the intensity of life wrapped around them like Cecilia did. Ellen felt an allegiance to her brother because he'd often run interference for her with Mam.

"Ellen's leaving a bit early this morning. She has an errand to run."

Patrick looked over at Ellen, but she just shrugged her shoulders. Grabbing a piece of wheaten toast and a banger she announced, "All right. I'm off then." She stepped out onto the stoop and looked up at the sky, a perpetual smudge of grey from the factories belching vast plumes of smoke. From one street over she could hear the trash wagons collecting refuse and clanging bells warning the street urchins to jump aside or be run over.

Ellen often thought of the old row houses here as sentinels standing side by side, woefully trying to block the ever present industrial odors and drifting soot, but without much success.

I do love Philadelphia, but life here with Mam will never be as good as my memories of sunlight dancing on the pastures of Dungannon with Da still alive. Regardless of what she thinks, I will make a success of myself in this city. Though I doubt either she or Patrick will help me.

A cacophony of voices, all with an Irish lilt, began in earnest.

"Good morning, Ellen."

"Hallo, Mrs. Fitzsimmons. Nice day, 'tis, isn't it?"

"Would be a nicer day if me Sean wasn't all excited about wantin' to become a soldier. Wants to get paid for fightin', so he does. I don't want my oldest boy goin' off anywhere."

"Send yer husband, then! At least he'd be bringing home steady pay," piped Mrs. Kenny, emerging from across the street.

"And I'll be thankin' you to keep your comments about me husband to yourself," snarled Mrs. Fitzsimmons.

"I'll say a Hail Mary that Sean won't be going off anywhere, Mrs. Fitzsimmons," Ellen said as she descended the three steps down to street level, thinking that maybe she would be more successful if she worked just with men and didn't have to put up with the friction that so often occurred between women.

Walking north along the street, she no longer even noticed how all the house fronts looked alike. America had been Da's dream, and she wondered what he would say now as the nation appeared to be dividing itself into two separate halves of North and South.

She turned the corner toward the church, and a lone figure hovered in the alley—watching her, but she was oblivious to his presence. She arrived at the church and realizing that early Mass was over, walked to the rectory. Knocking at the front door, she was surprised when the priest opened it right away.

"Ah, good morning, Ellen. Do come in. 'Tis a grand day to be alive, isn't it?"

She stepped inside. Father Reilly was such a good-looking priest that the high school girls had given him the nickname of Father-What-a-Waste. With his lean figure, jet black hair, and vivid blue eyes, he gave the ladies a stir, but to no avail. "Yes, Father, 'tis a grand day. And here is the loaf of barmbrack Mam promised you."

He looked a bit confused but accepted the bread and closed the door.

"Now Ellen, if you would like to sit here, we can discuss the particulars of the job."

"The job, Father Reilly? I don't know what you're talking about."

"The job for parish assistant. That is why you came, isn't it? Yours is the first name on my list. I have four other interviews after yours." Ellen said nothing as she realized her mother's duplicity. Mam had signed her up for this interview. She couldn't believe her mother's brass neck. The nerve!

"I'm sorry, Father. I fear a mistake's been made. I'm not here to interview for any job, just to deliver the barmbrack."

"But your mother bragged about your writing skills, and I need someone to help with my correspondence. The other women who are coming to interview can all clean and cook, but none of them finished high school like you. You'd be a welcome asset here."

"Clean and cook? I thought you said the job was for a parish

assistant?"

"Aye, 'tis. But I'm also in need of a noon meal each day. Even a priest gets hungry," he said smiling.

"I'm sorry about the mistake, Father." *As if I want to cook and clean.*

"Might you consider just a half day, then? Help me with the correspondence, fix a meal, and then you'd be free to go. I could really use your talents to help offset my work load."

As Ellen turned away trying to formulate a polite decline to his offer, she noticed an open doorway to a room overflowing with filled bookcases.

"Father Reilly, are all those books yours?" She pointed.

"Yes, but now they belong to the parish. 'Tis a source of pride in the diocese, this book collection of mine. I was schooled at Queens College in Belfast before heeding the call to become a priest, and I brought my books with me. My father worked at the Hall Library, and several of the discarded books found their way to our home and onto my shelves as well. So this collection is a bit diverse, but grand none the less. Are you interested in books, Ellen?"

"Yes, Father, I read every chance I get."

"Well, getting back to the business at hand. . . I know you were working at Cleary's Dry Goods. What made you leave?"

"I was let go when Mrs. Cleary's niece needed a job. I actually enjoyed working there, helping customers choose fabrics. I love being around material." Ellen smiled just thinking about textiles. She could identify cloth by its texture or sheen, or lace by the pattern it followed. Even though she wore cotton dresses on most days, Ellen could discern the luster of satin to the smoothness of silk and the noisy swish of taffeta to the exquisite silence of velvet.

"Mrs. Cleary pretended her fabrics were the latest in fashion and that the shop's lace came from Epsen's downtown, but I could tell by its quality it came from the Patriot Mill just a few blocks from here. In some ways, I guess Mrs. Cleary was glad to see me go."

Ellen turned her gaze back to the books, well aware that this could be the best collection in all of Kensington.

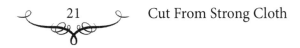

"Perhaps, Father, we could strike a bargain. I could come and do the correspondence and fix a noon meal as well, provided you give me open access to your library. In addition, I would require a salary. My family would be expecting that."

"Sounds fair to me." The priest grinned. "Please do not say anything about our agreement until tomorrow. I wouldn't want the other women to know I'd already hired you. And I promised your mother I would give you first consideration."

"'Tis a deal then, Father. When would you like me to start?"

"Would a fortnight provide you enough time?"

"Yes, Father. That would be perfect."

"Why don't you select a couple of books right now from my library? You can take them home and return them when you start work."

"Thank you, Father. I'd love that."

Ellen walked into the library room and took a moment to drink in the smell of the leather covers. Wouldn't Da be smiling at this good luck! She wandered over to the bookcases and saw that several volumes had bits of paper stuck between their pages. Instinctively she pulled one off the shelf and opened to the paper marker. It was the play of *Romeo and Juliet*. Maybe he hadn't always been Father-What-A-Waste after all! She forced herself to stifle a giggle.

Meandering further along the displays, she saw volumes of poetry, a novel by Charles Dickens, as well as several books about the history of Ireland. She let her fingers traipse along the spines until she found a treatise on Irish linen and she selected it, then a second book on the linen trade. She stood alone in the library and congratulated herself on negotiating the use of his library as a stipulation for the job. *I'll read everything he has on textiles. That will give me additional knowledge toward opening my own business in the future.*

"Good day, Father."

"Good day, Ellen."

Ellen started walking home. *If Mam is going behind my back to coax me into a job, then what in God's name might she be doing about trying to choose a husband for me? I won't fall into her traps. I'm not as green as she might think.*

 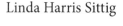

Rounding a corner onto Second Street, she careened right into a young man and spilled the two books she had been carrying. As she stooped to retrieve the first book, he picked up the other one.

"Beg your pardon, Miss, I dinna see you."

"Well that, sir, is obvious. No harm done, though."

"No harm? Then I think I must be having a lucky day."

"Now why would you be saying that?"

"Because you've just walked into my life. Michael Brady, at your service." He doffed his cap and made a sweeping bow, which in the middle of Kensington almost appeared ridiculous, but the gesture coerced a smile out of her.

She took in his jaunty manner. "Well, thank you for the compliment and the help in retrieving my books. But, actually, Mr. Brady, I have walked into no one's life and am not in need of anyone's service. But I do need that other book. They're on loan from Father Reilly."

"Father Reilly?"

"Yes, Father Reilly. He is allowing me to borrow books from the parish library."

"Well, Miss. . . ? You've not told me your name."

"No, I did not. And it wouldn't be appropriate for me to do so."

"Not appropriate? I just saved your last book."

"Mr. Brady, I am indebted to you, and your gallantry. Perhaps we will meet again in the neighborhood, or at St. Michael's. Then, I would tell you my name." She held out her hand for the last book, now with a smile softening her face.

"Then I will make sure that we meet again."

Ellen continued on her walk. *I wonder who he really is. I've never seen him in this neighborhood before.*

Once back at 1225 Fifth Street Ellen walked in to find her mother grinning, supposedly in perceived triumph. Ellen went on the initiative instead and caught her mother off guard.

"Mam, I canna thank you enough for sending me over to St. Michael's."

"Oh, really?" replied her mother, suspicion evident in her guarded eyes.

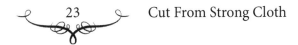

"Yes, Father Reilly indicated he needed an assistant and asked me if I might have any interest in the position. Since I'm not working for Mrs. Cleary anymore, I thought I would help him and see where the job goes."

"Will you, now? Where are those books from?"

"They're Father Reilly's. He's letting me borrow from his library." She waited, but Mam made no comment. "I think the job will go fine, but there's a part I'll need to work on. It requires that I fix him dinner each day, so I'll have to get some cooking lessons; unless of course, you wouldn't mind me experimenting here in your kitchen."

"I've never encouraged you to cook because I want you to become a lady, marry into money, and have someone cook for you. I know you don't always agree with me, but I do have your best intentions at heart."

"Looks like I'll have to learn after all, if I want the job with Father Reilly."

Cecilia was caught by her own deeds. "I'll speak to Mrs. McAllister. I know she gives cooking lessons from time to time, and that would be better than for you making a mess out of my kitchen. Just don't go around talking about what you try to cook. I don't want the neighbors to know."

"Mrs. McAllister will know."

"Aye, but she isn't a Kensington neighbor."

Ellen watched Mam's lip curl in victory.

***

Other than concocting soup, Ellen's limited culinary knowledge was almost non-existent. She was, however, a willing pupil. The lessons went well; the first meal for Father Reilly did not.

She planned on something familiar, like bangers and champ, but the rectory's ancient belching stove with its temperamental flu and fluctuating heat gauges got the better of her. The sausages burned and the mashed potatoes turned out lukewarm and lumpy. Even though she had been an apt pupil, her confidence evaporated with the unappetizing dinner. Father Reilly did not grimace; but Cecilia exploded.

"Jesus, Mary, and Joseph! How in the name of God did you burn the bangers? I thought you had practiced with Mrs. McAllister!"

"I did. But Father Reilly's stove is different from Mrs. McAllister's. I think I had the heat too high. But honest, Mam, he did not complain."

"Only because he's a man of God! You better start being more careful. I swear, Ellen, I don't understand how you can be smart in school, and careless in this. How did lumps get in the champ?"

"Perhaps I rushed and dinna warm the milk before adding it to the potatoes."

"Even a fool knows better than that. From now on you'll cook dinner here the night before you cook for Father Reilly. I'll oversee everything and try to fix what Mrs. McAllister has failed to instill in you."

Ellen stormed out of the kitchen. Damn her and damn the stupid cooking.

But by the end of two weeks, the meals improved, and the burden of correspondence dissipated for Father Reilly. Soon, helping Father Reilly with his correspondence in the early morning, followed by some quick sweeping or dusting, and then fixing the noon meal became a familiar rhythm to her routine.

***

"And what will we be cooking for Father Reilly today?" Mam asked.

"I'll be making pot roast. The butcher had some good beef yesterday. 'Tis a small hunk to be sure, but then 'tis only Father Reilly who'll be eating it. If I serve it with lots of carrots and potatoes, I can add some onions tomorrow, and stretch it into beef stew."

"The best stew is made with lamb."

"I know that, but good lamb is not available right now, is it? So beef will have to do."

"One would think you're planning to be a grand cook one day."

"What I'm planning is to have a grand future one day."

"Och, don't be making such proud statements. Words like that can come back to haunt you."

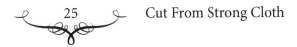

Cut From Strong Cloth

Ellen watched as her mother made the sign of the cross, one more facet of her annoying Irishness. Then Cecilia turned back to the stove while Ellen continued to set the table. The dinnerware might be old and chipped, but the cream-colored linen napkins sewn by Cecilia were a luxury in an otherwise working class kitchen.

"Mam, can I ask you a question?"

"Hmm."

"How did you get started in your sewing business?" She watched as her mother's eyes narrowed in a questioning glance.

"Now, why would you be wantin' to know somethin' like that?"

"I'm curious, that's all."

Cecilia waited a moment. "I altered an outfit for Bridget Donovan when she went to interview with the Reynolds' family over in Rittenhouse Square. Mrs. Reynolds complimented her on what she was wearing. That's how my reputation got started."

"But how did you get enough money to purchase a sewing machine?"

"I saved money from the alterations I did for Father Walsh. Remember him? He was the priest before Father Reilly." Cecilia peered intently at Ellen. "I know you, Ellen, and there's more to this conversation than you're letting on."

Ellen took a deep breath. "I've decided that I want to open my own business."

"Jesus, Mary, and Joseph! You couldn't possibly be a seamstress or a cook—you've got no talent for either."

"I'd like to buy and sell fabric."

"For the love of God, Ellen. Just get married like other girls your age do."

"I want more than just that."

"Well you're chasing dreams, just like your Da. And I hope you remember how his turned out."

Ellen felt like ice water had been thrown on her. Once again she felt the familiar pang of defeat with her mother. And Da's memory had been dragged out to boot. Ellen resolved not to show her hurt feelings. *I refuse to let her trample my dream.*

Cecilia returned to cooking with the hurtful words still hanging in the air.

✳✳✳

No one could deny that Cecilia hadn't worked hard to become established in Kensington. After many failed attempts, she finally had the opportunity to alter designs from *Godey's Magazine* and tailor them to fit the wealthy ladies of Rittenhouse Square. She saved every scrap of real lace for Ellen's clothes, determined to showcase her daughter as Lace Curtain Irish, the ultimate Irish immigrant dream.

Patrick had also had setbacks but was progressing now with his fledging wool import business. Cecilia needed both her children to become established in a proper way. She knew she would not be able to sew forever, and when that day came, Cecilia wanted her children to provide for her in comfort.

✳✳✳

"There's going to be a church social today," Mam called out from the kitchen. "I think it would be a good idea for you to attend. You never know who you might meet."

Ellen walked back to the kitchen.

"Thanks, Mam, but I already made plans to visit Brown's Bookstore. He's supposed to have a sale."

"For God's sake Ellen, you'll never meet anyone in a bookstore except dodgy old men with spectacles on their nose."

"I don't go to Brown's to meet anyone—other than the books." Ellen knew it was a flippant comment, but she rather enjoyed saying it.

"There are well-to-do widowers here in Kensington that have asked Father Reilly about you."

Widowers? All Ellen could think of was the ancient men who came to church tottering on their canes and reeking of unwashed clothes. She'd rather stay single forever than climb in bed with the likes of them pawing at her under the covers.

Cut From Strong Cloth

"Father Reilly has no say in who I should marry. So I am not in the least bit interested in any of his widowers."

Cecilia muttered under her breath.

Kensington did not possess a real bookstore of its own. Buying a book meant traveling all the way down Fourth Street to Brown's, but Ellen loved every visit to the venerable establishment. It was quirky in the way that many old buildings grow to become, and Ellen relished breathing in the smells of old leather mixed with new paper and bookbinder's glue. She felt welcomed as a patron and appreciated how the well-worn floorboards paid tribute to the many feet which had trod there before her.

Once she arrived, she headed past the classics, veered off to a room at the right, and scanned the books categorized as "industry studies," then claimed the one overstuffed chair in the section, thinking how Da would smile if he could see her there. A book on foreign textile manufacturing caught her eye and she thumbed through its pages. Most of the manufacturers, however, were English and had little relevance to Patrick's current woolen business or the business she hoped to start in the future. After an hour of searching, she decided on the purchase of two books.

Mr. Brown grinned when she came up to the register. She was the only Irish girl from Kensington who spent money in his store, and she always made an appearance on sale days.

"Hallo, Mr. Brown. I found two books I decided I had to have," Ellen said with a smile.

"Let's see." He took each book and read its title. "Are you planning on studying business?"

"I'm trying to learn everything I can about textiles."

"Last count I heard, Kensington has 228 different textile firms."

"Oh, I dinna realize there were so many."

"That's counting all of them, even those with only a few employees. Textiles are a big industry in Philadelphia. More than one man has made his fortune that way."

"Then perhaps a woman can, too."

"Oh, I don't think so. Never heard of any woman owning a textile business."

 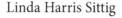

But that doesn't mean it canna happen.

***

An hour after Ellen returned from the bookstore, she retreated to her room and fell asleep reading. Mam heard a knock at the front door, and moments later Patrick popped his head into her sewing room.

"Mam, there's a gentleman here who says he needs to see you. He's arrived in a fine buggy and says his name is Louis Fallon from the Medical College."

"Medical College? What could he possibly want with us?"

Cecilia stood up and removed her tailor's apron and smoothed the front of her dark navy poplin dress. Giving a quick glance in the mirror, she rubbed some salve on her fingertips, tucked a loose strand of hair back into place, and pinched her cheeks to produce a light hint of color. Then she descended the two flights of stairs with a practiced grace.

"Mrs. Canavan?"

"Yes." She eyed the visitor with scrutiny. Judging by his clothes, he was well-to-do.

"I am here because you were recommended by Mrs. William Paxson of Rittenhouse Square."

"Mrs. Paxson?"

"Pardon my lack of manners. I should have properly introduced myself." He gave a short bow. "Dr. Louis Fallon, with the Medical College of Philadelphia. Mrs. Paxson is one of my patients."

"Is she all right?"

"Oh, quite so. Just some digestive upsets, correctable, once I convinced her to change her diet."

Cecilia blushed that Mrs. Paxson had recommended her. "How can I be of assistance to you, Dr. Fallon?"

"I am engaged, and soon to be married. Once my fiancée, Sarah Chambers, and I are wed, we will be returning to my home in Savannah. I would like to commission you to fashion Sarah's trousseau."

Cut From Strong Cloth

His southern accent softened the room, and for once Cecilia was almost speechless. To design a bridal trousseau would tap into every ounce of her talent, but would also bring in wonderful revenue.

"I would be honored, Dr. Fallon, to take on the commission."

"Delightful! When can you start?"

"I'll be delivering a dress to Mrs. Paxson next week. Perhaps your driver could pick me up there next Wednesday. Shall we say, one o'clock? Then he can take me to meet Miss Chambers. Would that be agreeable?"

"That will do nicely. Thank you, Mrs. Canavan. I will be forever in your debt."

With his farewell, he held her hand. She could not remember a gentleman ever holding her hand, not to mention coming to call at her house. The doctor nodded to Patrick before letting himself out. They could hear the horse and carriage trotting off down Fifth Street.

Cecilia and Patrick stared at each other and then grinned, both recognizing a windfall when they saw one.

Still napping, Ellen remained unaware of the visitor and how he would change the course of her life.

CHAPTER 3

September 1860

He struck the matchstick on the sole of his boot, watched the spark turn into a small flame, and tossed the burning match onto a pile of kerosene soaked rags. Then he darted off through an alley.

Twenty minutes later, the fire bell continued to clang as he arrived at the station and men swarmed into the hall like bees. Someone tossed him a hat and he hauled himself up on the back of the fire wagon as it lurched out into the road and up Masters Street. A mixture of apprehension, anticipation, and excitement settled on him as his brigade drew closer to the fire.

The wagon arrived at the destination with flames shooting out of an old wooden building. He watched the drivers maneuver the horses so the animals could not see the blaze. Then he jumped down and stood off to the side. Some men ran with axes, and others left to fill water buckets. Alone and transfixed, he felt that delicious twist of joy as the tongues of the inferno licked up toward the roof. Tongues he had set in motion not half an hour ago.

He stood entranced a moment longer, mesmerized by the hypnotic power of the combustion. Fires had fascinated him ever since he had been a young boy. The flames' fingers beckoned him. He gaped, longing to comply.

"All right men! Get your arses over here, now!"

Reality pulled him back, and he lamented to himself that the men would desecrate his work. One of them shoved an empty bucket at his chest, yelling at him to join the brigade. He morphed back into a firefighter, just like any of the other men running to get on the water line. But he knew he wasn't like the others.

"Hey, you. Watch out. A piece of burning timber can easily fall on you."

He acknowledged with a nod. *You have no idea of how good I am around the flames.*

The first moments of arriving on the scene were what he liked best because in the initial chaos, no one watched how he set himself apart and worshipped the fire-beast. It was like standing in front of an altar. Each time he stood before a blaze, power raced through his entire body, arcing toward the culmination of becoming one with the flames.

When the fire climaxed, exhaustion and exhilaration took over his effort of seducing the inferno. And like any prostituted love, an exchange of money for services performed was expected.

With a fire, he was omnipotent—wielding a power no one could ever imagine.

CHAPTER 4

September 1860

A rare blue sky matched Ellen's buoyant mood as she cleaned up from the morning's cooking. The bell sounded at the rectory's front door, and she went to the foyer to investigate.

"Mr. Brady! What a surprise to see you again." She realized she was wearing a gravy-stained apron and silently groaned.

"I have business here with the saints—and you. We made a bargain."

"We did? I'm not sure I know what you mean." She could feel her voice rising to an unintended higher pitch.

"You said you would tell me your name if we met again. Here I am. You gave me the name of your church, so you shouldn't seem so surprised to see me. You're not the type of girl who breaks promises, are you?" He looked directly at her and she felt the heat of blush crawl up her neck.

"Well, I'm not sure I would call it a promise. I had wanted to see if our chance encounter had been a pretense in flirting. You see, I don't flirt." She spoke the words with a bit of self-assurance, but felt butterflies whirling in her stomach. She was sure he could tell.

"I'm here now. So I think 'tis fair for you to introduce yourself."

She hesitated for a minute and Father Reilly appeared from a back room. "Ellen, do we have a visitor?" With the interruption of

Father Reilly's appearance she felt steadier on her feet.

"Father Reilly, this is Michael Brady, a new acquaintance of mine."

"Welcome to St. Michael's. Are you new to the parish?"

"I don't live in Kensington, Father. I just work nearby."

Then before the priest could ask him the name of the parish church he attended, Michael turned to Ellen and said, "'Tis good seeing you again, 'Ellen'. Perhaps we will meet at Mass."

As he walked out, her heart thumped. Michael's hazel gold-flecked eyes seem to send out sparks when he smiled and the jaunty swagger of his hips suggested a male confidence that quickened her pulse double-time.

***

Michael grinned as he walked straight into Whelan's, his favorite pub, itching to brag about meeting the attractive church girl.

"What'll it be, Brady? Same as usual?" The bartender quipped.

"Aye, give me a pint and let me tell you I have the prettiest girl in all of Philadelphia interested in me."

Hoots and hollers from men already at the bar greeted this proclamation.

Turning, he saluted them all and winked at the two better dressed men in the corner who barely acknowledged his presence. That didn't matter; these were the type of men who would make contact with Brady when a certain type of job was needed.

"So who is she?" A burly man with sweat-stained clothes edged his way to the bar and swigged down the last of his pint. "Is she prettier than the redhead you brought around last week?"

Another patron leaned in. "Or does she have bigger tits than the blonde? You know the one." Then he made the shape of an hour glass as more laughter erupted.

"Maybe she's got more than you can handle!" A gap-toothed man called out.

"No, this one has real class. I had to go over to St. Mike's to find out her name! Can you be believin' that?"

A new round of laughing exploded.

"You went to church to find a woman!"

Chortles swept around the bar.

He raised his glass in a mock toast, glancing sideways at the two men in the corner.

"Aye, I went to church. Anything to woo over this colleen." He drained his drink and left. The two men in the corner had watched his every move.

***

A week later in the butcher shop Ellen inadvertently discovered some information about Michael. The meat cutter's daughter was talking with another girl and indicated with a sly smile that she knew Michael Brady well—quite well, in fact. Ellen peered at the girl, acknowledging her full bosom but probably less ample wits, and tried not to let the off-handed comment bother her. But she couldn't quite push it out of her mind. What would Michael be doing with the likes of her?

Today was a new day, and as she finished putting away the clean dishes and saying good-bye to Father Reilly, she walked out in the street to find Michael standing on the corner in front of the rectory. Her heart skipped a beat. In spite of any misgivings she might have had from the incident at the butcher's, Michael's interest in Ellen made her feel special.

"Hallo. What are you doing here?"

"Isn't it obvious? I'm waiting for you. Can we walk together?"

Soon they were ambling down Second Street.

"What kind of work do you do for Father Reilly?"

"I write his daily correspondence and then cook his mid-day meal."

"And you're happy doing that?"

"He's a nice man, but I have other reasons why I work there."

"Like what?"

"Nothing you'd find interesting."

"You might be surprised in what I'm interested in. So tell me, what other reasons?" He smiled as he leaned closer.

Ellen felt drawn into his presence as if they were the only two

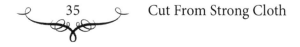

on the street. "I really took the job because of his wonderful library. Once I've read all his books, I plan on quitting and starting my own business."

"Your own business? Now where would you be gettin' that kind of money?"

"'Tis my dream, regardless of how much money it takes. My brother Patrick has been building up his wool company, so I'm hoping I might be able to ask him for a loan. 'Tis a lofty dream, I know."

"Well, I dinna know that about you. What I do know, is that high dream of yours deserves a kiss for good luck."

Before Ellen could protest, he turned and took her by the shoulders and kissed her full on the lips. Her heart soared with the thrill.

"I could get used to that with you." His eyes sparkled.

A bit embarrassed, she smoothed her dress.

He gently took her hand in his. "You don't mind, do you? If we hold hands?"

She felt a bit nervous but smiled at him. "All right." They resumed their walk. "What about you, Michael? Do you have a special dream?"

"Oh, I don't know. I get by. Someday I'll have money of me own."

"Do you have a plan for making that happen?"

"'Tis many different ways of making money, Ellen."

"What I meant was do you have a specific plan?"

"Yes, my specific plan is to become involved in your life." He grinned at her.

"Michael, I think you're making me blush."

"I am? Well darlin', that's a good sign. Perhaps we're destined to be together."

Ellen basked in the glow of feeling desirable and forgot about the question she'd asked concerning his future plans.

***

Weeks later the sound of whistling stopped Mr. James Nolan in his tracks. He had walked up Second Street, then east onto Jefferson

 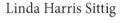

when he detected the distinct melody of a song he'd not heard since Ireland. The tune brought back haunting memories, tugging at his heartstrings for a life he had chosen to leave behind.

He continued a step or two and spotted a young woman sweeping the back porch of the rectory at St. Michael's. From this distance she appeared to be almost dancing the broom across the boards. Wisps of her chocolate brown hair escaped the ribbon at the nape of her neck, and he smiled in spite of himself, feeling a bit foolish for staring. He continued on his walk, but a few of her notes lingered in the air behind him.

Later that day, he arrived at 1225 Fifth Street for a business meeting with a new wool supplier. Ready to knock, he heard whistling again. He cocked his head. It was the same melody from the morning. A moment later the door opened and Patrick Canavan bid him welcome. James Nolan stepped inside the entrance.

"Hallo, Patrick. Where's the whistling coming from?"

"Oh, that would be my sister, Ellen. She's always humming or whistling one tune or another, but that one is her favorite. Do you recognize it?"

Just then Ellen appeared from the kitchen. "I thought I heard a visitor."

"The Derry Air, isn't it?" James answered Patrick, but looked at Ellen. She was indeed the same girl from the church and quite becoming now that he saw her up close. Her hair reminded him of the color of warm molasses, and he was caught off guard by eyes the color of summer moss.

She was looking right at him, and he straightened his frame. Tall and slender for an Irishman, he wondered what she thought about the slight wisps of grey at his temples and the somewhat faded scar on his jaw.

"Ellen, this is my new business client, Mr. James Nolan, proprietor of the St. John's Street Factory. James, this is my sister, Ellen."

"Hallo. And aye, I know that tune quite well, though I've not heard anyone sing or whistle it for some time."

She smiled back at him. "Mr. Nolan, would you like a cuppa tea? I canna offer you any good strong Irish tea, but I can brew a pot of Tetley's."

He didn't really want any tea, but he couldn't resist her pleasing

demeanor. "Yes, thank you."

When she disappeared back to the kitchen, he looked over at Patrick. "You dinna tell me you had a sister."

"Well, since this is the first time we've met at my house, this is your first opportunity to meet my family, or least my sister. Seat yourself here, James."

James glanced back at the kitchen, but then sat down. "So, do you have any new samples to show me? I must admit that I'm impressed with your eye for good wool."

"Thanks, I learned it from my Da."

"Your Da?"

"Aye, back home." Patrick retrieved the samples from the desk against the wall. "You pick the one you'd like to buy."

"How about you pick the one you feel is the best quality."

Patrick pointed to the sample in the middle of the display.

"Good. That was the same one I had already noticed."

Ellen returned carrying a wooden tray laden with all the necessities for tea. As she bent to pour the tea, the surprising scent of summer roses prickled his nose.

She smiled at him. "Your factory is on St. John's Street? Do you work with textiles other than wool?"

"At the moment my inventory is mostly wool, but I've been considering adding ginghams. Are you interested in textiles?"

"Actually I am. And I know that ginghams are usually good sellers, so that might be a wise choice. It has been nice to meet you, Mr. Nolan."

He stood up as she left the room.

Walking home, he found the melody of her tune popping back into his head. An unexpected single tear slid down his cheek with the memory of his Ulster youth, and he quickly brushed it aside. He was a grown man now; no need to revisit the hurtful parts of his past.

***

Several days later, James Nolan heard about a farmer out in the Perkiomen Valley whose wool was bringing in top dollar. It was the

perfect reason to stop in unannounced at the Canavan house. As he knocked on the door he reminded himself to make eye contact with Patrick first and not rivet a stare toward the kitchen, even though he was hoping to get a glimpse of Ellen.

"Hallo, James. Did we have an appointment?"

"No. This will be a quick visit because I came to alert you to a possible new supplier you might be interested in."

"My mother's on the other side of town and Ellen's not back yet from work. But I can offer you some tea."

James' shoulders slumped a bit at the news. "If you already have some made, I'll take a cup."

"Give me a moment."

As Patrick came back and set two cups down on the low table, James tried to act nonchalant with his next question.

"So where does Ellen work?"

"She's Father Reilly's assistant over at St. Michael's."

The front door opened and Ellen appeared.

"Oh, Mr. Nolan. How nice to see you again. I see Patrick offered you some tea."

He cleared his throat before speaking. "'Tis nice to see you again, too. So, Patrick tells me you work at St. Michael's with Father Reilly."

"That's right. I mostly handle his correspondence, and then cook his noon meal. In between time I borrow his books and study them."

"His books? Are you considering a religious life?"

"Oh, good heavens, no. I'm reading all I can to further my education."

Patrick interjected. "Ellen, would you be wantin' a cuppa tea, too?"

"No, I have a book I want to start, so I'll be leaving you two to conduct business in peace."

Ellen turned to go up the staircase. James' eyes followed her exit, smiling at her willowy silhouette. She reminded him a bit of his mother, buried long ago in County Antrim. When he turned his eyes back to the room, Patrick was grinning. James felt himself blush for the

Cut From Strong Cloth

first time in years.

Walking home later when the sun started streaking Philadelphia with the first vivid strokes of early autumn, James replayed his conversation with Ellen and acknowledged that he couldn't get her out of his mind.

***

The very next afternoon he ventured by St. Michael's to meet another business client and almost ran into Ellen walking with a young man. It would have been an uncomfortable situation, except that Ellen and the boyo were too caught up in conversation to even notice him.

As Ellen leaned into the rakish fellow, James struggled to breathe. Her laughter in the young man's company sent his brain reeling. His mouth went dry. *I should be the one out walking with her.*

"Is Ellen seeing anyone?" James sputtered as he and Patrick were examining a box of samples later that day. He had meant to pose the question in a casual manner, but the heat of his emotions sideswiped his intentions.

Patrick grinned. "Why, James, 'tis a peculiar question coming from a business associate. Is there something I should know?"

"Just curious, I suppose." He tried to cover his blunder. "She's young, so it would be reasonable for men to be interested in her."

"Young? Well, yes, James, but also attractive," he said with a wink. "We know she goes out walking with this Michael Brady fellow, a day laborer if you can believe that. Neither Mam nor I have met him. We aren't encouraging the relationship, but Ellen is quite headstrong, and as soon as you tell her she can't do something, she plunges in headfirst."

"Oh, a bit independent, is she?"

Patrick laughed. "Powerful independent, James. Been that way her entire life, and not likely to change." Then he hesitated a moment. "Oh, but I dinna mean that she wouldn't make for a good companion. Maybe even a wife. Life with Ellen would be a grand adventure—you can trust me on that."

James left Patrick and wasted no time in visiting Whelan's Saloon on Girard Avenue. The place smelled of hops and sweat-stained clothing. Wood shavings, intended to soak up spilled ale, littered the floor and as in most pubs, pipe smoke curled toward the ceiling and hung in tobacco halos around the room. A popular spot among the day labor crowd, he knew he didn't fit in here, and tried to act somewhat detached. He looked around and did not see Brady, which was what he hoped. The place thronged with men whose tongues loosened when plied with drink.

He leaned up against the bar and nodded to the other men already assembled.

"What'll it be?" the barkeep inquired.

"A pint will do, and an extra one for any man here that can help me in my quest." Raising his voice he announced, "I'm looking for a fellow countryman. Younger man, name of Brady."

At the other end of the bar a man dressed in loose fitting britches and a patched jacket spoke up. "I know a *Michael* Brady. Why would the likes of you be looking for him?"

"Oh, we're from the same area back home. Just thought it might be good to look him up, that's all. Do you know him well?"

The man elbowed himself next to James. The stench of body odor saturated the air.

"Pour me some stout and I'll tell you what I know. He works at Weikel Spice."

The barkeep filled up two glasses.

"*Sláinte*," the man said to James.

"*Sláinte*," James answered and raised his glass to the toast. "Has Brady married yet?"

"Married?" said one of the other men. "Michael Brady? He's a skiver, that one. Nah, no woman's going to get his name, only a bun in the oven by him."

The other men muttered in agreement.

"Let me tell you something, Mister," the body odor man interjected. "Fine looking gentleman like you, comin' in here where you don't belong, and fishin' for information that might not be your busi-

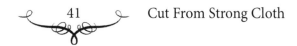

ness—I'd advise you to watch your step. We may be rungs down the ladder from the likes of you, but we ain't stupid. One ale don't get you much."

James held his ground. He hadn't always been a gentleman. Without thinking, his fingers reached up and touched the scar along his jaw.

"The other thing you should know is this," the man continued. "Michael Brady ain't someone you want to be doin' business with. He might be from your part of Ireland, but he sure ain't your kind now. He keeps company with men who. . . you don't want to know. Unless of course you don't mind getting your legs broke."

Snickers broke out around the bar.

James threw down a few more coins.

"Let my new friend here have another pint." Then tipping his hat, he walked out of the pub. Ellen deserved better. He passed a church and thought of stopping in to say a prayer, but then shrugged it off. Ever since Ireland, he and God were not on the best of terms.

***

He muddled over the Brady information for a day or two. Whether Brady would hear that someone was asking about him didn't matter. Cocky boyos like Brady never suspected there might be other competing suitors. Besides, right now all talk in Philadelphia centered on the upcoming national election and the four candidates whose campaign issues centered mainly on slavery. If the men in the saloon bothered to remember James at all, he didn't care.

He wanted to pursue Ellen and make his intentions known. The fishmongers' saying: "If you don't blow your horn, nobody buys your fish," came to his mind. He lived by that assertive rule in business, so he would need to become more active in pursuing Ellen, as well. Otherwise, she could become swayed by Brady instead.

He glanced at his pocket watch; Ellen would soon be heading over to St. Michael's. He impatiently waited another hour until he was sure she'd be out of the house and then he walked over to Fifth Street.

"Ah, welcome, James." Patrick greeted him at the door. "Are you here to discuss about some new wool or are you wanting some tea?"

"No tea. This time I just came to talk." As James wandered over to the sofa, he noticed a new pile of books on the front table. A copy of *Uncle Tom's Cabin* lay on top. Ellen must be reading it. He smiled. No other woman he knew read about current issues.

Patrick flopped down on the sofa next to him. "You know, James, I'm glad we've become business associates, you and I. And if you don't mind me saying, it seems you've done quite well for yourself, an Irish immigrant now running a factory. I hope to do as well as you one day."

"Thanks, Patrick, but my success came with a price. I lost most of my family in the Famine, and I would trade my factory business here for them to still be alive."

"Well, it seems you've had luck, anyway."

"Luck had nothing to do with it. I've worked hard these years in Philadelphia, and saved every penny."

Silence followed his statement. He sputtered a nervous cough and continued. "Patrick, what I came to talk about is. . . I am quite taken with your sister."

Patrick sat back, placing his arms behind his head with a broad smile spreading across his face. He turned and peered at James straight on. "I canna say I'm surprised, James. I've seen the way you look at her. Many of our business conversations could take place at the factory or elsewhere, but you almost always come here now instead. My mother and I suspected you might be coming to the house because of Ellen. It would be a comfort for us if you took her off our hands."

"'Tis an odd comment to make about your own sister."

"Oh, just kidding, though sometimes she exasperates even me. Have you told Ellen your feelings?"

"Of course not. The proper thing is for you to know my intentions first, and then perhaps Ellen and I could start getting to know each other. Do you think I stand a chance?"

Patrick shifted in his seat.

"Ah, James, who knows what goes on in a woman's mind? She

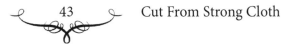

Cut From Strong Cloth

seems infatuated with this Michael Brady, but she smiles whenever you're around. I do think she likes you."

"All right then, 'tis up to me. The thing is, Patrick, I know I'm a good bit older, but I would be a gentleman suitor. Any suggestions of how I might win her favor?"

At this Patrick laughed. "Och! Women? I don't know, James, they're hard to figure out. We should bring my mother into this discussion. She knows Ellen better than anyone, and perhaps she can offer an idea from a female point of view."

"Good idea. I'll talk with her soon, then."

I'll just have to make sure I impress the mother, or I won't get anywhere near Ellen.

***

When Cecilia returned home later, Patrick had already gone out somewhere. She fixed herself a simple bacon sandwich and sat down at the table to read Father Reilly's latest gift to her—a month old copy of *The Irish Times*. No matter how long she'd been gone, she still enjoyed reading news of home.

The first two pages contained stories about the big cities of Dublin, Belfast, and Galway. But on page three, a name leapt off the page and sunk its fangs into her memory. She pushed back from the table's edge, as if the print were alive. *Oh God, he's still there.* Eyes darting furtively around the kitchen, she snatched the newspaper and took it over to the cook stove. Without a moment's hesitation, she stuffed the entire issue into the coals and watched as the pages caught fire and burned to ashes.

Still the monster was not subdued. She picked up her skirt and dashed up the two flights to her top room. Jerking the door open to her nightstand she took out a glass and a bottle and poured herself two fingers full of whiskey. Then she gulped it down. She sat on the side of her bed, waiting for the alcohol to work its magic. Soon her racing heart began to slow as the liquid coursed through her veins.

Walking back downstairs with a practiced composure that hid

the terror in her soul, she whispered, "Holy Mary, Mother of God, protect my daughter. Ellen must never find out, or both our lives will be ruined.

 # CHAPTER 5

October 1860

As the October weather shifted away from Indian summer, sporadic hints of winter dropped cooler temperatures on Kensington, and Ellen emerged from the rectory clasping a wool shawl across her chest. Michael Brady was leaning up against the corner street sign.

"My, and you are looking lovely today, Ellen. In fact, you look more beautiful each and every time I see you." He grinned as she crossed the street and stood before him.

"Oh, but Mr. Brady, I've heard that you say those exact same words to all the girls you go out walking with."

"Ellen, now where would you be hearing lies like that? Those words are meant for no one else but you. Are you done for the day? I'm free and canna think of anything better than to spend the time with you. Why don't we go get somethin' to eat?"

She linked her arm with his. Whether her mother or Patrick would approve did not bother her today. This was America, and she could walk with whomever she wanted. "That would be grand, Michael."

"So what did you cook for Father Reilly today?"

"Nothing special, just some shepherd's pie."

"Sounds special to me. My mam used to make that."

"Michael, you never talk about your family. Are any of them

here in America with you?"

"No, as far as I know they're all still back in Dublin."

"Have you no family here in Philadelphia, then?"

"Just a cousin. My family isn't important. Tell me instead, what other meals Father Reilly likes."

"Come on, Michael, you're not interested in my cooking."

"I told you before, what I'm interested in, is you."

She looked up into his lively eyes and boyish grin that together lured her into feeling that time spent with Michael made life feel glorious. In spite of herself, she grinned at his compliment.

Strolling arm in arm down the wooden sidewalks of Second Street, she hardly noticed the gripping mud and refuse that littered the road beside them. Odors of overripe produce and garbage from the vendors' outdoor stalls saturated the atmosphere, but Ellen concentrated instead on Michael's scent. She loved the way he smelled, a mixture of hard work and soap. As they held hands, the strong grasp of his fingers brought out the color in her cheeks. She loved the long walks they took, which were never long enough. They always parted before Fifth Street, although she wasn't really sure why.

"Fish for sale, fresh today, best price in all of Philadelphia!" yelled a nearby fishmonger as he blew a tin horn to attract buyers, and street children ran among the stands snitching any food they could grab. Michael steered Ellen away from the urchins almost crashing into her.

"Come on, Ellen, let's cross over Girard."

Passing dry goods stores juxtaposed with other shops and saloons that offered everything from oysters to oilcloths and whittle knives to whiskey, they headed toward Murphy's, with its weather-beaten siding faded with neglect, but the best fish and chips in the area.

Entering the restaurant, Ellen saw people look up and nod at Michael. She took it as a good sign; he must be known in this part of the neighborhood, so she shouldn't worry about Patrick and Mam's reactions. Just as Michael headed toward a seat, he stopped halfway, digging in his pockets and looked at her with a troubled expression. "Ah, Ellen, I loaned a friend at work some money this morning, and dinna have time to go back home and get more. Can you pay for us?"

Cut From Strong Cloth

"I thought this was your day off?"

He flashed his boyish smile. "Oh, did I say that? I meant I had the rest of the day off. I'm a soft touch when a friend is in need. I hope you don't mind."

She had just been paid by Father Reilly, and his noble act of helping out a friend appealed to her, so she dug into her purse and counted out some coins. Michael soon returned with two orders of fish and chips. He placed the plate in front of her, and beamed.

"Have I told you, Ellen, that spending a day with you makes my heart glad?"

"I enjoy being with you too, Michael."

As they began to eat, he stole a few of her potatoes as if in a game, and placed them one at a time in his own mouth, slowly licking his lips while she watched. Next, taking one of his potatoes, he reached over and placed it between her lips. They finished the meal between bites of conversation, hushed laughter, and engaging smiles.

"Ellen, the afternoon is still young. Why don't we walk in a new area? I know a wee small park where we could have a bit of privacy."

"All right. I just have to be mindful of the time because I promised to fix supper tonight."

They left Murphy's holding hands and walked down farther into the section of Philadelphia called the Northern Liberties. When they stopped, Ellen could see that the area was not a park at all, just a vacant lot with several clumps of trees.

But before she could question him, Michael pulled her over to the nearest tree and braced her up against its trunk. He leaned in and kissed her hard, not a teasing kiss, but a kiss that took her breath away. She pulled back for just a moment, taking in his toned body, strong muscular arms, and jaunty hips. His hazel-flecked eyes blazed with an unmistakable energy and then he cupped her head and began kissing her with a ferocity she never experienced before.

She reached up and ran her fingers through his hair, wanting to grab onto to him and never let go.

He drove his tongue into her mouth, darting it around behind her teeth. Stunned and pleased, she wasn't sure how to respond. She

didn't want him to think she was common, but her heart pounded with the intimacy of the act. With the bark of the tree pressing into her back, their kissing grew more and more intense. He rubbed his body against hers in a primal rhythm of passion and lust. Heat coursed through her arms and legs, and then an intense pulsing in her private area catapulted her body to a precipice. He thrust his hips on her, and pushed his hard cock against her pelvis, grinding with a fierce determination as his hands pulled at her dress.

Dear God, this was happening too fast. "Michael! Stop!"

But he was still clawing at her dress, fighting to open the buttons. She pushed hard and shoved him off her. He staggered back, his eyes now a glint of furious rage and his mouth a tight line, devoid of any affection.

"What do you mean, stop? We've been seeing each other long enough. How can you say stop, when I know you want it, too!"

"You know nothing of the kind! Of course I'm attracted to you, but I don't intend on this happening in a vacant lot, for God's sake. Michael, I'm not some whore. What were you thinking?"

"What was I thinking? I was thinking, Ellen, that if you want our relationship to continue, you need to think about us having each other. You're not a school girl anymore. 'Tis time you started acting like a woman."

Once spoken, the words could not be taken back. Her eyes flashed with fury, she squared her shoulders, held her head high, and declared, "I'm going home."

His eyes glared like shards of ice. "Go on back to the safety of your family and your own single bed. But listen to me, Ellen—I won't wait forever." Then he stalked off.

She held her composure, although confusion, passion, and anger were all competing for attention. When two people loved each other, she knew what eventually happened. But she believed it occurred once they were committed to each other and planned to marry.

He's never even said he loves me. Biting her lower lip, she retraced her steps home, reassuring herself that she had done the right thing even though her heart felt wounded.

"You're acting like Shanty Irish!"

Ellen stared at her brother. "What is it you're trying to say, Patrick?"

"Well for starters, why did you stay out so long after finishing work with Father Reilly? And why are your cheeks so red? You're not sick, and it isn't cold outside, so I'm betting you were with that Brady fellow!"

"His name is Michael, Michael Brady, and how dare you talk to me like that. You're not in charge of me!" Shanty Irish indeed! "This is America, Patrick, in case you forgot! I'm entitled to see whoever I choose, go out any afternoon I want, and I don't have to be accountable to you!"

Patrick tried a different tactic. "I only want what's best for you, Ellen. I was hoping you'd agree to the idea of James Nolan coming to see you. He's a fine gentleman."

Her back stiffened.

"You're being stubborn Ellen, not even listening to me!"

"If Da were alive he'd understand! I want to make my own choices. I don't intend to be dependent on any man. Da would know that I want to be my own person!"

"Ah, but he's not here, is he? I'm the one who's taken care of you and Mam ever since we landed in Philadelphia. Do you want to stay poor forever?"

When he saw how this stung, he stopped and lowered his voice.

"Ellen, James Nolan just wants to start seeing you. But also consider this—if you did marry someone like him, you'd be taken care of for the rest of your life. You'd be gentry Irish, with real lace curtains in every window of the house, not just a touch of lace like here. Think what that would have meant to Da."

She fought the tears that were welling up.

"I know you just came back from an afternoon with Brady. All I'm asking is for you to consider meeting with James Nolan. At least allow him to come visit you once or twice. If you got to know him better,

Linda Harris Sittig

I think you'd be surprised to find out what a gentleman he is. I know he's older than you, but even Da was older than Mam."

She quieted down. "Yes, Patrick, I'm sure Mr. Nolan's a decent man. But would he allow me my own independence? I won't marry anyone unless he honors me with my own freedom."

"So, does this Michael Brady you seem so fond of, does he honor you? Him, with his wayward ways, and never a penny to his name!"

"I would rather have a touch of lace and marry who I please than marry a man I dinna love!"

Patrick sputtered in exasperation and stormed out of the room.

Ellen sat alone. Feelings of confusion clouded her thinking. She loved being with Michael and wanted him to love her back. But a feeling of shame descended because he had taken her to an abandoned lot to pursue his physical desires. It had felt so cheap. She wanted more than just the physical. She wanted him to love her for who she was and to admire her for her goals. She wanted him to be proud of her and just as important—she wanted to be proud of him as well.

***

As Ellen prepared for sleep that night, she thought about the confrontation with Patrick and what he'd said about James Nolan. The fact that Mr. Nolan ran a business should impress her, but it didn't. The sixteen-year difference between them did not bother her either. She wanted the lace curtains in every window, but on her own terms. Ellen had no intention of staying poor forever.

She pulled the cotton quilt up to her shoulders and shrugged off the feeling she might be overlooking something about James Nolan. After all, he was nice looking with his dark hair and chocolate brown eyes, and he carried himself with an aura of a gentleman's confidence. But no one other than Michael could make her feel so alive. Worn out thinking about them both, she said her prayers and drifted off to sleep.

***

Cut From Strong Cloth

When she awoke fresh and eager to start the new day, she began as always with a prayer to the Blessed Mother. She often wondered how Father Reilly might react if she told him she believed Mary to be her own personal guardian angel. Surely he would tell her that the Virgin was too busy being the Queen of Heaven to take her on as a private case.

"Good morning, Mary. 'Tis me, Ellen. Hail Mary, full of grace. . ." Ending the ritual, she made the sign of the cross. Her Irish Catholic beliefs were tightly woven into her soul, even if she chided her mother for clinging to the same traditions.

She dressed in a dark blue wool dress to fend off the brisk October air and came to breakfast thinking about one of the presidential candidates, Abraham Lincoln. Patrick, already seated at the table, nodded in her direction. She joined him, giving a cursory smile to her mother, and then reached for a slice of warm barmbrack bread.

"Great barmbrack, Mam."

"Thank you, Patrick, I know 'tis a favorite of yours." Mam paused. "Ellen, cat got your tongue? Or don't you agree with Patrick?"

Ellen met the leveled gaze of Mam's steely blue eyes, signaling that a contest of wills was about to percolate.

"No, barmbrack's good. I've just been thinking about this upcoming election." She turned to address her brother. "Who do you think will win?"

"Some are predicting it's going to be Abraham Lincoln," he replied.

"I read an editorial last week that said if Lincoln wins, it might put the whole nation at odds with one another."

"And how would it be, Ellen, that you are suddenly an authority on politics? In my day women dinna—"

"Yes, Mam, I know. In your day women dinna involve themselves in much more than keeping house. But this is America. Remember, anything is supposed to be possible here."

Cecilia's eyes flashed with signs of anger and hurt.

But Ellen held fast. Giving in now meant giving in again further down the road.

Patrick carried on with the conversation. "Well for one thing, Lincoln's trying to stop slavery from spreading into the territories, so most Southerners don't want to see him in the White House."

"What are Lincoln's chances of winning?"

"Don't really know. It'll depend upon how many votes he receives. Can you pass more barmbrack?"

Mam picked up the plate and handed it over to Patrick with a smile. When she turned her focus back to Ellen, the smile evaporated. "What are the chances we could have a decent meal without all your talk about who might or might not win the election? I don't know why there's such a fuss over the Negros anyway."

"The real issue is slavery. Mam, you canna tell me that you approve of a practice where human beings are bought and sold?"

"What I think or don't think will have no effect on the election."

"If women could vote, then our ideas could affect major issues."

"Jesus, Mary, and Joseph! What in God's name, Ellen, ever gave you the idea that women should vote?" Cecilia almost screeched.

"Patrick, what if women could vote? Would that help Mr. Lincoln's cause?"

"I really don't know."

Ellen turned back to her mother. "Mam, wouldn't you vote if you could?"

"I swear, Ellen, I don't know where you get these grand ideas of yours. Too much reading, I think. First the Negros, now women voting! Why can't you just find a husband, settle down, and have babies?"

"I'd vote if I could."

"Aye, but you can't, and you might just as well get used to that. You should be thankful for the life you have, instead of always yearning for what's out of reach."

"Are you happy, Mam, with your life?"

Cecilia ignored the question. "You'll be late to work if you sit here much longer, and for heaven's sake don't say anything to Father Reilly about women voting."

"I wouldn't dream of doing that." Ellen pushed back from the table, strode over to the wash basin and plunked her dish in the water

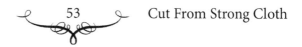

without first even bothering to sweep off the crumbs. Let her deal with the mess.

She picked up her purse, grabbed her cloak and bonnet, and stalked out the door. Perhaps this is the day she should talk to Father Reilly about her plans for the future. She hoped he might become an ally. As she approached St. Michael's, she squared her shoulders, held her head up high, and mounted the steps to the rectory. Pushing open the front door, she detected a faint wisp of incense in the parlor, indicating Father Reilly had finished his morning prayers.

"Ah, good morning, Ellen. How are you on this grand day that God hath made?"

"Good morning, Father. Yes, 'tis grand."

She hung her cloak and bonnet on the coat pegs.

"We have some new correspondence we'll be tackling this morning, as I plan to invite the Bishop to join us for an Advent service."

"Father Reilly, before we start in on the correspondence, do you have time for a small conversation with me? 'Tis of a personal nature."

"Personal? Do you wish to speak of it in confession?"

"Oh no, Father, 'tis not that type of personal. It has to do with my future plans."

"Your future plans? You're not happy working here?" His face registered dismay.

"Yes, of course I enjoy working here, but I've always had other plans. I want to go into business for myself."

Father Reilly's eyebrows shot up in surprise.

"You have been so gracious and kind to lend me the use of your library, and once I've read all your books, I should be ready. But what I need is a sponsor; someone willing to help me out, perhaps with a loan. With all of your contacts in Philadelphia, I thought you could introduce me to someone like that."

The priest let out a deep sigh. "Ellen, have you really thought this through? I don't think this dream of yours is very practical. Trying to open a business takes more than just money, and I really don't know of anyone who'd be willing to back a young woman. However, if this is a goal you continue to have, then I ask you to pray about it."

Ellen's shoulders drooped. She'd been so sure Father Reilly would see the worthiness of her dream.

"All right Father. I'll continue to pray and ask God to guide me. I'm thinking a small shop that specializes in a wide variety of fabrics would be a profitable business."

"Have you talked this over with your mother? She knows of your aspirations, I assume."

"Mam wouldn't part with even one cent for me to go into business on my own. All her money goes to supporting Patrick's business."

"You might be surprised as to what your mother would do."

Ellen looked askance at Father Reilly, when a loud voice boomed out in the side street.

"Boots! Boots, the iceman here!"

Ellen sometimes wondered if the iceman was practically deaf, because he always announced his appearance by yelling and then clanging his iron ice hooks together before bringing the block of ice into the kitchen.

She glanced back at Father Reilly, now sorting the morning's correspondence and obviously through with their conversation. She picked up the coin purse intended for vendors and waited on the back porch to pay the iceman.

"Good morning, girl. Do you need me to count out the correct change for you?"

Ellen didn't answer but glared at him, then counted out the exact change herself and plunked it down on the porch railing.

After he left, she took a broom to the back porch and attacked the floor with vengeance—sweeping and re-sweeping dirt that did not exist, but deserved to be pummeled because of the unfairness of life.

This won't set me back, Da. I'll figure out something.

Later, while preparing the noon meal, Ellen allowed her mind to drift and it settled on Patrick's suggestion of just getting to know James Nolan. It wasn't that she didn't enjoy his company; he was quite pleasant to talk to. Perhaps he could help her. At the very least he could have some good advice, and at best he might become a sponsor. And if Michael felt some competition existed with her seeing another man,

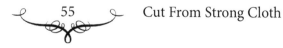

then he might try harder to win her affections. Perhaps it would be to her advantage to spend some time with James Nolan after all.

***

Autumn waned as the last day of October ticked itself off the calendar for the old Celtic holiday of Samhain. Kensington Irish still celebrated Samhain, although called now by its English name, Halloween.

This day signaled both the end of the ancient harvest season and the beginning of wool weather, when summer clothes were packed away and winter garments removed from storage. Ellen remembered Da hollowing out turnips, placing small candles in the cavities, and then positioning them outside the front door to scare away the dead on this particular night. Whether he believed in the old superstition or participated for the benefit of Patrick and Ellen, she never knew.

"Mam, I'm setting out candles for later. Are you going with me to the Flannigan's tonight?"

"Of course I am. Just because I work in Rittenhouse Square doesn't mean I canna enjoy a Kensington Halloween. I baked a tray of cookies to take over, but I think Patrick plans to celebrate with his own friends. I hope he still makes it to All Saints Mass tomorrow morning."

Ellen wanted to say that Patrick was a grown man and in charge of his own schedule, but she decided not to aggravate Mam, who seemed to be in good spirits.

The finale of Ellen's favorite season evoked in her a bit of wistfulness as the strokes of nature's brilliant colors withdrew from the city and Kensington cloaked itself once again in drab shades of browns and gray. But November also signaled the start of Advent and gift buying time. Ellen planned to purchase a woolen scarf for Michael and wondered what he might be giving her. Certainly their tiff the other day wouldn't stop him from celebrating Christmas with her?

Later at church, Ellen saw Michael peering in the poor box. Odd thing for him to be doing. He obviously did not know she was there, so she coughed.

"Oh, Ellen. Dinna know you were here."

"Hello. How has your week been?"

He shrugged. "Same as usual."

"Did you notice that we are putting up the Advent greens?"

"Never paid much attention to that."

"Well, Christmas will be here before you know it."

"Yeah, guess so."

Why was he being so distant? Was he still angry?

She decided to deflect the conversation to more neutral ground. "I've been reading about the presidential election and what might happen to the country if Abraham Lincoln wins." He made no comment, so she continued. "My brother Patrick feels the South will have a very negative reaction if Mr. Lincoln were to become president. He said fighting could even break out. Wouldn't that be terrible?"

"Aye. Violence is never good for anyone."

"Patrick also said that he and his business associate, James Nolan, might profit though from the situation."

This time he turned toward her. "How would anyone in Philadelphia profit?"

"If fighting does break out, additional soldiers would be needed, and extra cloth for their uniforms would have to be manufactured. I think Patrick and James Nolan are planning to bid for government contracts ahead of time so they can be prepared. Imagine that, Michael, Canavan wool might be the foundation for uniforms worn right here in Pennsylvania. I think the idea's wonderful."

When he didn't respond, she tried changing the subject again.

"Michael, let's not talk about soldiers and uniforms, then." She took a deep breath. "Would you consider coming to Sunday dinner with my family? For the start of the holiday season?"

"Ah. I'm sorry but there's talk right now that Weikel Spice might be laying off some workers. If that happens, it would mean me finding employment somewhere else. Of course I would send you word, but right now I canna commit to any dinner plans."

Then he cut the walk short, kissed her a hurried good-bye, and strode off toward the Northern Liberties.

Ellen felt deflated. As she stood alone on the street, she decid-

Cut From Strong Cloth

ed to start planning now on getting James Nolan to become an ally. It would be good for her business, and her relationship with Michael.

CHAPTER 6

November 1860

Sundays were his favorite day for setting fires. Most people were either at church or busy with family. Not that the day really mattered. As long as he set a successful fire and his benefactors collected the insurance money, he would always get paid. The money was what drove him to continue, or at least that is what he told himself.

He stuck to Kensington because it was familiar territory and he could quickly join his fire brigade and battle the blaze with them. Most times, he did not even inquire whose property he was setting fire to, but every once in a while he recognized the building as a familiar landmark. Like Delany's Glue Factory. It wasn't that he had anything against the owners; it was just business, pure and simple.

In reality, he needed the fires. He had a yearning in his soul that could not be quenched. He wanted to be somebody, somebody important. The fires made him invincible, and important men in the city depended upon his expertise. Without him, a fire was nothing more than a pile of refuse, waiting to be ignited.

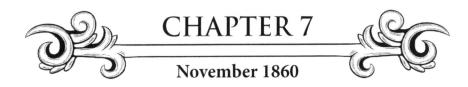

CHAPTER 7

November 1860

"Can you believe that ape from Illinois won?" a bar patron called out.

"I canna imagine who voted for him, other than them rich sons of bitches in high places," slurred another man.

The bartender kept pouring drinks. Politics always boded well for business.

"What do ya think he intends to do about slavery?" piped up a fellow at the end of the bar.

Several of the other men just shrugged; no one knew for sure how Lincoln's election would affect slavery, but they were all concerned how his actions might affect their jobs. James merely listened to their ranting because it didn't really matter who became President; these men would still complain about something, and politics was not as paramount to him as arranging a talk with Cecilia Canavan. He finished his food and left the pub. Back at work, he asked his factory manager, Jimmy Doyle, to take a note over to Fifth Street and wait for a reply.

The answer stated, "Delighted to have you call."

James appeared two days later. Cecilia opened the door wearing a modest but fashionable dress of navy wool trimmed with a narrow lace collar and showing pearl-colored buttons at the cuffs.

"Well hallo, Mr. Nolan, do come in."

"Hallo, Mrs. Canavan. Thank you for taking the time to see me. Patrick suggested I might talk with you about Ellen."

"Please join me over here. Patrick is out back rearranging some of the wool, so it will just be the two of us. May I offer you tea, or perhaps some Jameson?"

"A taste of the whiskey would be grand, thank you."

"I'll just be a moment. Please make yourself comfortable."

As she left for the kitchen, his eyes wandered around the room looking for signs of Ellen's presence.

Cecilia returned with a bottle of the Irish whiskey and two short glasses.

"Here we go." She set the bottle on the low table in front of the sofa and poured out two glasses with a steady hand.

He cleared his throat and then took a healthy sip. The warmth of the liquid brought a sense of calm to his nerves. "Mrs. Canavan, if I may be candid? I am quite enamored with your daughter and would like to court her, but I fear she might not be interested in me. The difference in our ages might be the problem."

"Mr. Nolan, 'tis not the difference in age I think that matters, 'tis the way a man courts a girl that counts. And since you were candid with me, might I be candid with you? What plans do you have involving Ellen? If I can understand that, then perhaps we can talk further."

He absentmindedly fingered his scar while collecting his wits.

"I plan to produce the best possible cloth in all of Philadelphia and own an entire mill, not just rent out factory space as I do now. I want to have Ellen by my side." When he finished speaking, he felt heat creep from his neck up to his cheeks.

"Well, Mr. Nolan, then let Ellen get to know the real you. Create time to talk with her. Engage her in conversation and show you are interested in what she has to say. She might be a bit outspoken, but she is quite knowledgeable on many topics."

They continued to sip their drinks and exchange pleasantries, but James realized the next step was up to him.

After draining his glass, he spoke up. "Thank you for your

Cut From Strong Cloth

honesty, Mrs. Canavan. Before I go, I'll stop outside to see Patrick, and I will take your words to heart."

He stepped outside and cleared his throat. "Patrick? Hallo!"

Patrick came out of a storage shed wiping the sweat off his face with a rag. "Have you talked with my mother?"

"Aye. I'd like to know what Ellen said when you told her of my intentions."

"James, I've told you that Ellen speaks her mind. She did not reject your offer, but said that she would not be dependent on any man and wanted to choose on her own who she would see and who she would marry."

"Damn. You said she had an independent streak, but I thought she'd be agreeable."

"Oh, she can be challenging, James, I guarantee you that. So I suggested she should consider having you come to visit—not really courting, you see. Once she gets to know you, maybe then you could court."

"The thing is, Patrick, I get tongue-tied when I'm around her, even though I have so much I want to say. Do you have any idea of how she might wish to spend an evening?"

"Dunno, James. I do know family's important to her. Perhaps you could share some stories about your life back in Ireland, before the Famine."

James grew quiet.

"Thanks. I'll plan on visiting Ellen soon." With that he picked up his walking stick and took off, leaving Patrick to stare after him.

* * *

A few days later a knock sounded at the Canavans' door and when Ellen answered, James stood before her.

"Mr. Nolan. My brother is out of the house on an errand. I'm sorry, but you've missed him."

"I'm not here to see Patrick. I came to ask if you would consider accompanying me on Sunday to a social function nearby. May I come in?"

Ellen appeared taken off guard. A social function? She hadn't thought about him attending social functions, but this would give her an opportunity to talk with him. He was picking at his sleeve. Could he be nervous, inviting her to accompany him?

"Why, of course, Mr. Nolan, do come in. What kind of social function would this be?"

"Supper with a local family. Informal, I can assure you, but I thought perhaps you would do me the honor of going along. This family has children and I will be bringing them some small gifts. I thought you might like to help me with that. And please, call me James. Mr. Nolan sounds so official."

"Of course I would be glad to go with you, James, and help in any way I can."

He broke into a surprised smile. "Grand. Well then, I will come for you at five o'clock Sunday evening." He shifted his feet. "Better get going, then. Good day."

Later that night, Ellen mentioned she wouldn't be home for supper on Sunday because she'd be going out with James Nolan instead.

Patrick grinned. "'Tis a hooley you'll be going to?"

"A party? No, of course not. Just visiting a local family for a meal. And I think it would be interesting to find out more about his factory, and his business."

Cecilia furrowed her brow. "I think he expects this to be a social event, so don't go bothering him with business questions. Act the part of a lady."

Ellen concocted a mischievous grin. "A lady can still show her interest in what the man does for a living."

***

On Sunday, Ellen chose her mauve and pink checked dress with fashionable black grosgrain bows accenting each sleeve. As with her other dresses, the belted waist and knife pleats showed off her trim figure, and the cuffs showcased real lace. She considered wearing a corset, then decided she did not have to compromise comfort just to impress

Cut From Strong Cloth

a man. But she did decide to wrap up a fresh loaf of Mam's barmbrack bread and take it along as a gift.

James was punctual, as Ellen surmised he would be, and a chill in the air added a festive feel to the evening. James helped Ellen on with her cloak and then guided her outside to his Phaeton carriage. A two-seater fashioned with upholstered ebony leather and a shiny black painted frame, it appeared worthy of carrying royalty. The magnificent white horse waiting in front of it made Ellen feel like Cinderella going to the ball.

Once ensconced on the front seat with a woolen carriage blanket thrown over her lap and the cylindrical stoneware foot warmer positioned under her feet, she smiled as James picked up the reins and began to drive. The nip of the evening air brought out the color of roses on Ellen's cheeks, and she let her fingers stroke the luxury of real leather seats.

"'Tis a short distance to this house where we'll be visiting, but with the night turning cold, I felt perhaps you would enjoy a ride."

"Oh, 'tis thoughtful of you, James, and your horse is so beautiful."

Almost as if in response, the horse snorted and shook his harness bells, which broke the stillness of the twilight.

"What's his name?"

"Lir. His name is Lir."

"Lir? Like from the story, 'The Children of Lir'?"

"Aye, the same one. But I promise you he'll not be turning into a swan."

Ellen beamed. The story of the four children of Lir who were changed into swans by their evil stepmother and forced to remain as such for 900 years had always been one of Ellen's favorite tales. She also sadly remembered that when the curse finally faded, the swans returned to human form only to die encircled in each other's arms. The message of loyalty was one that every child in Ireland knew well.

After several blocks, James stopped the carriage and Ellen realized they were down on Second Street, not too far from the exact spot where she first bumped into Michael. The houses here were modest row homes, three stories tall, with exterior fronts that showed both their age and their blue collar status. It was an immigrant block like so many

Linda Harris Sittig

others in Kensington, but the gas light that spilled out from the front windows made the homes appear more genteel than they actually were.

James tied Lir up to a hitching post, threw a stable blanket over him, and then came around to help Ellen. Before they could even approach the house, the door blew wide open, and children spilled out shouting, "James! 'Tis James!" Next, an attractive woman came to the door. He maneuvered Ellen in first.

"Ellen, I would like you to meet my sister, Mary Ready, and her family. Mary, this is Ellen Canavan."

Ellen stopped abruptly. "Your sister?" Turning to Mary she said, "Hello. James dinna mention this visit would be a family visit, or I would have brought more than just a loaf of barmbrack."

"Nonsense, you are welcome here, and we love barmbrack." Mary then hugged James.

As he took Ellen's cloak and bonnet and ushered her further into the house, Ellen stood transfixed as James began to dole out small gifts to the children. A man came over clapping James on the back, and James introduced him as his sister's husband, Ed. The children continued to swarm all over James. Ellen was speechless. *Could this be the same man who only carries on business conversations in our house?*

Then she remembered her manners. "Mary, is there something I could do to help with the meal?"

"Thank you, Ellen. I'd enjoy your company in the kitchen. We're having coddle for dinner because James loves that combination of sausage and potatoes. You can help by starting to fill up the serving dishes."

A short walk through a narrow hallway led them back to a kitchen with savory smells wafting in the air, and multiple tin pots and pans sitting on the stove.

"I hope you'll like the recipe, 'tis a family favorite because our mam often made it when we were young. She could take a few bangers and magically stretch them into a full meal."

"It smells wonderful."

"James told us he might be bringing a guest, but we had no idea he'd be bringing a young woman. He usually keeps to himself, so I know you must be special."

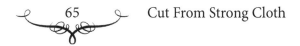

Ellen unexpectedly felt her heart jump. "Mary, I dinna even know he had family here in Kensington."

"I'm the only one. The rest of our family died back in Ireland during the Famine. When James and I survived, we decided to start new lives in America. Ed came too; we got married, and all our children were born here in Philadelphia."

Ellen felt comfortable with this easy, affable woman. She talked as if she and Ellen had known each other all their lives. Ellen walked over and placed her hand on Mary's arm.

"I'm sorry, Mary, for both you and James. I left Ireland as a young girl, and I must confess I don't remember much about the Famine, except often being hungry."

"You're lucky, then. I still have nightmares about it. But by the grace of God we endured and now have a good life here. James has become successful, I have a dependable husband, and all my children are healthy. Blessed, and I know it." She paused. "You've no memories of Ireland, then?"

"Oh yes! I remember my Da. He was a weaver who took great pride in his craft and won blue ribbons for his cloth on Fair Days."

"He never used shoddy, then, if he won blue ribbons."

"Shoddy?"

"'Tis when them skivers took used strips of rag wool glued and pressed together to look like a bolt of cloth. But as soon as it got wet, the material disintegrated and the buyer was left holding a sodden mess and nothing more."

"I've never heard that before, but I know my Da would never have allowed shoddy to be a part of his cloth."

"A good man then, your Da."

"But I did just read about a man named Thomas Burberry, an Englishman who experimented with combining different types of fibers to produce blended bolts of cloth. Do you think he used shoddy?"

"Oh, I don't think so. No one makes a name from using shoddy."

"Mary, is there food back there in the kitchen, or are you women going to talk all night?" a voice from the front room hollered.

"Mind your manners, Ed. We're coming with supper right now."

Linda Harris Sittig

The two women came out carrying bowls of food over to the large table, already laden with plates. Ellen placed the barmbrack next to the butter and then watched as James led the children in, pied-piper style.

The coddle, served alongside cooked carrots and canned peas, presented a simple but abundant meal, and the barmbrack disappeared with nine hungry bodies at the table. Ellen laughed with James over the children's antics and joined in with him on a discussion over Lincoln's election while they enjoyed apple cake for dessert. When it came time to bid goodnight, Ellen realized the evening had flown. She thanked Mary and Ed for their hospitality.

"Come back anytime you like, dear—with or without James, you'll always be welcome."

Out in the frosty air, James helped Ellen into the carriage. He spread an extra blanket down for her to sit on and told her to drape the woolen throw over her legs since the leather seat was now cold to the touch. Then he climbed back up in the driver's position.

"Did you enjoy the evening, Ellen?"

"Oh, I did. You just surprised me, not telling me it would be your family."

"I'm a private person, Ellen, and once I started my own business, I felt it would be better for Mary to keep a distance from me. There's always the possibility of strikes at a factory, and I wouldn't want anything to happen to her because of me. She's all I have left. We do see each other from time to time, but she and Ed have made their own life here in Kensington."

"I know, James. She shared a bit about losing your family in the Famine. I'm sorry."

No sooner were the words out of her mouth that she chewed on her lip. Somehow she felt mentioning the Famine was not appropriate. Too personal. But she put her hand on his arm in a display of genuine caring. James did not comment. For a brief moment, a look of melancholy washed over his face, but he let it pass and then tapped the reins and Lir started back toward Fifth Street.

"You might be a bit warmer if you leaned against me. Don't

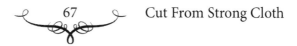

worry, I won't bite," he teased.

Ellen slipped closer to him till their arms touched.

"There. Better." He murmured.

"James, what made you decide to invite me to your sister's house?"

"Well, I thought if we were ever going to get to know each other better, you should see me apart from my life at the factory or in business meetings with your brother."

"And 'tis important that I get to know you better, is it?" she queried.

James did not speak for half a moment. Ellen could sense the rough wool of his coat sleeve brushing up against her cloak.

"Yes, Ellen. 'Tis important to me," James offered in a kind voice.

So this was James Nolan. Kind and good to his family, and respectful to Ellen. He'd make a fine business partner.

Once they arrived back at number 1225, James got out of the carriage, tied up Lir, and helped Ellen down to the street level. A dried leaf skittered in the road and a few soft flakes of snow drifted to the ground.

"Thank you for going tonight, Ellen," he said as he gently continued to hold onto her arm.

"James, it was a wonderful evening. I mean that."

"Really? How so? I was worried you might be bored."

Then Ellen walked over and stroked Lir, scratching the horse behind the ears. "Mary and Ed are so warm and inviting to be with, and their house felt happy with the jumble of all their children."

"You seemed to enjoy the children."

"Of course I did. Children are what make a family." She smiled.

"I'm glad you think that."

"Family is important to you, isn't it, James? I can tell by the way you acted with them, and even by the way you care for Lir."

James smiled. "Ellen, have you ever driven a carriage?"

"Back home I rode a pony once or twice, but nothing more."

"How would you like to learn to drive this carriage with Lir? We could go north of town where it would be safe to practice."

It was a strange suggestion, but an intriguing one. Since there had not been an opportunity to talk about business tonight, perhaps an afternoon outing would be more advantageous.

"I'd be delighted to, James. How about next Sunday afternoon, if the weather holds?"

His smile turned to a grin. "Sunday it shall be. I'll come for you at two o'clock." Then he walked her up to the door, kissed her lightly on the cheek, and bid her a fond goodnight.

As soon as she entered the house, Cecilia and Patrick looked up from the sofa where they had both been reading in total silence. In contrast to the Ready house, the atmosphere in the Canavan house felt almost gloomy.

"Well, how was supper with the local family?"

"The local family was his sister, brother-in-law, nieces, and nephews."

Ellen then watched in utter delight as both Cecilia and Patrick's mouths gaped open. "His sister?" they both said at the exact same time.

"Aye. There's an entire side to James that no one else in Kensington would ever suspect. I was wrong about him. He's easy to talk to, has solid opinions about Abraham Lincoln, and is interested in knowing my ideas. In fact, he's going to teach me to drive his carriage."

"Is he, now?" Cecilia tried not to show a reaction, but Patrick was beaming.

Cut From Strong Cloth

CHAPTER 8

November 1860

On Sunday, James showed up on time and chatted with Cecilia while Ellen finished dressing. The November air was a bit chilly, and never having been behind the reins, Ellen chose warmth, comfort, and ease of movement in her newest outfit, an innovative creation of Mam's. The caramel brown flared skirt and matching fitted jacket festooned with a black velvet collar and cuffs fit her perfectly. And it gave Ellen an ease of movement since neither a corset or petticoats were used. She also brought a short, tan, woolen cloak, Mam's Christmas gift from last year. Buttoning up her leather shoes snug and tight, she peeked in the mirror to check her appearance.

She skipped down the stairs and saw her mother's jaw set in stern disapproval at the unladylike descent. James had dressed in more informal clothes than usual. He was taller and thinner than Patrick, and Ellen saw that his trim figure was rather appealing.

"Hallo, James. Did you remember to bring Lir?"

"Now it would be hard to teach you to drive without a horse," he laughed. Then he helped her on with her cloak, and as they left the house Ellen felt the distinct lighthearted feeling of escape.

Out in the street, the carriage gleamed, a few more bells were now attached to the reins, and the black frame polished with gloss.

Even Lir's mane and tail had been combed till they shone. The horse shook his head from side to side when Ellen appeared, so she approached, stroking him and slipping him a bite of carrot that she'd been saving as a treat. Lir whinnied back at her, and James grinned.

"Now, Ellen, don't go spoiling him before we even get started."

James helped her into the carriage, climbed in himself, and then nudged Lir out into the road. They drove past unending blocks of row homes, each as drab as the next, but with the factories quiet, the afternoon felt peaceful. As they headed north toward the outskirts of the city, James began to hum a certain tune.

"Do you like how I can hum this tune? My Da claimed it was started by a fiddler up in Derry."

"I do, James. It reminds me of happy times when I was young. 'Tis my favorite. Does it remind you of Ireland, too?"

For a brief moment, James was silent. "Aye, it reminds me of Ireland. But now it also reminds me of you."

With a slight movement he flicked the reins, and Lir picked up a bit of speed. Ellen thought back to what his sister had said about losing their family in the Famine. No question that he would still have traces of sorrow. As they continued, the road narrowed and the buildings thinned out till the street traffic disappeared. James stopped the carriage.

Ellen had never been this far north before. A handful of run-down houses, more like shanties, sat by the side of the road, and empty fields spread out in all directions. In front of one of the dwellings she glimpsed a woman hunched over a cooking pot, stirring something greasy-smelling. Ellen thought it might be food. A scrawny pig dashed out from the back of another shanty chased by a small boy running barefoot even in this cold weather. These lands must belong to someone, but James didn't seem to be bothered with whose property it might be.

"All right, Ellen, here is the first thing you want to remember. Always approach a horse from the front, or near the front side, so it can see you coming. You never want to scare a horse by coming up from behind. The second thing you need to remember is to be firm at all times so Lir understands that you are the one in charge. Then the third

Cut From Strong Cloth

thing is keep your wits about you. Dogs or children can come charging out from anywhere. We don't want Lir to get spooked."

Like any other subject she tackled, Ellen believed that with concentration and determination, she would be able to master driving the carriage without a problem. James climbed down from the buggy. He went over to Lir and holding the reins, stroked Lir's neck, almost cooing to the horse. Then he looked up at Ellen.

"Let's start by you watching me. You saw how I first talked to Lir to settle him down. We both trust each other, but if he was a new horse, I wouldn't trust him until after I had driven him a few times."

With that, James climbed back up onto the carriage seat, picked up the reins and held them in both hands. Then with a soft "tsk" sound made by clicking his tongue on the roof of his mouth, he signaled to Lir that he was ready to move. Ellen watched as he first guided the horse straight ahead and then to the right or left by using just one side of the reins. To urge Lir forward, he tapped with both reins. When he was ready to stop, he said "whoa," and pulled back on the reins until Lir came to a standstill.

Ellen thought it looked simple enough. James stood up and let Ellen slide over into the driver's position. He sat back down, and she picked up the reins in both hands and made the same type of clicking sound she heard James use. Lir didn't move. She looked over at James with some exasperation.

"Aye, and did you talk to him before you started?"

"Well, sure I saw you do that, but I dinna think I would have to do it, too."

James just smiled. Ellen's independent spirit precluded her from asking for any help, so she got back down from the carriage on her own, walked away, and then approached Lir from the front. At sixteen hands high, Lir was a large and powerful horse, and Ellen tried not to show any signs of being timid around him, but concentrated instead by thinking of the swans in the fairytale. Standing on tiptoe, she gently whispered in his ear. The horse nickered back at her. She grinned at James and remounted the carriage seat. With a gentle flick of the reins Lir pulled out ahead and let Ellen drive him down the road.

"Congratulations and well done. Just what did you whisper to Lir that made him obey like a puppy dog?"

"I just told him that it was very important for me to impress you, and if he agreed to behave I had another carrot saved for him."

James laughed and, catching the scent of summer roses once more, asked, "Ellen how is it that you smell of roses even in winter?"

"'Tis rose water—my one indulgence. Mrs. Cleary gave me a bottle as a thank-you gift after I worked in her store. I must confess I do like to dab it on my neck and wrists. Does the smell bother you?"

"No, not at all. In fact, I find it quite pleasing. So, what did you and my sister talk about the other night? It seemed the two of you were deep in conversation in the kitchen, and I doubt you were talking about rose water."

"We were talking about weaving and making cloth. I told her how my Da used to win blue ribbons for his cloth on Fair Day. Mary told me about the process of using shoddy to trick the buyer into thinking they are purchasing full wool. Do you know about that?

"Aye. 'Tis a common way of beefing up sales."

"James, you don't use shoddy, do you?"

"Me? No. But there's plenty of them that do. Even the government has been tricked into buying shoddy and not knowing it until the cloth got wet. Of course by that time, it's too late. I'm not offended by the question, Ellen. I've nothing to hide with my business."

"Well then, can I ask a personal question as well? I know you're the proprietor of the St. John's Street Factory, but I don't know how you actually got started with your business."

"You really want to know?"

"Yes, I do."

"I came to America with my cousin Will about five years ago. We left the poverty of Belfast behind and planned to get jobs here as hand weavers. Our pay was less than four dollars a week at first, and we shared a room over on Mascher Street. Will wasn't so good about saving his money, but I scrimped and put away almost every cent I earned. Then the boldest thing I did was open an account at the Kensington Trust Bank so I could establish credit. Later, I went back there for my

first loan."

"So you need a bank account first before you can ask for a loan?"

"Aye, and money to put in the account, too. Why are you so curious? Is Patrick needing a bank reference?"

"Patrick? No. I'm just looking ahead to my own future and trying to get prepared."

"Prepared for what?"

"For opening my own business."

He looked surprised but refrained from making a comment.

"So, do you still live on Mascher Street?"

"No, I rent a three-room apartment in a house over on Sophia Street. 'Tis near the factory, so I can walk to work. Any other questions?"

"Just one. I've noticed the faint scar that runs down the side of your jaw. When did that happen?"

"When I was in Ireland, before I left for America."

Ellen stared at the scar and then for a brief moment, the whisper of a memory faint and distant came back to her; something about a stranger with a similar scar on the voyage to America with her. But as quickly as it came, like the sudden appearance of a hummingbird, the memory darted away.

"Ellen?"

"Just a memory from long ago. Nothing really." Shrugging it off, Ellen handed the reins back to James and let him take over. She liked being the driver, but felt content to sit back now and just enjoy the ride. As the afternoon progressed, James let down his guard and talked about his boyhood before the Famine, and Ellen tucked away the information about needing to open her own bank account.

As they returned back to Kensington, Ellen heard fire sirens and for some odd reason thought of Michael. It was then that she realized she had laughed and smiled more in this one afternoon with James than on any walk with Michael.

***

The first Sunday of Advent heralded the arrival of the Christmas season, when magic hung heavy in the air along with the fragrance of balsam and pine. This year, Christmas would be even more special because of the Ready family. Ellen already decided to make some small gifts for their children. Whether it was the merriment of the month, or something else, she found herself looking forward to spending time with James.

They had been out twice again with Lir, and she adored the horse, so extra carrots would be Lir's holiday gift. She wondered if it would be appropriate for her to give James a small gift as well. Her thoughts drifted back to Michael. He had not come back to the church for several weeks now, and she wondered when their time walking together would resume. She had loved being with him, but their last argument in the vacant lot had frightened her.

Instead of thinking about Michael, Ellen concentrated on what might be a suitable holiday gift for James. James so loved Lir. Suddenly an idea came to her. She would go to the tinsmith and ask him to fashion a small circular shape of four connected swans. The decorative piece could be attached to the top of James' walking stick. Then every time he went for a stroll, he would be reminded of her.

She needed to keep him interested in her because the business plan depended on it. Although she had never imagined that a business partner could be such enjoyable company.

Cut From Strong Cloth

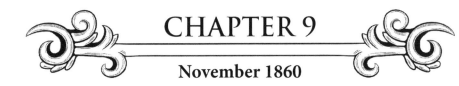

CHAPTER 9

November 1860

The next day she returned home from the tinsmith's, feeling quite pleased. He had agreed to design the circle according to the drawing she'd made. It would be a grand surprise for James. Upon entering the house, Ellen heard angry voices back by the kitchen. Walking down the short hallway, she discovered Patrick and James vehemently arguing, something she'd never witnessed before.

"Well, Patrick, if they didn't hear this from you, then just how do you suppose the McFadden brothers got wind of our idea? They'll underbid all the other mills now to get the best contracts!"

"Why would you think I'd be the one telling business plans? I saw Michael Brady over at Whalen's Pub last week. All of them clappin' him on the back and congratulating him for hittin' the jackpot. He wouldn't make eye contact with me, and he left the pub before I could introduce myself. I wouldn't be puttin' it past him to trade information for cash."

Michael? Ellen couldn't believe her ears. What on earth was happening, and how could Michael be involved in any of this?

"I tell you, James, I don't share our matters with anyone else. Why would I? What bothers me even more is that you believe I had a part in it. I thought you knew me better than that."

James glared at Patrick and then let out an exasperated sigh. "All right, it's hard for me to believe you'd be at fault, but I'm still furious that our idea was stolen out from under us."

Ellen entered the kitchen. Both men looked up and stopped talking. James broke the uncomfortable silence.

"Good day to you, Ellen. I'll be taking my leave, and Patrick can explain what we were arguing about. I have another appointment, and I'm already late."

He put on his coat, strode to the front door, and saw himself out.

"Patrick, what's going on?"

"Well, you won't be likin' what I have to tell. Someone got wind of our idea to bid early for government contracts. Whoever it was, they went to the McFadden brothers and sold our idea for cash. Can you believe that? Could even have been your precious Michael Brady." With that, Patrick got up and left the room.

Ellen steadied herself with the back of a chair; she had innocently given Michael that private idea about getting government contracts when they were out walking. Reality sunk in. Michael had taken words spoken in confidence and traded them for easy money. She felt betrayed.

How could she have been so blind? With a heavy sigh she unhooked her cloak and trudged upstairs. The day, so joyous moments before, now felt weighted with despair. She sat down on her bed and glanced over at the doll on the wall shelf. *Oh Da, how could I have been so stupid?*

"Hallo! Patrick, Ellen?"

Ellen got up and opened her bedroom door.

"Up here, Mam."

The catch of a sob in Ellen's voice must have alerted Cecelia to some sort of problem. She climbed the stairs.

"Ellen, what is it?"

"Oh, Mam, I've been such a fool!"

"What happened?"

Ellen looked up at her mother. "Patrick, James, and Michael Brady all happened."

77   Cut From Strong Cloth

"All three of them together? Sweet Jesus, how could the three of them be involved?"

"Because I trusted him. Michael Brady, I mean."

Cecilia's face registered her worst fear. "You didn't. . . ?"

"No, Mam, of course not. I dinna commit a mortal sin, if that's what you're worried about. I told him some private information, and he went behind my back."

"All right. Tell me the whole story."

While Mam sat by her side, Ellen recanted the saga from start to end. When she finished, her mother leaned forward and took her by the shoulders.

"Listen to me. It seems there are two issues here. One is your hurt over Michael Brady, and the other is the situation with Patrick and James Nolan.

"What can I say to you about Michael Brady? Nothing you want to hear. But I was young once and I know how a boy can make you believe that you are the center of his world. And I can tell you this—'tis better you found out the truth about him now. Think if you were married with babes on your lap and then discovered his dishonest nature—you'd suffer heartache for the rest of your life."

Ellen felt too distraught to see how anything could be worse than how she felt right now. Obviously he had never even loved her at all.

"Listen. I know you think I've been hard on you growing up, but I only wanted to make you tough and strong. Strong enough to survive tragedy or heartbreak. You're still young. The honest kind of love will come to you one day, and you will recognize it then."

"How?"

"Because in addition to the physical attraction, you'll know that life would be empty without the other person. Trust me on this. You are stronger than you know. The blood of the O'Neills flows through your veins. This is just a setback, one that you will grow from and become stronger for having gone through. Michael Brady is not the man for you."

Ellen's shoulders slumped.

"Your ancestors, the O'Neills, were chieftains back in Ireland a long time ago. Their courage and bravery are part of your heritage. How do you think I survived after I lost your Da? It isn't just us who came to America; we brought the spirit of the O'Neills with us."

"But Patrick told me about the flight of the O'Neills, how they ran from the British in order to save themselves."

"Well, every story has two sides. One set of O'Neills left because they feared their families would be killed if they stayed. But another branch remained in Ulster, and moved to safer grounds. If they hadn't, we wouldn't be here today. The O'Neills have always been a strong clan. Stay here a moment, there's something I want to show you."

Cecilia left and walked up to her bedroom. She returned with a folded linen napkin, inside of which lay a decorative metal object slightly smaller than the size of a closed fist.

"What is it, Mam?"

"An old brooch, fashioned long ago by one of the O'Neills."

"I've never seen it before."

"Aye, that's because 'tis supposed to be given to a daughter on her wedding day. My mam gave it to me and told me to keep it for my girl-child. It will be yours one day Ellen, when you know you've found the real love of your life. I hope you will recognize him before 'tis too late."

Ellen reached out and touched the pewter-colored heirloom. The body resembled a bold backward-facing capital letter C fashioned from twisted ropes of metal, and each endpoint of the "C" held an intricate Celtic knot. A long tapered stick went diagonal through the twisted strands of the brooch. "It looks old."

"'Tis. I only know what my mam told me, that it's been handed down in our family for generations, perhaps hundreds of years. From O'Neill mother to O'Neill daughter. My mam told me it might even have come from Kate O'Neill herself."

"Who was she?"

"The first wife of Hugh O'Neill, one of the Earls of Tyrone. It was said she had the 'sight' and saw in a dream that the British were on the move, coming to arrest the Earls and set fire to their homes. The Flight of the O'Neills happened a few days later. When the British ar-

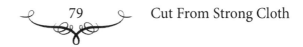

rived, those O'Neills were already on board ships, making their escape."

"Mam, how could a piece of jewelry survive all these years?"

"Anything's possible, Ellen. I like to think the brooch belonged to her."

"It feels too heavy to be a proper piece of jewelry."

"Brooches back then were used to keep cloaks fastened, so they had to be sturdy. Be careful, the tip is still quite sharp."

"Is there more to the story?"

"Not 'til the pin becomes yours, and you carry on the tradition."

"What about Da's family? Is there something I should be knowing about them, too?"

"Your Da's people were from Dublin. I never met them, so I dinna know anything to tell." Cecilia shrugged. "But right now, there is still the second issue you must face. You need to tell Patrick that you were the innocent instigator of this calamity. You owe it to your brother and James Nolan for them to learn the truth. Explain it all to Patrick, and then he can interpret the facts for Mr. Nolan."

"What do you mean, interpret the facts? If I tell Patrick, I should also be the one to explain the truth to James."

"Choose your words carefully, Ellen. We don't want James Nolan to turn from you." Cecilia gave Ellen a quick hug.

After Mam left the room, Ellen thought about what had been said. The long conversation was really the first time Ellen felt like her mother treated her as an adult. The brooch, the O'Neills, and Mam's empathy were unexpected discoveries. Although Ellen intended to be open and honest with James, perhaps she should take a cue from Mam and couch her words to soften the blow about her part in the debacle. There was no way she wanted to alienate him.

***

Ellen rose the next morning, and even though Father Reilly was out of town on a trip and she had the day off, she walked over to the church grounds where it would be quiet and she could clear her head. She needed to think over the situation with Patrick and James. Striding

down Fifth Street, she walked east along Girard and heard a newsboy shouting, "South Carolina threatens secession!"

A southern state announcing they intend to leave the Union? *God, perhaps things are worse than I thought.* However, that meant the government would definitely need additional uniform cloth sooner rather than later.

She continued up Second Street and approached the church, walking around the back of the property, and heading out into the cemetery. Wandering among the headstones and glancing at the inscriptions, she thought about these souls who had left Ireland to start new lives in America.

She walked to the back of the burial ground, took shelter against the cool stone wall, and thought of Da. What words of advice would he give? She knew he would tell her to be bold and have courage. Look the problem right in the face and spit in its eye. She squared her shoulders, picked her head up, and told herself she just had to figure out a way to rectify the situation.

Two sides to every story, wasn't that what Mam said? Just like the two parts of Da's weaving with the warp and weft on the loom. She thought about him holding his shuttles as the yarns ran over and under, creating a tight interface. Then she remembered Thomas Burberry's experiments of weaving different fibers together. What if she experimented with creating a special type of cloth, blending different yarns together to make a fabric more sturdy, yet comfortable—and free from shoddy? A cloth that would make superior material for soldiers' uniforms. That should certainly be of interest to the government, especially if she could show that her cloth would be more economical in the long run.

Would the government buy that? She didn't know for sure, but she felt her hunch was correct. A euphoric feeling swept through her body. How many of the other mills might use shoddy, she had no way of knowing, and she doubted anyone would admit to it anyway. This could be the perfect answer! The right mixture of wool and perhaps premier cotton could make the uniforms more durable. Her heart was lifted to think that out of Michael's duplicity came the answer for how to establish her business. Surely, Patrick and James would be impressed.

Cut From Strong Cloth

Finally she had a solid plan to help her go forward with her dream of becoming a businesswoman.

As she walked home, a million thoughts raced through her mind. Where could they get a source for the cotton? How much money would they need to start? Who would they contact in the government to buy the cloth? Did James' factory have enough space where they could dedicate a loom for this plan? The whole idea was a gamble, and she knew it. Suddenly she realized that by "they," she really meant the three of them. In order for this business venture to succeed from start to finish, Patrick and James might be necessary components.

Da, I have a brilliant idea, I do.

She fought wistful feelings about Michael. Her unwillingness to let him have his way with her no longer mattered. He belonged to her past and would not be a part of her future. She vowed she would never let any man break her heart again, or betray her confidence. Pacing down Second Street with a purpose to her stride, she arrived home and walked in hoping to find Patrick alone.

"Hallo, Patrick? Are you home? I need to talk to you," she called.

"Aye, I'm here. What's so important that you need to talk right now?"

"I have a wonderful idea that might put us back in the bidding process for government contracts. But first, I need you to listen to me with an open mind."

Patrick peered at her in a quizzical manner.

"Why an open mind, and what do you mean by 'us'?"

"Just let me talk. A few weeks back when I went out walking with Michael Brady, I shared with him the idea that you and James were thinking of manufacturing extra cloth so you could get an early bid for government contracts."

Patrick's mouth twisted into a rigid line.

"Of course I never expected him to go and sell that idea to a competing mill."

"Jesus Christ, Ellen. How could you have been so stupid?"

"Don't yell at me. I dinna realize he would go behind our backs."

"I always knew you'd grow up to be trouble for me, and now this

proves it," Patrick thundered as he shoved back his chair. He threw down the notes he'd been writing and clenched his fists as he glowered at her.

Ellen stood in shock. She had not anticipated such anger from him.

"Forget it, Patrick. We'll talk about this later when you're more reasonable."

He grabbed her arm. "Don't be assuming you've solved every-thing, little sister. You always think you've got the answers."

"Patrick, I only meant I have an idea that could help us out."

"I doubt that very much." He got up and stalked out of the room.

There had been arguments before, ever since Ellen was little; but this time Ellen saw more than just anger in his eyes. What exact emotion smoldered there, she could not tell, but it made her feel uneasy. Patrick's volatile explosion this time was actually a bit frightening.

***

On Saturday over breakfast, Patrick seemed to have shifted into a better mood. Ellen joined him, albeit with caution, at the table while Cecilia poured three cups of tea.

"Patrick, has Ellen consulted you about this tiff with James Nolan? It seems to be an ugly situation that needs fixing."

Patrick looked at Ellen, and then his face softened. "I'm sorry for our words yesterday. I know I spoke in anger. I guess you just caught me off guard. Go ahead and tell me your idea."

Ellen took a deep breath, half expecting him to blow up at her again. "I think we could purchase some premier cotton and use one of James' looms at the factory to experiment combining cotton with Canavan wool. Once the perfect balance is achieved, we'd manufacture several bolts of the fabric and bring samples to a government agent, showing how the cloth would make superior uniforms for soldiers."

Cecilia gave a long low whistle. "Not a bad idea, Ellen."

Ellen looked to see Patrick's reaction. Mam's opinion didn't count nearly as much.

"It might work as long as we don't price ourselves out of the market. How did you get this idea?"

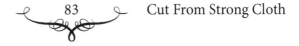

"I read that an Englishman, Thomas Burberry, started out in the drapery business but then progressed into creating textiles intended for outdoor clothing by using blended fibers. It started me thinking about combining wool with another fiber. I think we should tell James my idea as soon as possible."

"Your idea, huh? If we're going to use Canavan wool, then this 'solution,' as you call it, will not come from just you."

"All right, Patrick, we'll be in business together."

"Women don't go into business, Ellen. Women just work in business."

"No, Patrick, women do go into business. If you agree, then it will be our solution. Together in business. Now can we go tell James?"

Patrick waited and then pulled out his pocket watch. "I think his factory shuts down by one o'clock on Saturdays, so I'll go over there now."

"We'll go over together, and you'd better get used to me being involved."

He frowned at her. "Okay, grab your cloak and let's get going, but don't get too excited yet. 'Tis just an idea we're exploring."

At least James should be impressed with the idea, even if Patrick seems to have some misgivings.

The two siblings walked side by side down Fifth Street and took a left onto Girard. As Ellen made the quick turn south from Germantown onto St. John Street, she looked up to see a red-bricked factory looming on the horizon four stories tall. It dominated the entire block. Ellen felt dwarfed in its shadow. She knew his factory was only one part of the larger Globe Mills complex, but it was still impressive in its own right.

They approached the building, and Patrick pushed open the black iron gates. At the main entrance, Patrick knocked. When no one answered, he pushed open the left side of the heavy double wooden doors, and they walked in. For Ellen, the sounds emanating from the different rooms gave the entire mill a pulsating energy she'd never felt before. In the nearest room, huge machines in full operation looked like giant insects waving immense antennae. Women stood in front of massive looms, almost as if they were tied to them and children collect-

ed full bobbins of yarn and carried them off somewhere.

Back out in the hallways clerks scurried past them like ants in a line, sometimes stopping to fill leather fire buckets with water. Dirt and dust lay in piles everywhere, and Ellen detected the overpowering smell of rotten eggs. She wondered if anyone really ever got used to working in these conditions—especially the children. But the factory also possessed vitality, like the vibrant hub of a beehive, and as the workers dashed back and forth, Ellen found herself drawn into the energy of the place, in spite of the dirt and the odors. The deafening noise, though, caused her to cover her ears.

"Patrick, I can hardly hear!"

"Don't be acting the goat, Ellen. It only shows you're inexperienced. Next time, put cotton in your ears. That's what I usually do when I'm making my factory visits."

A man approached and she saw cotton stuffed in his ears. How did Patrick always know these things?

"Are ye here to apply for a position?" the man yelled.

Ellen smiled and shook her head no. "We're here on personal business with Mr. Nolan," she shouted back.

The man looked surprised. "I'll go get him for you," he hollered.

As James came out from the back he looked surprised, and maybe even a bit alarmed to see both Patrick and Ellen standing in the front hallway of his factory. "Ellen, Patrick, is anything wrong with your mother?"

"No, James, Ellen and I have a business matter to discuss with you."

James motioned for them to come over to his small office, where they would have privacy and a respite from the noise. Once inside, he closed the door.

"James, we have a timely idea and felt it better to come here to talk about it."

"All right, Patrick. Here, Ellen, let me take your cloak. Sit down, the both of you. I'm sorry I canna offer any tea, but at least I have two extra chairs. So, what is it you want to discuss?"

Before Patrick could steal her thunder, Ellen blurted out, "Pat-

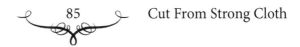

rick had nothing to do with letting Michael Brady find out about your business idea. I did."

"You?" James blanched, but then his eyes narrowed and he clenched his jaw. "I'd never believe you would betray either Patrick or me."

"I never intended it as a betrayal. You may know that Michael Brady and I had been seeing each other this past year and often went out walking in Kensington."

"Go on, I'm listening, and yes, I am quite aware that Brady has been trying to capture you. All of Kensington must know his intent by now."

"Well, James, I would hardly call it capturing, and I don't think 'tis fair of you to make such a comment about all of Kensington." Ellen squared her shoulders and did not lower her eyes.

Patrick stayed silent, but a sly grin spread across his face as he watched Ellen squirm.

"While Mr. Brady and I were out walking a few weeks ago, I shared the information about you and Patrick bidding for future government contracts. I guess I wanted him to think my family was clever."

At first, James said nothing. He jammed his hands in his trouser pockets and then caught Ellen off guard with his reply. "Ellen, 'tis not you that I blame. I'm sorry you were duped by this Brady fellow and ready perhaps to give your heart to a man who would never deserve you. Patrick and I may have lost the chance for early government contracts, but it would have been far worse to lose you."

Ellen did not immediately react. She hadn't realized until this point just how much he cared. It made her feel uncomfortable and awkward that James would speak in such a frank manner in front of Patrick. Did Patrick already know this information?

"Thank you, James, for your honesty, but I came here to explain my part in the current situation and to offer an idea that might counterbalance any bid the other mills make."

"All right. What's your idea?"

"I read about a British man named Thomas Burberry who combined different fibers—experimenting in manufacturing various types of cloth. So I'm thinking that Patrick and I could experiment using our wool and mix it with some premier cotton to produce a stronger, more

weather resistant cloth. We'd have to use one of your factory looms, but I'm sure the government would be interested. Don't you think so?"

Now it was Ellen's turn to have the tables turned on her. She expected James to congratulate her on her idea. Instead, she watched as his face turned crimson.

"I won't lower myself to use any bloody Brit's idea!" he exploded. "The British are the bastards who abandoned my family during the Famine! I'll never use any idea that came from them."

"But James, my idea has merit, it does!"

"You dinna know the horrors of the Famine, Ellen. I saw my little sister die from Famine Fever, my father weeping because he could not save her. My mother wasted away to a skeleton of her former self, and then died in my Da's arms while tears streamed down his face. No, I refuse to think of ever using an idea from an Englishman. So scrap your brilliant plan. I won't ever give the Brits credit for anything." A vein in his neck bulged.

She flared up at James.

"You're being pig-headed and stubborn. My idea is a good one, and it would make money for us all!"

"Go home, Ellen. You don't know a lot about me and what you see as stubbornness was born of tragedy that you never had to endure. I only have sad memories left from Ireland."

The room was deadened with silence.

"Right now, I think I need to be alone. In a few days I'll come to call and the three of us can sort this out. And for God's sake, stop trying to invent a business for yourself."

She grabbed her cloak and, not waiting for Patrick, stormed out of James' office. Fighting tears, she ran down the hallway and pushed open the front door and fled into the street. She swore never to let James see her cry, or admit her hurt feelings. With her cloak thrown around her shoulders, she stomped off the factory grounds and never glanced back.

Damn him! Damn all men!

***

Ellen pulled her cloak tighter across her body and brushed away the tears from her wounded pride. She crossed back over Girard, tromped up Second Street, and thumped on the Ready's door.

"Why, Ellen, what a pleasant surprise! Do come in. My, is something the matter?"

Ellen crossed the threshold and whipped off the cloak. Her flushed cheeks and blazing eyes betrayed the anger seething inside her.

"Mary, there's been a huge injustice done to James that I innocently caused. I went to the factory just now to try and set things right. He seemed to accept my apology until I suggested an idea to solve the dilemma. The idea came from that Englishman, Thomas Burberry, that I told you about. James began to rant and rave that he would never consider anything that came from the British, insinuating I'm too naive to understand. Please, Mary, help me. Even if it costs me the friendship, I want to understand why he reacted that way. I intend to right the injustice."

Mary gazed at the high color in Ellen's tear-stained face. "I'm sure he seemed obstinate to you. What has James told you about our family and the Famine?"

"He said your little sister died of Famine Fever and that your mother wasted away 'til death. He blamed the British."

"He told you the truth, Ellen. But I think perhaps you should have a cuppa tea. There's more to the story."

Mary went back to the kitchen and soon reappeared with a simple tray set for tea. "Sit down, Ellen, what I'm about to tell is not a happy tale.

"Most Irish dinna own their land out right, so the harvested crops were sent back to England by the Anglo-Irish landowners. Many families depended upon the one crop they were allowed to keep: the potato. You know that the potato crop failed four years in a row, and many people starved. But others like our family, got sick and then died from the complications. What James dinna tell you is that he also buried the girl he planned to marry. They'd known each other since childhood."

How could I have known, when James never shared any of this?

"What was her name?"

"Mary, just like mine. Our mam's name was Mary, too. We were told if we would renounce our Papist faith, we could gain entry to the soup kitchens set up for the Scotch-Irish. But James and Da refused to be called traitorous soupers. Mary got so sick that James found her one day crawling outside and stuffing grass in her mouth, then vomiting everything back onto the ground. By then her lively eyes were hollow and her spirit already dead. When she died a short time later, James blamed himself because he hadn't found enough food for her."

Ellen sat contemplating the information, and her anger began to subside a bit. She still felt that it would be foolish to sacrifice her business idea just to placate his feelings.

"What do I do now? I doubt James would have told me, so we'll keep this between us. My idea was a good one. I'd hate to think we'd lose out on a potential windfall just because it concerned an Englishman."

"Then get James to see the idea from a different point of view. 'Twas from an Englishman, right? That doesn't mean that James canna profit from it. Wouldn't that be a grand twist of fate? Irish making money off a Brit's idea!"

Mary's humor helped to dissolve Ellen's previous mood. "You're wonderful, Mary! That's how I'll restructure the plan. But I refuse to go back and see him. He'll have to approach me first."

Mary smiled. "Who's being the stubborn one now?"

CHAPTER 10

December 1860

After a week went by without any word from James, Patrick took matters into his own hands and walked over to St. John's Street.

He covered his ears as soon as he entered the factory. Looking around, he discovered James at almost the exact same moment that James saw him.

"So, Patrick, are you here because of Ellen?" James' lips retreated into a firm line.

"No, you eejit, I'm here because there's an excellent business plan that you are about to jeopardize. I'm going to make you listen to the idea, then you can decide to join us or not. I don't intend to beg."

The stubbornness in James' eyes softened as he beckoned Patrick over to his office.

"Okay, Patrick. Let's hear what you have to say."

"Listen, James. Both you and I can profit from this idea, and I won't sit still while you nurse your hurt feelings and let other mill owners rush to get the government contracts. I know your sentiments against the Brits, and I canna say I blame you. I figure this bloke might have a patent on his particular cloth, but what he doesn't have is good Georgia cotton. We have contacts where we can purchase the best cotton in America. Then we mix it in with the raw wool I already buy, and we can produce a superior blend. With cotton values dropping this year, we should be able to get a good price on the raw fiber."

He paused, waiting for James' reaction. "Open your eyes, James. With more southern states talking about seceding, I want to get to our contact in Georgia as soon as possible. Then if the country goes to war, we'll be in the best position to offer our superior cloth for uniforms."

James still stood with his arms folded across his chest. "And what if the country doesn't go to war? We'd lose money."

"Then we look into other means of selling my soon-to-be famous cloth. Ellen thinks there could be other buyers as well who need cloth free from shoddy."

"*Your* famous cloth? Sounds a bit grand." Finally his face relaxed. "I thought it was Ellen who came up with the idea of the so-called solution. And, may I ask, who is this contact in Georgia, and how do you see me fitting into the picture?"

"Our cousin, Tom Avery. Mind you, we haven't seen him since we were children. His family fled before the Famine and settled in Savannah. I'll ask him for help in contacting cotton sellers. Your part, James, would be to give up space in your factory for us to experiment with the weaving of this new cloth. In addition, we would need you to put up a financial stake, advancing the money to buy the cotton. Just say that you agree to the idea and I'll post a letter to Tom today. We canna delay. The McFadden brothers are gearing up production. Even the Globe is stockpiling wool. But none of them have Georgia cotton. 'Tis a brilliant idea, no?"

"I think that remains to be seen. Does Ellen know you're here?"

"Of course not. Do you think I tell Mam and Ellen about everywhere I go? No, I came on my own."

"All right, Patrick. I admit that Ellen's idea has merit. It's just that I hate the bloody British, and always will. If it hadn't been for them. . ." He fingered the scar on his right jaw. Go write to your cousin and tell him you'll be coming to Georgia to purchase some cotton. When do you think you should leave on your trip?"

"I'm thinking right after the New Year."

"Good, that's settled then. I think I need to do some Christmas

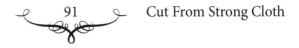

shopping. Buying a nice gift for Ellen might be the best way I can make amends for my harsh words. I do care for her very much. No argument, however big, could change that."

"Get whatever kind of gift you want. Just don't get sidetracked about our agreement."

∗∗∗

James left the factory and headed over to Foerderer's shop. Of all the gifts he could buy, a pair of pigskin gloves she could use when driving Lir might impress her the most. Entering the premise, he smelled the distinct scent of worked leather and the odors of tanned hides and neat's-foot oil. He looked at the displays of meticulously-crafted items. A wide assortment of gloves with various stitching and designs met his gaze. He knew he wanted to find a delicate set, yet durable—almost a reflection of Ellen herself. Perhaps he should be bold and say those exact words to her.

At last he selected a stunning pair in a beautiful chestnut that would match her short cape, the one she'd worn the first time they went driving. The shopkeeper wrapped the gift in plain paper, and James left the store whistling. On the way back to the factory, he decided to stop by Mary's and show her the present. Knocking on the door he was caught off guard when it opened to reveal Ellen staring at him, her hand on the door handle.

"Ellen, what are you doing here?" he stammered.

"Hallo, James."

Mary broke the awkwardness by coming from the kitchen to see who was at the door.

"Aye, James, I thought I heard your voice. Ellen came over to help me start some potato candy for the holidays. What brings you here in the middle of the day?"

She kissed him on the cheek and as he entered the front room, he dropped the wrapped parcel on a nearby end table. Then he tried to think of something clever to say. Looking back, he saw Ellen still standing by the door.

"Well, Mary, I came for advice."

"What kind of advice?"

He began to tap his foot. "I think I need some guidance about how to convince a certain young lady that I am indeed a stubborn and willful man, but kindhearted underneath. I won't apologize for my initial reaction, but I do need to tell her we're going ahead with her idea after all. We intend to make money off the Brit."

Ellen grinned. Then she walked over to James and standing up on tip toe, planted a kiss on his cheek. "I don't think you'll lose money on this venture, James. I think we'll all make money off the Brit!"

He laughed and looked at her with a longing he found hard to conceal. Damn, would she always be like this, getting her way?

"Ellen, why don't you and James go talk about the business plan? We can always continue our baking tomorrow."

"In fact, let me walk you home. I'm assuming you have no objection to us walking about in Kensington?" He arched his brow.

"No objection from me."

With the door closed behind them, and the package left with Mary, he held her elbow as they strolled up Second Street. "So, other than Thomas Burberry, what other information might you want to share with me?"

"Well, I've been doing some research. I went to Brown's Book Store recently and found mention of the Mercantile Library here in Philadelphia. 'Tis a special library where you can study about textiles and manufacturing. We canna stop the other mills from trying to get the government contracts, but I'm sure we can produce a better cloth for uniforms."

He cocked his head. "You really are serious about going into business, aren't you?"

"All I've ever wanted was to make something of my life and honor my Da. With this idea of a combined fabric I could become a real merchant in my own right and produce my own fabrics. So, yes, I am serious about it."

"I don't know of any woman in Philadelphia who's in the management end of a textile business. A mill's no place for that," he chided.

"I'm sure even your Da would have agreed on that."

"Why?"

"It takes a thorough knowledge about different fibers and balancing the books so a profit might be made. There are clients to be contacted for raw supplies and workers to be hired to run machinery. Managing a factory business is no life for a gentle woman."

Ellen looked at him with a leveled gaze. "But that doesn't mean a woman couldn't manage a textile business, only that it would be a challenge."

"Ellen, don't start getting fancy ideas that would only lead to disappointments later on. I would hate to see your dreams get crushed under the harsh realities of industrial competition." He admired her spunk and enthusiasm but did not want to see that spark extinguished by the cut-throat textile industry. Even if she got a government bid, she would have to outsmart the other mills in order to succeed.

"Oh, I don't intend to let disappointments or obstacles stop me, James. I intend to become a success in the industry, one way or another."

***

The month of December gained momentum. Even when money was tight, the businesses of Kensington made profits from their Christmas sales.

As Ellen shopped at the grocer's, she overhead two women complaining that Lincoln's election could mean trouble. Many young men now wanted to volunteer for military service instead of working close to home. Their talk buoyed Ellen's spirits with the fact that more soldiers would mean more opportunity for Ellen's business plan to succeed.

By nightfall, carolers paraded with their faces aglow by candlelight and added to Ellen's festive mood. Even the pubs were promoting Christmas music alongside the livelier strains of tin whistles and fiddles. Holiday baking sent whiffs of tantalizing aromas adrift from every window left slightly ajar, and the magic of the season drifted in and out of households on every block.

It seemed that Christmas was the one time of the year when everyone relaxed, even Cecilia. The yearly shift in her mood could be clocked by the calendar. As soon as Advent rolled in, Cecilia softened. Whether this was a nostalgic throwback to her childhood, no one would ever know.

Ellen and Cecilia were in the kitchen together, assembling the dried fruits, glacé cherries, and raisins that formed the key ingredients to Cecilia's special Christmas cake. The stove had been stoked, and Mam had turned the kitchen counters into an assembly line in order to whip up multiple cakes. When done, each Christmas cake would be a rich brown loaf teeming with colorful bits of fruit and plump raisins, and a tablespoon or two of Mam's hoarded rum.

Holiday baking often induced a feeling of gaiety and family bonding, something that did not always come to the forefront during other times of the year.

"Mam, you never talk about Ireland."

Cecilia let out a deep sigh. "'Twas a long time ago. There's nothing of interest to talk about."

"Can you tell me something about the Famine? How did we survive?"

"The Famine? A terrible time. Thank God you don't remember it." Cecilia's shoulders sagged with the burden of the memory.

"Why did no one in our family get sick?"

"Your Da got sick." Cecilia's voice held the hint of suppressed tears.

"What do you mean?"

"Your Da caught the con, and it eventually killed him."

Ellen suddenly grew very pale. "I don't understand."

"The con. Consumption, Ellen. Your Da died from the lung fever he contracted."

"But I always thought. . . "

"You thought what?" Cecilia shook her head. When Ellen didn't reply, Cecilia continued but with a faraway look in her eyes. "He was already sick when we got on the boat for America. The voyage in the crowded hold and the damp cold sea weather only made him weaken faster. I had hoped he would live to make a new life in America. But

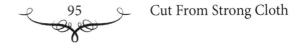

that dinna happen."

Ellen felt her stomach flip-flop. This meant she had not killed her father after all. Impulsively, she ran over to her mother and threw her arms around her in a tight embrace. "Oh, Mam, I never knew! I am so sorry at how hard the voyage must have been for you."

A small shrug from Cecilia seemed to indicate that she had dealt with the sad emotions a long time ago.

Ellen pulled back, visibly more calm.

"Can I ask then, how we left Ireland if Da was so sick?"

"I sold your Da's loom and most of our possessions, and we rode away from our cottage in a donkey cart to Belfast. From there we got on a ship to Liverpool. All he brought from home were his precious weaving shuttles—so sure he'd be needin' them in Philadelphia. We set sail for America on a late March afternoon with a stiff breeze blowing us away from the shore. That's all I want to remember."

"I'm glad you gave me the shuttles. He told me once that the threads would sing when they moved under and over each other."

"Sentimental old fool, your Da. Like putting the birth wool in your luggage when we left home."

"Birth wool?"

"Aye, the piece of wool a weaver puts in his newborn's tiny fist so the babe will always be connected to the father's craft."

"I have that piece of wool tucked away in a box up in my room, but I dinna remember it being called birth wool. All I remembered is that it came from Da."

Again, Cecilia shrugged. "We should be getting back to our baking."

The moment of tenderness between the two of them expired like a candle flame, and life resumed as usual at 1225 Fifth Street. After they finished baking, Ellen went up to her room and knelt by the bed. *Hail Mary, Blessed art thou among women. Thank you for this gift of finally being freed from the burden that I had caused Da's death.*

The guilt she had carried for the past five years had finally been extinguished.

Ellen watched some children running in the streets enjoying the first few snowflakes of the season. She paused to realize how much she wanted children of her own. At one time she had dreamed that might happen with Michael. He had made her feel desirable, and she had falsely believed he would propose to her one day. She realized now it had all been a sham on his part, and she had allowed him to steal her heart. Even though she resolved to move forward and forget him, it was easier said than done. He was probably off charming some other poor young girl.

She took a deep breath and vowed to be more careful with her feelings about James. She wasn't about to let her heart get broken again.

In the last week before Christmas, she rewrapped the blue scarf purchased for Michael and put Patrick's name on the tag instead; then she walked to the tin shop and picked up the four connected swans she had designed for James. Last on her list was a soft woolen shawl in tones of saffron yellow for Cecilia. By the fourth Sunday of Advent, all her gifts were wrapped and ready to give.

***

For the Catholic community of Kensington, Christmas spanned a course of three days. First came Christmas Eve, followed by Christmas Day, and ending on St. Stephen's Day. Ellen and James had decided to exchange gifts on Christmas Eve and planned to see each other on the other days as well. Ellen thought she would have to coax Mam for permission to go with James to the Ready's house on Christmas morning, but Cecilia did not object. The one stipulation was to be home in time for the Canavan Christmas dinner.

Christmas Eve arrived with a perfect dusting of snow. Kensington, which normally wore a mantle of drab gray in winter, now had its edges softened by the ivory flakes. Ellen peered out into the night sky, enjoying how the gaslight cradled the evening with a romantic glow. Gently-falling flurries lent a hush and solemnity to the winter air. For

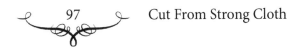

Cut From Strong Cloth

dinner, Cecilia cooked a small but memorable meal of oyster stew and fresh rolls, and a handed out a glass of stout for each of them. Tomorrow afternoon they would feast on her Christmas dinner of roasted chicken, creamy mashed champ, boiled peas, orange glazed carrots, yeast rolls, and celebratory glasses of special Madeira—followed, of course, by tea and her famous Christmas cake.

James arrived later that evening, stepping into the mingled scent of lighted candles and fir boughs as he entered the foyer.

"James, do come in, and Merry Christmas!" Ellen's excitement shone in the rosy apples of her cheeks.

"Merry Christmas, Ellen." He produced a sprig of mistletoe over her.

"James, wherever did you get mistletoe?" laughed Ellen.

"I have my sources." He smiled. "Now, I think I am entitled to a mistletoe kiss."

Ellen did not stop him, and he gave her a lingering kiss. "That's to last you till at least St. Stephen's Day." He winked. "Now show me all the decorations."

Ellen pointed out the candles placed on each window sill and sprigs of evergreen boughs she had tacked up over the front door transom. "Look over here, James. It took us days, but 'ta da'!" She bowed to the solo pine tree in the middle of the room which had been strung with whimsical white paper stars.

Just then Cecilia walked in from the kitchen.

"*Nollaig Shona*, Mrs. Canavan."

"*Nollaig Shona*, to you, too. Patrick is upstairs taking a nap before Midnight Mass, and I need to rest as well. We will see you later, Mr. Nolan?"

"Yes."

As soon as her mother went upstairs, Ellen led James to the sofa. Her heart was beating fast with the excitement of impressing him with her gift and she was relieved they would have some privacy. "James, come here. I want you to open your gift first." She clapped her hands in childish glee. James untied the ribbon and paper, and then stared at the tin piece in the box.

"Ellen, 'tis the Legend of Lir, right here on this circle! Wherever

did you find such an incredible gift?"

"I had it made for you at the tinsmith, with my own design. 'Tis meant to be attached to the top of your walking stick."

"You did? 'Tis beautiful. Thank you." He held it up to the light, smiling at the four silver swans entwined together.

She felt delighted that he was obviously impressed with both the gift and with her ingenuity in creating it.

"Here, Ellen. Now open yours." He smiled, placing the box in her hands.

Her fingers tore off the wrapping. When she saw the beautiful leather gloves, she gave a small cry of delight. "Thank you, James, they're lovely."

"They can be used as driving gloves. I wanted you to have them for when you drive Lir. It seems that Lir inspired both our gifts."

She put the gloves under her nose and drank in the heady smell of quality leather, then stretched the supple pigskin to glide over her fingers. The gift was quite a luxury. She had never owned pigskin gloves in her life.

James reached over and held both her hands in his.

"I think 'tis only appropriate that we also exchange a real Christmas kiss."

Ellen nodded in agreement, and he leaned in and kissed her passionately on the lips. Her heart quickened and she felt electricity in the air. "Why James, that was quite . . . impressive. And I am not just referring to the gloves." She smiled back at him with an impish grin.

He paused a moment. "Ellen, I care deeply for you. I am not here for just a casual relationship."

She felt she was blushing. While his kisses were delightful, she wondered if he would still consent to be her business sponsor if she did not agree to a personal commitment. *I've been through these beginning feelings before, and I don't want another relationship where I can get hurt. Am I being fair to him? I do want his sponsorship, but might I want him in the other parts of my life as well?* She hesitated. "James, give me a bit more time before we talk about a promise that could change our lives."

Outside snow continued to fall, swirling in gaslight circles, and keeping Kensington unusually quiet. A reverent hush covered the room as well.

"All right, Ellen, I'll wait." He paused. "How then should we spend the time tonight until Midnight Mass?"

"Midnight Mass?"

"Aye, I already asked permission to be your escort."

Ellen was thrilled to think of what the neighbors would say when they saw her on the arm of Mr. James Nolan, well-to-do factory proprietor.

"James, I'm delighted. Thank you. But could we talk just a bit about business first?"

"You want to talk about business on Christmas Eve?"

"Aye, I do. I want to learn all I can about your factory and how you produce your cloth."

"'Tis an unusual request for Christmas Eve, but if that's what you want, I can give you at least a short explanation of the process."

As he began to explain the steps involved in producing a bolt of cloth, she found that his business acumen deepened her admiration of him, and gave him an attractive aura of authority. She glanced at the faded scar on his jar and the wisps of grey at his temples and realized he was striking in a mature way that Michael Brady would never achieve.

After he finished talking about his factory, Ellen paused before going up to dress for Mass. "James, I loved hearing about the factory. Thank you." She began to climb the stairs and then turned back smiling at him. He was watching her with a tender smile that in itself, was a gift.

***

Later, stamping the snow off their shoes, they entered St. Michael's while strains of "Once in Royal David's City" hovered in the air. Patrick walked in first with Mam, and James followed, ushering Ellen down the aisle. As she had predicted, heads turned and tongues wagged. Mary Ready smiled up at them as they found their seats. Ellen wore her best dress for this occasion and removed her cloak as soon as

Linda Harris Sittig

they entered the church so her outfit would be visible. The lovely brown and black plaid taffeta silk with thick ebony ribbons swished as she walked. She felt beautiful.

The interior of St. Michael's Church belied the fact of Kensington being a poor city ward. Almost completely destroyed in the Nativist Riots of the 1840s, the rebuilt church now gleamed inside with alabaster tones of white and gold, highlighting the frescoes of the large center alcove.

"'Tis beautiful here, isn't it, James?"

"Aye, 'tis." He put his hand in hers and gave a slight squeeze.

Father Reilly began his Christmas homily with a reference to the military tension in Judaea when Joseph and Mary journeyed to Bethlehem to pay their taxes. Then he continued by asking the parish to say special prayers during this solemn season that the nation not be torn asunder by the differing viewpoints on slavery, and he admonished one and all to strive for peace in their own family as well. Ellen looked aside at Mam who did not appear to catch the implication of the priest's words.

Later, when Ellen went forward for Holy Communion, she lifted her head while kneeling at the rail. She let her gaze fall beyond to the multiple tiers of pure white marble supporting the altar and the exquisite white arches curving upward to the fresco of Christ in the Crucifixion. The magnificence of it all humbled her.

"Corpus Christi," the priest intoned as he offered the Eucharist to her. Ellen answered, "Amen." Then she turned and walked past the statue of the Blessed Mother looking down from a private niche. Ellen drew in a breath and whispered a prayer of gratitude for life's blessings. Returning to her seat, she realized James had not gone forward to receive the Eucharist. Puzzled, she knew Mam would have noticed his decision not to take Holy Communion. It bothered Ellen that on this, the holiest of nights, James would refrain from a sacrament. Why? What possible reason could he have? But that was his business—not hers.

When the foursome returned home, Cecilia served tea with Christmas cake, and James stayed long enough to give Ellen a celebratory holiday kiss and the verbal promise of seeing her tomorrow.

Cut From Strong Cloth

***

Christmas morning dawned bright and clear. Ellen selected her butternut brown and cream striped dress and then added a Kelly green shawl for a dash of holiday color. She gathered up her hair with a matching green velvet ribbon and carried her new gloves as the final component to her stylish ensemble. James arrived as planned, and she saw with delight the swan circle attached to his walking stick. Together they piled the gifts, including one of Cecilia's Christmas cakes, in the back of the carriage and drove with Lir over to Second Street.

Once inside the Ready house, Ellen participated in the gift-giving ritual where each child had to guess what might be inside each modest box. The small number of gifts did nothing to dampen the holiday magic, and Ellen relished the wonderment accompanying the innocence of childhood on Christmas morning. *I hope I'll have a family like this someday.*

She looked over at James and blushed at her own thinking. Just before they sat down to the late full breakfast, a knock sounded and James registered pure surprise when Mary opened the door to find their cousin Will Nolan standing before them.

"Good God, James, I dinna know I'd find you here, too!" Will exclaimed as he entered the house. "Merry Christmas!"

"I thought you'd gone to Boston!"

"I did. But not many good jobs there anymore, so I decided to return to Philadelphia. Anyway, the girls are prettier here." He winked. "And now just who might this be?" he asked as he walked over to Ellen.

"Hallo. I'm Ellen; James'. . . friend." She replied.

"Friend? Good God, James, dinna tell me you are allowing her to be just a friend?"

"Ellen is a special friend," answered James. Then he turned toward her and added, "Until she indicates she wants to be more than that."

The children clamoring to begin the meal diffused the awkward moment, and Ellen was relieved that she did not have to answer the tease. She avoided eye contact with James for a while, but watching him

interact with his family she realized she did want to be more than just a special friend. She just didn't want to rush the relationship.

Mary's breakfast table held her best dishes. Tiny painted rosebuds lay in the center of each creamy white porcelain plate, giving an air of delicacy to the room. The table itself groaned under the multiple servings of fried eggs, black and white pudding, rashers and bangers, potato boxty, and pots of tea. Cecilia's Christmas cake would be saved for later. When James announced they must go, the children did not beg him to stay. The girls were playing with their new dolls and the boys were staging mock battles with their new toy soldiers.

"I see the boys are playing war," Will said. "Good thing they're still small. From what I've heard, lots of Irish are thinking of signing up to be in Lincoln's army. They're hoping for better pay than they get as common laborers."

"Now, Will, where would you be hearing that kind of gossip?" Mary admonished. She looked at her husband for confirmation.

"You only have to go in any pub and you'll hear the fervor of young men wanting to fight," Ed replied.

Mary shot a look of fear mixed with fierce love at her sons. "Well, they're too young to become soldiers. God willing, this will all die down soon."

"I'm not so sure about that, Mary." Will spoke up again. "When I was arriving at the Philadelphia train station, newsboys were shouting about South Carolina voting to secede from the Union."

"All right! No more talk of war. This is Christmas, for God's sake."

***

Later, as Lir trotted back towards Fifth Street, Ellen brought up the question of when would be a good time to travel to Savannah.

"You mean for Patrick? A trip after New Year's would give him ample time to make cotton connections in Georgia."

"How long, James, do you think a trip like that would take?"

"Assuming Patrick travels by steamship, it should take about two and a half days to reach Savannah. Then once he meets up with

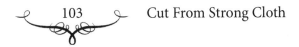

your cousin, it would take ten business days to draw up contracts and arrange for shipping with the various merchants. I'd guess a two-week stretch should suffice. Then he would want to get out of the South, I assume. Why all these questions?"

"I want to understand all the components of this business venture."

"Don't worry. Patrick will take care of everything."

"Do you think it will be safe to travel to Georgia?"

James' smile faded. "There's no telling what the other southern states will do. I certainly hope Georgia doesn't secede. But I'll say a prayer for Patrick's safety."

Ellen nodded, but made no further comment.

CHAPTER 11

December 1860

Snow drifted gently as Christmas morning moved into Christmas Day, but tension gripped Ellen's shoulders because of the announcement she was about to make. She sat pious as Cecilia asked Patrick to give the Christmas blessing.

"Bless us oh Lord and these, thy gifts, which we are about to receive, from thy bounty, through Christ our Lord. Amen."

At the end of the holiday dinner, Ellen offered to serve dessert. She could sense her mother's shifting moods from the years of studying Mam's behavior. Something was brewing under Cecilia's skin.

"Always serve from the left, Ellen. I thought I'd taught you that before."

Not wanting to further fan her mother's irritability, Ellen moved to the left and set the dessert plates down one by one. She cleared her throat twice and addressed Patrick. "James tells me you plan to leave for Savannah after the New Year."

"That's right. I've posted a letter to Cousin Tom and I'm waiting for his reply."

"Will you travel by steamship?"

"Aye. Why all these questions?"

"Because I'm going with you."

"Jesus, Mary, and Joseph! Over my dead body will you be going to Savannah!" Cecilia slammed her hand down on the table.

Ellen had prepared herself for her mother's total opposition, and directed her comments only to Patrick. "This business solution was mine, Patrick. 'Tis only fair that I get to meet the Savannah merchants, too."

"Did you hear me, Ellen?" Cecilia fairly screeched. "I said no! If you are so well read as you pretend to be, then you would know that northern ships are having a hard time getting into some southern ports. What in God's name makes you think you belong anywhere in the South just now?"

Ellen shot her mother a look of total defiance and turned back to re-address Patrick.

"Well?"

"You canna go, Ellen."

"Why not?"

"Well for starters, you're a girl."

"A *girl*! Are you wearing blinders or what? I'm a young woman, Patrick. Or haven't you noticed? I've grown up."

"Aye, you've grown up, but that doesn't give you the right to make the trip, and that's final."

"No, 'tis not final. I intend to go whether you like it or not."

"How about your safety? And we'd have to get two rooms on the ship and in the hotel. You'd double the expense."

"Come on, Patrick, I'd have you to protect me. I'm entitled to make the trip, and you know it."

"Entitled!" Cecilia burst in. "You're only a part-time cook, Ellen. The men you'd meet would think you're common—traipsing around the country putting on airs and pretending to be more than you are."

"No, Mam. I would be a young female merchant, thank you, traveling with her brother— her partner in fact, and yes, *entitled*."

"Partner? Is that what this is all about?" Patrick shoved his plate away.

"Ellen, you'll be the death of us yet. What will the neighbors say? How could I explain this to Father Reilly, when he depends on you for his daily sustenance? I'm the one who got you that job."

"Really, Mam? I thought I qualified for that job on my own. Mrs. McAllister can work for the two weeks we'll be gone. And 'tis none of the neighbors' business where I go."

"Ellen, what gave you the idea that you could become my partner?" Patrick growled.

"I intend to start my own business, but for right now I'll be your full partner. There's no reason why I shouldn't. I've helped you reconcile the books each week and write to the delinquent clients, so I understand the finances. We'll both have a better background for negotiations on future purchases this way."

Patrick looked at her straight on. "Does James know you intend on becoming my full partner?"

"He hasn't asked, but if he does, I'll inform him."

"Well, you've just ruined my Christmas," Cecilia declared.

***

James and Ellen planned to be together on the day after Christmas, when most of the Irish went out socializing with friends or family. Since they had already visited both the Canavan and the Ready households, James had come up with a different option.

He chatted with Cecilia, who seemed unusually reserved, while he waited for Ellen to come downstairs. "Ah, there you are Ellen," he said as she entered the room.

"Good morning to you, James."

"Here, let me help you on with your cloak. There will be a chill where we're going." He nodded to Cecilia, and maneuvered Ellen out the door.

"Where are you taking me?"

"No need to visit our families, so I thought I'd take you someplace special to me, and I think for you, too. We're going to the St. John's Street Factory for a grand tour."

"'Tis not the usual place to visit on St. Stephen's Day."

"You wanted to talk business on Christmas Eve, so I thought you'd enjoy touring the factory and seeing the operation up front. First

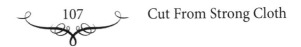

hand, so to speak."

"I canna think of a better idea."

When they arrived at the factory, James opened the gates and then unlocked a side door and led her inside. Even though the mill was closed for the holidays, the unpleasant smell of greasy wool mixed with harsh cleansers permeated the still air.

What an awful smell. I dinna remember it to be this bad. She wrinkled her nose in distaste.

"Ah, yes. The smell does take a bit of getting used to, but if you want to understand the entire process then you need to experience what happens in each room. The boilers have not been lighted since 'tis not a work day, but if you keep your cloak on, you shouldn't feel the cold so much." He ushered her into a large room filled with a variety of tables. "Ready?"

Ellen nodded in assent.

"First the fleece comes here to be sorted by similar lengths and quality, and then put on tables with wire netting so that dust and impurities can fall through. Fifty per cent of the raw weight can actually be particles of dirt." Ellen sneezed.

"Oh boy, I hope you're not allergic to wool," he teased.

"I think 'tis the dust. I hope I'm not allergic to anything else."

"Unfortunately, dust lingers throughout the factory. We try to sweep it up, but it keeps reappearing." He smiled as he pointed to a door. "Over here, the next room is called the scouring room. 'Tis where the fleece gets washed to rid it of its yolk."

"Yolk? I thought that was only in eggs!"

James laughed. "Well, 'tis in wool, too. That's what the grease in the wool is called. You'd better prepare yourself for where we go next, the smell is pretty strong."

Ellen put a hand up in front of her nose. The odor still got through to her. "What is that, James?"

"You're lucky we don't use the old method of soaking the fleece in stale urine and then beating it," James said. "The current technique is to wash the wool in a series of giant washbasins filled with detergents, as you see over there. The last soak is in a solution of sulfuric acid.

That's the left-over odor you smell now.

"Once the wool has been scoured, it goes through a drying process where it has to be heated to 212 degrees. The high temperature carbonizes any leftover matter, but doesn't harm the fibers because wool is heat resistant. Ready for the next room?"

No way will I use stale urine.

As he held the door open for her, James asked. "Did your Da spin his wool or buy from others?"

"He bought the yarn from local spinners. Mam said she never learned to spin and dinna intend to start."

James smiled. "Sounds like your Mam. So, this is one of our largest rooms where mechanized cylinders card or pull the fibers out into a teased fine web of wool. If we are going to manufacture a blended fabric, then the cotton and wool would have to be carded together at this point to produce a continuous intermingled mesh of loose threads called slivers—that is before it can proceed to a spinning room." James stopped and looked at Ellen.

"Is this too much information for right now?"

"Not at all. I'm fascinated by each and every step. I just wish I had brought some paper so I could be taking notes."

"We can always come back another time and take notes then."

"I'd love to come back." *This is where I'll learn the real facts about textile manufacturing.*

"The spinning rooms are near the back," James continued. "But there's not much light without the lamps lit, so it would be hard to see. Can we just go on instead to a dye room nearer the front?"

"Yes, of course. I want to see as much as I can."

They walked into the last section. "So this is where the spun wool comes to absorb color?"

"Right. Then it goes to the large looms where the yarns will be woven into cloth."

"I must admit, James. The entire process is ingenious."

A noise in the foyer alerted them and the factory manager, Jimmy Doyle, appeared.

"Jimmy, what are you doing here on St. Stephens Day? You

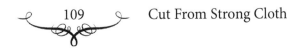

should be home with your family."

"Aye, Mr. Nolan, but I came back to spend an hour going over the books. Everything has to be recorded before the end of the year."

"I'll be taking the books home myself. Go on and enjoy the day off."

"Thank you, Mr. Nolan. The missus will be glad to see me back so soon." He wasted no time in departing.

Ellen made a mental note that all the factory books had to be in shape by year's end. To the casual observer she might have seemed to be a polite listener, but in reality, her mind was ticking away every bit of information. She understood the process of weaving but now realized she would have to be schooled about the entire operations of a factory. One tour in a cold, dim facility would not suffice. She would need to return many times. She shivered.

"Let me take you home, Ellen. 'Tis almost dinner time, and I promised Mary that I'd stop over there later."

"James, the factory is amazing. You have no idea of how much I enjoyed the tour."

"Glad to hear that."

Before they left the factory James leaned in, enveloping her in his arms and kissed her with a long, hard kiss.

Ellen did not pull away and decided that his kisses were delicious in a sultry sort of way. Business partner or not, she enjoyed it each time they kissed. They walked back to Fifth Street and before Ellen went inside, she and James exchanged a last kiss that any bystander would recognize as belonging to new lovers.

***

As James headed home, he saw Patrick walking around from a different block. Still enveloped in the happiness of having spent time with Ellen, he waved over to Patrick.

"Hallo."

"Hallo, James. Been visiting Ellen?"

"I took her on a tour of the factory. She has such a keen interest in the business that I thought she might enjoy seeing how it all oper-

ates. I was delighted that she had so many questions."

"Oh, I bet she did. Did she tell you she plans to go with me to Savannah?"

James stopped. "What do you mean she's planning on going with you? Patrick, are you daft?"

"I've tried to warn you that Ellen can be awful stubborn. She's gotten it into her head that she should become my full partner and be involved in every aspect of this deal."

"Well, you're just going to have to persuade her that she can't go. What the hell is she thinking? This business idea is giving her a swelled head."

"Ah, you've no idea of how tough Ellen can be. I'd wager she's already upstairs packing her bags."

"Let me talk some sense into her, then. Surely your mother's opposed to this idea?"

"Aye, we're both against it. Seems our opinion doesn't matter. But you go right ahead and talk with Ellen. Good luck, by the way. I'll look forward to hearing the outcome."

James lost no time in walking right back in the house with Patrick. When he entered the kitchen, Ellen had started peeling some apples. She turned and seeing him, broke into a grin.

"James? Is there something you forgot?"

"No, Ellen, there's something you forgot. What's this idea of yours about going to Savannah?"

Patrick removed himself to the front room, although he was close enough to the kitchen that he could hear the conversation.

"I plan to go with Patrick. 'Tis as simple as that."

"No, 'tis not as simple as that. I canna understand why you feel the need to go, and I must say I don't like the fact that you didn't mention it to me at all."

"Well, 'tis not for you to like, nor understand, now, is it? The decision is mine, and mine alone."

"Have you thought at all about safety?"

"Safety? Of course I've thought about safety. I'll be with Patrick and Cousin Tom. If two grown men canna defend me, then I'll defend

Cut From Strong Cloth

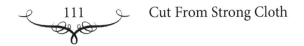

myself." She put up her fists in a mock boxing pose.

James did not react with any humor. "Who's the one being pig-headed now? You've read the papers. You know the South is in turmoil over Lincoln being elected. South Carolina has already voted to leave the Union. Don't you understand that Georgia might not be far behind? You've heard the news in the streets, and you've seen the Union bunting hanging from the mayor's office. What in the world do you think you'll accomplish by going to Savannah?" Without realizing it, James had allowed his voice to become louder and more agitated.

"So what would you propose? That I sit back here in a safe little job with Father Reilly for the rest of my life, while Patrick has the opportunity to negotiate the business deals?"

"At least I'd know where you'd be. I can be the one to take care of you."

"Then you don't know me as well as you think. Remember when I told you I wouldn't let disappointments interfere with my dreams of success? Weaving is my legacy from Da. I was meant to become a textile merchant all along. And I don't need anyone taking care of me. I can take care of myself."

"Ellen, your Da's been dead for years. You don't owe him a thing."

Her eyes stormed as she held her head high. "How dare you speak of Da that way! Aye, he's dead, but his dream isn't. I'll succeed for him because he never got the chance."

James shook his head. "If I canna talk you out of this foolhardy scheme, then I won't be giving you my blessings for the trip."

"I dinna ask for them."

★

An uneasy truce settled into place around Ellen's travel plans. Little talk centered on the trip, only a fortnight away.

"Patrick, I'm only allowing Ellen to go on this trip if you promise to keep her safe."

"Aye, I won't let any harm come her way. But I'm also hoping she won't be a pain in the neck, trying to interfere with the business meet-

ings. She told me she needs to be present at each and every meeting."

"She'll be fine. Just remind her of her place."

"Has she said anything to you, Mam, about her real motives?"

"Patrick, she's your sister. I doubt she has any dark motives. Just keep her from trying to dominate the transactions. You know she'll steal the upper hand if you let her. Explain to her that it would be improper. The man is supposed to be the one to hold the reins."

Patrick listened, but his faced showed skepticism. "I still wager she has something more up her sleeve," he grumbled.

Ellen, meanwhile, pulled out all the clothes she owned, checking which pieces might do for appropriate traveling attire. Cecilia had started refashioning Ellen's outfits into four business ensembles suitable for Savannah's winter season. Her experience in producing the trousseau for Sarah Chambers had given Cecilia some knowledge about southern fashions. Ellen would travel in style.

***

Although annoyed with Ellen's insistence about going to Savannah, James still wanted to spend the New Year's celebration with her and invited her to dine with him down on Sansom Street. Revelers were already making noise in the streets by the time the carriage brought them to Center City.

James helped her down from the carriage and then opened the door to the restaurant, ushering her inside. A waiter motioned them over to a corner table, and James helped Ellen remove her cloak.

"I hope you're impressed with my choice of how to celebrate the evening with you."

"'Tis lovely, James."

Ellen had never dined in a fancy city restaurant before. The white damask tablecloths, carved mahogany wooden chairs, and beautiful silver flatware on each table impressed her. So this was what money can buy. She smiled to herself.

James pulled out her chair and she demurely sat down. Not wanting to ruin the evening, she still felt she needed to break the stalemate.

"James, let's not allow the trip to come between us. I am serious about my aspirations of becoming a businesswoman, born out of respect for my Da. Patrick will watch over me. I just want to learn all I can about the value of cotton so that I can be more knowledgeable about the industry."

"I'm still worried about you venturing into Georgia when hostilities could explode at any time. Escaped slaves are pouring into Philadelphia with tales of unbelievable violence. Men who help a slave escape can be hanged in the South. I don't want you in danger."

"We won't be helping any slaves, James. I give you my word I won't do anything foolhardy." She shuddered though with the information about possible hangings.

"We'll let the hare sit on this for tonight, but I still have my concerns."

Ellen breathed a small sigh, hoping that he might relent some of his fears. When James worried, it made her worry, too. "James, have you ever been to the Mercantile Library?"

"Aye. I'll take you there some time if you like. Now may we call a truce and enjoy this evening with no more talk of business, textiles, or the trip? I'd like to just spend the time together welcoming in the New Year."

"Aye, James. A truce it will be."

As the dinner progressed, Ellen relaxed and admitted to herself that she wanted a relationship with James that went beyond business. She just didn't want her heart broken in the process.

***

Two days later with a raw blustering wind enveloping around her, Ellen stood bundled on Library Street in front of the Mercantile Library, gawking at its edifice. The library towered over the other buildings on the downtown block, and although the cold nagged at her feet, face and mittened hands, the imposing structure caused her heart to race with excitement.

Da, it looks just like a university, it does.

The white block front of the building, with its six Grecian columns supporting the overhang portico roof, displayed an air of refinement and class. Not even the frozen mud in the street could dampen her enthusiasm at being able to study in this magnificent place. She stamped her feet, trying to knock off any mud before entering such a venerable establishment.

"Does thee need help?"

Ellen turned to find a woman, dressed from head to toe in a heavy cloak of gray wool and matching bonnet, standing nearby. She appeared to be several years older than Ellen.

"I'm sorry, what did you say?"

"Does thee need help?"

"Oh no, I'm just admiring the building. Are you a library patron?"

"No, I am a nurse next door at the dispensary, on my way back from running an errand. It is rather cold to be standing here. Would thee like to come inside to get warm?"

"No, thank you. I am here to study at the Mercantile Library. This is my first time, and I wanted to take a moment to appreciate the building."

The look on the woman's face seemed to indicate she thought it strange to be standing outside on such a freezing day. Ellen noticed her features, a fine, chiseled face with bright blue penetrating eyes, and a no-nonsense chin.

"Well, if thee needs help, my name is Catherine Biddle, and I am just next door."

"Thank you. My name is Ellen Canavan. I hope to be coming to the library on a regular basis, so perhaps we'll meet again."

"Good day, then." The woman with the strange way of talking headed into the dispensary.

Ellen walked up the steps to the entrance of the library, pushed open the heavy front door and stepped inside. Just breathing the air of lemon oil polished wood touched off a thrill of anticipation, almost like opening a present.

"May I help you, Miss?" A kind looking older gentleman appeared at her side.

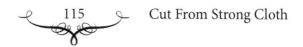 115   Cut From Strong Cloth

"Yes, thank you. I would like to use the library to study about the textile industry."

"Very well. May I ask if you are a member, or are you representing a particular enterprise?"

"I am part of Canavan Wool," Ellen answered.

"Then I will just have to check that a Mr. Canavan is a member in good standing."

"Oh, I don't think my brother, Patrick Canavan, has a membership. Could you check instead for Mr. James Nolan? I will be representing him."

"Nolan, you say?"

"Yes, Mr. James Nolan, of the St. John Street Factory."

The man shuffled over to consult a ledger which she supposed held the names of all the members. Ellen crossed her fingers behind her back, hoping her hunch was correct. James would have a membership if he had already visited here, and hopefully wouldn't mind her using his name. By the time he found out, she would have gained the information she sought.

"Yes, his name is here. May I show you around the library?"

Ellen followed after the gentleman, trying hard not to act like a child in a confectionary shop. She slipped off her cloak, draped it over her arm, and followed him deeper into the main foyer where the marble floor looked like it belonged in a palace. The cavernous space was hushed with silence, but Ellen was sure her heart was beating loud enough for anyone to hear.

"This building dates back to 1845," the man whispered. "We started with 300 members, but today we have about 2,450 subscribers. While we are indeed focused on the textile industry, we also carry works of great literature."

He led her through the stacks. She wished that Da could have lived to see this, his own daughter being allowed to study in a building devoted to education for the business class. After the tour of the first floor, the gentleman explained that the second story housed the newspaper collection, and then he left her on her own. Ellen found her way back to the shelves dedicated to various textile fibers and decided to

concentrate first on cotton. Later she could explore the books dealing with manufacturing. Locating several books with promising titles she went into a reading room, sat down at a table, draped her cloak and bonnet on a side chair, and began to turn the pages of the first book.

"And just what do you think you're doing, Missy?"

Ellen looked up, shocked to discover the question directed to her. A portly, red-faced man peered over his spectacles and glared at her. The cut of his morning coat indicated he belonged to Philadelphia's elite business class.

"I am studying."

"Not in here, you're not! This is a men's reading room and the rules state—no women allowed!"

"I'm sorry. I had no idea."

"You don't belong here."

Flushed with indignation, Ellen gathered up the books, her cloak and hat, and beat a hasty retreat back to the front desk.

"Excuse me. Is there a particular desk where I can study?" she asked the attendant.

He glanced up at her and pointed to a side room she had not noticed on the tour. As she walked over to it she felt every man's gaze following her. Reaching the space she saw a sign that read, Women's Reading Room. *That old goat. Why didn't he just tell me I had to read in this room?* Once inside, she placed the books on an empty table and sat down. Her earlier bravado now gave way to self-doubt. *Everywhere I turn, someone is trying to discourage me, or block my way. It shouldn't have to be this hard.* She smudged a tear away. *Damn them. Damn them all. I will succeed, Da. I promise you.*

Hours passed, and the daylight turned to dusk. Closing up the last book and placing it on the corner of the table, she donned her cloak and bonnet, and left the library with a sense of accomplishment. She couldn't wait to get home and write down everything she had learned. Stepping out onto the street, a gust of bitter wind swirled around her and the other pedestrians hurrying along the frigid ground. Just then the door to the Philadelphia Dispensary opened and out stepped Catherine Biddle as well.

"Hallo!" Ellen waved to the woman, and Catherine tromped over to her.

"Hello, Ellen. Lucky chance we should meet again so soon. Was thee successful?"

"Yes, I found books I can study, but some of the men in the library were not very friendly. I sat in a men's reading room and they demanded that I leave. It was very embarrassing."

Catherine shook her head in dismay. "Thee had every right to sit in any chair. There is no law that says women must sit separately from men in a public building."

"'Tis not a public building. 'Tis a membership library," Ellen explained.

"That does not give them the right to belittle thee."

"Well, I hope next time it will be easier since now I know where to sit." She rubbed her mittened hands together. "'Tis very cold out here. I need to be taking the streetcar at Chestnut and Fifth Street. Which way are you going?"

"I take the same route," Catherine replied.

"Oh, good. Let's walk, then. At least it will help us keep warm."

The two women fell in step with one another.

"Ellen, thee needs not feel defeated. Women are allowed to study there," Catherine commented as they walked along.

"I know. But, 'tis not enough just to be able to study in the library, I should be able to sit wherever I please."

"Yes, thee is correct. But until women have the documented right to vote, it is very difficult to change the rules that favor men."

Ellen turned to look at Catherine straight on. "So you, too, believe that women should be allowed to vote?"

Catherine nodded, and then let her smile turn into a wide grin. "Indeed, I do."

By now they had arrived at the end of the block just as the horse drawn streetcar pulled up. Both of them climbed inside, juggling for seats with the other passengers and thankful for the enclosed roof. The new streetcars on iron tracks provided a smoother ride than the old omnibuses. The driver clicked the reins and the roan flared his nostrils,

Linda Harris Sittig

exhaling great steamy breaths as they continued north up Fifth Street.

"Catherine, I couldn't agree with you more. I wish I could convince my mam about women having equal rights with men."

Catherine lowered her voice. "I am a Quaker, Ellen, and raised to believe that we are all equal in God's eyes. So yes, I think that women deserve an equal place in society. Not everyone agrees with that, but I can teach thee some polite, confident phrases. Like, *Thank you, I'll take that under consideration.* Use that in the library so the men will know thee is serious about studying."

"That would be grand. I've never met any other woman who thinks as boldly as you do. I'll start practicing on my own family. I need to learn to become more confident as soon as possible."

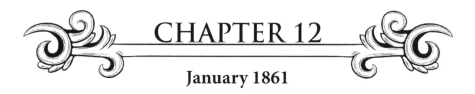

CHAPTER 12

January 1861

He loved the fires most in winter when the flames competed with the early night stars to light up the sky. As much as he enjoyed the companionship of the other fire fighters, he savored the drama of racing to the destination and the competitiveness of arriving on the scene ahead of another station. The brigades often fought bloody street battles in which the victors earned the right to extinguish the fire. Although the insurance companies only paid the brigade that put out the flames, he was employed by certain men to set the fires. He became adept at setting a blaze, rushing to the fire station to join his brigade, and later collecting the arson payment.

The fires gave him authority and transformed him from poor immigrant to something more powerful. They energized him with their capability for destruction, and the roar of the inferno set his heart racing as the wood crackled into oblivion. Malevolent colors from the fires made his pulse quicken and the heat made his breathing more rapid, almost like drug-induced euphoria. Here, success was always in his pocket.

Setting fires became more than just a profit; it became his secret addiction and his weapon of choice.

CHAPTER 13

January 1861

A block from home, Ellen pulled the bell cord to let the street-car driver know she wanted to get off. He reined in the horse, and she climbed down into the street, waving good-bye to Catherine and walking quickly to her own front door.

"Patrick? Mam? Hallo?" The savory aroma of stewing chicken, onions, and herbs caused her stomach to growl, reminding her she had skipped the noon meal in favor of studying at the library. Looking to share her day, Ellen headed for the kitchen where Cecilia stood at the stove with a matchstick clenched between her teeth to stop onion tears.

"Mam, I spent the entire afternoon at the Mercantile Library and learned so much about cotton!"

Cecilia gave a weak smile and looked up toward heaven but did not offer any comment. Ellen ignored the condescending gesture and, taking off her cloak and hat, walked instead to the front room. Gathering up some clean sheets of paper, and grasping the ink bottle and nib-tipped pen, she sat down at Patrick's desk to write out the facts she had just learned about cotton. In the margin she jotted Catherine Biddle's words: "Thank you. I will take that under consideration."

Patrick returned home a half hour later, wiping soot and ash off his face. "It took all we had to battle the fire, and in the end, the building went down anyway."

At least he was safe.

He appeared distant, like he sometimes did after fighting a blaze. Ellen and Mam both knew his brigade had a reputation for quickly throwing the first punch in order to stop another brigade from venturing onto their turf and claiming the pay.

He's scowling because his brigade probably missed out on getting the money.

Patrick went out on the back porch, took off his sooty jacket, and then splashed his face and washed his hands in an old chipped basin. Cecilia stopped him as he came back into the house.

"Change your clothes." She smiled. "I've been slaving over a hot stove and want no talk about fires or cotton while we eat supper."

Ellen laid down the pen, covered the inkwell, and ventured into the kitchen. Patrick came back in the kitchen wearing clean clothes, but no smile. She decided not to ask for any details about the fire. He obviously wasn't in the mood to talk about it. Then the three of them sat down to a quiet but satisfying meal of chicken fricassee and fresh rolls. Ellen forced herself to wait until they had finished eating before engaging him in conversation.

"Mam, the meal was grand. Why don't Patrick and I do the dishes and let you relax?"

Patrick eyed Ellen with suspicion, but Cecilia took the offer and went upstairs to rest.

"Thanks for volunteering me to do the dishes," Patrick grumbled and grabbed a towel, which meant Ellen would be doing the washing up.

"I'm not going to let your mood ruin what I have to share."

"Go ahead. Looks like I have little choice in the matter anyway."

Ellen gritted her teeth. "I spent the entire afternoon down at the Mercantile Library on Library Street. James has a membership, and I used his name to gain entry. I read volumes of pages devoted to the production of cotton. Then I met the most unusual woman, a Quaker."

"A Quaker? What's she got to do with cotton? You'd better be careful, Ellen. You know how Mam feels about non-Catholics."

"Well, I'm not asking Mam to become friends with her."

"You know perfectly well what I mean. Heed my words and don't get too close to her. You canna trust her kind."

"Patrick, you're as suspicious as Mam."

"Well, we were right about Michael Brady, now weren't we?"

Ellen turned her head away so Patrick wouldn't see how the words stung.

"So, James let you use his membership. 'Twas generous of him."

"He doesn't know I'm using his membership. But I'm sure he won't object." *And I loved how it felt to be there.*

"You're pretty bold to be using someone's name for your own purposes."

Ellen stopped the washing and held a lone soapy dish in her hand. "Patrick, what's wrong? You're being unusually negative, almost like Mam."

He shrugged. "Just hoping for some peace and quiet tonight, that's all. Never mind. Go ahead and give me the highlights of what you read in this library."

"For starters, I learned that there are four main textile fibers: cotton, flax, silk, and wool. Cotton and flax are from plants, while silk and wool come from animals. But of course, you already knew that."

Before he could answer, Ellen charged ahead with a full-bodied enthusiasm, relegating him to the role of silent listener in a one-sided conversation.

"Then I studied comparison figures about the four fibers in regard to abrasion resistance, strength, elongation, absorbency, elasticity, and even sunlight resistance. Cotton beat wool every time, except in terms of elasticity. Therefore, I'm thinking that our new cloth needs to have a strong presence of cotton with the wool.

"I read, too, about the different types of cotton fibers, and learned that staple length is the most important factor in determining quality because the longer the cotton fiber, the stronger the yarn produced. There are upland cottons, long staple cottons, and short staple cottons. We need to make sure our Savannah purchases will include long staple. James already told me that there are mills here in Philadelphia producing mixed fabrics, but I doubt any of them are using long

Cut From Strong Cloth

staple coastal cotton because of the price."

"So why would we use a more costly fiber?"

"Because we want our cloth to hold up in wet weather, and be comfortable for the soldiers to wear. Of course that also means the long staple cotton will have a higher purchase tag, so we'll have to factor that in for each woven bolt. Did I mention too, that I read 'tis the Quartermaster of the Army who purchases the cloth and issues the contracts?" Ellen passed him a plate wet with rinse water. "Patrick, you haven't said much. Isn't this all very exciting?"

"I'm just waiting for you to take a breath so I can get my two cents in. So, long staple cotton will be included, and we'll work toward using a higher percentage of it in the cotton mix we present to the Quartermaster."

"I can't wait to go back to the library. I want to learn everything I can. And Patrick, 'tis a beautiful building. Just as grand as any library in Belfast or Dublin could be. Da would be proud of both of us. Now tell me what's wrong? I know you, Patrick, and you're hiding something."

"I'm not hiding anything, Ellen. I just fear that in your typical excitement, you haven't thought through the realities of the situation. Looks like the nation is definitely heading to a fight, maybe an all-out war. But if we move forward in haste, we could lose money. All you're thinking of is success, not the risks. This could force me to neglect business right here at home."

"Patrick, I have thought of the risks. But without risk, we canna have any gain. We should only be gone for two weeks in Georgia. Canavan Wool can survive for that amount of time without you. The government is going to need cloth, if not for soldiers' uniforms, then for something else."

"Something else, huh? Just what might that 'something else' be?"

"I don't know yet, but perhaps we'll find the answer once we're in Georgia."

"Well, just don't go making any blunders to further complicate my life."

Ellen's thoughts were already racing ahead to tomorrow's library

visit and whatever new information she might learn. Patrick's attitude could not diminish her excitement, even in the frigid weather.

***

The next morning Ellen used some charm, asking Father Reilly to adjust his schedule so she could serve his noontime meal each day at eleven-thirty. This would give her full afternoons at the Mercantile Library. If Father Reilly was amused at her choice of where she went to study, he did not mention it.

After she gave him a steaming bowl of ham and bean soup, and a loaf of hot baked soda bread, she wrapped her sturdy cloak tightly across her body, tied on her hat, and dashed out the rectory. Double pacing down Second Street, passing street vendors and shoppers, she turned at last onto Girard Avenue and walked toward Sixth Street.

While waiting for the next streetcar heading south, she saw a private street carriage ramble by. It gave her pause. *What if I don't really qualify to study at the Library? What if 'tis meant for only upper-class businessmen? Am I forcing this, to study where I don't fit in? Or can I thumb my nose at all of them and see how long I can last?*

By the time she arrived at the library, she swallowed her fears and steeled herself to be assertive. With a gulp of gumption, she bit her lower lip, whispered Catherine's words to herself, and opened the door.

She waved to the front desk attendant, marched into the stacks, and pulled several new titles off the shelves. Not hurrying, she smiled at two male patrons as she sauntered off into the women's reading room. The two businessmen glanced at one another other, and Ellen pretended not to hear their words as she passed by.

"Pretty saucy of her to come in here parading through the stacks and acting like she's a part of us."

"In the old days, they would never have let that happen," grumbled the other one.

As before, the hours flew by, but Ellen had come prepared with an inkwell, pen and paper. Leaving the library at the same time as yesterday, she discovered Catherine Biddle emerging from the dispensary.

"Hallo, Catherine!" She waved at the other woman, who walked over to her.

"Did thee have a better experience today in the library?"

"Aye, I kept my head up and dinna let the men know they had gotten to me yesterday. Thank you for those phrases. They gave me courage. See? I took a lot of notes."

"Thee carried an inkwell to the library?"

"I had to in order to remember all the information. Shall we take the streetcar together?"

The two of them walked together and Catherine asked, "Tell me what thee learned."

"Well, I learned that cotton fibers were first cultivated in ancient India." Ellen hesitated a moment. "Do you know where that is?"

"Of course I do. Quaker women are educated right along with men. I have read about India, although I did not know they were the first to harvest cotton."

"I envy you your schooling, Catherine. I've had to teach myself beyond what the nuns did. No one in my family believes a woman needs an education. Well, my Da did."

"Your Da?"

"Aye, my father. But he died when I was a young girl."

"I am sorry for thee, Ellen. I lost my father at an early age, too. Even though I had two older brothers, no one ever replaced my father."

"I feel the exact same way about my Da."

Ellen thought about Da, and felt certain he would have liked Catherine Biddle.

"So, I read all I can to further my knowledge. For now I work for Father Reilly at St. Michael's, but I intend to live out my Da's dream one day."

"What dream is that?"

Ellen smiled. "To seize the world."

"Well, that's a formidable dream, but certainly not impossible," Catherine replied. "Is Father Reilly a good man?"

"Oh yes, he's given me open access to his personal library. Then about twice a month I visit Brown's Book Store down on Arch Street.

That way I've been able to keep up with my learning."

"Brown's Book Store? The Friends Meeting House is right across the street. Just think Ellen, while thee shopped in the book store, I might have been nearby reading in the Friend's Library. Of course, the majority of the titles concern our beliefs."

Patrick's words of caution echoed in Ellen's mind.

"Thee works for the priest at St. Michael's. So, thee is Catholic?

"Yes."

"Was thee born a Catholic?"

Ellen laughed. "Yes, that's how most Irish get to be Catholic. But I canna imagine being anything else. St. Peter himself started the Roman Catholic Church."

Catherine listened, but did not offer a reply.

"Catherine, can I ask you a personal question? Why are some people suspicious of Quakers?"

"Perhaps because we keep to ourselves, shun fancy clothes, and speak in a different manner. We believe that everyone has inherent worth—there is that of God in everyone—and therefore differences should not be a factor in how one is judged."

"Because you are Quaker, are you also an abolitionist?"

Catherine lowered her voice to a whisper. "That is not a topic we should discuss here."

***

When they met on Monday, Catherine presented Ellen with a gift of a paper bound journal and a new writing implement called a pencil. Approximately five inches long, crafted from a fragrant wood stained an acorn color, the pencil's width was slim as a finger. Ellen quickly saw how much easier this would be for taking notes in the library. No longer would she need to carry an inkwell, pen, and loose sheaves of paper.

"Thank you, Catherine, the gift is quite thoughtful."

"Thou art welcome. The gift is also quite practical."

For two days they rode the streetcar together at dusk and talked

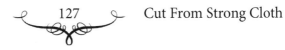

over the day's happenings. In spite of the differences in their ages and religions, Ellen felt a connection to Catherine and took her suggestions to heart. Catherine was really the first true female confidant Ellen ever had.

"Always appear gentle, Ellen. Smile when you say, 'Thank you, I will consider that suggestion.' Then the adversary will feel confused because of thy calm disposition and will wonder if perhaps he has won after all. Which, of course, he has not. Thee has only offered to consider his point of view—not act upon it."

"Oh, I doubt my brother Patrick would ever refer to me as gentle, and my mam. . . well she's like many Irish, tenacious in her beliefs and stubborn in what you call disposition."

"Just remember that thou can catch more flies with honey than with vinegar."

"Catherine, I love how you use words! I'll try to remember about the honey."

Ellen got her first chance to use Catherine's words just an hour later.

"Mam, see what I have? 'Tis a journal. You take notes and use this to write with, it's called a pencil. Look, see how easy this is." Ellen took the pencil and opened to the first page in the journal and wrote out her full name, Ellen Anne Canavan. "Isn't it clever?"

"I hope you dinna waste your hard earned money buying into such a foolish idea. Real businessmen would never use such a thing. Only the poor buy inexpensive objects."

Ellen swallowed the seething anger ready to escape her mouth. "Well, thank you for telling me your opinion. I'll think on your words." *Catch her with honey? Even Catherine would have a hard time with that.*

***

The next day the weather warmed to just chilly and not bone-biting cold. The two women were able to walk at a leisurely pace as they headed back towards Chestnut Street at the end of the day.

"Catherine, we're alone out here. Can you answer my question now about being an abolitionist?"

Catherine thought for a moment before answering.

"Ellen, I cannot say for all Quakers, but yes, I am opposed to slavery and would gladly help another escape those bonds. There are many others who share my same views, not just Quakers. That is how the Underground Railroad was started—to help slaves escape their imprisonments."

"But the Underground Railroad is breaking the law."

"Whose law, Ellen? The laws of those who support slavery? Does thee believe in slavery?"

"No, I am opposed to it as well."

"Then we are not so different after all. Think of me as thy friend first, and a Quaker second. I do not let thee being a Catholic interfere with my caring about you. Let us remain friends."

"Catherine, do you think that slavery exists because it is men who make the laws and hold the power?"

"Anyone who makes and enforces the law always has the power. But until women are given the right to vote, which we do deserve, changing laws will not be easy."

"I am so glad that we met and have become friends."

Catherine's acceptance of Ellen as a friend, coupled with her words of wisdom, gave Ellen a renewed sense of her own capabilities.

***

On a frigid January day, Patrick and Ellen boarded a steamship at the very same Philadelphia docks where they had first stepped onto American soil over five years ago. Ellen mused that back then they arrived with only a few possessions, and now they were traveling in modern style with fashionable woolen coats. She glanced down at her pigskin leather gloves and pulled them tighter onto her fingers.

Gulls still soared over the docks and even in the biting cold one could still smell the ever-present odor of the fuel-stoked ships. She knew that they had held fast to Da's dream of a new and better life in America, but as the ship sailed down the Delaware River she smiled to realize that this trip embraced *her* dream.

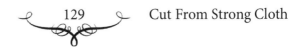

Cut From Strong Cloth

The vessel churned through the icy river, pushed out into the Delaware Bay, then plowed through the currents until bursting into the choppy waves of the Atlantic Ocean. Ellen had not been on a boat since the voyage from Ireland on damp April seas, and now she felt the icy winter wind seeping through the walls into her second class cabin. She had brought the new journal so she could record her thoughts about the trip, and decided to pencil in details right away. It would help take up some of the dead time in the cabin.

On the second afternoon of the trip, the chill abated. Deciding she needed some fresh air, she ventured on deck. The salty tang of the ocean breeze and the rolling gait of the ship brought back memories of Da's funeral; but she had grown past the tears and misguided guilt, and now kept him in her heart.

Turning around, she saw Patrick approaching.

"'Tis better weather now that we are further south."

"Aye. But before we land, I want to remind you that James and I set a cap of $2200.00 for the cotton venture. Once we're with the sellers, don't do anything stupid like overriding our decision and offering them even one penny more."

"Patrick, why would you be thinking I'd go behind your back and make a counter offer? We're in this deal together and I expect us to totally support one another, conferring on all decisions."

"Just so long as you stick to that, little sister."

She smiled back at him. Remember, catch the fly with honey.

***

Around noon the following day when the boat turned into the Savannah River, the two travelers saw the Fort Pulaski flag waving briskly in the breeze. They scanned the mudflats along the river trying to get a glimpse of the docking destination. Seagulls swooped down and followed the ship all the way into port.

"Patrick, look!" Perched forty feet above the wharf and high on a bluff, sat the city of Savannah—nothing like Philadelphia where the streets ended almost at the river's edge. "I never expected the city to be

up so high."

"Aye, well don't gape."

Their boat pulled into a jumbled scene reminiscent of home. The groans of ships' timbers mixed with men's voices shouting directions as cargo was unloaded. Even the rhythmic stamping of horses' hooves provided a familiar dockside clatter. Amidst the port menagerie was a large assortment of vessels—barques, schooners, and steam packets all tied up at the wharves. The port of Savannah had entered its winter transport shipping season and soon businessmen of all callings would be making deals.

But along with the normal port noises they heard the chants of enslaved laborers calling out to one another as they stacked cargo crates destined for outbound ships.

Ellen shuddered when she saw livid scars on many of the slaves' faces and how their eyes were always cast only on each other, never looking into the crowd. *I'm glad Catherine is not here to see this.*

As they stepped on the wooden planks of the docks, they saw two men arguing with a third, loud enough for them to hear every bit of the conversation even though they could not quite identify the men's accents.

"We don't care how hard it was to get through. We depend on these shipments from Hazard Powder to add to our arsenals."

"I'm telling you, that with all the troubles brewing, my packet ship was stopped twice out on the waters. I don't know if I'll be able to get through with another transport."

"You'd better get through, if you know what's good for you. You Yanks don't mind making money down here, but you get yellow-bellied with fear of blockades."

Ellen tensed, expecting a fight might break out. Patrick stepped toward the men, ready, it seemed, to join in. Ellen grabbed his arm.

"Patrick, 'tis not our argument."

He waved her off, and then shrugged. "All right, 'tis not our argument. . . yet."

"Now wasn't it lucky I came along on this trip, to help you restrain your Irish temper?"

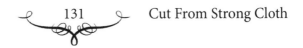

Patrick made no comment but hoisted their traveling bags and started to follow the other passengers climbing to reach the city proper. Upon gaining the top of the bluff, they looked around and observed three-storied brick warehouses and offices lined up in a row. In front of them, men in fancy morning coats paced back and forth along the ballast-paved street. Far from the rough scene of the Philadelphia riverfront, Ellen felt that Savannah evoked a more genteel feeling along its perimeter, and she found it rather pleasing.

Their cousin Tom had suggested they stay at the Planters Hotel on Bryan Street located a few blocks from the riverfront and frequented by travelers conducting business affairs in the city. Ellen felt a strong pull to walk right to the cotton offices but resisted the urge and let Patrick inquire instead about directions to the hotel. Then they walked over to the address and procured two rooms.

"Patrick, let's go out right away and see the city."

"Do you think that's a good idea? You heard those men by the docks. Yanks aren't in favor down here."

"We just won't pay any heed to the words of some roughnecks."

"You always have an answer, don't you?"

"Don't be silly. Of course I don't always have the answer. But give me ten minutes to change clothes."

Ellen had never stayed in a hotel before, and the excitement of the trip energized her. Her small room adequately held a bed and night stand, wall pegs for clothes, and an oval mirror hanging on the wall. Shaking out her garments and hanging them up to minimize any wrinkles, she stepped into one of her refashioned dresses, an apricot-colored cotton trimmed with horizontal cinnamon-hued ribbons and scalloped buttons. Grabbing her short cape and traveling bonnet, she dashed downstairs to meet Patrick.

They left the hotel and began to wander the streets, soon recognizing the layout of a grid pattern similar to Philadelphia. Smaller, but with a more intimate beauty. Savannah contained numerous city squares flanked by magnificent stately trees with feathery silver-grey vines that seemed to dance with the breeze.

They admired the gardens they chanced upon and the gracious

houses that anchored them. Street after street boasted magnificent townhomes made from brownstone or white brick, or even a material that they later learned was called stucco. Many of the homes sported ornate black iron railings—worthy rivals of even the best houses of Rittenhouse Square in Philadelphia. Even in the dead of winter, Savannah displayed refinement.

Ellen wondered why there did not seem to be the loud boisterous talk of war they had expected to hear from people in the streets. Other than the men at the docks, she overheard few discussions concerning politics, even though Mississippi had just announced secession a few days ago. Do they only talk about war and politics behind closed doors?

Women swished down the streets in hooped skirts, carrying market baskets, or on the arms of gentlemen in silk hats. People smiled at Ellen and Patrick, and no one gave any indication that they feared a possible attack. Perhaps anti-Northern sentiments were really brewing just below the surface of this polite society. Regardless of Mam's fears and James' concerns, Ellen vowed to enjoy every bit of this trip.

Within an hour Patrick and Ellen traversed the city from one end to the other. Hungry for a change of taste from what the ship had offered, they stopped at a neighborhood inn and had their first experience with southern coastal cooking. Starting with a richly flavored fish gumbo, and then proceeding to piquant fish cakes served with red beans and rice, they washed the meal down with a glass of ale for each, and commented on the contrast to Mam's cooking.

"Even the beer tastes different down here," Patrick declared. "'Tis a bit weaker than ours."

"Well, let's not be critical. We should both act like business travelers who are used to different types of food."

"I prefer to act like myself, and not have my little sister tell me what to do."

"Of course, Patrick. I just want us to fit in, that's all."

Cut From Strong Cloth

CHAPTER 14

January 1861

Tom Avery met them at the hotel the next day, and they spent some time getting re-acquainted.

"So, why do you need our fine Georgia cotton, and what type of cloth will you be making with it?" Tom queried in a low voice.

Patrick and Ellen looked at each other, but before Ellen could reply, Patrick jumped in with a voice that appeared to sound nonchalant. "We want to fashion a special cloth that would be a blend of wool and cotton. Then we intend to sell it for the making of clothes."

"Clothes? What type of clothes? Fine suits and fancy dresses, I hope."

"We're not sure what will sell best."

"Then, who are the customers you'll be selling to? Not the military, I hope. Down here the growers have been selling their cotton to Northern mills for years. But I don't think they'd be wanting their cotton to be used for military purposes against other Southerners."

"But Tom, you just said that Georgia cotton has always been sold to Northern mills. Why would our purchases be any different?" Ellen asked.

"Ellen, you might not be aware of what's happening to the nation, but I'm sure Patrick has read the papers."

"Actually, Tom, I'm quite well read myself, thank you. Mississippi and Alabama voted to secede from the Union, just a few days ago."

"This is the way I see it," Patrick interjected. "We're going to offer top pay for top quality. The merchants here will make a profit, and we hope to as well. Who knows in the end who'll be buying our cloth? The fact still remains that the Savannah growers will make money. This business venture can be a boon for us all."

"All right. I'll ask around and see who might be interested in selling cotton to you. But I canna guarantee any sales. One more thing; down here the men who negotiate the sale of cotton are called cotton factors, not merchants."

Ellen's eyes shot up in surprise. *Why dinna I discover that term before we left home?*

"So don't be calling them merchants or they'll know for sure you're a greenhorn. You'll be going to their offices located on Factors Row. Another thing, brush up on using your brogue. If anyone asks where you're from, tell them County Tyrone, Ireland. 'Tis a smarter answer right now than advertising you're from up North. I should be able to give you a list tomorrow morning of the factors most likely to receive you."

Then he turned to face Ellen. "In the meantime, what will you be doin', while Patrick's making the business rounds? Will you be shopping?"

"I fear Patrick dinna explain everything. We're business partners, he and I, and I'm on this trip to help with the transactions, not to shop."

Tom's face registered surprise. "Ellen, down here a woman's business is in the home. They might find it queer for you to be involved with buying cotton."

"I don't care in the least if they find me queer or not. I want to be able to purchase the best cotton Savannah has to offer."

"Full of ideas, isn't she, Tom?"

"Well then, let Patrick speak first. I think you'll find that business in the South is conducted in a different manner than in Philadelphia."

Ellen flashed him a dazzling smile. "All right, Tom, thank you for your honesty. I'll take that under advisement. Would you mind placing a star at the most important name? I want to make sure we see that gentleman first."

Cut From Strong Cloth

***

Walking home, Tom Avery whistled, "He'll be having his hands full with her."

***

Monday morning dawned with a playful nip in the air, and only a few winter clouds made their presence known by hanging low on the horizon. The brisk but somewhat gentle morning breeze provided a delightful reprieve from the harsh winter winds of Philadelphia.

Ellen knocked on Patrick's door. "Patrick, are you ready?"

"Aye, give me a moment."

She stood in the hallway waiting. Patrick emerged wearing his best suit. Together they went down to the breakfast room and each ordered a meal of fried eggs, rashers of bacon, and hot rolls called biscuits. Ellen then watched as other diners spooned a concoction that looked somewhat like porridge onto their plates, but seasoned it with butter, salt, and pepper. She had seen this ritual yesterday as well, so she did the same. Patrick smirked at her overzealous attempt of appearing knowledgeable about southern breakfasts.

An hour later they were headed for the area called Factors Row, armed with the list of names Tom Avery had prepared for them.

"Why did you ask Tom to tick the most important name?"

"Because if we put forth a good showing with that merchant, I mean factor, word will spread and the other factors might be more agreeable to doing business with us."

Patrick gave a silent nod in her direction, but didn't acknowledge the merit of her idea.

Ellen drank in the salty air of Savannah, now mixed with the heady overtones of excitement and potential success. Wearing one of her favorite dresses, the caramel check with a cream-colored shawl, provided her with an extra boost of confidence. Being away from home infused her body with the thrill of independence.

As they walked the streets toward Factors Row, Ellen scrutinized the dresses of the women she saw out walking and blessed Mam's talent for providing her with clothes that did not stand out in Savannah. Once they arrived at the factors' offices, Ellen glanced at the names on each door. They found the name they were seeking, and Ellen whispered "St. Brigid" to herself. With a smile and a nod of assurance to each other, Ellen squared her shoulders while Patrick opened the door.

"Good day. May I be of assistance?" They were greeted by a middle-aged gentleman who got up from a desk littered with paperwork.

Patrick spoke, as planned. "Good day to you, sir. We would like to meet with Mr. Francis."

"Do you have an appointment?"

"No, but we have traveled a great distance to see him."

"Very well, if you would wait a moment? And the nature of your visit is. . . ?"

"We are textile merchants seeking to purchase future cotton harvests and would like to conduct business with Mr. Francis."

Ellen noticed that Patrick had used the term "we," which meant they were off to a good start.

The man opened a door and disappeared to another space, but neither Patrick nor Ellen could quite tell if it was an office or small corridor. After a few moments, the door reopened and he returned, walking this time behind an older gentleman.

"I understand you are looking for me. Who might I be addressing?"

Ellen noted the definitive cut of the older man's clothes, the expert tailoring evident in the fit of his jacket, and how his shirt had been recently pressed. He obviously took great stock in appearances, and she silently thanked Mam again for dressing her well.

"Good morning, sir. I am Patrick Canavan and this is my sister, Ellen. We have come to inquire about purchasing future cotton harvests."

The man turned to look at Ellen rather than Patrick, and she smiled back at him in her most confident manner.

"Yes, Gerald said there were textile merchants come to see me. I assumed that there would be two gentlemen. I did not expect to be meeting a young lady."

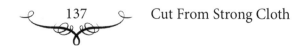

137   Cut From Strong Cloth

Ellen had promised herself not to jump into any conversation until necessary. But she found it unbearable to remain silent.

"Mr. Francis, I am indeed the other textile merchant. My brother and I are business partners."

"Business partners? Still, how unusual that you would bring your sister to a business negotiation."

Patrick looked like he wanted to wring Ellen's neck. They had agreed she would not talk until Patrick brought her into the conversation. Mr. Francis appeared somewhat amused at Ellen's presence. But before Ellen could further alienate Mr. Francis, Patrick took command of the conversation.

"I think, Mr. Francis, you will find us both knowledgeable about cotton purchases. We are prepared to offer solid cash for any transactions agreed upon."

Mr. Francis eyed the two of them. "Your voice betrays you, sir; you are not from these parts."

"No, our family is from County Tyrone, Ireland."

"Ireland? Do you have any letters of introduction or references, then?"

"This is still America, isn't it? I dinna think that we would be asked to prove our legitimacy."

"Yes, Mr. Canavan, this is still America, but this is also Savannah, and here we expect common courtesy, even in business transactions."

Ellen spoke up. "Mr. Francis, my brother and I don't have any letters of introduction, but we do have a local reference."

She saw Patrick glare and supposed he thought she would mention their cousin Tom. A local Irishman working in the lumber yard would hardly be the type of character reference this gentleman was seeking, and she knew that.

"Dr. Fallon will vouch for us."

"Louis Fallon, the surgeon? How are you connected to Dr. Fallon?"

"He is a family friend."

"Indeed? Well then, Miss Canavan, before we can proceed with any further formalities, I will need to contact Dr. Fallon. Perhaps you

can both return tomorrow morning around eleven o'clock? That will give me ample time to check your reference. If Dr. Fallon does vouch for you, we can continue."

"We shall see you tomorrow then, Mr. Francis." Ellen suppressed her feelings of irritation. Never had she expected to be challenged on references.

"Thank you, sir, for your time," Patrick stated.

He and Ellen exited the office together but once on the street, Ellen marched out ahead of him, striding back toward the hotel.

"Ellen, wait." He grabbed her arm. "Where are you going?"

"Patrick, just keep walking. We'll talk when we turn the corner."

When they rounded the block, Ellen exploded.

"The nerve of that pompous ass! He thinks he's calling our bluff. Won't he be surprised when Dr. Fallon gives approval?"

"Ellen, calm down. You must have known the factors might be taken back a bit to have a woman arrive to conduct business. We'll just wait until tomorrow and go back after he sees Dr. Fallon. Now walk by my side, not out in front."

"We will do nothing of the kind. We're going to pay a call to Dr. Fallon today. That way we can reconnect with him and ensure success for tomorrow."

"All right, but in the meantime, let's get something to eat. I'm hungry."

They found a small restaurant near Bryan Street and asked for tea, much to the surprise of the waiter who was used to patrons arriving later for the main meal of the day. They sampled some fresh hot cornbread along with the tea.

"Patrick, I think we should find the nearest Catholic Church and go say a prayer. We dinna attend Mass yesterday. Perhaps that's the reason we encountered the unexpected difficulties."

"I doubt our going or not going to Mass had any bearing on Mr. Francis, but I'll go with you if you like."

The closest Catholic church happened to be the only Catholic church, St. John the Baptist on the corner of Drayton and Perry Streets. It was more than twice the size of St. Michael's and constructed completely out of brick; they couldn't help but be impressed with its exterior. Crossing the threshold, Ellen gazed inside to the large crucifix poised over the altar, genuflected in homage, and entered a pew. Kneeling, she felt the old familiar and welcomed sensation of being at peace with God. She offered a silent prayer and then looked around in awe at the size of the interior, which could seat a thousand people. Ellen felt humble in the expansive space, but secure with the feeling of sanctuary that being in church always gave her. She bowed her head once again and began in earnest to ask the Virgin to bless their cotton endeavors.

Back outside, she asked Patrick, "Did you say three wishes?"

"Aye, I did."

Ellen pulled the address of Dr. Fallon out of her string purse and suggested they walk over to his residence on West Broad. They started west on Perry, passing the graceful Chippewa Square where Ellen noted a church that resembled the Mercantile Library. She hoped this was a sign of good luck. They continued past Orleans Square and turned right onto Jefferson. Holding Tom's crude map, they proceeded along Jefferson under a canopy of trees laden with Spanish moss. Blocks later, after crossing York, they came across the most magnificent townhome Ellen had ever seen; in fact she wondered how one family could inhabit such a large residence. Built of red brick and solid as a bank, its classical design bespoke money. It appeared to occupy the entire block.

"That's how the very wealthy live, Ellen. With luck, we'll get a piece of that." Patrick grinned.

They continued up Jefferson until they came to the city market at Ellis Square, another reminder of Philadelphia with its noisy market stalls. Ellen began to feel more comfortable in this southern city and hoped it was not a false sense of ease.

***

An older man swept the front walk as they arrived at 64 West Broad, and Ellen wondered if he was a slave. He looked up at their arrival, but upon seeing Ellen, dropped his gaze as if perhaps he had been

taught his place over the years. Ellen thought immediately of Catherine Biddle and how this sight would have bothered her.

Three stories tall and built of oyster-colored stucco, Dr. Fallon's house showcased money as well, including full-length ebony shutters flanking the windows to provide symmetry. As with many Savannah homes, the front door opened at the top of a balustrade of steps and a row of ornate cornices lining the front of the roof lent elegance to the entire structure.

Ellen knocked, and the door opened to reveal the blackest woman Ellen had ever seen, dressed somewhat like an Irish house maid.

"Good day," Ellen said.

"Yessum, how can I help you?"

"We are here to pay a visit to Dr. Fallon and his wife."

The woman stared for a moment at Patrick and Ellen.

"The doctor, he's at de clinic, and the missus, she be out."

"Well, can you please tell them that Patrick and Ellen Canavan came to call?"

The woman waited for a few moments, then asked, "Don't y'all got a calling card to leave?"

Ellen stammered. "I'm not sure I understand you. What do you mean by a calling card?" The servant seemed surprised. "If'n you don't have no card, I just be telling the Missus you was here."

"All right, thank you."

The woman nodded and shut the door, leaving Ellen and Patrick perplexed out on the front stoop. Ellen tried to think of what the woman was referring to.

"Patrick, we need to get some calling cards."

"What are you talking about, Ellen? That woman made no sense."

"I might know. Come on, there's still time to find out what those cards are and where they might be sold."

Upon Ellen's insistence, they walked back to the hotel and asked the desk clerk where the closest store might be that dealt in paper stationary. Armed with an address, they headed off to the destination.

"Patrick, I know you want to be in charge. But in this instance, please let me do the talking."

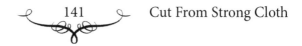

Cut From Strong Cloth

"Don't think I can handle the transaction? Or are you trying to gain the upper hand?"

"Patrick, please. Just go along with me on this."

At the assigned address they found a small wooden shop with a simple sign indicating paper goods.

"May I help you?" asked the clerk from behind the counter.

"Yes. We lost our calling cards on our trip here to Savannah and would like to have a new set made."

"Would that be engraved or printed?"

"Printed would be fine, thank you."

"What type of stock would you prefer?"

"Stock? Oh, you mean paper. Please show me a quality example, but one within a reasonable price range."

"You from Georgia?" the clerk asked with a quizzical expression.

"No, we hail from County Tyrone, Ireland. Now would you be so kind as to show us the stock, and perhaps some samples of calling cards that you sell."

The man disappeared into a back room and came out with several sheets of paper and a small box of cards. Ellen peered into the box and thumbing through the cards, saw that they all announced someone's name and place of residence. Some also stated information about the person's business. All the cards were about the same size, but the quality of the paper, or stock, differed. She also noted that all the cards were printed in black ink, but with varying scripts. She leafed through the sheets of paper and chose one of good quality.

"This is the stock I would like, and I would like the cards printed with this type of lettering in black ink. Here, I'll write out the text."

> *P. Canavan and E. Canavan*
> *Textile Merchants*
> *Kensington*

"Now would this Kensington be the name of your home?"

"Yes, that is where we live."

"How many cards do you need?"

 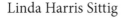

"I think thirty would be sufficient."

"All right, we can have this ready in a few days."

"Oh, I am sorry, we need those cards before eleven o'clock tomorrow morning. We have an appointment with Mr. Alexander Francis, the cotton factor. He's expecting us."

"You're doing business with Mr. Francis? Well then, there'll be a surcharge for a rush job."

"We are prepared to add ten percent to the bill, for your inconvenience of having to rush," Ellen replied.

"Make it fifteen and I can have the order ready by ten in the morning."

"Twelve percent and I will not mention to Mr. Francis that you tried to gouge us once we mentioned his name."

The clerk's eyes smoldered, but he agreed.

Out on the street, Patrick whistled.

"Brilliant, Ellen, I must give you credit this time."

"Patrick, I won't let anyone take advantage of us just because we're not Southerners."

"Why didn't you list my full name as Patrick Joseph Canavan? Wouldn't that have been more proper?"

"No, because then I would have to write out my first name, and anyone reading the card would see that I am a woman. We need to impress these people, and no need for them to be prejudiced against us right from the start because I am a female."

"Well, you chose expensive paper."

"I had to. Just like you know inferior wool when you touch it, paper products also have a feel to them. Appearances mean more down here than I realized. Tomorrow we'll pay a quick visit back to Dr. Fallon's and leave our new calling card, and then proceed to Mr. Francis's office. Let's hope Dr. Fallon has already put in a good word for us."

"All right, but don't try and get me to agree to any more unexpected expenses."

Ellen ignored the comment.

***

Cut From Strong Cloth

The next morning they walked back to the stationary shop and picked up their order. Ellen wanted to shout out loud, seeing her name in print as a textile merchant, but she kept her composure.

After dropping off their calling card to the Fallon's residence, they ventured back to Factors Row. Patrick opened the door to Mr. Francis' office and guided Ellen in ahead of him. The same gentleman from yesterday stood up to greet them.

"Good day, Mr. and Miss Canavan. Mr. Francis is expecting you. One moment, please."

He disappeared through the other door and then came back and motioned them to enter.

"Good morning, Mr. Canavan." Mr. Francis stood up and came over to shake hands with Patrick. "Miss Canavan." He nodded in her direction.

A bit taken back by his coolness toward her, Ellen hoped that nothing was amiss. Taking a moment to look around the room, she noticed fine mahogany book cases lining the side walls, and a prominent window behind his desk gave a splendid view of the river. Various ledgers covered his large desk, the main focal piece in the room. Underneath the piles she could still catch glimpses of a well-polished surface. Looking up, she saw a stunning wall clock that looked down on her as if to declare this domain belonged to a successful businessman.

"Miss Canavan." He pulled out a chair for Ellen and then motioned to Patrick to seat himself. "Perhaps I should begin by saying that Dr. Fallon did assure me I would be dealing with a reputable family. However, he also told me your home is in Philadelphia, not Ireland as you had indicated."

"We answered your question honestly; we are indeed from County Tyrone, Ireland. However, we now reside in Philadelphia and the mill where we conduct our business is located in the Kensington area of Philadelphia." Ellen could tell that Patrick struggled to keep his temper in check.

"Very well, but I do hope from now on we will be completely honest with one another."

"We have nothing to hide, and I don't like your tone insinuating that we're not the honest kind," Patrick countered, his pride and anger now kindled.

Ellen had held her tongue, but now edged her way into the conversation. "You will find that we are honest, Mr. Francis. We're simply interested in buying cotton from you. If you do not wish to conduct business with us, please be forthright and inform us of that now."

The factor remained impassive. "All right, tell me about the type of cotton you wish to purchase."

"We'll be needing at least two types, some long staple coastal and upland cotton as well," Ellen replied.

"Are you aware, Miss Canavan, that long staple coastal is more expensive than upland cotton?"

"Yes, of course. For every five bales of long staple coastal cotton that we buy, we would purchase an additional fifteen bales of upland cotton. I assume you would be agreeable to twelve cents per pound for upland and fifteen cents per pound for long staple? Then each upland bale would be sixty dollars per five-hundred pounds and seventy-five dollars for each coastal bale of the same weight. We are prepared to sign a contract to that effect."

Mr. Francis let out a long slow whistle.

"Now, would you be able to furnish us with cotton, or should we conduct business with other factors as well?"

"I can see, Miss Canavan, that you came prepared. And you, Mr. Canavan, are you in accord with this proposal?"

Patrick steeled himself not to look at Ellen. "Aye. We speak for one another in these transactions."

"I hope you have also calculated four cents a pound for shipping? That is the going rate. So, might I ask what the mill will do with our cotton once you receive it?"

"We'll be making cloth," Patrick interjected.

"Ah yes, Mr. Canavan. Well, I did assume that—cotton is a textile fiber after all. Perhaps I should have been more specific in my query. What type of cloth will you be making, and for what purpose?"

"Does it matter? You'll make your commission," Patrick almost

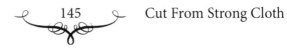

Cut From Strong Cloth

sneered.

Mr. Francis' face went white. "Down here, sir, we consider it crass to speak of commissions."

Ellen sensed a moment of panic that Patrick might ruin everything, and she grabbed command of the conversation.

"What my brother means to imply is that we have several potential buyers for our cloth. We intend to manufacture a blend of cotton and wool that would produce cloth suitable for all weather wear. We, as well as you, sir, are in this to make a profit."

She waited.

Mr. Francis studied first her face, then Patrick's.

"All right, Miss Canavan, I can live with that. I'll have Gerald draw up a contract. And yes, I can arrange for you to receive the number of bales requested. If I cannot provide you with the adequate number myself, I will requisition cotton from other factors."

Patrick spoke up to prevent Ellen from having the last say.

"One more item, Mr. Francis. We would need to purchase two bales right away—one of upland and one of long staple, both to be shipped as soon as possible to Philadelphia. Will that be possible?"

"Yes, we still have cotton available and ready for shipment. Once Gerald draws up both contracts, I will introduce you to Mr. Nash Finch, who handles all our shipping contracts. Perhaps, Mr. Canavan, I can put you more at ease about doing business here in Savannah by joining me for a drink and cigar tomorrow night at my club. Mr. Finch could also attend. You wouldn't be opposed to that, Miss Canavan, would you?"

Ellen felt annoyance with him arranging a gentlemen's night that would preclude her from being present. Clever on his part and she knew it, so she smiled and murmured, "I think you two deserve a drink together. Just remember, Mr. Francis, we are Irish, and my brother knows good whiskey when he sees it."

"Oh, I don't doubt that one bit, Miss Canavan."

***

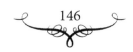

The next day Patrick and Ellen took time to explore more of Savannah, from Factors Row to Forsyth Park. The mild winter weather made walking a pleasure. On their way they sampled more southern cooking: first a spicy shrimp soup, then some chicken pilau, and even peas with bacon. A decadent concoction called Crème Brulée was their dessert.

Savannah at first had seemed to present itself as a quiet model for English architecture and culture. However as they walked around the city they heard Irish brogues spilling out of pubs, Portuguese cooks haggling in the markets, and Jewish men in black caps offering prayers outside a synagogue. African women singing with baskets on their heads often passed as they walked through the streets. Ellen found the colorful mix of cultures to be fascinating.

But the sight of chained slaves being paraded from pens shocked Ellen as they continued exploring the city. She knew that every society had its servants, but servants still retained freedom. Seeing the slaves in Savannah strengthened her resolve to ask Catherine Biddle what could be done to help the abolitionist cause. To Ellen, slavery cast a blight on Savannah, and she wondered if the rest of the South was the same. She also wondered how James would react to slavery. From an economic point of view he used men, women and children as his labor force, but all of them were paid labor.

***

The morning after Patrick's night out with Mr. Francis, Ellen could hardly wait to ask Patrick to share the details. He told her that Nash Finch had joined them at a special club and together the three men had drinks and cigars, just like Mr. Francis had indicated.

"What is a gentlemen's club, Patrick?"

"Like a fancy pub, where all the patrons are businessmen. No ruffians at all. 'Twas easy to hold my own. And I was careful not to out drink them or become too loud with the whiskey. They wanted, I think, to see if I could carry myself within their social circle."

"I'm sure they did, Patrick, and 'twas calculated to exclude me as

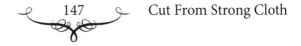

Cut From Strong Cloth

well. When tomorrow arrives, we'll be signing our first contract, and I do intend to be present for that, putting my name right alongside yours."

**

The next morning dawned with the invigorating air of imminent success. They walked to Mr. Francis' office and together signed the first cotton contract promising to pay twelve hundred and seventy-five dollars for the first future shipment and one hundred and thirty-five dollars for the first immediate one. That meant they would have some superior cotton arrive at the mill within a few weeks and they had stayed under budget.

Ellen took a stolen moment to look down at her signature, Ellen A. Canavan, and reveled at the ink marking on the paper. *I told you I'd succeed, Da. I'm on my way at last.*

They both shook hands with Mr. Francis.

"I am sorry that the shipping contracts will not be ready until next week, so I hope you will not be inconvenienced by staying a few days longer in Savannah."

"Why not at all, Mr. Francis," Ellen purred. "We plan to visit Dr. Fallon on Sunday, so we would be staying into next week anyway." *There, you old goat. Let's see how you react to us making social visits here in Savannah.*

But Mr. Francis did not rise to the bait. "Very well, then. Do enjoy the rest of your time here in our fair city."

As they left Factors Row, Patrick suggested they return to the hotel for dinner and then spend the afternoon shopping for a gift for Mam. Upon entering the hotel they noticed a man seated on a horsehair sofa in the front lobby, reading the newspaper. He lowered it, and they were both astounded to see James Nolan behind the paper. He looked at them with genuine delight and strode over to Ellen.

"James, what are you doing here?" she stammered.

"I regretted not coming with you after your departure. So I decided to come down and see Savannah for myself."

"We never expected to find you here in our hotel," exclaimed Ellen.

Linda Harris Sittig  148

"I hope there's nothing you're trying to hide from me," he said grinning.

Patrick replied, "Nothing to hide, James. We stuck to the agreed price, and I've not let Ellen out of my sight, if you were worried about that."

James took Ellen by the arm and led her out of earshot from the curious hotel clerk.

"I'll be staying here at The Planter, too. I think we can have a week together before we return home. Let's make it memorable and just enjoy being together. No quarrels."

Ellen stared at him for a moment, and then realized he was being genuine, and oh, so himself. He had come to Savannah to savor and share in the success of the purchases. She chided herself for her petty insecurities. Had she only been gone from him for a few days? Suddenly she realized that she was delighted to have him here with her in Savannah.

"Of course, James, it'll be grand having you here, and showing you the city. We were just about to have our midday meal, and then shop. Would you like to join us?"

"Wild horses couldn't keep me away."

***

The next morning, January 19, 1861, Ellen was the first one down to breakfast. There was a discernible buzz in the lobby as most of the patrons were reading the morning newspapers and excitedly talking aloud.

"Hard to believe that Georgia has actually seceded from the Union," one man exclaimed to the gentlemen on his right. "Seems natural they are following their fellow Southerners."

Ellen stood shocked. Georgia seceded? Oh God, this changes everything. Will Mr. Francis still sell us the cotton? Will we be considered as enemies? Instead of going into the breakfast room, she turned and fled back up the stairs to alert Patrick and James.

They spent the remainder of the morning discussing how this one single event could impact their plans.

Cut From Strong Cloth

CHAPTER 15

January / February 1861

"Patrick, open up, we need to talk," Ellen said as she knocked on his hotel door the following morning.

From within she could hear him mutter, "Hold on, hold on. I'm coming."

When the door swung open, Ellen marched in and closed the door behind her.

"I won't go back without you," she declared.

"Ellen, don't be stupid. You have to go home. Georgia's no longer a safe place to be, and fighting could break out at any moment. We're Northerners now in enemy territory."

"Don't over-dramatize this, Patrick. We're no more enemies of Georgia than the man in the moon. And besides, even if fighting did break out, women wouldn't be involved."

"You are so naive! All the rules of polite society disappear in war. Women could be in just as much danger as men. For once I'm taking the upper hand—you are going home, whether you like that or not. I made a vow to Mam that I would not let you get in harm's way."

She thought of the young waiter who had been friendly to her since the beginning of their stay, but since yesterday avoided speaking to her at all. Could sentiments change that quickly? Were they really at risk in Savannah? Was she being naive? But her pride eclipsed worry. Just yesterday morning she had written in her journal about the excitement of seeing all the contracts secured.

"Patrick, I just want to stay until all the contracts have been locked down—including the shipping ones. Then we can both go home together. I promise I won't ask to extend the trip."

"No. We've got to focus on your safety. 'Tis the most important thing right now and you won't be missing anything here except possible danger."

"I'd be safe with both you and James to protect me."

"Jesus, Ellen, try to see this from someone else's point of view. Mam was reluctant for you to travel at all. Now that Georgia has pulled out of the Union, she'll be fearful every day until you return. Dinna you hear all the celebrating out in the streets?"

"Of course I heard the noise."

"That noise is people rejoicing in secession. We canna let you stay. James and I will remain behind and get the shipping contracts signed, and then as soon as possible we'll buy return tickets on the next Philadelphia bound steamer. We need to get you back to Pennsylvania, now."

"Patrick, If I dinna know better, I'd say you're attempting to send me home so you can take solo credit for the shipping arrangements."

"Good God, Ellen, I dinna get Georgia to secede! The state did that all on its own. Don't go blaming me for this interruption in your plans."

A light knock sounded, the door opened, and James leaned his head into the room.

"Are you needing re-enforcements?" He grinned at Patrick, stepping inside and closing the door after him. "I could hear your voices even out in the hallway."

"Very funny, James, but I don't see any humor in this." Ellen glared.

"Ellen, 'tis not our fault Georgia decided to secede. A person of your intelligence should recognize the danger of being a Yankee down here right now."

"I want my name on those shipping contracts along with Patrick's."

"Your name will be on the shipping contracts, just not your signature, "James assured her. "But isn't your signature on the cotton

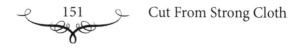

151   Cut From Strong Cloth

contracts? That's far more important than the shipping licenses. Three steamers a month leave for Philadelphia, and tomorrow is one of the sailings. We'll both breathe easier once we know you're outward bound. I promise we'll both be home by the first of February."

Ellen's mood inclined her toward sulking, but she realized it would be to no avail. This time she wouldn't win, nor would she get to visit Dr. Fallon and his wife. With an infuriated sigh, she stomped back to her room and started throwing clothes into her valise. *'Tis not fair, Da.*

***

By the next day, Ellen found herself back on board a ship. This time, the journey did not hold even one ounce of excitement or any hint of adventure. The weather alternated sheets of rain mixed with sleet, preventing her from going out on deck at all. She felt frustrated about everything: the weather, the secession, the shipping contracts, even Patrick and James staying on without her. Without any other outlet for her anger, she wrote out her emotions in her journal.

On the second morning she awoke from an ugly nightmare where she dreamed she was running through a forest being chased by an enemy. The dream left her unsettled. For the rest of the trip she could not shake the lingering sense of unease that the nightmare added to her already despondent feelings.

Three days from departure, the steamer pulled into the port of Philadelphia, and Ellen paid a hack driver to take her to Fifth Street. Carrying her traveling bag and walking up to the front door, she saw how their soot-dusted row house appeared shabby in comparison to the grand homes with wisteria arbors she had seen in Savannah. With a deep sigh, she pushed open the door.

Cecilia came out from the kitchen with the familiar scent of fried potatoes trailing after her. "Ellen? Oh praise God, you're home safe." Then looking around, she asked, "Where's Patrick?"

"He's still in Savannah with James. The two of them stayed behind to get the shipping contracts signed. I only came back because Georgia seceded."

"James Nolan?"

"Aye, he showed up in Savannah."

"Dear God, Georgia's secession means I was right all along worrying about the possible dangers. I'm surprised with you so good at getting your way, that you couldn't convince Patrick and James Nolan to return with you."

"They'll both be back in another week or so. They gave their word."

***

By the last week in January, all shipping contracts had been signed and secured, and Patrick and James were ready to return home. They invited Tom Avery to join them at a local saloon on Congress Street for a farewell evening. The combined odors of human sweat, pipe tobacco, and ale drenched bar rags clearly illustrated they had chosen a working man's pub. A thin film of sand loosely scattered over the floor soaked up spilled beer, and the packed tables gave an indication of the pub's popularity. All the spots were occupied by drinkers, card players or both, but Tom found them three empty seats near the back.

Patrick bought the first round, James the second, and Tom the third. Succeeding rounds followed, and with all the drinking came a loosening of their tongues. Tom announced his love for his current lady friend, and Patrick professed a love for all women.

"Well, I'm goin' raise my glass to the woman I love—your sister, Patrick!"

"Whoa. Have you told Ellen this?" Patrick laughed at James.

"Not exactly. She's a might bit hard to convince of what a wonderful man I can be."

"She's stubborn, James, that's what she is."

"Aye, but I love her. She makes life worth livin'," James declared.

"You're doomed, James, if you're that much in love. Women have a way of taking over your life," Tom chuckled.

James grinned and downed his pint. They began to congratulate each other on how lucky they were to be good-looking Irishmen who stood to make a killing off Georgia cotton. Soon the brogue of their

childhoods took over and they appeared to be Irishmen well on their way to getting soused.

***

Three ragged men sat drinking in the corner and watching the Irish trio.

"Lousy Micks, that's what they are," whispered one of the harsh looking men.

"Yankee Micks," chimed in another as tobacco juice dribbled down his chin.

"Trying to act like big shots, coming in here and bragging loud enough so we can all hear how they're getting rich off our cotton."

"We need to teach 'em a lesson," piped the first man. The other two nodded in agreement.

They watched as the man named Tom begged off, saying he needed to leave. Then the loud one called Patrick proclaimed they should have one last round and then call it a night. The three tattered strangers in the corner got up and left.

From their hidden vantage point they saw the Tom man swagger out of the saloon and stumble off into the night. The leader of the gang shook his head *no*. They waited. Fairly soon the other two drunken Irishmen tottered out the door and practically stumbled into the road. The leader nodded *yes*.

The three thugs stepped out of the darkness with sticks and clubs.

"Hey, Yank!" When Patrick looked up, one of the men viciously hit him over and over, around the arms and shoulders before swinging the bat at Patrick's chest. Patrick crumpled. Meanwhile, the two other men had beat James unconscious. "Take that, yer lousy Mick", one of them shouted as he kicked James in the stomach and then clubbed both James' legs with the sickening sound of cracked bone infiltrating the night.

"Search their pockets, and take whatever they have."

"All right, shove them in the back of the wagon."

The robbers drove the crude buckboard southwest down the

Ogeechee Road.

"Stop here." The leader walked to the back of the wagon, took a large draught of whiskey from the bottle he carried and then spit the liquor all over Patrick. "Take that, yer stupid Mick."

The other two robbers proceeded to do the same. Then they rolled Patrick off the back and left him in the road. They drove off into the night. A few miles further, they stopped and dragged James' body out of the wagon and dumped him in a nearby field.

"Hope this teaches you that you ain't welcome in the South."

Laughing at their escapade, they drove off into the night.

***

When Patrick woke the next morning, every part of his body ached. He lie by the side of a road and tried to reconstruct the events of the previous evening. The facts stood that he had been in a saloon with James and Tom, and that they all consumed too much drink. Now his head throbbed and his chest hurt when he coughed. Peering down at his body, he didn't see any gashes or evidence though of bloody wounds.

Tentatively, he attempted to stand and grabbed onto a tree branch for support. A wagon rumbled into view and he started to hail the driver. But when he let go of the branch, he fell into the road and passed out.

***

The driver of the wagon reined in the horse and looked up ahead. There seemed to be a man lying in the road. The choice was to either ignore him or see if he needed help. Approaching with caution, she stopped the horse and stepped down from her buckboard with a small revolver concealed in her cloak. As she drew nearer, she detected the overpowering stench of whiskey clinging to his clothes. She nudged him with her shoe and then nudged him again a bit harder.

Patrick groaned. When he came around, he held his arm up, blocking out the bright morning light, and his face registered shock,

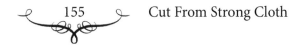

155   Cut From Strong Cloth

presumably at seeing a woman standing over him.

"Sweet Jesus, who might you be?"

"It seems to me I should be the one asking the questions. Who might 'you be,' and why are you lying in the middle of the Ogeechee Road?"

"Ooch," he winced as he tried to talk. "My name is Patrick Canavan, and I am a wool merchant on business in Savannah."

"Business? By lying in the middle of the road?"

"My partner and I were celebrating, a wee bit too much last night, and I think we were bushwhacked."

"Your partner? And where might he be? Is he in the middle of a different road? Where are you from, sir? By your accent, I can tell it's not Georgia."

"I'm an Irishman from County Tyrone, but now I make my home in Philadelphia."

The dilemma had worsened. He was a Yankee, Irish or not. Could she rationalize that helping a Yankee would not bring trouble? But some instinct prompted her to stay. "Well, Mr. Canavan, let me help you into my wagon. I'm Magdalena Fox, a pharmacist by trade, and on my way back to Savannah. I know a doctor in town who can examine you."

As Patrick climbed up into the wagon, he smiled. He appeared to be clear-headed enough to notice that the driver was a beauty.

***

A young boy ran through the fields, intent on climbing the old hickory tree with the broken swing. Instead, he stumbled upon James in a heap on the ground. James' normally-groomed hair was matted with dried blood and flies crawled over his silent face.

"Hey, Mister, you okay? Are you dead?"

The body did not respond, but the boy could see the chest give a slight rise and fall. The man was still breathing. Peering back toward a dilapidated cabin, the youngster took off at full speed.

His mother looked up from sharpening knives on the sagging

porch of her home. Her son jumped the board fence, and streaked across the yard.

"Mama," he panted. "There's a man, lying out in our field. Hurt real bad, but alive I think."

"Tommy Walker, if you're playing me for a fool to come with you, there better be a good reason—a really good reason."

The boy began to pull on her arm trying to tell her that the man needed help. Still young, he was unaware of the grudge she bore about life. All he knew is that his pa had died out in one of their fields and now there was a stranger lying in another one.

The woman put down the knife and, hiking up her thin dress, followed after her son. When they got to the area, they both looked down and saw the pitiful body of a man barely alive. The twisted leg, deep head wound, and unconscious body should have alerted them to the possibility that the body was in shock.

***

Like other country women who lived far from town, Emma Walker did all the family nursing. Skilled as she was, she had not been able to save her husband when a gash from a rusty scythe developed into a fatal infection. He had died in her arms. After that she no longer bothered with her appearance and had little desire to spend any time with the children, who soon learned to fend for themselves.

She knew folks in town called her a "poor cracker," but the man lying in her field deserved a chance to live.

"Tommy, get the girls quick and meet me at the barn."

As Tommy took off running once again, she made a dash to the barn and hitched up the old swayback horse to the farm wagon. When her two daughters came pell-mell after Tommy, all of them worked together using two poles, some clamps, and a slightly moth-eaten horse blanket to rig up a crude stretcher.

"You three, jump in back." Then she urged the horse toward the stranger who had fallen into their lives.

Once they reached James, Emma fashioned a crude splint from

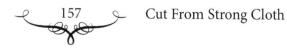

Cut From Strong Cloth

the club the robbers had tossed next to his body. Then the children helped her carefully move James onto the stretcher and into the wagon. Once back at the cabin, they struggled to pull him through the doorway and onto her bed. His state of unconsciousness was merciful; otherwise the jostling would have caused unbearable pain.

"Jesus Christ," Emma muttered as she removed the splint and cut away his pant leg, revealing the broken bone. This was beyond her expertise.

"Tommy, you run and go get Selma."

Once more Tommy took off across the fields, this time to a distant cabin where a black woman named Selma lived. A rarity in the Deep South, Selma was a free Negro who treated white and black folks alike with a healing knowledge that had been passed down through the ages.

When Selma arrived, she said nothing but set about washing his leg and setting the bone, securing the injured leg with a new splint of thin crabapple shanks and torn strips of old bedding.

"I'm beholden to you, Selma. This man was dumped in our side pasture."

Selma nodded. "I helps you now. There'll be cause when you'll help me. Right now I needs to clean his scalp and stitch up this here wound."

Emma stood quiet at Selma's side in case she would need assistance.

"Done. Now here's some tree bark. Brew him a tea. Should help speed the healin'. Watch for fever. If'n pus begins to seep, send Tommy to get me."

Emma nodded. "Thank you, Selma."

The black woman just nodded in acknowledgement.

***

Little more than a rundown shack, the Walker cabin could have done with a good strong spring cleaning, but Emma saw no use in fixing what would just become dirty all over again. She left James to sleep on her meager mattress and pulled a ragged curtain behind her.

By the next morning his body temperature began to climb. Emma brewed more tea from Selma's dried willow bark, wondering if Indian Sage would have been a better choice. She spooned the liquid between his feverish lips, but by afternoon he began to moan as she mopped his sweating brow.

All through the remainder of the day she stayed by his bedside, laying cold, wet rags over his forehead and forcing him to swallow dribbles of the herb tea. In the throes of the fever, James started to thrash. "Go get me another clean rag," directed Emma to one of her daughters.

"Ellen? Is that you?" He shouted and then fell back against the pillows, where the fever reclaimed him and dragged him back into the darkness of sleep.

Emma stayed by his side throughout the entire night. She dozed toward dawn, only to be awakened with the sound of her daughter's voice yelling, "Mama! Mama! Look!"

She bolted awake to find James sitting up, his eyes opened but glazed over.

"I did what I had to!"

He was yelling at someone, but neither Emma nor her daughter had any idea who.

"The coins were just laying there! I found them first! They were mine to keep!"

Then James fell back, exhausted from his ranting, and slipped into a stupor. Emma felt his brow and prayed he would survive the fever.

"Mama, what was he talking 'bout?"

"Don't know. Let him sleep."

The fever could be serious, but so could the oozing head wound. The clean fracture of his leg had been set, and although he might walk with a small limp, at least he would be able to walk again. What Emma feared most were signs of the dreaded pus.

"Tommy, go get Selma. Tell her I just want her to look at him again. Tell her I'm feared of an infection."

Selma returned, inspecting the leg and then the scalp. "I needs to ride into town and get some stronger medicine."

Cut From Strong Cloth

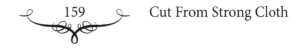

"Town? Selma, you know I can't afford anything from town."

"I do a favor for a man there last month. Tells me to come back if'n I need strong medicine. You wait here."

***

Selma left the property and rode bareback on her old horse out the Ogeechee Road. Close to an hour later she stopped near the outskirts of Savannah at an old ramshackle building where a doctor of sorts would perform any needed request—if you had the money.

With no need to knock, she walked in. The pungent odor of opium smoke wafted from the back room. She coughed, the agreed upon signal, and within a minute a greasy-haired man appeared, his bloodshot eyes glazed over in a drug-induced euphoria. His tobacco-stained teeth and filthy fingers disgusted Selma, but Emma needed the medicine that only he would sell.

"I needs that powerful medicine you told me about," she announced.

"Well, well, if it ain't Selma come back to see me," he slurred.

She stood her ground. "You told me to come if'n I need the strong medicine. I be needing it now."

"What did you bring in trade?"

"I don't owe you nuthin'. Remember?"

"Well, who you need it for?"

"Some white man, dumped out of town. His head wound be real bad."

He grew impatient with her chatter and, retreating to the back room, came back with a vial full of salve.

"Use this sparingly, thin dabs at a time, 'cause it's all you're goin' get."

She left the building, with the unpleasant stench of the white man lodged in her nostrils.

Later, the two women began to treat the festering wound on James' head. They used up most of the vial.

***

Back in town, Magdalena took Patrick to a local doctor near the Savannah Poor House Hospital, who checked him over for any internal injuries. The examination showed only bad bruises, which would eventually heal.

"All right, Mr. Canavan. The question is what do we do with you now?" Magdalena asked.

"I have to look for my partner. I'm hoping he's here in town," he said.

"Let me ask around to see if any out-of-town Irishman is wandering about the city."

"That would be great. I hate to ask another favor, but could I catch a ride with you over to the Planter Hotel on Bryan Street? I need to collect my belongings. My cousin lives in a boarding house over by Washington Square, and I'll see if I can bunk with him while I search for my friend."

"Certainly. I can take you over there."

They pulled away. "You've had quite an experience in our city. I am sorry you met up with some of our more unsavory characters."

"I think I'm lucky to have only bruises. I'm hoping my friend is all right. I've no clue where he might be."

"I'll keep my fingers crossed that your friend is safe and that the two of you will be reunited soon."

Patrick smiled, but inwardly he harbored fears that something bad had happened to James. *Canna shake the feeling that he's in trouble and needs me.*

Magdalena turned the burnished wooden buckboard west, pulling her bonnet to shield her face from the sun. As they drove along, Patrick thought how pretty she was and how lucky he had been to be rescued by her and not just some dirt farmer in the area. He felt the urge to whistle, but his mouth hurt too much. They arrived at the Planter in a short amount of time, and he thought about a way to get her to stay with him a bit longer.

"I'll just be a few minutes." He walked gingerly upstairs to retrieve all the bags and tried not to wince from the bruises. His muscles ached. It had been some time since he had been in a fight, and the last

time he was the victor. Bags in hand, he came back outside.

"All set? I'll head toward Washington Square and you can show me the boarding house where your cousin stays. Do you have any friends here in Savannah other than your cousin?"

"Not really."

They arrived at Washington Square, and Magdalena reined in the horse. "Keep me informed about your partner," she said with a friendly smile. "I work at Solomon's Pharmacy on Madison Square."

"Thank you for the help. Might I be able to repay you for your kindness in rescuing me?"

"Oh, I'm sure we'll meet again. Savannah is a small town." She smiled, snapped the reins, and drove away. Patrick watched until her wagon disappeared in the soft winter light of the Savannah afternoon.

***

Tom Avery showed up an hour or so later, coming off his shift from the lumber yard. When he saw Patrick leaning up against the front wall of the rooming house, with obvious angry purple-blue bruises glaring out from his neck, Tom frowned. Now what the hell happened to him? He furrowed his brow and cocked his head. "Patrick, what's going on? Are you all right?"

"James and I were attacked last night after we left the saloon. They beat us, stole our money, and dumped us outside of town. I ache all over, but the real problem is—I canna find James anywhere."

"You were bushwhacked?" Tom lowered his voice. "Was it because you're Northerners or Irishmen?" He came over closer.

"Maybe both. After you left, we stayed a bit more. I think the men who beat us did so for the money they thought we were carrying."

"Did they get a lot?"

"Na. I dinna have much cash on me at all. James had made sure of that. We were celebrating the prospects of the contracts. But now I'm worried about him."

"I don't suppose you got a look at the men?"

Patrick shook his head. "I think we were too much in the bottle."

"Right. We need to concentrate on finding James, then. Until we do, there's no need contacting your mother or Ellen. They're not expecting you home for a while, and they would just worry if you told them about James' disappearance. We'll make the inquiries, and in the meantime, you can stay here with me."

"I'd like to start asking about James as soon as possible. I keep getting a bad feeling about what might have happened to him."

"Why are you saying that?"

"Don't know. Just a bad feeling, that's all."

"We'll start first thing tomorrow. I'll ask around the lumber yard if there's any gossip about some Irishman getting beat up. Sooner or later he has to reappear."

Jesus, I hope so. Because Ellen will blame me for his disappearance.

***

For the next few days Patrick canvassed all of Savannah, annoyed each time someone asked about his bruises. His aches and pains were of a secondary concern because James had seemingly vanished in the night.

Where the hell could he be? I'll have to stay here until I find out some information on him. And I'll have to post a letter to Ellen and Mam explaining my delay.

Today, after making his daily check with the Savannah Police about James' disappearance, he found Solomon's Pharmacy and wandered in, pretending to look for merchandise. A door from the back storage room opened and Magdalena emerged, smiling as soon as she spied him.

"Why, hello Mr. Canavan. Have you found your friend?"

He took her smile to be encouraging, as well as her interest in news about James. "I'm afraid I haven't been successful in locating him. I've been out walking the city every day looking, and walking makes me hungry. Could you recommend a place nearby where we could get something to eat? Perhaps have some tea?"

"Are you asking me to join you, Mr. Canavan?"

Cut From Strong Cloth

"Aye. That I am." He felt his heart skip a beat. Then he chided himself on being nervous. It wasn't as if he did not have experience with women. But he normally did not feel awkward around any females.

"Give me a moment; I'll need to close out my receipt drawer." She grinned.

They walked to a nearby inn where, in addition to a light meal, they discovered a shared interest in good food and the beginnings of chemistry between them. They lingered over tea and some Irish Lace Cookies, stretching out the hours, not in any hurry to end the time together.

Patrick walked her home as Magdalena's light-hearted laughter filled the air.

∗∗∗

As time wore on, Patrick found himself stopping in at Solomon's on a daily basis and relishing how she always appeared glad to see him. They began to share the late afternoons together, strolling the streets and sometimes taking meals in local inns. Today they were sitting in a restaurant having tea and sesame seed biscuits.

"Magdalena, you know I eventually have to return to Philadelphia. I've left my business and my family behind. Both are being neglected."

"Haven't you written your family?" She reached over and placed her hand on his arm and he covered her hand with his own.

"Aye, my mam and my sister know I'm here. I had intended to stay for only a week or so, but now. . . " He smiled. "I find that I am not in a rush to return north. However, I don't like leaving my business in my sister's care."

"Then until you have to leave, let's make sure we enjoy however much time we have together."

The days soon turned into one week and then another. If Patrick felt guilty about not finding James, he no longer mentioned it to Magdalena because he was too caught up in his emotions toward her. Cupid's arrow had finally pierced his heart.

"Patrick, I need to drop off some supplies to a doctor on State Street. Would you like to go with me?" Magdalena asked when they met up one day in early February.

"Sure."

They arrived at the address and walked in the infirmary door. When the doctor came out to see who the caller might be, he immediately addressed Magdalena and then looked at Patrick with some sort of recognition, but not with any clarity.

Patrick stepped forward to introduce himself.

"I am Patrick Canavan, and I get the feeling, sir, that we may have met before; however, I canna understand where we might have made each other's acquaintance."

The doctor's face broke into a wide grin.

"Canavan, you say? Could your mother be Cecilia Canavan?"

"Aye. And you sir, are . . . ?"

"Dr. Fallon, Dr. Louis Fallon. We briefly met at your house back in September when I came to call on your mother and asked her to fashion my wife's trousseau. To what pleasure do I owe this call? According to Alexander Francis, I thought you and your sister had returned to Philadelphia."

Magdalena watched in utter surprise as Patrick and Dr. Fallon began to chat like long lost friends. Patrick told how Ellen had returned home; but that he and his business partner, James Nolan, had stayed on to sign the shipping licenses. Patrick ended with telling the unfortunate incidence that led to James' disappearance.

"When Alexander Francis asked me to vouch for your reputation, I assumed you were in the city for only a short time. We did get your calling card. But when Georgia seceded, I naturally thought you returned to Philadelphia. How can I help in this search for your missing friend?"

"I'd be much obliged for any help. I reported his disappearance to the local police, but they haven't found any clues. I don't know what

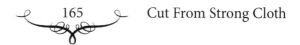

else to do."

"Perhaps you could come by our home this Sunday. We can get caught up on the details of his disappearance, and you can tell us how your mother is doing. My wife, Sarah, joined a women's group, and they can get word out about your missing friend. Please Magdalena, do come, too."

"We'd be delighted to visit. Right, Magdalena?" Patrick clasped her hand in an almost adolescent expression of exuberance.

Magdalena smiled at Patrick. "I am amazed that the two of you know each other." Turning to Dr. Fallon she added, "And, yes we'd love to visit on Sunday."

"For the time being, Patrick, there is no need to advertise that you are from Philadelphia. If asked, say that you are staying in Savannah to visit us. No one will question your allegiance that way," Dr. Fallon advised. As he walked back toward one of the examining rooms, he turned and added, "By the way, next week is St. Valentine's. I hope you both enjoy it." He winked.

CHAPTER 16

February / March 1861

Back in Philadelphia, Ellen had no news about Patrick or James. She was beside herself with worry and tried not to openly show her concerns around Mam. She'd expected them home by the first of February and became more and more frightened as February dragged its heels.

Today she grabbed her cloak and walked over the Ready's.

"Hallo, Ellen. 'Tis nice to have you call. Is James back from Savannah, too?"

"No, Mary, he isn't. James and my brother sent me home because Georgia had seceded and they worried about my safety. They stayed behind to sign the shipping contracts, but no one has heard from them since. I even wrote a letter to our cotton factor, Mr. Francis, but he knew nothing."

Ellen stopped when she saw Mary's face pale with concern.

"How bad is Georgia with the secession?"

"Honestly, Mary, I don't know. I left so quickly. All I know is what I read in the newspapers. But I don't think they've mustered troops yet. If you do get a letter from him, will you come to 1225 Fifth Street and let me know?"

As she turned to leave, she spied a jacket she knew belonged to James hanging on the hall tree. Instinctively she walked over to it and rubbed her fingers along the wool, as if by touching the fabric, she could hurry him home.

The following week the nightmare from the boat returned once more, and Ellen now believed it was an omen; something disastrous had befallen either Patrick or James. She decided if she did not hear anything from them within one more week's time, she would go back to Georgia herself and look for them.

Later that morning, as she came downstairs, Ellen heard her mother putting the kettle on for tea.

"Ah, Ellen."

"Mam, are you all right?"

"Just tired, I suppose. I'm not sleeping well with Patrick gone, and me reading about how some of the southern states have actually banded together to form, what did they call it, oh yes, the Confederate States of America. I'm frightened for Patrick, being down there."

Ellen nodded and glanced at the gloves James had given her for Christmas. James was forefront on her mind every morning as soon as she woke. Another trip south would be even more dangerous now, but she could not go on any longer without knowing what had happened to him. Dear God, let James be safe. Let them both be safe.

She decided to visit James' factory, in spite of a day drenched with rain, and see if anyone there had heard from him. If not, then her resolve to travel to Georgia would be even more important. Hurrying along the street, she arrived and shook out the umbrella. A man approached her as soon as she walked inside.

"Miss, can I help you?"

"You are Jimmy Doyle, are you not?" Ellen asked.

"Aye. How can I be helping you?"

Ellen saw sprouts of unruly red hair tucked under his work cap, and a broad swath of freckles that made his face look years younger than the age she suspected him to be. Fingertips stained deep blue and with the odor of vinegar clinging to his clothes made her surmise he must have been working in the dye rooms that week.

"My name is Ellen Canavan. You might remember that I was

Linda Harris Sittig  168

here with Mr. Nolan on St. Stephen's Day. We are personal friends."

"Are you now?"

"Yes, and I have come to inquire if you've heard from him these past few weeks?"

"Well, if you are a personal friend, then you'd be knowin' that Mr. Nolan is in Georgia."

"Mr. Doyle, I happened to be in Georgia at the same time that Mr. Nolan was there. My brother and I met with James. . . Mr. Nolan. However, I returned to Philadelphia and have not heard from him since. I thought perhaps he'd been in communication with you."

"If he's not gotten in touch with you, Miss Canavan, perhaps he has his reasons."

Ellen resented his cheeky manner, but then remembered Catherine's words of advice. Recomposing herself, she smiled demurely. "Oh I am sure you're correct on that matter, and there is nothing to worry about. However, we do have certain business contracts with Mr. Nolan. Would there be a way for me to post some money into his account in the bank? Of course that would require an official signature."

The manager's shoulders sagged a bit.

"Aye, well, truth be told, we've not heard from him after he left for Savannah. He set up a special account with the bank so I can pay the workers in his absence, but I had expected him to return by now."

"Have any cotton shipments arrived from Savannah? My brother and I calculated that at least one shipment was scheduled to arrive by early February."

"Aye, it did. We have the cotton in one of our storage rooms. Mr. Nolan left instructions for me to store any shipments in his absence and to wait until he returned from Savannah. Would you like me to contact you, Miss Canavan, as soon as we hear from him?"

"Yes, thank you," she smiled. "I would appreciate that."

Pulling on her gloves and wrapping her cloak across her body, she left the factory smiling. She had forged a success with the factory manager. Taking Catherine's words to heart, she had caught another fly with honey.

On the way home, she started rehearsing the words she would use on her mother. Getting Mam to agree on Ellen going back south

would be a far more difficult challenge than the factory manager had been. Ellen squared her shoulders, held her head up high, and said to herself, *Oh Mam, I can understand your worry, but here is my plan. . .*

***

At the end of the next day, when the dim winter light necessitated turning on the gas lamps at supper, Ellen waited until they had finished eating before she reiterated her plea.

"Don't you see Mam, it's the only way. Neither of us knows what's happened."

"Absolutely not! 'Tis bad enough Patrick's in the South amidst all the troubles. I won't be letting you go back!"

"But you said Mrs. Chambers was anxious about her daughter living in Savannah. I can travel with Mrs. Chambers, posing as her private nurse. With your talents, you can sew me a special outfit, maybe out of dark brown muslin, and no one would be the wiser. I'll pay to send a telegram ahead to Dr. Fallon, telling him we would be sailing for Savannah on the sixth of March."

"I am not in favor of this idea, regardless of Mrs. Chambers. And why haven't we heard from Patrick?"

"You know the mail's having a hard time getting through. Perhaps he's written and it's just been delayed."

Ellen took a deep breath and continued. "Look, Mam, once we're in Savannah we'll be under the protection of Dr. Fallon. As soon as I find out about Patrick and James, I promise I'll send word. Before you know it, the three of us will be coming home together."

"You think you have this all figured out, don't you? I tell you, Ellen, the way you are worried about James Nolan seems to me he's more important to you than I realized."

"Aye, I do care about him. I need to know that both he and Patrick are safe."

"Well, don't go 'round wearing your heart on your sleeve. Men don't buy a cow when milk's cheap."

Ellen flushed. What in hell was her mother insinuating? "That

was an ugly comment, Mam."

Cecilia shrugged. "Remember, I am grooming you to become a lady."

"So, will you agree that I can go, if I promise to act like a lady?"

"If it is the only way to find out what happened to Patrick, then yes. But I won't be able to sleep a wink with both of you down there. At least Mrs. Chambers will be paying the fifteen dollars for your ticket."

"I promise, nothing bad will happen to me and I will act the part of a lady. With luck, I'll find Patrick as soon as I land, and hopefully, James, too."

But Ellen felt sure something bad had already happened. She knew Patrick might not realize the importance of writing to them, but James would. They were supposed to be home weeks ago, and if there were some sort of delay, James would have alerted her.

∗∗∗

Patrick had written a letter and asked a young barefoot boy walking down the road to post it. Patrick had even offered the boy some coins to mail the letter.

"You talk funny, Mister."

"Aye, that's because I'm from Ireland."

"Where's that? You ain't a Yankee, are you?"

"No. Ireland is a country far across the ocean. Here's money for the stamp, and a tip for helping me. I'm in a hurry to meet someone, or I'd be going to the post office myself."

The boy had stared at Patrick and then shrugged. Once Patrick put the coins in the boy's open palm and walked away, the boy looked at the envelope. But since he couldn't read, he stuffed it in his pocket and on his walk home he met a friend who told him the catfish were starting to bite in the nearby river.

By evening, he had caught three catfish and forgotten all about the letter.

∗∗∗

 Cut From Strong Cloth

Ellen began assembling a travel bag when she looked up in surprise to see Cecilia enter her room.

"Ellen, I have something to give you for the trip." She brought forth a beige linen napkin, which when unrolled disclosed the O'Neill brooch.

"But, Mam, you said this was passed down on the daughter's wedding day."

"Aye, 'tis true. But the pin is mine to give, and I want it to be your good luck charm. You can pin it to your cloak just like the other O'Neills did."

Ellen looked at her mother. This was not typical for Mam at all. "But you also told me the pin had to wait until I found my true love."

"And I believe he might just be in Georgia at the moment. Come here and take it."

Is James my true love? Is he my destiny after all?

"I don't know what to say, Mam. How can I be sure of who my true love is meant to be?"

"Remember that I told you to think how life without that person would feel?"

Ellen nodded.

"If your life would be empty without him, and fuller and richer with him, then I think you are already in love with that person."

Maybe I am.

***

JEFFERSON DAVIS ELECTED AS PRESIDENT OF CONFEDERACY!

The headlines caused Ellen to wince as she thought about Patrick and James. She knew that in two days the headlines would applaud Abraham Lincoln's inauguration as President of the United States, but right now she had no time to brood over politics. Today she was advancing to the next step in her plan. Today she was opening her own bank account before leaving on the return trip to Savannah.

Throughout the time she worked at the Cleary's, Ellen had

managed to keep some of her pay. She shook out the bills stashed in the old baking powder tin and counted them one by one. Her entire savings amounted to less than twenty dollars, but she hoped it would be enough to prove her good intentions.

She chose her most professional outfit, a dark blue dress with ebony trim on the sleeves, and fixed her hair with extra care, dabbing rose water behind her ears and on her neck. Then she left the house with a confident air and walked the few blocks over to the Kensington Trust Bank.

Once inside she approached a window at the counter.

"Good day, Miss, can I be of service?"

"Yes, thank you. I wish to open an account."

The man peered over his spectacles, looking behind her.

"Are you alone?" He asked with an air of incredibility.

"Yes."

"Did you bring a letter of guarantee?"

"A letter of guarantee?"

"Yes, from your father, or perhaps a brother." A vestige of annoyance appeared on his face.

"No, my father is dead and my brother is on a trip."

"I'm sorry, but without a letter of guarantee, and a signature from a male family member, you cannot open an account."

Ellen held up the cash. "This is perfectly good American money."

"I can see that. But the rules state that a woman needs her husband, father, or brother to sign for her." He lowered his eyes to her chest and then let his gaze linger. "Are you married?"

"No."

"Then I suggest you find someone in your family—maybe an uncle—to come back with you to open an account."

Ellen's throat went dry. She didn't have an uncle. "What about a gentleman family friend?"

"I'm sorry, but I am very busy and unless you can comply with the rules, I will have to ask you to step aside. Next! Who's next in line?"

She attempted to stay put, but the male customer behind her elbowed his way to the counter. Ellen felt the heat of anger on her neck

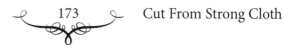

and face as she walked out of the bank with as much dignity as she could muster. *I won't let them win, Da. I won't.*

✳✳✳

As the voyage to Savannah began, Ellen wondered if Mrs. Chambers would ever stop talking. Even as they began the supper meal, Mrs. Chambers kept a steady verbal stream going.

"So you see, my dear, I am worried to death that my only child is stowed away in the South. Of course, she has married a doctor, so I should be grateful for that at least. What about you, Ellen? Do you have a beau?"

"No, mam, not at present." But the image of James with the wisps of gray in his hair came instantly to her mind.

"Well, my Henry has been gone for fourteen years now, God rest his soul. Did you know I was betrothed by the time I was sixteen?"

Ellen gave a half-hearted smile as she dragged the bent spoon through the watery pea soup. The shriveled apple slices that accompanied the hard tea biscuits held little appeal either, but at least by eating she could not reply to Mrs. Chambers.

Being at sea gave Ellen time to think about James. She did care for him, perhaps even love him, but she also needed him for her plan to succeed. But committing herself to him—would that interfere with the business?

Ellen sighed when the ship pulled into the mouth of the Savannah River and she spied the Fort Pulaski flag saluting her. It felt good to be back there.

As they pulled up to port, Ellen overhead two deck hands talking about how Alexander Stephens, the new elected Vice President of the Confederacy, recently made a speech to the Georgia delegates about the natural order of slavery that the North was trying to erase. She shifted her feet and turned away so they would not see her expression of disgust. How could anyone honestly believe that slavery was intended to be a natural occurrence?

Upon leaving the ship, Ellen saw a new type of vessel moored

in the river, one that did not seem to be carrying passengers or cotton cargo. She spied multiple kegs of gunpowder being unloaded from the ship. Were they stockpiling weapons already?

They hailed a porter, who carried their bags up to Bay Street, and signaled for a driver. As they rode through the streets, Ellen inhaled the gentle fragrance of magnolia and jasmine and began to relax as the warm Savannah air caressed her shoulders. She drank in the heady offerings of early springtime in Georgia, delighted to be a recipient of its gifts once again. Even the swaying wisps of silver-gray moss seemed to be welcoming her return.

When they arrived at Dr. Fallon's home, the elegance of his residence made her smile. Ellen stared up at the ebony front door with its matching sidelights, remembering how she and Patrick had stood at the front entrance, not even knowing about calling cards.

Dr. Fallon opened the door and called out a greeting, then descended the steps with agility. He kissed Mrs. Chambers on the cheek. Sarah Fallon followed right behind and ran to embrace her mother. Then Dr. Fallon saw Ellen.

"You must be Ellen. How can I ever thank you for bringing my mother-in-law down here to be with us?"

"The pleasure was mine, Dr. Fallon." Ellen bit her lower lip, and felt a bit shaky with nerves, but she had to find out as soon as possible about Patrick and James. "I know we have just arrived, and I hope I'm not showing bad manners, but may I ask if it is at all possible that you have seen or heard from my brother Patrick during the past six weeks?"

Ellen saw a look of surprise on Dr. Fallon's face, but before he could answer, Mrs. Chambers declared, "I am so fatigued from the journey. Louis, could we please just enter the house and then carry on conversations?"

Ever the gentleman, Dr. Fallon asked the driver to bring the suitcases inside as he ushered the ladies up the stairs and held open the door for them to enter. Once inside, Ellen tried not to stare, but the front room displayed the finest furniture she had ever seen. Against the back wall a camelback sofa swathed in a burgundy tufted fabric sat between two large mahogany wing chairs covered with cushions of

Cut From Strong Cloth

striped burgundy and cream. In front of the sofa, a long Queen Anne style table held two large matching cut glass bowls sitting on a runner of pure lace. Additional mahogany chairs were positioned near a lady's elegant writing desk, and over in the corner rested a small piano—something Ellen had never seen in anyone's home.

She walked further into the room and as her feet sank into the lush Oriental carpet, she looked up and saw tall windows nestled by sheer bisque curtains. No need for lace curtains at the front of this house—the entire residence displayed its wealth.

Was this the same type of house that Mam frequented at Rittenhouse Square? If so, how could she return home to Kensington each time without feeling poor? Ellen suspected Mam had yearned for a Rittenhouse life once upon a time, and now her only hope was for Ellen to marry into it. Of course her mother would never dream that a woman could create that lifestyle on her own by becoming a success in business.

She followed the maid upstairs and entered the guest room where her bags had been taken, then thanked the woman for showing her to the room. After the maid left, Ellen went over and stroked the coverlet on the bed, running her fingers across the fine woven linen. There were fresh flowers on the side table in another cut class bowl, and the sheer curtains had been drawn to let in the afternoon light. The room exuded the luxury and serenity of the privileged class, and Ellen drank it in like elixir.

Once she had unpacked and taken the light refreshments provided on a tray, she went back downstairs and waited for a moment alone with Dr. Fallon. Only then did she bring up the subject once again about Patrick and James. "Dr. Fallon, as I mentioned earlier, I am worried about my brother and his business associate, James Nolan. We've heard nothing from them in over six weeks."

Dr. Fallon paused before he answered.

"Ellen, what do you know about their business here in Savannah? You do understand these are difficult, even dangerous, times? Yes, I did meet with your brother Patrick. I had assumed he'd been in contact with you. If for nothing else I thought perhaps he would have

written to you about Magdalena."

Now it was Ellen's turn to be surprised. "Magdalena? I have no idea who you're talking about."

"Several weeks ago, Magdalena Fox, a family friend and pharmacist who works here in the city, came to see me accompanied by a young man who turned out to be your brother. I realized we had met briefly last September, in Kensington. Then he told me how he and his friend had been here on business when they were beaten and robbed just prior to their planned trip home. That occurred, I believe, near the end of January. Patrick was discovered along a road outside of town by Magdalena. Together they have been making inquiries about the other gentleman. However, he is yet to be found."

Ellen felt slightly sick but steadied herself.

"I am sorry to be the bearer of this news."

"Thank you, Dr. Fallon, but since James has not yet been found, then there is still a chance he could be alive. Is Patrick staying with our cousin here in Savannah?"

"Patrick left two days ago on a steamer bound for Philadelphia."

"What? I don't understand."

"I believe he went home because he needed to tell you in person about James Nolan. He expressed concern about being gone so long from your mother, and said he needed to check on the factory shipments." Dr. Fallon paused. "Ellen, here in Savannah your brother and his business associate would be looked upon as undesirable Yankees."

"But Dr. Fallon. . ."

"No, please listen. Since Georgia seceded from the Union, Savannah is no longer hospitable toward Northerners. There are Federal troops stationed in Charleston. If the country goes to war, battles could very well be fought on southern soil. In that case, Patrick and your friend would be enemies of the South."

His last few words helped her to rally. "Thank you for your candor, Dr. Fallon. Patrick and James are textile merchants, buying cotton and shipping it north. They would not be taking sides in a war; they would be impartial businessmen."

"Ellen, you are thinking in a rational manner, but if the country

goes to war, then I will be a southern surgeon, giving medical help to those in need here in Savannah. Your brother has already gone home, and you will need to return north as soon as possible."

"Thank you for your concern, but I am not leaving Savannah until I find out what happened to James. If you will excuse me, I need to lie down. The journey has tired me out."

"Of course. I did not mean to upset you."

Ellen went back up to the guest room and sat on the bed. She felt an ache in her chest, and her legs were heavy with exhaustion. Later she would start looking for James, with or without the help of Dr. Fallon.

She lay down on the bed and before she could recite the prayer to St. Brigid, sleep overcame her and she slept soundly, not even rousing for supper.

***

But part way through the night, worry about James penetrated her dreams. When she wakened, instead of being refreshed, she felt tired throughout her entire body. Quickly dressing in a simple lime green dress, she tucked her hair and tied it back with a cream colored ribbon.

"Good morning everyone," she forced a weak smile as she entered the dining room for breakfast. Delicious odors of rashers frying in the kitchen and hot rolls emerging from the oven stimulated her appetite.

"Good morning, Ellen. I trust you slept well?"

"Not completely, Mrs. Fallon, but thank you. I think my mind raced from one concern to another."

"Ellen, please call me Sarah. I would feel better if we weren't so formal with each other."

"All right, Sarah."

She seated herself at the long dining table, which could accommodate ten, marveling at the amount of food being passed and the possibility that they ate this way every Sunday.

"I hope you'll not be offended if I leave the house right after breakfast. I'd like to attend Mass at St. John's. Would that be all right?"

"Certainly. Will you need the driver to take you there?"

"Oh, no. I would much prefer to walk, thank you."

She wanted to be left alone with her thoughts. Patrick home safe. Well, safe at least on his way back home. They could have passed each other on the open sea. And James—the fact that his body had not been discovered gave her some hope.

The time frame bothered her the most. The attack had happened near the end of January and now they were almost into the second week of March. Shouldn't someone have found James during all this time? She shook her head. He had to be alive.

Walking later in the fresh morning air felt invigorating, and Sunday Mass always soothed her spirit. She arrived before the start of the next service and walked to a side alcove where a statue of the Blessed Mother hovered over an array of candles. She pushed her offering in the slot of the candle box and taking a long match stick, lit it from one of the burning candles. Then, she lit a new candle and bowed her head. *Hail Mary, full of grace, 'tis me, Ellen. Thank you for all the times you have been by my side. I come to you now in supplication, asking that James be found alive, regardless of why I have not heard from him. Please protect him, as you have always protected me. Amen.*

On the walk home she decided she would ask Dr. Fallon if she could stay on for an extended visit, and in exchange she would be willing to help him in his infirmary. She would write Mam and explain the need to stay in Savannah a bit longer. By the time the letter arrived, Patrick should be home. She couldn't worry about Father Reilly; Mrs. McAllister would take care of him.

Ellen lost no time in approaching Dr. Fallon as soon as she returned to the house.

"Dr. Fallon, I would like to make a proposal. I need to stay in Savannah for a while, to find the whereabouts of Mr. Nolan, but I can't impose upon you and Sarah forever. I was thinking that in exchange for room and board, I could help out at your infirmary—perhaps relieve you of some clerical duties?"

Cut From Strong Cloth

"That is very kind, Ellen. But you are more than welcome to remain here as our guest."

"No, Dr. Fallon, I canna do that. I need to contribute to my stay. Besides, by working in the infirmary, I would be in the heart of the city where perhaps I would hear something about James."

"Well, my clerical needs are small, but I can always use an extra pair of hands with the patients. Have you had any nursing training?"

"No, sir, I haven't. But I am a willing and quick learner. I do know how to use some herbs for medicinal purposes. For example, I know which ones help quell indigestion and which herbs help to reduce a fever."

"What about blood? Does it make you feel faint?"

"Not that I know."

"When would you want to start?"

"Tomorrow is Monday, is it not? I would like to start first thing in the morning. I'm good working with people, and I don't think you'll be disappointed in me."

"Very well, I've been hiring temporary help since my former nurse left to take care of her elderly mother. I'll welcome your assistance, but only for the time necessary. I still insist that you start making plans to return home."

***

The next morning, Ellen became a part of the Savannah workforce.

Dr. Fallon's driver delivered them to State Street so the doctor could show Ellen around the infirmary before any of the morning patients arrived. The outside of the infirmary could have passed for a nice row house in Philadelphia with a brick front and three double hung windows running from side to side on each level.

"We'll dispense with any correspondence this morning and just let you get a feel for how the office operates." Dr. Fallon chuckled. "My, I did not intend that as a joke." He laughed as he unlocked the front door.

He led her into the front reception room where at least everything smelled clean. Ellen could detect the faint odor of vinegar and wash water, just like Mam used back home. But unlike home where the furniture felt cozy, this front room contained only six wooden chairs lined up against sterile white walls. A desk and chair sat opposite the entrance. Cheer was lacking.

"This is where the patients wait until they're called back to an examination room, and this is where I could use you the most," Dr. Fallon explained. "You'll ask them to sign in on the daily log so we know who arrived first. Then you write down the patient's name and complaint, and then bring the paper back to the examination area where I will read it. When I am ready, I'll ring a bell, and that will be your signal to bring the patient to me. Here, let me show you the rest of the office."

A center hallway led from the front waiting room back to the actual infirmary. A few pictures of pastoral lake scenes chosen perhaps to evoke a sense of serenity hung on the walls. Otherwise, the hallway was bare. Halfway back, two small examination rooms flanked each other. A smaller room held storage, and across the hall there was an indoor toilet. What a luxury! At the extreme back of the building sat the operation room—used for small surgeries. The exam rooms and the surgery room each contained two or three chairs, a cabinet which held various medical supplies, and a long rectangular table hugging the wall where the patient could sit or lie down to be examined. The tables each contained a pile of fresh linens at one end, and a chart containing random letters in different sizes hung above them.

Ellen hoped she wouldn't be asked to assist in any surgeries, yet. She needed to get her feet steady before anything complicated like sewing up a wound would occur.

The first patient of the day turned out to be an older woman who came in complaining that her one ear had stopped working and she couldn't hear a thing out of it. Ellen took down her information and reassured the woman that Dr. Fallon would be in soon.

"Heh? What's that you're saying? Isn't he here now? Who are you anyway, and where are you from? Your people aren't from Savannah, are they?"

Ellen realized she had made a mistake by not introducing her-

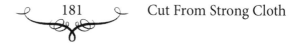

self. Manners were of utmost importance down here in Georgia, and she needed to qualm any misgivings this woman might have.

"I do so apologize. My name is Ellen Canavan. 'Tis true I am not from Savannah, but my family has been friends with Dr. Fallon for quite some time. I am helping out here for a few weeks. Now just make yourself comfortable Mrs. . . ?"

"Johnson, my name is Mrs. Albert Johnson."

"All right, Mrs. Johnson. Dr. Fallon is in the next room and will be right over."

Ellen left, closing the door behind her, then leaned up against the hallway wall and let out a deep breath. She had survived her first patient interview, and learned that manners mattered in medicine just like anywhere else. *Holy Mary, give me the ability to do good work here.*

CHAPTER 17

March 1861

He had forced himself to take a hiatus from the fires. The Philadelphia Police had been investigating a series of suspicious fires, and he had not wanted to attract any attention. But now, he could hold off no longer. He needed the fires, just as much as they needed him. He slithered through a series of alleys in Kensington, always mindful of traveling unseen. When he reached Thompson Street, he was ready to dart inside an abandoned house when he saw a girl up ahead. For a brief moment, he thought it might be—her. But of course, it wasn't. This was just some neighborhood lass. Christ, had she seen him? He didn't think so, but he decided to wait until she passed by. He couldn't risk being identified. Even if he were in jail, his benefactors had a way of getting to their fire-setters and silencing them.

A full hour passed while he stayed in the shadows. Then he slipped into the building. Inside the back door was the can of kerosene, waiting for him. Standing still, he quieted his breathing. The appearance of the girl had rattled him, and he needed complete composure in order to set a perfect conflagration. In his mind, he envisioned another building, one he would love to set fire to. Taking several deep breaths, he reminded himself that he alone held this magnificent power. Then he opened the kerosene container and walked around the first floor rooms, sprinkling the fuel as calm as watering flowers.

Being a criminal did not bother him in the least. You had to grab whatever chances life presented. Only the dumb let themselves get caught.

CHAPTER 18

March 1861

Emma woke before the children. Sitting up on the makeshift bedding on the floor, she gazed over at James lying in her bed, still asleep. Then she quietly got up and moved to the kitchen where she splashed water on her face and for the first time in months looked into the cracked, chipped mirror on the wall. She frowned. *Lord almighty, look at my hair. Wonder if I can get Selma to give me a decent hair cut.* Then she peered down at her rough hands and silently went to the shelf, pulled out a can of lard, and massaged some of the grease onto her hands. *Maybe he'll like me if I clean up some.*

Emma often slept in the same clothes she had worn the day before, but this morning she began to take more care with her appearance. She changed out of the dirty dress from yesterday and silently gave herself a quick sponge bath in the kitchen, although she had no real sponge, so she used the same rag she had used to wash the dishes from the night before.

She slipped into her one semi-clean dress and ran her fingers through the tangle of her hair, or at least attempted to. *I'll definitely have to get this mess cut.* Then she pinched her cheeks, licked her forefinger and ran it up her eyebrows.

James stirred and she walked over to the bed. "Good morning."

He peered up at her, but said nothing. His eyelids began to close again.

"Hey, notice anything?"

But he had already fallen back asleep.

Her lips reverted to a single straight line. "No, guess not." She exhaled in a rush of rancid breath. "God damn men," she uttered under her breath. "Don't do no good dressing up for them anyhow."

She stalked back to the kitchen. *I'll fix him. I'll see to it that he don't go nowhere, and I don't need to clean up to do that.*

***

When Ellen awoke she prayed the words of the Hail Mary and the prayer to St. Brigid, ending with, "Please let today be the day I find James." The recitation gave her renewed strength in her purpose. "Look fear right in the face and spit in its eye." Those had been Da's words, and she was trying to emulate his fearless approach to life.

Ellen's plan was to work with Dr. Fallon and then walk in the city during the noon meal break. Even though her cousin Tom and Dr. Fallon had both made a missing person report to the Savannah Police, Ellen planned to talk to as many people as possible in her search for James. Having a plan made her feel more active.

Her first two working days in Savannah were filled with patients from morning till late afternoon. There had been children with bazaar situations like the one who had stuffed raisins up his nose to the young girl with a serious cough, reminding Ellen of Da. Older patients had come in complaining of earaches and toothaches and aches in their bones. Ellen took down each notation and also took the time to talk to each patient before they went back to see Dr. Fallon. Knowing very little about actual nursing, she watched everything Dr. Fallon did, and wrote down copious notes which she read back to herself at the end of the day.

Her only confidence came when Dr. Fallon dispensed medicine, because she realized most of the formularies were derived from the homeopathic herbs she already knew. Before closing the infirmary at the end of business, she tidied up the examining rooms, noting with surprise the shabby quality of the patients' linens. They were nothing like the beautiful fabrics Dr. Fallon had at home.

On the third work day, Ellen congratulated herself that she had made it through the first two without disaster. She had just opened the infirmary and tied on her day apron when the front door opened and a man came in holding his hand wrapped in a bloodied handkerchief.

"Oh my! Please sit down, sir."

"Is the doctor in yet? I seemed to have made an unfortunate mistake with a knife, and fear I have almost sliced off the tip of my thumb. It will require stitches, I am certain."

Ellen looked away from the thumb, and to the man. He appeared dressed as a gentleman in a fine cutaway form-fitting jacket, under which might be riding breeches, and he was wearing a shirt of quality linen. His tousled hair did not quite fit with his impeccable outfit, and she also noticed his moss green eyes were similar in color to her own. She averted her gaze, lest he discover her inspecting his handsome features.

Without warning, he began to undo the bandage, and fresh blood spurted.

Ellen had not dealt much with wounds before, other than the bloody scraped knees of childhood, so she startled a bit at the sight of the mangled thumb. Before she had to take any action, Dr. Fallon walked into the infirmary.

"Oh, Louis. I'm glad you're here. It seems I have cut myself, rather badly, I must admit."

"Let's take a look at it, Nash. My yes, this is a dandy. Ellen, will you take Mr. Finch to the surgery room while I get my instruments."

Ellen eyed the visitor now with some curiosity as she led him down the hall to the back room. "Please sit here," she said as she ushered him into the patient area and over to a chair. "Are you Nash Finch, the shipping agent?"

"Yes, I am. But you have me at a disadvantage. You are?"

"Ellen Canavan. I believe that you met my brother Patrick some weeks back when he and I were arranging shipping details with our cotton factor, Mr. Francis."

Cut From Strong Cloth

"The Irishman from Philadelphia? Yes, I remember. You are the other business partner? Your brother never mentioned his partner was his sister, and such a pretty one at that."

Ellen felt herself blush, and then Dr. Fallon entered the room and began preparations to suture the thumb.

"If you don't need me, Dr. Fallon, I will go back up front and see if we have any new patients." She lingered, however, just outside the door to listen for a moment longer. Then chided herself for eavesdropping, and returned to the front room.

"You really smashed this thumb, Nash. How did it happen?"

"The dogs barked at something, and I turned my head. Instead of cutting off a chunk of cheese, I sliced my thumb. But the trip over here has now turned out to be a pleasant one. How is it you've nabbed such a delight to help in the infirmary? Especially a textile merchant from up North."

"Ellen? Her family and I are friends. She's searching for an acquaintance that seems to have disappeared in our city."

"Disappeared?"

"The gentleman and her brother were conducting some business, and they were bushwhacked late one night. Her brother resurfaced the next day, but the other man has not been seen since."

"When did this happen?"

"Back in January. She's determined to stay in Savannah until she finds out what happened to him."

"Well now, perhaps we should make her feel most welcomed. After all, Savannah can always use another pretty young woman."

"Hands off, Nash. The gentleman she's looking for is quite important to her."

"But he hasn't been found?"

"No, not yet."

"Then I may still entertain the possibility of also becoming a friend," he grinned.

"Still sit, this is going to hurt while I stitch up the cut."

Nash turned his head away, steeling himself. Later, as he prepared to leave the infirmary, he stopped by Ellen's desk. "Thank you,

 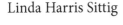 

Miss Canavan, for your assistance earlier. I am sorry if I offended you in any way with my bloody thumb."

"Not at all, Mr. Finch. While I'm helping Dr. Fallon, I should expect to see blood from time to time."

"Are you here in Savannah with your family?"

"No, I accompanied Mrs. Chambers, Sarah Fallon's mother, down here for a visit."

"Wonderful! Then I must make it up to you that I so brutishly interrupted your peaceful morning. Please allow me to meet you after work today, and I can show you around Savannah."

"That is very kind of you, but I have been in Savannah before and explored its squares."

"But not with someone who knows all the best stories about the people of the city. Please, let me at least take you for afternoon tea. If you like, we can even discuss the shipping details of your cotton purchase."

"All right. Thank you. That would be acceptable."

"Fine, I will call for you at four o'clock then." He grinned as he opened the door and left, heading in the direction of Solomon's Pharmacy.

***

Tea with Nash Finch started out to be an enjoyable experience, even though Ellen felt a bit nervous. This was only the third time in her life that a man other than Patrick had taken her to an eating establishment. She couldn't help but notice how the other women in the tea room smiled at Nash. Well, he was good looking with his wavy dark hair and lively green eyes, not to mention his trim physique. *What am I thinking? He is our shipping agent, nothing else.*

"So, Miss Canavan, now that we are having tea together and I have filled you in on the tonnage requirements of the cotton shipments, may I address you as Ellen?"

His formal request to call her by first name seemed almost silly, but then again this was the South, and she acquiesced with a hint of enjoyment at his manners.

"All right, Mr. Finch. You may call me Ellen."

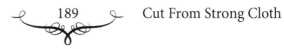

Cut From Strong Cloth

"Well, I do have one condition. You must call me Nash."

"Isn't this a bit quick to be on first names with each other?"

"Not when you consider we're in business together." He winked. "So, Ellen, tell me what you think of our city."

She waited a moment before replying. "'Tis quite lovely. Much more genteel than Philadelphia—other than the issue of slavery, of course."

Nash arched an eyebrow, showing surprise. "Ah, yes, being from Pennsylvania, I expect you do not understand nor condone the practice of slavery."

"Of course I do not condone a practice where human beings are bought and sold. I'm not sure there is much to understand about that."

"Yet, you are willing to conduct business with a product based upon slave labor," he mused.

"The fact that I am purchasing cotton has nothing at all to do with my beliefs about the unfairness of slavery," Ellen stammered.

"What if I told you that without slave labor, there wouldn't be any Georgia cotton for you to purchase?"

"Paid workers could harvest cotton for the South," Ellen countered.

"Have you studied economics, Ellen, or are you just trying to make money for yourself?"

"I think, Mr. Nash, our tea is over." Ellen tossed her napkin down at the plate.

"What? Giving up in your argument so soon? Don't be quick to judge, Ellen. The economy of the South is quite different from what you know in the North."

Ellen stood up. "Forgive me for not staying any longer, but we have nothing more to say to one another. I hope this won't affect the shipping agreements."

Nash stood up as well.

"Of course not. I rely on the shipping contracts to make money. It's all part of the cotton economy," he said with a rakish smile.

"Good day, Mr. Finch." Ellen marched out of the restaurant.

"It was my pleasure, and I do hope we see each other again," he called out after her.

Ellen did not look back. But what Nash Finch had said about

her part in the slave economy bothered her. Of course she didn't condone slavery, but she had to face the fact that their business would depend on slave labor in order to prosper. Was there any other way she could purchase cotton not harvested by slaves? Why hadn't she thought about this before? Good God, by purchasing Georgia cotton she was actually supporting slavery.

Determined to stay true to her goal, she would have to come to terms with this dilemma.

***

She jabbed the key into the infirmary door, still irritable with Nash Finch from the day before. She knew she needed to dispel her mood before Dr. Fallon arrived, but she was bothered with the notion that her business would be supporting a slave economy. Somehow, there must be an answer. All morning she worked with the usual load of patients, but her mind kept mulling over the slavery issue.

Right before noon, she looked up as an attractive young woman entered the infirmary. Ellen noticed right away the woman's lemon and cream striped dress with matching bonnet. The color perfectly complemented the woman's curly auburn hair. She did not appear to be ailing, so Ellen wondered why she had come there.

"May I help you?" Ellen asked.

"Yes, I believe so. I received a note from Dr. Fallon, inviting me to come to the infirmary today to meet you."

"To meet me? Why, whatever for?"

"Because of Patrick."

Confused at first, Ellen smiled. "Are you Magdalena?"

"Yes, I am." A generous smile spread across the woman's face. "And you are just as Patrick described."

"I hope he had nice things to say."

"He spoke as a brother who loves his sister. It's almost the noon hour and instead of having your dinner with Dr. Fallon, how about dining with me instead? It would be nice to get to know you better."

"Why, that would be grand. I'll just go in back and tell Dr. Fallon."

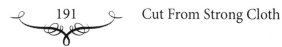

191   Cut From Strong Cloth

They ate at the same establishment where Nash Finch had taken her for tea. She hoped she would not run into him again. As they ate, Magdalena wanted to hear as much as possible about the Canavan family.

"I know Patrick was born in a place called County Tyrone, and came to Philadelphia at the age of twenty-four. But other than that, I don't know much about your lives."

"Well, in Ireland we lived in a small village called Dungannon, where our Da was a weaver and Mam took in sewing. I was fourteen when we left, so Patrick would have stronger memories of home."

"And you've lived in Philadelphia ever since? I'm curious as to why Patrick hasn't married."

"Married! There must be hundreds of girls in Kensington who tried to catch my brother. He's a flirt, I'll admit to that. But, marriage? No, that hasn't happened. What about you?"

"I was married. My husband John died of yellow fever four years ago, along with my parents. I never remarried because I felt no one could replace him. The way I feel about Patrick, though, is different. It's not that he's replacing John, it's rather that I am starting life over."

Ellen's eyes opened wide.

"Oh. Well, have you lived your entire life here in Savannah, then?"

"Yes. My parents worked at Solomon's Pharmacy and from the time I was a little girl, I knew my way around its counters and displays. So I guess it was only natural I wound up working there."

"How about you, Ellen? Patrick told me that you had a keen interest in textiles."

"Mam is a seamstress, so ever since I can remember I played with scraps of fabrics and leftover notions. Our Da was a weaver and I used to watch him at his loom. So I guess that explains why I want to own my textile business."

After the meal ended and the two women parted, Ellen realized how much she enjoyed Magdalena's company. No wonder Patrick was attracted to her.

***

Emma Walker looked at James lying back asleep on her bed, his frame positioned under a thin quilt. Many times she sat watching him like this. Often he would half-wake with fever, thrash with agitation, and mumble, "Where am I?" before slumping back into a deep sleep.

She knew every inch of his body. He appeared to be strong, but his hands were soft, like a gentleman. He was neither a Southerner nor a farmer, but that didn't matter. At least she had a man back in her life.

"You rest," she whispered to him. While he was deeply asleep, she often took one of his hands and placed it on her bare breast, rubbing his fingers over her nipples. After all this time living alone, taking care of the three children and sleeping cold under a single blanket, she often sought her own physical release and now that a man was here, she did not want him to leave.

"How can I make you stay?" she mused by his bedside. "What matters is that I got time. You'll stay all right," she murmured with a crooked smile.

***

Little by little, James' body began to heal, and he managed to stay awake for longer periods. Finally he managed to sit up in bed on his own and carry on a conversation.

"Where am I again?" he asked.

"My farm," she tersely replied.

"But where? And how?"

"You're in Old Canoochee country, about seven miles south of Savannah. You was dumped in one of my fields and left for dead."

"What is your name?"

"Emma Walker. I own this place."

"How long have I been here, Mrs. Walker?"

"A while. When my son Tommy found you, you was unconscious and left with a broken leg. Whoever dumped you out here gave you a nasty head wound, too. It became infected and you developed a fever. But you've survived."

"Where did you find a doctor out here?"

Cut From Strong Cloth

"Hmph! What makes you think a doctor treated you? We tended you ourselves. My children and Selma been watching over you."

"Selma?"

"Local nigra woman. A healer."

"Then the angels and saints must have been watching over me." He gave a faint smile for the first time.

"I don't put much stock in angels and saints, Mister. Just rest and take it easy. You got a long ways to go before your strength will come back."

"But I canna just stay here."

"Don't worry 'bout that. We'll work something out, though I doubt you're used to any farm work. You look more like the city type."

"At home I run a factory."

"A factory, huh? Then you can read and write. Well, maybe we can trade. I'll keep on takin' care of you, if 'n you teach my boy his letters and numbers. Out here, very little schoolin' gets done."

"I thought I saw three children here."

"Girls don't need no school bookin'. As soon as they's fifteen they'll be off and married. It's better for them to learn how to clean and cook."

"Perhaps they should learn numbers and letters, too," he responded.

"Suit yourself, Mister. But the girls got to finish chores first."

***

The day arrived when his appetite returned and he hungered for a real meal, not just the watery soups she had been feeding him. By now, he'd had numerous conversations with the three children; Tommy, Samantha, and Emily.

"Emma."

She turned to look at him lowering his legs over the side of the bed and standing on his own, though still a bit shaky.

"I'd like to join the children and you for the supper meal you're preparing."

She nodded and went over to his side. Her husband's old crutch

leaned up against the wall. "Here, use this stick to steady yourself."

Later the children smiled when he sat down on the bench across from them.

"Hey, that's the spot where our daddy used to sit. He was—"

"Be quiet, Samantha. Our guest don't have no need to know family business," Emma retorted.

All the children fell silent as she ladled out a thin stew and set out a pan of biscuits. After the blessing and the biscuits being passed, Tommy looked askance at his mother and then turned to James. "Hey, Mister. Do you want to hear how we found you in our field?"

"Tommy, don't you go botherin' our guest," Emma shot out. "Didn't you hear what I said to Samantha?"

"Of course I'd like to hear the story. You rescued me, Tommy, didn't you?" James smiled at the boy.

Tommy beamed. "Well, you was lyin' in our field, and I thought you was dead. I ran and got Momma, and together me and Momma, and Emily and Samantha, got you back to the cabin. You was hurt real bad, but my momma healed you."

Here Tommy paused and looked at Emma, who did not bother to acknowledge his praise.

"Then you took sick with a real bad fever and just thrashed for days. We all took turns watchin' over you. But then one day you opened your eyes and peered around, and looked real confused. So I said, 'Hey, Mister. You're awake!' Do you remember that?"

"Yes, and I asked your name, and you told me you were Tommy Walker. And 'tis a blessing that you found me."

Tommy grinned, the girls giggled, but Emma remained mute— her lips in a perpetual hard line.

***

Dr. Fallon often left the house early on workdays, and Ellen enjoyed the exercise of walking to the infirmary on her own—unless it was pouring rain, then she accepted the offer of a ride over to State Street.

When Ellen arrived at work this morning, she saw that Dr. Fallon had an unusual expression on his face.

"Ellen, I don't want to be giving you any false hopes, but another doctor in town heard a rumor about a disreputable man who sold some medicine to a Negro woman a few weeks back. She claimed she needed it for a white man with a bad head wound."

Ellen straightened her shoulders. "Dr. Fallon, do you think it could be James?"

"I'm not sure, dear, but I could ride out this afternoon and investigate for you."

"Dr. Fallon, I very much want to go with you."

"This fellow, Oliver Burke, calls himself a doctor, but I and the other doctors refuse to have anything to do with him. We all know that his main business is opium. But perhaps we should follow up on this piece of information anyway."

Later that day Dr. Fallon drove his wagon out on the Ogeechee Road with Ellen as his passenger. The matched pair of sorrel horses had pulled them a few miles beyond the outskirts of town when a run-down building came into view.

"Well, this fits the description," Dr. Fallon said.

The building hardly looked inhabited. Weathered timbers had been shoved under a sagging porch roof to stave off collapse, and mountains of trash littered the yard. Some of the windows were open to the elements, while others sported tattered strips of flour sacks moving with the breeze.

Ellen shuddered with an uneasy feeling.

Dr. Fallon saw her reaction. "Let me do the talking. We'll leave as soon as possible." They approached the door, swaying on two of its three rusted hinges. The overpowering stench of unwashed bodies and accumulated goat and pig filth permeated the air. Ellen tried hard not to gag.

"Hello?" Dr. Fallon called out.

A moment later a greasy-haired man emerged, tucking a food-stained shirt back into his dirty breeches. His bloodshot eyes zeroed in on Ellen and he licked his lips, revealing several yellow-stained broken

teeth. A shiver ran through her when she spied a small black boy in tattered rags standing just behind him. A feeling of unnaturalness draped the scene.

"Does your lady friend here need to dispose of something?"

"No, this has nothing to do with her. You are Oliver Burke, I assume, and I am here for information only," Dr. Fallon replied.

The man registered a look of disappointment.

"What kind of information?" he asked.

"We're looking for the name and whereabouts of a Negro woman you sold some medicine to last month. She came here claiming she needed it for a white man."

"Is that so?"

"I'm not here to turn you in for selling opium. I just want to find out who she is and where she lives."

"What's it worth to you?"

"If you can tell me her name, I will make it worth your while," Dr. Fallon responded.

He pulled out a small wad of bills.

Burke shot out a skinny arm, fingers like talons, trying to grab for the money, but Dr. Fallon pulled his arm back.

"Not until you give me the information."

Burke eyed him with suspicion but offered no reply.

"Perhaps I should rephrase my request. How much is it worth to you that I not go back into town and report what you're doing with that slave boy?"

This statement took Burke by surprise. "You can't prove nothin'. Anyway, I own him. He's my property, not yours."

Dr. Fallon held his ground but then waved the small wad of bills up in front of the man's face.

Oliver Burke licked his lips once more. "Selma. Where she lives, I don't know. Somewhere down the road. Who the man was—don't know neither. Just know she needed to treat a bad wound. That's all."

His greasy hand reached for the money, but Dr. Fallon pulled out only a few bills, threw them down on the table and without looking back, ushered Ellen outside.

"Now get the hell off my property!" the voice from inside hollered.

Ellen and Dr. Fallon drove on, stopping at every farmhouse or shanty they encountered for several miles. But each time they asked about a Negro woman named Selma, they were met with a look of amusement in the other peoples' eyes. "We got several Selma's around here. Which one do you want?" Even when they explained they only wanted to ask about a white man she might have treated, none of the inhabitants came forward with any useful information. With heavy hearts they drove back to Savannah.

"I'm sorry, Ellen. I thought perhaps we might have had a lead."

"That's all right, Dr. Fallon. The white man could still be James, which means he might be alive. I'm not giving up hope. I'll stay on in Savannah. I've wanted to check on our cotton shipments anyway."

"Is Patrick buying cotton? I thought he dealt in wool."

"'Tis not just Patrick. I am a part of the business as well," stated Ellen.

"I never heard Patrick mention anything about your involvement."

"I started out by helping with the books for Canavan Wool, our family business. Then I began to handle the weekly correspondence on the accounts as well. He buys raw wool and then sells it to factory owners in Philadelphia. But then with the troubles that seemed to be brewing, we decided, he and I, that we could manufacture a blended type of fabric using cotton and wool to make a special material for soldiers' uniforms. We plan to make a superior product, free of the shoddy that other mills use."

She saw a look on concern pass over Dr. Fallon's face.

"I know you're thinking we mean to manufacture the cloth only for Northern soldiers' uniforms. But the cloth will be sold to anyone who wants to purchase it, and the southern cotton growers will make a profit, regardless of who buys the material."

"Where does this James Nolan fit in?"

"James has the factory space and equipment we need to manufacture the cloth. He also has the money we need for the beginning cotton purchases. Eventually I want to branch out on my own and I'm hoping that James will be my sponsor."

"I see." Dr. Fallon urged the horse back toward Savannah. He

spoke little on the return journey, almost as if he was lost in thought. Ellen remained quiet as well, trying hard to believe that James was still alive somewhere. But her heart hung heavy in her chest with the unspoken fear that he might truly be dead.

***

By the start of his second month of recovery, James regained some stamina. His legs no longer gave out when he tried to stand without the aid of the crutch, but he still required two naps a day. By now his appetite had come back completely.

"Emma, I'm getting stronger every day. I think 'tis time we switched—let me sleep on the floor and you get your bed back."

"I don't mind the floor, and you're not yet healed."

"Just a few days more, then I insist you return to your bed. I see that you keep a hatchet next to the pallet. Are you afraid of me?"

"You? 'Course not. There's bad people in these parts. You ran into some of them a month or so ago. Remember?"

He accepted her answer but still wondered about the hatchet.

After the noon dishes were cleared, he brought the children to the kitchen table and using the sole book in the cabin, a dusty old Bible, he began to read to them stories from the Old Testament. The passages seemed to cast a magic spell on the children, perhaps lifting them out of the drudgery of their lives. They especially liked the story of David and Goliath, and begged for him to re-read it on a regular basis.

"I bet I could hit Goliath with a rock, too," boasted Tommy one day.

"Yer just braggin', that's all," quipped Samantha.

"Well, I can knock a 'coon out of a tree."

"I bet you're a great hunter, Tommy." James smiled. Tommy beamed.

After the stories, the children would scramble outside and James would follow, albeit at a slower pace, and begin to scratch letters for them in the dirt. Within a few days each could write their name.

He saw Emma watching them from a distance with somewhat of a scowl on her face. He suspected she was either jealous of what the children were learning or angry that he should be doing more than

Cut From Strong Cloth

teaching the children their letters.

Through the next week as he convalesced at the Walker cabin, he started planning how he would get back to Savannah and then home to Philadelphia. *Just got to get my strength back.* He had told the Walker family how he was an Irishman who had landed in Philadelphia, worked in cloth, and had come to Savannah on cotton business. By now, the children called him, James.

One afternoon he decided to broach the subject to Emma about him leaving.

"Emma, 'tis hot out there today. I came in for a glass of water."

She went over to the jug by the crude sink and he saw her look around for a cup.

"You know I canna be staying much longer," he said. "Is there a chance I could send a letter home to alert them of what has happened to me?"

"No post out here, I don't get no letters."

She turned her back to him, but he thought she might be pouring his drink. He could not see that she kept a small vial hidden in her apron pocket. Then she went over to the honey jar and scooped out a generous spoonful of the amber sweet substance.

"Here James, I've added some wild honey to sweeten the well water."

He sat down, accepted the cup, and drank it empty. A few minutes later he got up from the chair.

"Must be the heat. I'm a bit tired. Think I'll rest a while."

The rest turned into another two-hour nap.

Emma continued to slip a potent drop of distilled mandrake into his daily beverage. Stirring in the wild honey, she camouflaged any possible bitter taste, and it kept him drowsy enough so he had energy for interacting with the children, but not enough to leave the farm.

CHAPTER 19

March 1861

On a warm March day, Dr. Fallon announced that he wanted to go explore further along the Ogeechee Road. He felt certain the Selma woman lived out in the area referred to as Old Canoochee. Ellen insisted once more on going along, and soon the team of sorrel horses was pulling the wagon out of town.

"Ellen, why don't you tell me more about this business idea of yours?" Dr. Fallon asked as the buckboard rumbled down the road. "I'd like to hear the details."

"I read about this Englishman, Thomas Burberry, who experimented with mixing together different types of fibers to produce a fabric better suited for outdoor wear. I thought that we could combine wool and cotton to produce a superior cloth that wouldn't fall apart once it got wet. Patrick and James decided to go forward with my idea and so we'll be manufacturing a blended cloth, possibly military uniforms.

"Once we have acquired the first profit, I want to start my own small business with my own loom. 'Tis a gamble, I know, but I want to have my own independence with making and selling textiles."

"Quite ambitious of you. Although I hope you'll find additional uses for the cloth, and not just designate your business for military textiles."

They continued driving further and further out along the Ogeechee Road, stopping at every farm house, shack or cabin to ask about a healing woman named Selma. No one seemed ready to give up any information.

When they were almost seven miles from the city, Dr. Fallon peered down the road and said, "I don't see any houses in the distance. Perhaps we should turn back here and search again another day."

"Okay. All I can see is an old tree with a broken swing. Nothing else." Ellen let out a deep sigh.

***

James decided it was time for him to return to Philadelphia. He had searched in vain for some paper in the Walker cabin on which he could write at least a note back to Philadalphia, but found none. He wanted to be done with this place now.

"Emma, you know I canna be staying any longer."

He saw her jaw clenched along with the hard set of her mouth. "Yes, I know you want to get back to your factory. But you'll have to trust me in what's best for you. You're not strong enough yet to make the travel."

"I am still tired every day. By now I should be back to normal."

"Some people heal fast, others don't. Your body's just taking longer, that's all. You'll leave when the time is right."

A few days later Emily knocked over his cup of morning tea. Emma flew into a rage.

"You stupid child! Now look what you've done!"

"Emma, 'tis only a cup of tea," James admonished, and then saw the fury in her eyes.

"All food's precious here, and no child of mine will be wasteful." Without warning she slapped Emily across the face, and the frightened child began to whimper.

"Emma, that wasn't necessary. She dinna do it on purpose, and I can do without tea for today."

Emma looked like she might protest, but then just shrugged.

"Clean up this mess," she demanded of her tearful daughter.

That day James found he didn't need much of a nap, and later in the afternoon felt some energy for the first time since he had been at the cabin. What had changed all of a sudden? Then he realized it had been a day without any tea.

He decided to decline tea the next day, too, and Emma became visibly upset with his decision.

"James, the tea I brew is good for you. You need it to speed your healing."

"Maybe tomorrow. I just need a break from it for a while."

"I don't think it's good for you to skip the tea. Here, I'm making more."

"Emma, I don't want any tea. I'm tired of it."

"You'll do as I say!"

"I'm not one of your children who can be ordered around. I'm staying off the tea for a day or two."

She stormed out of the cabin.

That afternoon, after he helped the children with their reading, he walked outside and began to look towards the road, trying to figure out which direction was north—the way back to Savannah. Judging by the position of the sun, he could easily figure out east and west; then he calculated north. The full moon which had occurred while he sojourned here made him suspect that more than one month had passed.

I've got to get away from here now, as soon as possible.

***

He watched Emma planting her second crop of spring potatoes. It has to be the middle of March by now, just when all the St. Patrick's Day festivities would be starting back home.

"Are you admiring my straight rows of seedlings?"

"Aye, I am. You work hard here, Emma."

"You know, there's no reason you have to leave. I could use a good strong hand around here, and once you've healed, you could stay on. I'd make it worth your while. I can clean up real good, if there's a

man around."

He felt a shiver run up his spine with the thought of becoming Emma Walker's lifelong inmate.

"I dunno, Emma. I have many people back home who work in my factory. They would lose their jobs if I don't return, and there's another woman in my life. Her name is Ellen."

She ignored the comment.

"It's not fair, me being left to work this miserable land by myself. Men always seem to be leavin' me. You know, I once knowed a woman who got herself knocked up with child. The babe's father was going to leave her for another woman, so she killed him. They never did find his body."

She didn't bother to look at James as she walked off. Her message rang clear.

Jesus Christ. Drugging me might be just the beginning. James decided he would need to leave that very night.

Once everyone had climbed into bed, he feigned sleep but willed himself to stay awake. A few hours later the light from a crescent moon peeking in the window helped him see around the cabin. Emma snored on the pallet next to his bed. He took care to ease himself up, trying not to make the old rope bed creak. Glancing down he saw a strip of burlap tied to each of his boots, and the other end to Emma; an obvious alert if he moved his boots in the middle of the night.

Shifting his weight to the side, he swung his legs over the frame and bent down, carefully untying the fabric strap from his boots while listening to her snore. Looking over at the children, he saw that all three were deep in sleep. Then with an agility born from desperation, he picked up his boots and avoiding the parts of the cabin flooring that squeaked, began his memorized dog-leg path to the cabin door.

He heard someone shift in their sleep and he held his breath, hoping no one would wake. Young Emily must have been dreaming, and whatever had caused her to stir now caused her to fall back asleep. He looked over at Emma. Had she noticed? Her body remained still as stone, so he moved his feet one at a time, closer to the door. He dared himself not to breathe as he grabbed his crutch, reached the latch and quietly lifted it, then slipped out into the night.

The cool spring night air refreshed him as he put on his boots and headed straight for the road. Using the moon as his guide, he turned north on the Ogeechee Road and limped-ran as fast as he could to get away from the Walker cabin and the woman who would have become his jailer.

A mile or so down the road he slowed to a fast walk, his weaker leg giving him an achy reminder that he was not the same virile man he had been at Christmas. Remorse for Emma's children tugged at his heart, but he couldn't change their lives, and desperation for his own survival drove him onward. By watching the moon rise in the night sky, he kept some track of time and figured he could keep to a rate of at least two miles an hour. For the first time in decades he whispered a prayer. *Dear God, please let me make it back to Savannah.*

Vulnerable out in the open, and with his muscles in the wounded leg throbbing, he still felt a surge of power from taking back his freedom. A barn owl called to him from an overhead branch, and he whistled back to the nocturnal watchman witnessing his escape.

He tried to keep a steady pace so he wouldn't become chilled and wished he had grabbed one of Emma's shawls for warmth. But then a thought surfaced from long ago when he had taken something that had not belonged to him, and the dire consequences of that act still reverberated in his soul.

Periodic bursts of wild forsythia added spots of color by the side of the road, and spring peepers serenaded his journey, but no human crossed his path. As the first lights of dawn flushed the sky pink, he reached the outskirts of Savannah.

***

When he made it to Bryan Street, he limped into the Planters Hotel and asked the clerk if he could rent a certain room where he had stayed before, number twenty-four.

The clerk looked at James' unkempt clothes and ragged hair. "Yeah, that room's vacant, but you'll have to pay in advance. You got

Cut From Strong Cloth

cash? We don't let rooms on credit."

"Just let me check in, and I promise you that I should be able to pay for the room within half an hour. If not, then you can throw me out."

"Okay, Mister, but thirty minutes is all." The clerk took out a pocket watch and checked the time for emphasis.

"Much obliged," James said, and then climbed up the stairs, holding the railing to steady his shaky legs. As soon as he entered the room and closed the door, he went over to the corner wash stand and moved it away. Next he lowered himself down on his knees and pried up a loose corner of an oaken floor board. Reaching under the floor, he retrieved a small leather bag.

Relief flooded his face as he opened the bag and found his cash still intact. Although he had brought enough for the two week trip, he had also had the forethought to hide most of the money when he and Patrick had gone out celebrating. He'd taken a small amount with him to the saloon. Although his valise no longer rested in the corner, he hoped Patrick had retrieved it. What had happened to Patrick?

He splashed water on his face, walked back downstairs, and paid the astonished clerk in cash for the room, well under the thirty-minute timeframe. Then he retreated back upstairs and stretched out on the bed. The escape had completely exhausted him. Within moments, sleep claimed him still dressed in his clothes.

***

While James slept at the hotel, Ellen joined Magdalena for a post-St. Patrick's Day meal of corned beef and cabbage at a local inn. "Magdalena, did you see the parade on Broughton Street? I looked for you yesterday."

"Of course I saw the parade—well part of it, anyway. March 17th is the anniversary of John's death, so I always watch a bit of the parade and then go to the burial grounds to visit his grave. I place a small stone on his marker and stay to say some prayers. He died four years ago, but sometimes it feels like I lost him just yesterday."

"I'm sorry, I dinna mean to bring up sad memories."

"That's all right, Ellen. You couldn't have known. Let's change the subject, shall we? Have you decided how long you'll be staying in Savannah?"

"Until I either find James or at least find out what happened. I thought Dr. Fallon had discovered a clue, but it turned out to be a dead end. I keep checking the hospital and even St. John's church, but I've gotten no new information."

"Tell me then, what's James like?"

"He's older than me and a fine-looking man. Reserved when you first meet him, but put him around his nieces and nephews and he softens."

"Does he have a sense of humor?"

"Oh, not like Patrick. James does have a temper, though, just like Patrick. But James also broods over things. I've watched him from afar, and I sense that sometimes there is a terrible sadness about him."

"Patrick has a temper?"

"Just a wee small one. Patrick may blow up over something, but he's back to his smiling self in no time."

"Is James Catholic?"

"Of course he's Catholic, but he doesn't go to church."

"Have you pledged yourselves to each other?"

"No. Our relationship is mostly business, but personal in a way, too."

Magdalena cocked her head. "I thought it was more than just business for you."

Ellen blushed and smiled, both at the same time.

"I'm sorry you haven't found him. But had they not been bush-whacked, I may never have met Patrick."

"Magdalena, I'm glad for you and Patrick. I am. But I need to ask something. How serious are you about my brother?"

"Ellen, before I reply to that, first there is something you should know about me."

"What?"

"I'm Jewish."

Ellen felt a moment of pause. Was Magdalena playing a joke?

Not sure what to say, Ellen composed herself.

"Really? Does Patrick know?"

"Yes. It is part of the reason he left for Philadelphia. He needed to check on your mother and the factory; but he also went home to tell your mother about me—the fact that I'm Jewish and we intend to live as husband and wife."

Ellen didn't know how to react. She had assumed that Patrick and Magdalena were serious about each other, and she didn't really have a problem with other religions. But no one in her family, or entire neighborhood, had ever married outside the church. Everyone she knew went to St. Michael's, except for Catherine Biddle.

"Does this bother you?"

"No, it's just that I've never known anyone Jewish, that's all."

"Yes you have," Magdalena smiled. "Dr. Fallon is Jewish, too."

Ellen's jaw opened in surprise. "What? Are you sure?"

"Yes, quite sure. Dr. Fallon is the reason I stayed on in Savannah after John and my parents died. As pharmacists, my parents counted many doctors among their friends. Dr. Fallon's aunt suggested I take my parents' place in the pharmacy. I had no one else, so Dr. Fallon's extended family became my adopted family."

"Magdalena, why didn't you tell me this before? This changes everything."

"Why? You must have suspected by now that Patrick and I are a couple. The only difference is, now you know I'm not Catholic."

"But you can never be married in a Catholic church, and how will Mam ever cope with news like this?"

"We know that neither a priest nor a rabbi will marry us, but a judge can. It doesn't matter to Patrick or me that we are of different faiths. All that matters is that we want to be together for the rest of our lives."

"But what about children, and where will you live? You canna live in Kensington among all the Irish Catholics! Oh, Mam would die if Patrick were to move away."

"We won't be moving anywhere. We'll find a neighborhood in Philadelphia where people are tolerant of different faiths. As for children, they can be raised Catholic. But they would still be Jewish because I

am Jewish. In Judaism, the lineage is passed through the mother."

"Magdalena, I don't know what to say."

"I know this is a big surprise for you, but I hope it does not change our friendship."

"Of course not. If it doesn't matter to Patrick, then it doesn't matter to me. But Magdalena, I don't know of any neighborhood in Philadelphia where people of different faiths marry and live. And I doubt any Catholics would be welcoming Jews into our neighborhood. Do you understand what type of life you'd have?"

"I didn't say it would be easy, Ellen. But Patrick and I will make it work. I'm used to sticking up for myself and my family background."

"If you're willing to leave everything you have ever known and move north among people who are not your kind, then I think you are very brave, Magdalena, and very much in love with my brother."

"I do love him, Ellen, with all my heart. Here, I don't think he'll mind if you read his latest letter." Reaching into her pocket, Magdalena passed it to Ellen.

Ellen opened the stationery and felt a quickening of her heart when she saw Patrick's handwriting. Had it only been two months since she had seen him?

My Dearest Magdalena,

Mam continues to ask more questions about you every day. I have already told her how your parents were pharmacists, although Mam would call them chemists. She wants to know what Savannah is like. 'Are there many Irish there', she asks and of course, I have to explain that there is a large Irish section. I think she would love Savannah, but I don't see her ever traveling south. I am still surprised she let Ellen return.

I'm happy to hear that you and Ellen have become friends. Tell her I read that Lincoln has refused to meet with any of the ambassadors of the Confederacy, so he won't have to validate them as having left the Union. Also, there are rumors that he is talking about sending additional troops to Fort Sumter, which you know is in Charleston Harbor. Magdalena, if anything serious should happen in Savannah—leave for Philadel-

phia immediately.

I know we talked about reuniting by the start of summer, but I do not want you in any danger. Much military activity is occurring here in Philadelphia as talk of volunteering is on everybody's lips. I count the days and hours until we can be together again. Don't worry about me; I won't volunteer for anything, except being your husband.

Love,
Patrick

Ellen felt a pang of loss after reading the letter, and she did not know why. She realized that life in the Canavan household would never be the same again, now that Patrick had chosen to marry. She wished Catherine Biddle could be with her, so they could talk. How would Catherine react to Patrick marrying a Jewish woman? But then she already knew the answer: there is that of God in everyone.

So Patrick would be getting married. She fingered the brooch Mam had given her, attached to the bodice of her dress. God willing, she would have a daughter to pass it on to. She smiled at the thought of possibly having children with James as the father.

***

Savannah had changed Ellen. Regardless of what Mam wanted, or even what Patrick might have in mind, she knew her world could no longer be confined to the boundaries of Kensington. She intended to grab the horns of success and make a name for herself. Her eyes had been opened to both the good and the bad. She still shuddered when a line of manacled slaves marched through the Savannah streets, but she was determined to succeed and use that success to help other people as well. Hopefully, Catherine Biddle would give her some ideas of how to help the abolitionist cause with certain textiles.

Today she decided to pay a return visit to cotton factor Alexander Francis. Pushing open the door to his office vestibule, she found herself caught off guard to see him talking with Nash Finch.

"Why, hello, Miss Canavan. I heard you had returned to Savannah, so it is nice to see you again. Have you met Mr. Nash Finch, our shipping agent?"

"Ellen, how delightful to see you again—so soon." Nash grinned at her uncomfortable gaze.

"Yes, Mr. Francis, Mr. Finch and I are acquainted, thank you." Ellen replied in a tight voice.

"You see, Alexander," Nash said, "Ellen does not condone certain economic practices here in Savannah, and we had a rather large disagreement over the matter." Then he turned to face Ellen. "When you left in haste the other day, you did not give me time to explain my background on the situation."

"I am not concerned with your background, Mr. Finch. What matters is that we have an impasse regarding our opinions about slavery." *There, I've said what's on my mind.*

The men did not respond, and Ellen wondered if she had crossed some invisible line.

"You might be interested to learn that Mr. Finch's family is not from the South, but from Maryland," Mr. Francis announced.

"You're a Northerner?" Ellen shot a surprised look back at Nash.

"Not completely. My father's family was from Annapolis, and my mother's family, the Bedwell's, was English aristocracy. Unfortunately my grandfather disowned my mother when she wed my father, an American. I guess you could say that I am part British, part American, and full-time Southerner. I still have cousins who work in the Annapolis shipyards."

"I had no idea, Mr. Finch, of your complicated past."

"It's fortuitous for you and your brother that I still have connections in Maryland. My ships are not being stopped as they sail, while other boats are being detained in port. That means you'll receive your precious cotton." He winked at her.

"That is very comforting, Mr. Finch, but it still doesn't change my feelings about slavery. I intend to make a profit with my business, but also to make a difference in peoples' lives. I came here today to make sure our shipments would not be detained, now that Georgia has

seceded. I did not expect to be seeing you again."

"I can assure you, the shipments will go through," Nash replied.

"Good day to you then, Gentlemen."

Once she left, Nash turned to Alexander Francis. "She's got spunk, that one." Nash said. "My money's on her succeeding in both endeavors."

***

James had been back in Savannah for a few days. He considered contacting the police about Emma Walker, but it would be his word against hers, and deep down he felt a measure of pity for her. If she were to be arrested, what would happen to the children? So he let the matter drop.

At the noon meal in the hotel dining room he couldn't help but notice an attractive young woman seated at the table next to him carrying on a conversation with another gentlemen. Seeing another young woman of Ellen's age made his heart quicken. It seemed like an eternity since he last held Ellen in his arms. Just thinking about Ellen produced a swelling in his loins and he quickly covered himself with his napkin.

"So you see, Uncle Harry, I hope all this silly talk about the possibility of war won't hurt Frank's cotton profits. I'm sure that the upriver plantations will not be affected."

"War can change many things, my dear, including family fortunes."

She looked up in time to notice that James appeared to be listening to the conversation.

"Why, suh, are you eavesdropping on us?" she smiled.

"Guilty as charged, I guess," James admitted with a grin. "My firm just purchased cotton a few months back from Mr. Alexander Francis, and I wondered whose plantation the cotton might come from."

"Your firm?" the uncle inquired.

"I am a textile merchant, but my firm is small. You wouldn't know it," answered James.

"You're not a Yankee, are you? Your voice is not a southern one."

"I'm from County Tyrone, in Ireland."

 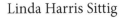

"See, Uncle Harry. Don't go ruining this man's dinner by calling him a Yankee. Successful textile merchants don't just pop into our lives." Then she turned toward James. "I'll be meeting my brother later today at Market Square. Perhaps you'd like to join me and meet him. Everyone 'round here knows Frank Dunne, and his reputation for producing fine cotton. The two of you could discuss his plantation production cycle and perhaps you could buy some of his cotton."

"Oh no, I wouldn't want to impose on your family."

"Suh, are you turning down a lady's request?"

"No. . . I guess not. I would be happy to be introduced to your brother and learn from him as much as I can."

"Then meet me back here at half past three, Mister. . . ?"

"Nolan. James Nolan."

With that he finished his meal, stood up and nodded at the couple, and left the room.

CHAPTER 20

MARCH/APRIL 1861

Easter came early, on the last weekend in March, and Holy Week coincided with the Jewish Passover. Dr. Fallon explained to Ellen about the Seder meal that he and his family would celebrate, and she decided to buy some flowers for the special occasion.

"I'm off, then," she called out to Dr. Fallon as she finished for the day. "I'll be stopping at City Market on my way home. Is there anything Sarah needs for tonight?"

"Thank you, Ellen, but I think the larder is set for the next few days. I'll see you at the Seder gathering."

Ellen took off the long apron she wore over her day dress and hung it on the wall peg. Leaving the infirmary, she walked out on State Street and turned north. She had sent her mother a letter talking about the work at Dr. Fallon's infirmary and ending with a note of relief that Patrick was back home safe. She did not feel the need to mention that Magdalena and Dr. Fallon were Jewish. She intended to let Patrick be the one to break that news.

As she walked up toward the river, thoughts ran through her mind of how much longer she would be able to stay. Magdalena must be anxious to join Patrick, and Ellen wanted to get back so she could start experimenting with the production of the new cloth. But without James, the excitement of her plan felt hollow. Being without him these last eight weeks had made her realize how empty life without him would be. It was as if he completed her in a way she had never felt before.

Holy Mary and St. Brigid, please let James be alive—wherever he might be.

As she reached Market Square, the sights and sounds were reminiscent of home with the various stalls filling up the market place. The mixed aromas of flowers, produce, baked goods and seafood competed together under the one large roof. Vendors called out special sales while butchers in blood-stained aprons haggled with customers and various black women offered sweet grass baskets for sale. There was vitality here, just like in the stalls in Kensington.

Amid the jumble of noise and activity, Ellen wistfully looked over at Miss Sally's, known for the scrumptious bakery items. She licked her lips as she anticipated the taste of fresh hot cross buns dripping with sugary icing for Easter and headed over to buy some.

Then she came to an abrupt halt.

On the other side of the market, gaily chatting with a woman, was James! Ellen felt her breath stop in her chest—he was alive! She balanced herself against a counter, her knees having turned to jelly. It took a full minute to regain her normal breathing and steady her wobbly legs. Her first instinct was to run to him, but she heard his laughter with the other woman and she suddenly felt immobilized. She was hidden by the stalls and could see him, but he could not see her. He seemed to be a tad thinner than before, but no worse for the wear.

My God, is this Michael all over again? How could I have been such a fool, believing that I was a special part of James' life? He practically told me he wanted to marry me and I believed him. Now I find him with another woman!

As Ellen watched, she saw the woman take a step, bob a bit, and James reach out his arm to steady her. Ellen's eyes narrowed as the woman began to openly flirt. All the pent-up anxiety about James' welfare drained from her body, along with any pity she was beginning to feel for herself. Those emotions were replaced with anger. How had he

Cut From Strong Cloth

managed to stay hidden in Savannah when so many people had been trying to find him? Perhaps he's living with this hussy? Was he starting a business with her now? Her heart thumped with fury.

Without thinking of the consequences, Ellen walked directly to him.

"Well, what have we here? The famous factory owner from Philadelphia due to return by early February?"

"Ellen! What in the world are you doing here?"

"I work here for a doctor. And from the looks of what I just saw, I can see you are quite at home in this city."

"Ellen, I was just joking with Miss Dunne about a funny incident that occurred this morning at the hotel."

"Really, James? I see nothing funny at all. Are you even aware that Patrick and others have been searching for you for months? That you have turned my life upside down with worry of what might have happened to you?"

"Ellen, 'tis a long story. But I can explain what happened to me, and how I just now got back to Savannah."

"I'm sure 'tis a long story, but I'm quite busy myself. In fact, I'm on my way home from work. I live at 64 W. Broad Street now."

Ellen turned to walk past him, but he grabbed her by the arm. His face now registered anger of his own.

"Not so fast. I can tell you're powerful upset about something. We need to talk this out before you go making a fool of yourself."

"What you need to do, sir, is to take your hand off my arm. A true gentleman never grabs a lady." What she really wanted to do was slap him in the face, but she fought that urge. Instead, she jerked her arm away and strode across the square without looking back. Tears streamed down her face, but pride and determination kept her walking ahead.

James stood in the square with a puzzled look on his face. Then he glanced over at the woman next to him.

"I'm sorry, she usually isn't like that. Rude, I mean. I've never seen her act that way before."

"It is obvious, Mr. Nolan, that she thinks you and I are well acquainted. You didn't mention to me that you were already spoken for. You would be best to let her cool down and then go over to that address

with some flowers."

By the time Ellen arrived at Dr. Fallon's she had convinced herself that James had been living in disguise these many weeks; even if he had been robbed and beaten in late January. That woman in the market certainly seemed to know him well. She felt humiliated. What was wrong with her that she could not see the truth about men? She needed to get back to Philadelphia and get on with her life as soon as possible, and find a more reliable sponsor than James Nolan. She could not admit to herself that she had allowed her heart to be broken again.

No one else seemed to be around, so she went straight to her room, sat on the bed, and dissolved into sobs. She wanted James to come and take her in his arms and explain that it was all a mistake, that he loved her and only her. But she knew that would not happen. Her face became swollen with all the crying and her body trembled from the weeping of heartache. She cried forcibly for a good twenty minutes until she was spent. Then she forced herself to get up and wash her tear-stained face. She needed to start making plans about returning home to a life without James.

***

As departure plans flew through Ellen's mind, James walked over to West Broad with the number 64 written on a scrap of paper, and a bouquet of flowers in his hand. He arrived at the house and felt a stab of emotion halfway between foolishness and irritation.

My God, if she had just let me explain back there in the square. She could at least have some sympathy for all I've gone through.

He climbed up the steps and knocked at the door. When a maid answered, he announced he needed to speak with Ellen Canavan. The woman beckoned him inside and a few moments later a lady entered the foyer and addressed him.

"Good day, Sir. I am Mrs. Fallon. I understand you are here to see Miss Canavan?"

"Aye, I need to talk to her right away."

"And your name, sir?"

"James Nolan. She knows me."

The woman's face registered surprise, but she nodded. "Please wait here a moment." Sarah Fallon climbed the stairs and knocked on Ellen's door. "There's a man downstairs claiming to be James Nolan."

Ellen opened her door, her eyes hopeful. But then her stubborn streak took over her emotions. "Tell him to go away. I have no wish to speak to him."

"Ellen, is this the man you've been searching for?"

"Aye, but it seems he's been here all along. I no longer trust him."

"Are you sure?"

"I saw him with another woman in the market this afternoon. He was holding her elbow."

"Her elbow? For goodness sake, that doesn't mean anything in Savannah. I think you should go downstairs and talk to him. You might both owe each other some explanations."

Ellen shrugged but got up and descended the stairs. She reached the bottom of the stairs and simply stared at James.

"Before you go and say or do something we will both regret, let me tell you that I have only been in Savannah a few days. The woman you saw me speaking to, her family owns a cotton plantation nearby. There is nothing between us."

Then before she could shoot a volley back, he continued. "I was beaten and left for dead back in January. A poor family who lives on a farm several miles outside Savannah found me and nursed me back to life. I sent you a telegram as soon as I got back to Savannah. Of course I sent it to Philadelphia. Never did I dream that you'd be here."

"How do I know you're telling the truth?"

"I had a very different reunion planned for us. That is the truth, Ellen."

"You sound sincere, James. But I've heard mock sincerity before, from someone else."

"Good God. I hope you're not comparing me to that Brady fellow. That would be an insult and make me think I might have misjudged you."

"Misjudged me! I'm not the one defending myself, now am I?

I trusted you James, and I was so sure you'd write if anything delayed your return."

"Listen to me. I couldn't write. Hell, I couldn't even get out of bed for weeks, and when I started to get better, they. . . she. . . drugged me to keep me on the farm."

"Drugged you? That's a pretty strong accusation. Why would anyone do that?"

"I told you, the woman wanted me to stay."

"Oh, so at least two women here in Savannah have been able to detain you. First some woman on a farm, then this hussy in the market place today. It all sounds pretty farfetched to me."

"Farfetched? Why in God's name would I be lying?"

"To cover for where you've been for eight weeks."

"So you kept count on how long I went missing?"

"We all did." Then her voice cracked. The embedded fear of the last two months broke with a flood of tears.

"Ellen, why did you come back to Savannah?"

"I came back to find you." She tried without success to choke back her sobs.

He crossed the floor, took her in his arms, and kissed her full on the mouth with an embrace of deep and passionate love. Then he held her in his arms. Neither of them spoke for a few minutes.

"When I thought I was dying, I only wanted to see you one more time." He pulled her closer and let her head fall against his chest. He hummed her favorite tune and stroked her hair.

She stopped crying and turned to him. "My greatest fear was that I would never see you again, or be with you. I was so afraid I had lost you forever."

"Hush." He placed his fingers over her lips. "We're together again, that's all that matters."

***

Later as James and Ellen sat down as guests at the Seder, Dr. Fallon took time to explain the significance of the dinner to them. Ellen

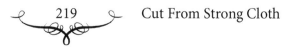

mused that the importance of family and traditions were as important to Jews as they were to Catholics. She was reminded once again of Catherine's words, *that of God in everyone.*

After the meal James turned to Ellen, "The weather is still nice. Why don't you and I take a walk?"

"Just stick to this neighborhood and stay on the side of the street with gas lights," Dr. Fallon interjected. "No telling what hoodlums might be using secession as a rationale for violence."

"We'll be careful, Dr. Fallon." Now that she and James had reconnected, she felt safe.

Once outside, James put his arm around her shoulders. "So, why don't we begin with you telling me how you came back to Savannah?"

"Dr. Fallon and my mother were acquainted back in Philadelphia. I accompanied Sarah Fallon's mother back down here. The Fallons have let me stay as their guest and I decided to work in Dr. Fallon's infirmary so I could be in the city and look for you and Patrick.

"I should also tell you about Magdalena."

"Who's that?"

"She's the one who found Patrick lying by the side of the road after the beating. It seems that while Patrick stayed in Savannah looking for you, he fell in love with Magdalena. They plan to marry. And I should tell you that Magdalena is also Jewish, just like the Fallons."

Before he had a chance to answer, two shadowy figures stepped out from a darkened alley. Ellen felt her heart skip in fright, as James' body went rigid. The two men however just tipped their hats to the couple and continued a zigzag path through to a different alley across the street.

James exhaled a big breath of air.

"Were you scared?"

"Aye, for a moment. The memory of my attack is still pretty clear. Perhaps we should heed Dr. Fallon's words and stick to the main streets, away from any nearby alleys."

Ellen nodded.

"James, can you stay in Savannah a bit longer? It would be nice to have some time together. I can finish up helping Dr. Fallon, and you

could check on some possible future cotton contacts. Then we'll make our way back to Philadelphia and get on with our lives."

As an answer, he took her in his arms and kissed her with unbridled passion under a sweet-smelling spring breeze of wisteria and azalea blossoms.

***

After Easter weekend, Ellen invited Magdalena to come meet James, and he instantly saw the attraction Patrick had discovered. While her smile did light up a room, it was Magdalena's vibrant personality and wit that gave her certain flair.

Dr. Fallon suggested that Ellen cut back on her hours so that she and James could spend more time together. They decided to meet each day at 3:00 p.m. and explore more sections of Savannah, but always getting Ellen home before dark when the streets could possibly become more dangerous.

"Let's start by visiting some more squares today, James. I have a few favorites and bits of history to share along the way. I've been all over the city with Magdalena, and she's the one who explained the importance of many of the landmarks to me." They walked down the street, her arm linked with his.

"All right. You're the leader today. May I say, I've noticed your new brooch? 'Tis pretty."

"Mam gave it to me as a good luck charm to wear in Georgia. I've been wearing it ever since I arrived. Here, James, take a look at it. It belonged to Mam's mother and grandmother. Did you know that Mam was an O'Neill?"

"From *the* O'Neills? Dinna know she came from such a famous clan." James looked carefully at the brooch. 'Tis beautiful workmanship, and I'm sure it already brought you luck. After all, we've been reunited." He smiled.

"James, I have an idea. Let's dispense with the squares for today and make a visit to St. John's instead. The pastor there is Father O'Neill. Would that be all right?"

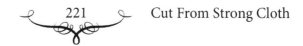

Cut From Strong Cloth

"Another O'Neill? Is he a relative of yours?"

"No, not at all. I like going there because most of the parishioners are Irish. It reminds me of home."

They made their way west along East Perry until they arrived at the church. Together they walked inside, went to a pew, made the sign of the cross, and then knelt to offer prayers. James took a moment to look around, admiring the impressive stained glass windows, statuary, and prayer alcoves. When Ellen finally stood up, so did he. They both genuflected once more, and then retreated outside.

"Did you make your three wishes?"

"My three what?"

"Mam always told Patrick and me that whenever you visit a new church for the first time, you are entitled to make three wishes, and the angels will listen to your petitions. Did you make any wishes?"

"I canna say I ever heard that custom, so I dinna make any."

"We could go back, and let you re-enter the building."

"I'll save my three wishes for another time. I promise."

"All right. Here, up ahead is my favorite square. This one is Chippewa, and the Savannah Theater is located nearby."

"I thought we were done with squares for the day?"

"So you are paying attention to what I say?"

"Only when it benefits me." A mischievous smile spread across his face. "Ellen, there is something I would like to talk about."

"What would that be?"

"I'd like you to consider the idea of letting me take care of you once we are back home in Philadelphia."

"Take care of me? How?"

"I could provide for you so that you would not need to work, anywhere. I could give you a life of leisure."

Ellen's face drained itself of color. She waited before answering.

"James, you know how much I deeply care about you. When I thought you might be dead, my whole body felt empty at the prospect of life without you. But, please do not ask me to choose between you and my dream of starting my business. 'Tis not a fair request."

Now James' face drained of color. "Are you telling me that be-

cause you are choosing business over me?"

"Don't force me to make a choice."

"Will I ever be your priority?"

"Just help me get my business started; then I can concentrate on my life with you."

There's no reason why I canna have both—James and the business.

***

As Ellen prepared to leave for the infirmary the next morning, Dr. Fallon asked her to join him in his carriage. He dismissed the driver and took hold of the reins himself. Ellen looked perplexed.

"I have a private matter to discuss with you," he said as the sorrel horses pulled away from West Broad and turned east. "Ellen, I have watched how you work in the infirmary and I believe you have a gift of working with people."

"Thank you."

"I want to help in your quest to start a business. When you are ready, may I provide you with a loan that will allow you to purchase the needed equipment?"

Ellen found herself at a loss of what to say. "Dr. Fallon, I'm touched by your generous offer."

"Then say yes. It will be a good business decision for both of us. I know you will succeed, and I'll write out an I.O.U. without a due date. I'll loan you the money at a low interest, and you'll repay it when you can. We'll both profit from working together."

"Dr. Fallon, I canna thank you enough. But I've not been able to open a bank account on my own. The bank in Kensington refused me because I am a single female with no male family member to co-sign for me. I don't want Patrick involved. Without an account, I don't know how your loan could be dispensed."

"I still have many contacts in Philadelphia, including a good friend who is a banker. If you agree, I'll see to it that he allows you to open an account in his bank on Chestnut Street. Neither Patrick nor James Nolan needs be involved."

"Now I am truly indebted to you, Dr. Fallon."

"Should we shake hands on our deal?"

Under a cobalt blue sky with the tang of salt in the air, Ellen sealed her first business loan by shaking hands with a man she had come to deeply admire. She felt exhilarated with the prospect of knowing she could now open a bank account, but with just a twinge of guilt that she was excluding James in this endeavor.

***

A week later, Ellen woke earlier than usual as a mockingbird welcomed the dawn outside her window. With streaks of mauve and pink just beginning to color the sky, she tunneled back under the covers. Later the sound of a gunshot bolted her awake. She peered out the side window and saw a large crowd of people dancing and singing in the street. Then all the church bells in Savannah began to ring. She dressed quickly and dashed downstairs. Sarah Fallon stood stock still at the bottom of the staircase.

"Did you hear the shot, Ellen?"

"Aye, I heard it. What's happening?"

"Louis went out to investigate. Someone told him that Fort Sumter was fired upon very early this morning in Charleston Harbor. Apparently the Federal soldiers retaliated by shooting back, and a cannon volley was started. This is serious, Ellen, it means the Confederacy will probably go to war. I don't think it would be safe for you to go to the infirmary this morning, not with the type of crowds that will be swarming."

"Fort Sumter attacked? But that's in Charleston, not Savannah."

"It's a federal fort, Ellen; federal property that lies within the South and therefore stands as a symbol of Northern authority to every Southerner. Louis feared that something along these lines might happen."

Outside people began to chant, "Long live the South!"

"Sarah, how do you feel about all of this? You're from Philadelphia, like me."

"Yes, but I was born in Ashland, Virginia. We moved to Phila-

delphia when I was quite young, and Daddy had been offered a position with the bank. After his death, Mother and I stayed."

"Did you have slaves?"

"No. And neither Louis nor I condone the practice of slavery. That is why we hire free people of color to work for us."

"I'm glad to hear that, Sarah. I was not prepared for seeing the humiliation of slavery so up close here in Savannah."

"I still believe, though, that the government does not have the right to step in and tell a state how it should operate. What if Lincoln outlawed all textile factories in the North because working conditions were hazardous? How do you think the Northern states would react?"

"But Sarah, Lincoln's not trying to outlaw slavery. He just doesn't want to see it spread to new states and territories. I think he's content to allow the South to continue their way of life."

"I'm not so sure, Ellen."

"Have you become a complete Southern sympathizer, then?"

"I believe the term is 'copperhead'—someone from the North who sympathizes with the South, but hopes to avoid war."

Just then the front door opened, and Dr. Fallon rushed back in.

"All the riffraff in Savannah are rubbing elbows with decent folk out in the streets. The crowds are feverish with southern patriotism."

A moment later, an insistent knock sounded at the front door, and in came James with Magdalena.

"Thank God you're safe. As soon as I heard the news at the hotel I left to come here. Then I ran into Magdalena." James caught his breath.

"This is serious," Dr. Fallon stipulated. "The firing on Fort Sumter changes everything. You and Ellen need to plan your return journey as soon as possible now. I'll look into getting you traveling accommodations, and hopefully we can get you on your way in a day or two. I'm afraid you'd no longer be safe in my house."

Ellen gulped.

"Dr. Fallon, you've been so kind to both of us, and I will always be in your debt for your hospitality and assistance. But we're not the only ones who need to get back North. Magdalena needs to get to Phil-

adelphia as well; she must be reunited with Patrick."

Dr. Fallon turned to Magdalena. "Are you trying to tell me that you and Patrick have promised yourselves to each other?

"We have."

"Then the three of you will be traveling to Philadelphia together?" He sighed deeply. "There's talk at my club that Lincoln might issue a blockade of all Southern ports. If that occurs, you'll not be able to return by steamship, so the other choice would have to be by train. Journeying that way could be dangerous. If the other travelers realize that two of you are Northerners, all your lives could be at risk."

Ellen's heart raced. "Dr. Fallon, what if we, meaning Magdalena and I, travel as private nurses? We could each carry a medical kit, and James could be a recovering patient. That way we might not arouse so much suspicion."

"It will still be dangerous going through Confederate lands, but I could provide you with a letter stating that you've been in my employ and are transporting a patient further north for additional treatment. I have a friend from medical college, Dr. Philip Jackson, who now has a practice in Fredericksburg, Virginia. You'll go there and seek him out, carrying two letters. The first one will be official, in case you're stopped. The other one will be sewn into Ellen's hem and given only to Dr. Jackson. I hope he'll be able to help you."

"God bless you, Dr. Fallon." Ellen ran over and hugged him.

"What I am is a Confederate surgeon helping two Northerners escape and take a Southern defector with them. God help me." He sighed. "If you are stopped, use the medical bags as proof of your mission. Without any quinine, no one will rob you. The two letters should help."

He smiled encouragingly at the trio. Magdalena gave a small smile, James nodded his head in appreciation, and Ellen tried to quiet the fear escalating in her heart.

***

Magdalena and Ellen spent the next two days selecting what clothes they could carry.

"Look, Ellen, this is the dress I wore when I married John. I hope he would forgive me, leaving it behind."

Ellen walked over and gave Magdalena a hug. "Are you as scared as I am? I know we put up a brave front for Dr. Fallon, but what if we are discovered on the trip north? I have heard that they hang spies, even women spies."

"We are not spies. We are nurses honestly taking a patient further north for better care."

"I wish I was as cool as you, Magdalena."

"You'll act the part once we're on the trains. I have faith in you. Right now I have to make some painful decisions of what to put in storage and what I will need to sell."

By the end of the day, Magdalena filled three trunks with her most prized possessions, including family silver, fine china, lovely woven linens, and the painted portraits of her parents. She would store the trunks at Dr. Fallon's house and have them shipped to Philadelphia once the nation settled back into peace. Her furniture and household goods would eventually go to auction, and Dr. Fallon would oversee the selling of her home on Marshall Row.

By nightfall, both women had sorted through everything and packed only the few clothes necessary for the trip.

***

Three days later Dr. and Sarah Fallon, plus the three passengers, walked the few blocks to the Savannah train station. The crowded Monday morning street scene of ladies in spring frocks carrying parasols against the sun and men in fine morning coats strolling through the streets made Ellen wince when she wondered how Savannah might eventually change with war. Even though she had walked past this station before, she now took a moment to look at its fine red brick front and nine double hung windows on the top matching similar windows below.

She wanted to remember this as the last sight of Savannah because only God knew if she would ever return. When Ellen went to kiss Dr. Fallon good-bye, silent tears flowed down her cheeks. Words would

 Cut From Strong Cloth

never be able to convey the deep gratitude and love she felt toward him. Both Fallons held her in a tight embrace and bid her a safe journey, promising they would see her again. Dr. Fallon bent to give Ellen one last hug and whispered in her ear, "I will still provide the loan."

They went inside the terminal and located the track for their train. Ellen scrutinized the rail cars with some trepidation. She had never ridden on a train before, and now she was fleeing on one. The exterior wood paneling of a smoky yellow pine with the words *Charleston and Savannah* painted in bold black script along the sides intimidated her just a bit. Would they be able to pull off this escape?

Sarah Fallon blew a kiss to the trio, and Dr. Fallon tipped his hat to them, looking for all intents and purposes as saying good-bye to special guests.

As the travelers approached their chosen car, a porter placed a small stepstool down on the platform for the women to climb on and James maneuvered his injured leg, and then swung their valises up the steps.

He told Ellen and Magdalena to find two rows where the seats could turn to face one another in the center of the car where less soot would swirl through the air. As the women walked toward the middle, he saw Ellen stroke the top of a gleaming red leather seat, a luxury compared to the plain wooden seats of Philadelphia omnibuses. They found two rows of facing seats and sat together, giving James the full length of the opposite row to stretch out his achy leg.

Once seated, Ellen looked out the window to see both Dr. Fallon and Sarah still standing near the platform. She detected shared looks of nostalgia laced with threads of despair as they waited for the train to depart. Ellen realized then that the Fallons were more than just her friends; they were like family. She brushed away tears.

The engines started, and Ellen took a deep breath because she was not only coming home with James, she was also shepherding the woman whom Patrick would marry. She felt the need to get back to Philadelphia as soon as possible, before any type of calamity could strike.

CHAPTER 21

April 1861

The train lurched away from the platform just as Ellen overheard two men snickering that the President had publically asked for 75,000 volunteers for his Northern army. Southerners would readily volunteer on their own for the Confederacy. They wouldn't have to be asked.

Ellen turned to Magdalena with a whisper. "Perhaps you should do most of the talking for the three of us while we are still deep in the South. Your Southern accent will be less suspicious than either of our Irish lilts." Then she turned her head to the side and tried to become an invisible passenger on a train.

Once the cars pulled into Charleston, they disembarked from one platform and climbed onto another, waiting to board the North-eastern line. When the train finally pulled in, they threaded their way to the center of a new car. Two women boarded the train after them and sat across the aisle from Ellen's small party. Ellen could tell by the way they were dressed that they were Catholic Sisters, but their habits were so unusual with their prominent starched white winged caps that Ellen had no idea of their order. Just seeing the two nuns made her suddenly nostalgic for Kensington and relieved at the same time. Nuns meant that the presence of God was with them on the train. Ellen smiled and whispered, "Good day, Sisters." The two women acknowledged her with a smile in return.

As the train sped north, they stopped and changed lines again in Florence, South Carolina. Each train may have been built out of different woods, but they all contained leather seats, either in red, green, or dark brown, and Ellen was thankful for the comfort. The party was grateful too that Sarah Fallon had provided them with provisions for the first day of the trip; they saw the other passengers having to buy food from the local women who magically appeared on the platform selling fried chicken, ham sandwiches, and bottles of cider.

The two Sisters continued with them on the journey, sitting in the same car across from the travelers. Ellen's curiosity finally got the better of her and she leaned forward and asked in a quiet voice, "I beg your pardon, but what is your order? You do not dress like the Sisters of St. Joseph."

"We belong to the Daughters of Charity," the Sister closest to her replied. "We are heading north to Richmond where we will be assigned as nurses at the Alms House Hospital." Then looking closer at the bags near Magdalena's feet, she continued, "You are nurses as well?"

Ellen hesitated for a moment. "Yes, we are private duty nurses on our way to Fredericksburg, Virginia, taking a patient there for special treatment."

"Then it seems we will have the pleasure of each others' company on this long trip. Fredericksburg is the stop after ours," the first nun commented.

Ellen tentatively smiled back, worried now that she had volunteered too much information. The other passengers would have heard her talking and possibly detected her northern accent. She looked around the car, but most of the women were involved in animated chatter about fashions it seemed, and the few groups of men on board were playing cards and not paying any attention to Ellen or her small group.

Then, almost as if the Sisters could hear her thinking, one of them replied, "As civilian nurses I am sure you've taken the same vow we have—to treat the sick, the wounded, and the dying, regardless of their political leanings or where they come from."

"Yes, Sister, you are correct. We have made that same promise."

The Sister nodded and gave Ellen a small, almost knowing smile. Could this woman know they were not real nurses? Or was she helping Ellen to feel safe? Ellen closed her eyes, fingered the Rosary beads in her pocket, and prayed the Hail Mary to quiet her nerves.

By the next day they had passed Wilmington, North Carolina, and were now traveling on the Wilmington and Weldon Line. New passengers had boarded the train and several of them appeared to be backwoodsmen all complaining of how the damn Yankees were trying to ruin the South. Ellen slouched on her seat and avoided making eye contact with anyone.

A new conductor got on. As he made his way through their car Ellen could hear him asking for tickets and chatting socially with many passengers. Magdalena was napping so Ellen took the three tickets out for him to inspect.

"Where you headed, little lady?"

Before Ellen could gather her wits to speak with an Irish lilt, she replied, "We're going to Fredericksburg, Virginia."

He stared at her suspiciously for a moment. "Where you from? Cause you don't sound like a Southern lady." He leaned in closer and twirled his moustache, but his eyes hardened into narrow slits. Jerking his head toward Magdalena and James he spat out, "Could be, that you're really Yankees. Then I'd have to report you."

Ellen could feel her heart pounding and thought she might actually throw up, but before she could summon her voice, the Sister who had spoken earlier now addressed the conductor. "Why, sir, I am sure you can see that these two women are nurses, just as we are." She indicated the other Sister and herself. "As nurses we have all made a promise to minister to the sick, wounded, and dying wherever they may come from. So in that vein, sir, we will be looking after Southerners and Northerners alike. Remember we are all God's children."

The conductor listened to the Sister but then leaned down and kicked at Ellen's traveling bag. "What's in here?" he growled.

By now Magdalena had awakened. In her genuine relaxed Georgian drawl she murmured, "Why, Ellen, show the gentleman our kits, then," and she beamed her best smile at the conductor.

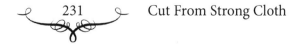

Trying to quell her fingers from shaking, Ellen opened her bag first and then Magdalena's. Both kits held many different types of powders, tinctures, and salves, each one in its own special wrapping.

"Yeah, that proves nothing," the conductor sneered. He pointed at the first container. "So what does that one do?"

Magdalena spoke up. "Why suh, that is dried elder. It is used to treat a fever, or when a person's bowels are. . . indisposed. I think you know what I am referring to." She lowered her eyes with proper discretion.

The conductor stared at her for a moment. "Hand me them tickets." He punched each stub and then continued on in the aisle, but not before he turned back to Ellen. "I got my eyes on you, Missy. And don't you forget that."

When he entered the next car, Ellen visibly shuddered and gave a sigh of relief. She whispered, "Magdalena, how did you remember the first vial was elder?"

"I didn't. But I thought if I mentioned bowels, he might not want any further discussion."

"You're brilliant."

Then Ellen peered over at James. They had given him two drops of laudanum in order for him to sleep most of the journey and therefore appear to be a patient in need of medical help. He was oblivious to the recent encounter.

Ellen looked over at the Sisters. "Thank you," she mouthed.

"You will be called on yet to serve God by helping others. And your patient there will need more than just physical healing for the trials he's gone through."

Ellen wondered what the Sister had so discerned about James that she could feel he needed healing in other parts of his life. She remembered Catherine Biddle telling her that when God closes a door, somewhere he opens a window. Was this journey back home a window of sorts? Exhausted, she put her head back and fell asleep.

***

Wednesday morning dawned bright and clear. The last stop

had been in Weldon, North Carolina, the night before, where they had waited for two hours to change onto the Petersburg Railroad, and eaten only some ham sandwiches for dinner. The Sister who had done the talking on the trip nudged her shoulder.

"We'll soon be coming into Richmond, our final stop. Your party will change there for the train to Fredericksburg. Sister Mary Margaret and I want to wish you Godspeed on your final journey, and to remember that God always listens to prayer, wherever we might be. God bless."

An hour later she heard the conductor announce, "Richmond, Richmond, Virginia," and the Sisters picked up their bags and left. Ellen hated to see them go. *I wish they could have stayed with us all the way to Fredericksburg.* Fingering the rosary in her pocket as she and Magdalena picked up their traveling valises and helped James to disembark, she thanked the Blessed Mother for putting the Sisters on the trains with them.

The last leg of the rail journey started. Ellen looked over at James. He was fully awake now.

"Just a bit further, Ellen. Have courage," he whispered. She got up from her seat and sat down next to him, sliding her hand into his. Then she leaned her head back and rested.

Soon she heard, "Fredericksburg! Fredericksburg, Virginia! All passengers disembark!"

Ellen took a deep breath. Even though this final depot in the South meant they were closer to home, they were still in Confederate territory. The trio picked up their valises and descended onto the depot platform. Ellen looked up, surprised that there were actually two depots. There was one for passengers, and a second, larger one looked like it was designated for freight. She saw a look of surprise on James and Magdalena's faces as well.

"Let's act like we belong here," she murmured to them. "Magdalena, you do the talking until we find Dr. Jackson. I don't want anyone else commenting that I don't sound like a Southern lady."

Magdalena scanned the crowd, and then walked over to a well-dressed man. "Why suh," Magdalena purred. "Would you be evah so kind and tell us where we could engage a driver? We are expected at the

house of Dr. Philip Jackson."

The gentlemen she had singled out rewarded her with a smile.

"Dr. Jackson, the new physician? It would be my pleasure, Miss. Are all three of you going there?"

"Why, yes indeed, we are. I would be evah so grateful for your help."

"Let's walk over there." He pointed. "Then you can wait in the shade while I find you a hack."

Ellen stood in stunned amazement. Magdalena had transformed herself into a helpless female whose syrupy voice poured over the gentleman like melted butter. James poked Ellen in the ribs. "Don't be staring after her like that. Remember, we supposedly belong here." He smiled.

The trio followed the gentleman through an area of landscaped boxwood hedges until they came to the street, and he signaled a man standing next to a buggy. Within minutes the three of them were riding into Fredericksburg proper, a quiet little town with tidy wooden houses lining a main thoroughfare interspersed with shops. As they drove further along, Ellen noticed a huge home located across the river, perched on the heights. Must be money here, too.

Within a short amount of time, the driver halted in front of a comfortably modest two story house on Williams Street. A sign read, "Philip Jackson, M.D." After they climbed out of the hack, Magdalena paid the driver with Confederate money. Ellen congratulated herself that she insisted they carry both Federal and Confederate currency. A woman answered the door, and Magdalena explained in very business-like terms that they had been sent by a mutual friend, Dr. Louis Fallon, to see Dr. Jackson on a private matter.

The woman invited them in and asked them to wait while she took the message to Dr. Jackson. A few moments later an attractive man with startling blue eyes and curly jet black hair came out to the parlor and extended his welcome. "Hello. You are friends of Louis Fallon? I haven't seen him since leaving medical school back in Philadelphia. How is he, and how may I be of assistance to you?"

This time Ellen spoke up. "He is doing well, thank you. I have been working with him as his assistant in Savannah. This man, James

Nolan, is a patient of Dr. Fallon's and Miss Fox is a family friend. Certain events have transpired that have made it necessary for us to transport the patient to more superior hospital facilities. Here, I have a letter of explanation from Dr. Fallon."

Dr. Jackson took the short letter and skimmed it. "Hmm, I see. Well, if Louis Fallon is vouching for you, then you are most welcome in my home. Please, stay the night and then tomorrow I can get your patient checked into the hospital here in Fredericksburg."

The three travelers looked at one another.

"Dr. Jackson, may I have a word with you in private?"

"Of course." He led Ellen into his study and closed the door.

Ellen asked to use a pair of scissors and then ripped out a small back portion of her hem. Dr. Jackson seemed a bit perplexed at her unusual behavior, but said nothing as she retrieved the much longer rolled note from Dr. Fallon. Ellen handed it to him. It read:

April 1861

Dear Philip,

It has been too long since we have seen each other and I hope you are happy in Virginia. By now you know that I am practicing in Savannah. The three travelers who have arrived at your home are all friends of mine. The real reason I have sent them to you is that they need to get to Philadelphia. Ellen Canavan is a Northerner, as is "the patient," James Nolan. Magdalena Fox is from Georgia, but engaged to Ellen's brother. These are difficult times, and I fear they will only get worse before any type of settlement is reached. Will you help them on my account? Any expense that you incur I will repay. Ellen's mother showed great kindness to my wife, Sarah, and I must insure that these travelers reach their destination. Please burn this letter. I will be in your debt.

Sincerely,
Louis A. Fallon, M.D.

Ellen watched Dr. Jackson's face for any negative reactions but saw none.

"Well, I see now why you are here." Dr. Jackson crossed the room, lighted a match, and proceeded to burn the letter in a copper bowl.

"Let's rejoin the others. I assure you I will help all I can and also provide you with a letter of safe conduct."

Dr. Jackson rang for the woman who had opened the door. "Thank you, Martha. Our three weary travelers will be staying the night. If you would be so kind, please set the table for extra places, and arrange bed linens for them. Stretch the meal anyway you can. Thank you."

Martha nodded and went into the kitchen.

"Martha is my housekeeper. I'm afraid I've been so busy setting up my practice that I haven't joined the social scene here in Fredericksburg, nor married."

Ellen smiled because with his good looks, many young women had certainly tried to set their cap for him. The three travelers followed him to the study, where he pulled out a map.

"Here we are in Fredericksburg. Washington, D.C., is northeast of us. However, even with a letter, taking the main roads would be risky. You'd be better served to start out on Kings Highway, but then veer off at Boswells and get on the Williamsville Road. Martha's brother-in-law runs a store two miles further up; it's called the Mountjoy Store. You'll be safe spending the first night there. After that you'll be on your own for accommodations."

He saw concern on all of their faces. "I'll provide you with a wagon, blankets, and a canvas in case you need to sleep out in the open. Watch me as I trace the route." His finger moved up, over place names like Bell Fair Mills and Independent Hill.

"This Bristow Road will lead you to Brentsville. There's a hotel and the courthouse there, but you'd raise too much suspicion, so before you come to the village, take the Brentsville Road. It twists and turns into the Lucasville Road, but will lead you to an area called Tudor Hall. Nearby is Manassas Junction. But keep driving, and once you get to the Centreville Road it will be less than 30 miles to Alexandria. From there you'll be able to cross into Washington, D.C."

He looked up to see the three of them earnestly studying the map. "Here, I'll write down the names of the roads and the approximate mileage between stops. Then I'll also sketch a map. Now, which one of you will be driving the wagon?"

"We can all drive and take turns," James replied.

Ellen stole a glance at James. Thank God he had taught her how to drive Lir.

"All right. The first letter will be from me explaining your presence here in Virginia—you're visiting some cousins in a place called Centreville. The second letter will be to a Dr. Stone. He's a doctor at the Washington Infirmary. It will explain why you need to get into the city. Now you better rest before dinner. We'll have tomorrow to get the wagon outfitted, plus acquire feed for the horse. Once you're on the road, you'll have to set a pace of almost sixteen miles a day. Even with good weather it will take you at least four days to reach Alexandria. And one more thing: Washington may be across the Potomac River, but it's still considered to be a Southern city. You'll have to be on guard."

"Thank you, Dr. Jackson. How will we ever be able to repay you?"

"This is a courtesy to an old friend. Dr. Fallon would do the same for me. Once you reach Dr. Stone in Washington, you'll leave the horse and wagon with him. He'll contact me about returning it. God willing, you'll arrive home safely."

At the supper meal that evening, Ellen offered the blessing. "Dear God, thank you for all the kind people who have helped us on our way. Please continue to watch over us and keep us safe." She looked up and noticed that the housekeeper had continued to stand near the table.

"Amen." The events of the last few days made her more cautious with her words than usual. In her mind, no one was above suspicion.

***

Ellen felt as though a herd of elephants had trampled her body; each and every muscle ached. The days on the train had been exhausting. However, time was closing in on the trio and she knew they could not dally, so she climbed up in the buckboard next to Magdalena and took the reins. With James bundled as a "sick patient," she drove them over the Rappahannock River and onto Kings Highway.

No one spoke, each presumably lost in their own thoughts as mile after mile of hillsides adorned with wild cherry and blooming dogwoods flanked the road. As the sun dipped toward the horizon, they arrived at the Mountjoy Store.

James tied the horse to a hitching post, and Ellen and Magdalena walked in the store. The front counter display advertised everything from licorice treats to lye soap, and the man behind the counter asked if they needed something.

"Yes, we do. We spent the last two days at Dr. Jackson's home in Fredericksburg. He indicated that we might seek refuge with you and your wife, here tonight."

"Of course. If Philip Jackson passed our name onto you, then you are welcome. I'll stable your horse and secure the wagon. Go next door to our home. My wife will see to you."

Ellen's shoulders relaxed for the first time in days. Could this family be trusted? She prayed that they would not ask many questions and just offer safe haven.

The trio tromped over to the house and knocked on the door.

"Yes?" A pleasantly plump woman with a friendly face answered.

"Mrs. Mountjoy? Your husband told us to come over and meet you while he is tending to our horse and wagon. We are asking for hospitality for the night. We're friends of Dr. Jackson."

"Philip Jackson? Of course, come right in. I'm afraid all I have to offer is bean stew and cornbread, and quilts on the floor for sleeping. I hope those accommodations will do."

"Yes, they will do quite nicely, thank you."

After a full day of travel in the open air, the warm meal made them drowsy. As soon as the stars came out to dot the night sky, all three wrapped up in soft quilts on the front room floor, and quickly dropped off to sleep.

Mrs. Mountjoy, however, did see the man's arm draped itself across the girl lying next to him, as if even in his dreams he was trying to protect her.

Their bodies ached even more by the second day traveling as the hard wooden wagon seat jostled them along every mile. To alleviate some of the boredom and numb bottoms, each took a turn at driving, and the other two rotated who got to stretch out in the back of the wagon. By the end of the day, Ellen joined Magdalena on the driving seat and allowed James to rest in back. They would have to stop soon.

Ellen consulted Dr. Jackson's rudimentary map and calculated they should be quite near Brentsville. Wistfully, she thought how wonderful it would be to stay in the hotel. She honestly thought she would trade the horse if she could be guaranteed a hot bath and clean sheets. A mile later, they turned onto the Brentsville Road. Chestnut, elm, and locust trees shaded the road, and a nearby gurgling creek gave promise of a nighttime lullaby, but the bucolic nature of the landscape was lost on the travelers who were dead tired.

A figure stepped out of the tree line up ahead. He appeared to be a federal soldier, but alone. Ellen saw Magdalena stiffen. "I'll handle it," whispered Ellen and snatched the reins from Magdalena's hands.

As she pulled the wagon up closer in the road, she stared at the soldier from under her bonnet. Familiar strains of Irish brogue reached her ears as he addressed them.

"Whoa, now, ladies, and where would you be going off to at the close of day?"

Ellen loosened her bonnet and let it fall back against her shoulders.

"Ellen?" A stunned Michael Brady stood before her.

"Aye, 'tis me. Might I be the one who should be asking what you're doing here? Perhaps you are selling confidential ideas to the army? Like you did to the McFadden brothers back in Kensington."

Michael recovered from the surprise of seeing her. "Ellen, what are you saying? 'Tis true I was short on cash back then, but there's no law against sharing ideas in a pub."

"Sharing ideas? I have firsthand information, Michael, that you betrayed me and my family. Your traitorous behavior might have ruined

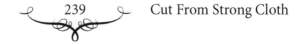

our chances of getting contracts. But we, that is. . . James Nolan, my brother, and I, have figured out a way to make a hefty profit in spite of you."

She had not intended to let this venom fly between them, but once the words were out of her mouth, she did feel some vindication.

Michael's eyes hardened. "I think you best be careful who you're callin' a traitor, darlin.'"

"I'm not your darlin', Michael. By betraying my confidence, you destroyed any feelings I had for you. Now let us pass."

"Ah, Ellen, pretty as ever, and anger only brings out the beauty in your gorgeous green eyes. But who is this James Nolan you're speaking about? You canna tell me that you are involved with someone? When I last saw you in December, I thought I was the special person in your life."

"Flattery doesn't work with me, Michael. Or have you forgotten?"

Michael walked to the side of the wagon and peered in the back, seeing a poor fellow who did appear to be ailing.

The long-buried anger in Ellen rose once more to the surface. "So why are you here in Virginia?" Ellen demanded. "I suspect you're somehow making money off the deal."

"I volunteered early, expecting the war, and got assigned to this small scouting unit."

But before the conversation could continue, another form stepped out of the woods, this time, an officer.

"Corporal Brady, what have you found here? Some Confederate belles, I assume."

Ellen's bravado of the past ten minutes evaporated, and she shot a pleading look at Michael, not knowing what he might say.

Michael saluted the officer. "Well, Captain, believe it or not, I know these people. Miss Canavan here, was. . . an acquaintance of mine back in Philadelphia."

The captain walked around the wagon.

"And this fellow, he's one of your 'acquaintances,' too?"

Ellen turned to address the officer.

"Sir, I am Ellen Canavan, a private duty nurse employed by Dr. Louis Fallon of the Medical College of Philadelphia. I am bringing this

sick man, a patient of Dr. Fallon's, to a Federal hospital."

The captain returned to the front of the wagon and glanced at Magdalena, who remained silent.

"Then who might she be?"

"This is Magdalena Fox, my assistant. We're on a medical mission here, transporting this patient, and we are Northerners—just like you, sir."

The captain's voice took on a hard edge. "Lady, you can dress in any kind of outfit and still be a spy. Do you have papers proving who you are?"

"I do."

Ellen's hands shook as she took the letter from Dr. Jackson out of her medical bag and handed it to the captain, who took the time to read through the entire correspondence. "So, you're supposed to be on your way to Washington. Well then, just what are you doing on this particular road? Maybe you plan to visit friends over at Clover Hill?"

"I do not know any Clover Hill. We're just trying to get to the Centreville Road by nightfall."

"Why should I believe you?"

"Well, didn't Corporal Brady, vouch for us?"

The captain remained silent. "Why the Centreville Road?"

"We hope to have quarters there with cousins of mine who recently moved to Virginia."

"But you are arriving from the south."

"Yes, we missed a turn and have gone several miles past where we should be. That is why we are hurrying now to get to the Centreville Road." *Holy Mary forgive me this lie.*

The captain laughed. "Well your cousins picked a poor time to move south. War's about to start, in case you didn't know. I can't risk having you leave now, and you couldn't make the Centreville Road by nightfall, anyway. We'll let you stay here close to our camp, and in the morning I'll have an escort lead you on your way.

"You do know, I assume, that Virginia just voted on an ordinance calling for secession? That means Virginia will soon become part of the Confederacy, and no Northerners will be safe here, including

you. I'm only letting you stay because of Corporal Brady; otherwise, I might consider that you really are spies. As soon as it's light, you'll need to be on your way. We're a few miles south of Manassas Junction, and from there you can get on the Centreville Road."

"Thank you." She picked up the reins and guided the horse off the road to a narrow path leading to an opening in the trees. She saw a spot where they could have some protection and be able to sleep in the wagon. She did not look directly back at Michael, but dipped her head in the slightest acknowledgement of his help. *Of course I have no knowledge about the secession ordinance. Oh God, please let us be on the correct road.* Then she climbed down from the wagon.

James, a bit groggy but now awake, led the horse over to graze while Ellen and Magdalena prepared a simple meal of sandwiches and hard cheese given to them by Mrs. Mountjoy.

As dark settled in, each of them found themselves exhausted, both by the ardors of the trip and the stress of still being in Southern territory. Ellen changed out of her dress in an attempt to keep it clean but shivered in just her chemise, so she wrapped up in her cloak to stay warm. Then they all climbed into the back of the wagon and huddled together under the blankets. Deep slumber quickly overtook them.

Much later, Ellen stirred. She had to relieve herself and knew she would not be able to fall back asleep until she did. Moving aside the rough woolen blanket covering her, she inched away from James and Magdalena and slipped down from the wagon. The darkness of the night made it difficult to see, but she remembered a copse of trees where she could have some privacy and headed toward it.

Once concealed in the thicket, she took off the cumbersome cloak and hung it on a nearby branch; then she hiked up her chemise and, squatting, opened the split crotch of her drawers. Her hair hung down in a braid behind her neck. Almost at once, she detected the faint odor of stale cigar smoke mixed with the fragrance of springtime blossoms. The traces of the smoke evoked uneasiness in her. Then the audible snap of a nearby bough quickly made her straighten up, all her senses heightened.

Fear rolled over her. She dropped the hem of her chemise with

nervous fingers, and peered back in the direction of the wagon. Her breath caught in her throat. No one knew she was here.

The shadowy figure of a large man emerged from the trees.

"Well, what have we here?" he slurred.

Ellen could see he was a Federal soldier, but he appeared to be soaked in alcohol. She tried to ignore him and leave, but he prowled closer and cut off her avenue of escape.

"You're not thinking of running off, pretty one, are you?"

Ellen spun in an attempt to flee, but the man lunged, grabbing her and clamping a dirty hand over her mouth. Her heart raced with the terror of a trapped animal. She tried to scream, but his huge paw completely covered her mouth. Then he relaxed his grip ever so slightly and in a primal surge of rage, Ellen jerked her head and sunk her teeth as hard as she could into his grimy fingers.

"You bitch!" he snarled and slapped her hard across the face—making her head snap backward. Then he wrenched her braid back with brutal force, leaving her no alternative but to appear submissive. She tried to twist away from him, but he slapped her again with a force driven now by fury. He grabbed the front of her thin cotton chemise and ripped it down to her waist, exposing her breasts.

With a vicious shove, he threw her to the ground, momentarily knocking the breath out of her. As her body lay motionless, he fumbled with the opening of his crotch. She came out of the daze to see his disgusting male organ flopping out of his pants like a fat snake poised to strike. A single ragged sob escaped her mouth.

Bending closer, he pinned her to the ground with one hand gripping her throat. He leaned over her, an ugly sneer distorting his face. His fetid breath made her gag.

By God, I won't let you rape me. I would rather die.

She tried to kick her legs at him, but to no avail. Twisting her head a bit sideways, she saw her cloak lying now on the ground next to her body. With a wild fierceness, she grabbed the brooch with one outstretched hand, and then jerked the pin out of the cloth. She wildly stabbed at his head. On the third jab, the sharp point went straight into his neck.

He staggered to his feet, his eyes registering shock and his hands flailing in desperation to locate and pull out the tormenting instrument. But he lost his balance and fell backward, his head hitting a large protruding boulder. Blood spurted as his skull cracked and he lay motionless.

Ellen stared at his lifeless body and then sobs wracked her body. Slowly she eased herself to a sitting position, clutching her torn chemise and stared over at him. The snap of another branch made her jerk around in fear. She jumped to her feet in panic, only to see James step through the trees.

"My God, Ellen. What happened?"

He ran over to her and held her tight, waiting till she stopped shaking. "'Tis all right, I'm here. I promise you're safe."

When her sobbing subsided, he reached down to the ground, picked up her cloak, and draped it around her body. "Tell me what happened—exactly."

Ellen took a small breath, her throat throbbing with bruising pain. "He was going to rape me and I fought him. I stabbed him with the pin of my brooch. Then he fell. Oh God, James, I killed him. I know I did."

"Shh. It was self-defense, and no witness to say otherwise. I'll get the pin, and then we'll let the bastard stay where he is. By morning when he's discovered, we'll be long gone and they'll assume he died from taking a drunken fall, hitting his head on the rock. Wait here. I'm only leaving you for a second."

James walked over and pulled the brooch pin out of the soldier's neck. The puncture wound may not have killed him, but the substantial head gash from the rock would have been hard to survive.

"You got what you deserved, you bashtoon." Then he wiped the blood off the pin with some leaves and made his way back to Ellen.

"Listen to me, Ellen. We will forget what happened here tonight. I should have told you when I asked you to choose between me and your business, that no matter what you answered, I would stick by you and love you forever. Nothing could ever change that. From this night on, I swear to always protect you. We may be only business partners right now, but I will wait for you to become my partner in life—no matter how long it takes."

She remained silent as they slowly walked back through the woods, his arm around her providing a measure of safety. When they reached the wagon, he retrieved a blanket and wrapped it around her shivering body. Then he sat on the ground against a wagon wheel and motioned for her to sit down. As she leaned her body into his, he cradled her in his arms and began to hum the Derry Air.

"I want you to know that I intend to love you for life and help you forget the ugliness of what happened here." He lifted Ellen's face and kissed her with the promise of a lifelong love. She returned the kiss with a feeling of commitment that surprised even her, and stayed wrapped in his arms accepting the warmth of security he offered.

Unbeknown to them, a witness lingered out of sight.

Michael Brady had been watching Ellen all night, and saw her stab the soldier. But he did not come forward, remaining instead near the thicket. Now as he watched the intimacy of the two lovers in an embrace, he felt a lump in his throat for the first time in his life as the unexpected emotion of jealously penetrated his usually unaffected demeanor.

Much later when James climbed back into the wagon, Ellen stripped off the torn chemise and put on one of her dresses. She rolled the ripped garment into a ball she would burn later and threw it on the ground. No evidence could be left behind to tie her to the soldier's death. As she climbed in next to him on the wagon floor, Ellen spooned her body into his. Her scalp and face throbbed with pain from the ordeal, and her arms ached with a weakness she could not even describe. But as she nestled into his space, she wondered if perhaps she had at last found her perfect fit.

Cut From Strong Cloth

CHAPTER 22

April 1861

Before dawn, Ellen gingerly crawled out of the wagon. Her entire body hurt beyond belief. Her face, scalp, throat and arms were bruised from the struggle with the soldier, but they needed to leave before the army encampment awoke. Cooking would have to wait till later; they would simply have to eat whatever food they still had, cold. As she packed, Ellen made a conscious effort not to let the events of the previous night subject her to any further fear.

"Ellen, come quick. I think something's wrong with Magdalena!"

The worry in James' voice made her turn to the wagon, where she saw glistening sweat bead along Magdalena's forehead. Ellen reached out and felt Magdalena's face—it was hot with fever, and her eyes barely open. She remembered the dried elder in their medical kit; she would brew some elder tea after they had cleared the camp. She wished she could make soaked cracker toast for the fever, but she had neither crackers, nor sugar, nor milk.

"I think Magdalena needs a doctor," James voiced.

"If this is the type of fever I fear it could be, then she needs a hospital. We need to get to Washington now, as fast as possible."

"Ellen, do you hear what you're saying? We're supposed to stick to the back roads."

"That was before Magdalena got sick. She needs medicine, James, not just herbs. And frankly, I don't want to be on any more back roads. We might encounter other scouting parties. Dr. Jackson said there was a depot at the crossroads of Tudor Hall. We must be just a few miles away and can hopefully take a train from there. We'll have to leave the horse and wagon behind."

"We can't just abandon the horse, and how will you buy train tickets?"

"I watched Magdalena back in Fredericksburg flirt with that man. I can pose as a Southern lady if I have to. The important thing is to get all of us on a train."

"And Dr. Jackson's horse and wagon?"

"We'll have to find someone who can take care of that. Then we'll write to Dr. Jackson and explain what happened. We canna delay. We need to get out of here fast."

James just shook his head. "I don't see how it can work."

"Just help me, then."

They quickly wrapped Magdalena in blankets and wedged her body against the rolled canvas in the back of the wagon. Then they nudged the horse back onto the Lucasville Road. Slowly at first, and then urging the horse to a faster pace, they came to a crossroads at what their map named Tudor Hall, even though both the Federal captain and Dr. Jackson had referred to it as Manassas Junction.

Across from the tracks they spied a small wooden building which looked like it could be a railroad depot. Ellen drove over and then reined in the horse, jumped down from the wagon, and tied up to a nearby post. Mustering her courage, she held her head up high, squared her shoulders, and tried to remember everything she had seen Magdalena do. She took a deep breath and smoothed the front of her dress, then pulled her bonnet full onto her face so the bruise marks would not be so easily seen. Lastly, she grabbed a small tin cup from their supplies.

She opened the door to find one single man inside the station, pouring a steaming beverage into a cup.

"Good morning, Miss. Can I help you?"

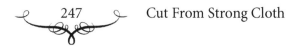

Cut From Strong Cloth

"Why yes, suh. If you would be evah so kind. I am in need of three tickets to Alexandria. My two patients need to be transported to Washington. They'll be receiving medical treatment at the hospital there."

"Are you a nurse?"

"Yes, a private duty nurse." She peeked up at him from under her bonnet with a shy smile.

"Washington, D.C.? You'll be crossing into federal territory. Do you have southern connections up there?"

"Why yes suh, I do. But even as a private nurse, I have taken the vow to assist wherever I am needed. Here, I have traveling papers from Dr. Philip Jackson of Fredericksburg."

She held out the papers and tried not to show any nervousness, but act the role of a Southern belle. The man read through them. "This looks official. Wasn't the hospital in Fredericksburg good enough?"

"Oh, these patients need long-term medical care, and Dr. Jackson felt the hospital in Washington has better equipment. He was trained there, you see, and knows the facility quite well."

"All right, I can get you three tickets."

"Thank you evah so much. May I ask two more favas? I need to make some tea for one of the patients and I need to find your local doctor."

"Local doctor? We ain't big enough for a full-time one, but Dr. Kavanagh makes the rounds when he can. You're in luck 'cause he's here today at one of the nearby farms. Can't miss it, it's the plantation house south of the railroad tracks, built of red brick. I can give you some hot water, though. Kettle's on the stove. How much do you need?"

"Just one cup would be sufficient. What time does the train depart?"

"You've got a little over an hour before it's due."

"Thank you, suh. I won't forget your kindness."

Ellen paid for the tickets and picked up the tin cup filled with hot water. In a genteel manner she sauntered back outside.

James had positioned himself at the back of the wagon watching over Magdalena.

"I did it, James, I got three tickets and some hot water. I want to

 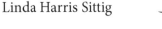

make Magdalena a medicinal tea. Then we have to find the local doctor and convince him to take the horse and wagon."

James looked around to see if they were being watched. He gave out a low whistle. "This, I want to see."

Ellen concocted a weak tea, and then her hands began to shake. "James, can you get Magdalena to drink this? I need a moment to settle myself."

James held out the tea to Magdalena and tried to coax her to sip it, but she fretted and tossed her head from side to side, refusing to drink even a drop. James gave up, tossed the tea and repacked the tin cup. "I couldna get her to drink any of it."

"At least we tried. Perhaps we can try again later."

Ellen climbed back in the wagon and steered them southeast of the tracks where they soon found the wide lane that led to the plantation home. She pulled the wagon up to the front of the house, taking only a moment to admire its two story structure of russet brick. Mustering courage once again, she gently descended from the seat, walked to the door, and knocked. A dark-skinned woman answered the door.

"Good day. Is your mistress at home?"

The colored woman looked at her with some interest.

"Who's do I say you are?"

"I am Ellen Canavan, and I'm here to confer with Dr. Kavanagh. I understand he is making his rounds."

"Yes 'um, the doctor's here. Please wait and I'll go get him."

A moment later a young man came to the door.

"I am Dr. Kavanagh. How may I be of assistance?" He glanced over at the wagon.

"Dr. Kavanagh, my name is Ellen Canavan. I'm a private duty nurse trying to get my two patients to the hospital in Washington. We have traveling papers from Dr. Philip Jackson in Fredericksburg, and we have tickets for the train that is coming through here in an hour."

"Yes. What do you want with me, then?"

"We had intended to drive to Alexandria, but my assistant awoke with a fever this morning and I am afraid that she needs to get to the hospital as soon as possible."

Cut From Strong Cloth

"Again, pardon my asking, but I don't understand how I can help you."

"We need someone who can take care of the horse and wagon until Dr. Jackson can retrieve them. I am asking you, suh, as a Southern gentleman and a doctor, if you can take the horse and wagon for us. I will be writing Dr. Jackson once we reach Alexandria. But I have to find someone I can entrust the horse and wagon to."

Afraid to relax for even one moment, Ellen worried she might betray herself.

"But I already have a horse."

"Oh no, suh, I did not mean to imply that you would have to stable the horse, only that you would be dependable to see that the animal was cared for until Dr. Jackson could come get him. This would be a fava from one doctor to another."

The young doctor looked at her for a moment. "I took an oath to treat the sick and help the wounded. Nothing in my training ever indicated I should have to take care of a horse, but I guess I can help you." He smiled. "I'll see to it that the horse is stabled here with one of the local families until your doctor from Fredericksburg can fetch it. You can write to him and explain our agreement. He can reach me through the station master here in the village. I do have another patient to see today, but it's not urgent. Do you need a ride back to the depot?"

"Why yes, suh, I would be evah so grateful."

Ellen walked back to the wagon, giving James a wink. A few moments later the doctor came out of the house and approached the wagon. The man in the wagon did not appear to be sick, but the woman was feverish.

"What have you given to help with the fever?"

"I made some elder tea, but she would not drink any of it."

"Well, I would have tried the same remedy. Do you need me to treat your bruises?"

"No, thank you. I am all right."

He raised an eyebrow but did not question her further. "Let's get you and your patients to the depot then."

As they pulled away from the plantation, James tossed a rolled

bundle of fabric into a smoldering trash pile. He watched as the material caught the flame and burned.

Within the hour they boarded a train heading east. James supported Magdalena in his arms, and she slept as a light drizzle began to fall. So far, they had managed to escape detection, but still had many miles to go. Ellen could not concentrate on anything other than getting Magdalena to the hospital. If she took a turn for the worse, how would Ellen ever be able to face Patrick?

As the train sped through the countryside, telegraphs were reporting that Virginia ports had just become part of the federal blockade and all ships were being quarantined.

⁂

Ellen could not fully appreciate the beauty of the Northern Virginia countryside even though the terrain sported a riotous mixture of lilacs, wild cherry trees and redbuds. She lowered her window to catch some fresh air after the rain stopped. The genteel feeling of the Virginia countryside belied the fact that war was progressing.

As they pulled into the Alexandria Station and climbed down on the platform, Ellen overheard two men discussing the news that the Norfolk Navy Yard had been burned by federal troops earlier in the morning. *Thank God we are almost back in Northern territory.* She looked around and tried to catch a glimpse of the bridge that would carry them across the Potomac River into Washington. James retrieved their valises, and Ellen helped support Magdalena as they walked away from the train.

Dear God. Where is the bridge? "James, I don't see any bridge. Do you?"

"No. Are you sure Dr. Jackson said you could get into Washington from Alexandria?"

"Of course, I'm sure. Oh God, James. What if he was wrong?"

A man approached them.

"Begging your pardon, but would youse be needin' transport?"

"Well, we need directions at the very least. We're looking for the

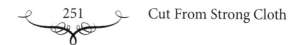

bridge that goes into Washington," Ellen stated.

"That would be Long Bridge, Miss, but 'tis five miles upriver."

"Five miles! Mother of the God, we canna walk that far."

"No, Miss, you can't. But begging your pardon again, do I detect a wee bit of the ould country in your voice?"

Was this a trick? A Southerner trying to determine if they should be detained? She took a chance.

"Yes, you do. I was born in County Tyrone, but I've lived in America for the last six years now."

The man's face lit up with a big smile.

"I'm from up Derry way myself; been here in the states as long as you. Five miles is a fair piece to travel, but you're in luck. I'm a wagoner. My horse is just over there, and for a fee I can take you and your friends to Long Bridge."

"I see, Mr. . . . ?"

"Quigg. Mr. James Quigg, Miss. I drive people out to the bridge all the time."

"What if we gave you an extra amount of pay? Could you take us across the bridge and into Washington?"

"You do know Washington City is federal territory? Southerners been leavin' it for days."

"We are expected at the Washington Infirmary to see a Dr. Stone. I have traveling papers you can inspect."

She held the papers out to him. "Can't read much, Miss. But I can take you across the bridge. In fact, I can take you all the way to the infirmary if you like. Though people here abouts call it the E Street Infirmary. You'd only have to hire a driver on the other side, anyway." So saying, he collected the valises from James, tipped his cap to the two women, and ushered Ellen, with James supporting Magdalena, over to his wagon. If he noticed Ellen's bruises, he was too much of a gentleman to comment on them.

"What's wrong with your friend?"

"She's feverish, but nothing you could catch, so don't worry. We feel most grateful to you, Mr. Quigg, helping us in this way."

She peered at Mr. Quigg's profile. He could have easily been

any one of the men she had known in her childhood back in Dungannon with his freckled face, unruly reddish brown hair, and the light of Ireland still shining in his eyes. That thought gave her some feeling of comfort.

The five-mile uneventful journey led them through a landscape bursting with golden yellow forsythia. When they reached the vicinity of the Long Bridge, Ellen squinted in the fading afternoon light, appalled to see the large sprawling shanty area that preceded the bridge. The buildings were no better than hovels. As she watched, she saw a woman beckoning in a doorway to a group of men outside. The woman wore only enough fabric to cover the essential parts of her body. Ellen closed her eyes in disgust, wondering for a moment if Michael had ever frequented women like that back in Philadelphia.

"That there is Jackson City. No place you'd want to visit, Miss. Offers every vice known to man." Mr. Quigg gave James a knowing wink and urged his horse to keep on going.

As they approached the planks of the bridge entrance, Mr. Quigg stopped the wagon. Two militiamen in grey caps were guarding the span. Ellen handed her traveling papers to the wagoner, who gave them to one of the guards. The older guard took his time inspecting the letter; but then indicated that the party could cross.

Mr. Quigg guided the horse and wagon onto the bridge, cajoling the beast with gentle whispers. The late afternoon sun shone down on the water, causing the river to sparkle like tiny stars, but Ellen's eyes were on the horse, which reminded her of Lir.

Once on the other side, they were greeted by two Federal pickets, who waved them through. With a click of the reins, Mr. Quigg prodded his horse into the city. Ellen knew this was the capital of the United States, but one would not know that from the entry onto Maryland Avenue. Up ahead she could spy outlines of distant buildings, but here at the border, the swampy ground appeared to be not much more than squatters' territory or a breeding haven for insects.

They pulled further ahead, and off to the left she saw a huge white obelisk jutting up into the air, but she had no idea of its purpose. Then as if to punctuate the shabby entrance to Washington, two pigs

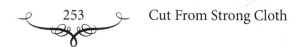

and some geese suddenly ran out into the muddy road, snorting and grunting their way through the littered refuse. Shocked at the rough condition of the city, Ellen couldn't help but contrast it to the beauty of Savannah and the orderliness of Center City Philadelphia.

After proceeding down Maryland Avenue, they turned left on Seventh Street, and several blocks later, they turned right and spied the hospital. Looking around E Street, she could see a scattered assortment of buildings and City Hall. The neighborhood could best be described as a ragtag assortment of working-class boarding houses and saloons crowding the blocks that led down to the unfinished Capitol Building in the distance. Hucksters abounded, just like in Kensington, all of them plying their wares. But the number of slaves attending their owners surprised her.

"We're here now. And if you don't mind me saying so, you might want to consider wearing a secesh cockade on your dress while you're in the city."

Ellen looked puzzled.

"You know, one of them fancy ribbons that show you're loyal to the Confederacy. That way no one should bother you."

"Thank you so much, Mr. Quigg, but as private duty nurses we do not favor either side. Now, how much do we owe you?" Ellen knew he could gouge them with an unfair price, and she wouldn't know the difference. But the mention of County Tyrone must have touched a soft chord and he helped them down with their bags, accepted a modest pay, and bid them goodbye.

Ellen looked at the few coins he gave her in change. She bit her lip. Their travel money was dwindling and they would have to be careful to make it last till they reached Philadelphia.

James assisted Magdalena up the infirmary steps while Ellen held open the door. Once inside, a plain-looking woman came over to them. "Can I help you?" she addressed Ellen.

Ellen took a moment to look at the woman who wore a drab gray dress, lacking any collar or cuffs, and covered by a dingy apron. Her mousy brown hair was pulled away from her face with a severe center part and gathered into a tight bun at the back of her neck. But

her smile was genuine. She reminded Ellen of Catherine Biddle, although this woman did not appear to be a Quaker.

"Yes, thank you. We are here to see Dr. Stone. I have papers from a physician in Fredericksburg who wanted Dr. Stone to examine our patient, Mr. Nolan. However, in our journey it is my assistant who now needs the medical attention."

"Dr. Stone is out of town for a few days, but Dr. Randall is working. Let's see if we can find her a bed. I'm a volunteer here myself. Normally I clerk at the Patent Office, but I came over just now to get some supplies for the soldiers of the Sixth Massachusetts. We'll get a doctor to look at her." She eyed James. "The other patient, I assume, sir, is you?"

"Aye. But 'tis Miss Fox who needs the attention."

"Are you going to check in here at the hospital, or wait to be seen later?"

"I'll stay at a hotel nearby. I don't think there's a need for me to be in a hospital anymore. Ellen, I'll go and make sure we can get rooms."

"You can stay here overnight, if you wish." She directed this comment at Ellen.

"Thank you, but I am in dire need of a hot bath. I'll stay the night in a hotel as well."

"It looks as if you were injured. Do you need someone to examine those bruises?"

Ellen's fingers flew to the marks on her face, realizing she had let her bonnet slide back. "No, that won't be necessary. I was attacked by . . . an insane patient. I'm afraid the brute left his marks on me, though."

The woman scrutinized Ellen's face.

"It appears that the skin isn't broken, so the bruises should heal well. I'm sorry you had to endure that. An insane patient, you say?"

"I'm a private duty nurse; he was actually another nurse's patient," mumbled Ellen. *How did that lie come so quickly out of my mouth?*

The no-nonsense volunteer nurse wheeled Magdalena into a nearby ward while Ellen followed.

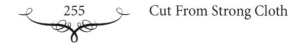

"I'm sorry, I dinna catch your name."

"Just call me Clare."

"I'm Ellen."

Ellen stayed until Magdalena dozed, then left and looked up and down the street to find James. He was waiting for her across the road and waved her over.

"I've found adjoining rooms in a small hotel close by, though I fear their kitchen has closed. Are you hungry? Maybe we can find something to eat in one of the local oyster saloons."

"Actually, I'm starved." They set off walking and located a reasonable establishment just a few doors down the street. In the dim light of the saloon, no one commented on her bruises.

"How long do you think Magdalena will need to stay in the hospital?"

"I'm not sure, but we should find out tomorrow." She studied his face. "Is something wrong?"

"No, everything is right now that we're almost home. But I did receive a telegram from my manager Jimmy Doyle the day before we left Savannah. He suspects that someone has been pilfering from the factory. I am worried about that."

"Do you think maybe you should return to Philadelphia right away, then?"

"I can wait. Magdalena should be released tomorrow."

"James, there's no guarantee of that. Why don't you return home tomorrow and I stay and wait until Magdalena is released? I really don't mind, and I want to meet the Quartermaster of the Army anyway and talk to him about buying our cloth. It should only mean a few more days for me."

"All right, as long as you are safe here, then I'll go on home tomorrow. Now, let's eat these oysters."

***

After the meal, they walked back to the hotel. James went to speak to the night clerk and then they climbed up to their rooms on the second floor.

"I know you must be exhausted, so I will kiss you goodnight here and let you get a well-deserved night's rest." James took hold of her shoulders and kissed her firmly on the mouth. "However, I am just next door if you need me."

"Good night, James." Ellen closed her door, but a few moments later a knock sounded. She opened the door a crack to find two maids holding buckets of hot water for the bath. She couldn't even remember the last time she had been able to wash, and she yearned to scrub away both the grime from the trip and the memory of the soldier's hands on her body.

Once the maids left, she filled the bath, disrobed, and then slowly lowered herself into the delightfully warm water. Inhaling, she smelled the essence of rose water. James must have remembered and arranged for the scent to be added to the bathwater. She smiled at his thoughtfulness and then stayed in the tub for a long time, letting the water begin to dilute the horror of yesterday.

After the bath, she inspected herself in the mirror and found that the bruises mottled her skin with purple and yellow discoloring. As Clare said, they would fade. Perhaps she could purchase some pancake makeup and cover them up a bit. She'd look for a store on Monday. Right now she needed sleep. She dressed in a clean chemise and eased herself down on the bed.

She slid between the sheets. Sleep, however, eluded her.

I could have died yesterday. What if I do die young, sudden, like Da? What kind of legacy would I leave behind? Who would mourn me? Who would carry on with my dream? Without children, would I even be remembered?

She thought of James next door, and felt the need to be with him. Climbing out of bed, she walked over and tapped on the door separating their rooms.

"Yes?"

"James, 'tis me."

She turned the handle and finding it unlocked, opened the door.

He raised himself up on one elbow, peering at her silhouette in

257   Cut From Strong Cloth

the night. "Are you all right?"

"Yes. Can I come in?"

"Of course."

She stepped just inside the door. "So much has happened in the last few days. . . can I stay here with you for a while?"

He pulled the sheet more securely over himself as she crossed the room and stood next to his bed for several moments, just looking at him. She felt as if all the clocks in the world had stopped. Without any hesitation, she slipped the chemise off her shoulders and let it slide to the floor.

"Ellen, do you know what you're doing?" he whispered.

"Aye James, I do. I understand now, truly for the first time, how short life can be. I want to be with you tonight, before you leave for home.

He moved, making room for her next to him.

"But I dinna want you to think. . . "

"Shhh, don't say anything. Just coming to me of your own free will is enough."

He gazed at her bruises as she sat down on the edge of the bed. Tenderly he pulled her to him and began to caress her face and then lightly traced his fingers over her hairline, telling her his love would wipe away the memory of what she endured in the woods. He moved the sheet aside, and she slowly lowered herself down next to him, although she did not look at his lower body.

"Ellen, you are beautiful."

She had heard almost those same words from Michael, but they had sounded like mere flattery. This time, she felt deep within her bones the sensation of being cherished.

He gently kissed her shoulders and moved to her neck. Ellen had no idea of what she was supposed to do, but her body became aroused. This was nothing like the afternoon in the vacant lot with Michael. This felt completely right and honorable.

He moved and kissed the top of her arms, then gently cupped one of her breasts and kissed it. When she did not object, he took the breast into her mouth and began to slowly suck the nipple.

Oh my God. She shuddered with delight. He moved and suckled

the other breast as well. Then he slowly slid his hand down her stomach and stroked her thighs with his fingertips.

Is this the way it is supposed to feel? No one ever told me it could be so explosive. She became wet, and a new type of energy surged through her body. Ellen could not have stopped, even if she had wanted to. She felt her virginal body demand that he take her, and she knew in that split second that no one else would ever be able to claim her. This act was a defining moment, and it would banish forever the young naïve girl she had been. For once, this had nothing to do with business, and everything about the man she had come to love.

Soon they were together, limb to limb, with an insatiable need for each other. James had proceeded gently at first, but then her body responded with such urgency that he surrendered to the need to be inside her. Her nipples became erect and her body arched as he entered her and drove himself deep within. She grabbed his buttocks and held him tight. They pulsated against each other, escalating till their bodies crested and exploded in a fit of raw climax that dropped them both back onto the bed in an exhausted ecstasy of delight.

For the remainder of the night, she never left his side.

***

Hours after Sunday dawned, she looked over at his sleeping body and marveled that this love had been waiting for her all along. She tiptoed back to her room, gave herself a cold sponge bath and dressed for the day. She felt different and realized that Mam had told her the truth. With the right person, love is a beautiful and shared gift. She had never felt so complete. The physical seal had bonded them in a way that nothing else could. Everything about being with James now felt completely right. She knew she wanted to be with him for the rest of her life. All she needed was the right moment to tell him those exact words. But perhaps with her bold gesture of coming to him last night, he already understood.

Downstairs at the breakfast table, she murmured a shy "Good morning." After a quick cup of tea and some toast and eggs, James paid

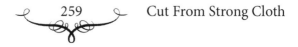

their bills, retrieved the valises, and walked outside with her, arm in arm.

"I best be going if I don't want to miss the train."

When he bent down to kiss her, she clung to him for a moment.

"Ellen, 'tis not like I won't be seeing you again," he chided.

"I know, but I don't want to be separated."

"Just a few days more." He leaned over and kissed her firmly on the lips. "That's so you won't be forgetting me."

"Och, James, I think you're making me blush."

Then they parted, waved to each other, and she watched as he became swallowed up in the crowd on his way to the train station. Ellen crossed back over the street to the infirmary and found her way to the wing where Magdalena lay sleeping. Dressed in her private duty nurse dress, Ellen felt confident that she could continue to pull off the charade, at least a little bit longer.

She placed her valise under Magdalena's bed and then checked for any charts. Finding none, she decided to search out a nurse or doctor that would give her information on Magdalena's condition. A few moments later, a doctor walked onto the ward.

"Excuse me, doctor, but I was wondering what you could tell me about this patient lying over here. She is a friend of mine, and I canna find her chart."

"Let me check my records. Magdalena Canavan—brought in last night. Fever, chills, and malaise."

"Canavan? No, the patient's name is Magdalena Fox."

"Well, according to this chart, her name is Magdalena Canavan. She's made it through the worst of the fever, and she'll survive. So will the baby."

"The baby? There must be a mistake. Her name is Magdalena Fox, and to my knowledge she's not pregnant."

The doctor gave her an imperious look. "How well do you know her then? Because you should be able to recognize the signs of a pregnancy. Now excuse me, I have other patients to see. Are you working here or just visiting?"

"I'm visiting." Ellen gave him a nod, and once the doctor left, she sank in a nearby chair.

Dear God! Who would have written down the name Magdalena Canavan, and how could she be expecting a child? Did Patrick know Magdalena was pregnant? Was that the real reason he had left in such a hurry to return to Philadelphia? As Ellen considered all this new information, Clare appeared.

"Ellen? Good morning. How is your friend doing?"

"Good morning. She's asleep, so I've not been able to speak with her. Clare, do you think hospital records ever get mixed up?"

"Of course. I'm sure it happens. Why?"

"I checked Magdalena in here myself last night, and now this morning one of the doctors referred to her under a different name, and informed me that she's pregnant."

"Mistakes can happen, but not usually when diagnosing a pregnancy. You didn't know?"

"No, not at all."

"Well, I'll be helping with the morning rounds. You could accompany me if you like until she gets up. Then you can ask her outright. Doing rounds might mean changing a bed pan or checking with a patient to see if there is anything he or she needs. I'd welcome your company."

"I'd be glad to help in any way I can."

"Good. We'll start in the women's ward. They're usually in worse shape than the men because women seem to come to the hospital only when they are very sick. Often they've waited too long, and no one can help them. The least we can do is to try and make them comfortable."

They entered the women's ward, and Ellen's heart sank to her stomach. The women in the beds were all thin and looked like they would benefit from a warm bath. Ellen and Clare went patient to patient, bed to bed, reading the charts and talking to the women, trying to offer at least a bit of empathy and compassion. Dismayed at the thin blankets and the poor quality of their weave, Ellen bent down to examine the fabric. Each blanket felt coarse to the touch and upon closer inspection they appeared to be mostly shoddy. None of these blankets would last through the first washing. What a waste!

"Clare, are you aware of how pitiful these blankets are?"

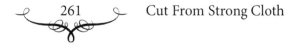

"It's a hospital, Ellen. They use what they are given."

An hour later, Ellen went back to check on Magdalena, now awake.

"I'm feeling much better. It appears I had a strong fever, but I've pulled through."

"Aye, Magdalena, we're all grateful. But I think we need to have a talk."

"You've seen my chart?"

"The doctor told me about your name, and supposedly a baby. What's going on?"

Magdalena's face betrayed the truth. "I'm sorry I didn't tell you everything before we left Savannah. I had planned on it once we were across the Confederate lines, but then I fell sick. Patrick and I were married the first week of March at the courthouse in Savannah. We had four nights together as husband and wife before he left to return to Philadelphia. But those four nights were enough to start a family. He doesn't know yet about the baby. So help me keep it a surprise."

"Why? A baby is supposed to be an occasion for celebrating. Are you worried about how my mother might react?"

"I just want to surprise Patrick myself, before everyone else hears the good news."

"All right, I won't tell. Has the doctor said when you can leave?"

"He said either tomorrow or the next day. You go do what you need to. I think I need to rest some more."

Ellen slipped outside the hospital and looked to see if there was a church nearby. She wanted the solitude of prayer. Last night with James had changed everything, and although she knew she should go to confession, she felt instead the need to offer a prayer of thanks.

She walked a block west and found St. Mary's Catholic Church. Inside, only a handful of people were scattered among the pews. Ellen genuflected in front of the crucifix, then entered a pew and knelt to pray. *Holy Mary, thank you for watching over us and bringing us closer to home. Thank you, too, for bringing James back to me and opening my eyes to his love.*

Once finished, she sat back in the pew and drank in the peacefulness of the space. She noticed a small booklet left behind on the seat

and saw that it was written in German. Strange to think of Germans as Catholics. Everyone at St. Michael's was Irish. Perhaps Magdalena and Patrick would find acceptance in Philadelphia after all.

Before leaving, she made her three wishes: one for James's safe return home, another for a productive meeting with the Quartermaster, and the last one for Magdalena's acceptance by Mam. Then she left the church. No stores were open on Sunday, so she meandered over to H Street. Here were poised the stately mansions of Washington, complete with six-pane double-hung windows. Oddly enough, they made her nostalgic for Savannah.

The afternoon slipped away. Tired, she made her way back to the infirmary, stopping first for a bowl of oyster stew in a small but reputable-looking oyster house. She felt lonely without James to share the meal, and the knowledge that Magdalena was carrying Patrick's child made Ellen wonder if she could have become pregnant from last night. As much as she wanted children, she didn't want them quite yet.

She tried to remember what the early signs of a pregnancy might be.

Cut From Strong Cloth

CHAPTER 23

April 1861

A solitary man pushed away from the other fellows who were too involved in talk of how stupid those Southern states were to secede. They hardly gave him a second thought as he left. God, the war was already complicating life.

He stepped outside and peered at his surroundings. Not having heard from his benefactors in weeks, he felt disconsolate. Perhaps he should look elsewhere for men who better appreciated his talents. As he walked, he came across a small fire and three men huddled around it, seeking its heat. Almost at once, his pulse quickened, even from just this small flame. The men in front of him had no clue.

He left them and sought solitude, wanting to bring back the image of his last fire. A few minutes later, he was alone. He remembered how the odor of the room had smelled when the kerosene sprang to life and started the ecstasy. The hint of tobacco taste came back as he envisioned how he had puffed on the cigar and then tossed it into the largest mound of rags before him. The fire had ignited and flames roared to life, hopping from one pile to another.

In his mind he saw the blazing inferno as the flames had danced in front of him, climbing higher and higher. Now his eyes glazed over with the seduction of the memory. He didn't even realize the actions of his hands, until he climaxed.

CHAPTER 24

April 1861

Monday dawned with an early morning rain, but Ellen had always loved a springtime shower, and the plop of raindrops hitting the roof soothed her. By today, she assumed James would be home. After checking on Magdalena, she wrote a letter to Dr. Jackson explaining about his horse and wagon left behind at Manassas Junction and hoped he would not be angry. She would post it later that day and also ask about the location of the Quartermaster's office. One of the orderlies had implied that Ellen might have to offer a bribe to get in to see the Quartermaster, since she had no government connections. *Like hell I will.*

Borrowing an umbrella from the hospital, she walked the few blocks over to Lansburgh's on Seventh Street. Here the hustle and bustle was so reminiscent of Center City Philadelphia, where shoppers choked the sidewalks and huddled under store awnings to inspect the latest displays of merchandise. She walked in and purchased a round tin of pancake makeup and a small mirror. Asking to use the toilet, she held up the small mirror while applying the makeup to conceal the bruises.

Now where would I find the Quartermaster of the Army?

The rain had stopped, and she left, peering up Seventh Street. She saw the massive U.S. Patent Office where Clare worked, with its eight Greek columns and high front staircase. She doubted any information about the Quartermaster would be found there. Looking around for a constable, she spied a familiar figure walking up the street.

"Clare! Good morning. Are you on your way to work, or to the hospital?"

"I'm on my way to work. Are you out shopping?"

"Lansburgh's had the makeup I needed, so now I'm looking for the address for the Quartermaster of the Army."

"I believe he's housed at the War Department, which is just past the President's house at Seventeenth and Pennsylvania. But why would you need the Quartermaster?"

"My family runs a small woolen business in Philadelphia. I've only been working as a private duty nurse for a few months, and I'm heading back home in the next few days. The two patients, James and Magdalena, are actually friends who are accompanying me."

"Ah. . . that explains why he addressed you directly as Ellen. Is he only a friend? He seemed to look at you with fondness." She stopped. "I'm sorry, that's none of my business."

"Well he is more than just a friend. He and I are planning to be. . . a permanent couple."

Clare smiled. "But it doesn't explain about your need to see the Quartermaster."

"I intend to manufacture cloth that would be superior to the shoddy produced by others, and sell it to the Quartermaster for use in the war."

"My goodness. Are you doing all this by yourself?"

"No, my brother Patrick, and James are both involved. We want the cloth to be used for uniforms. But after what I've seen here in the infirmary, I would also like to make quality blankets for hospitals."

"I wish you the best of luck and hope you succeed. There'll be a great need for cloth, I fear, for both uniforms and hospitals. I'm scheduled to work all day today, but I always stop by the infirmary after work. Will I see you there again?"

"Yes, I'll be back later, after I find the Quartermaster."

"Good-bye, then."

 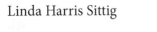

Clare turned to walk up to the Patent Office, and Ellen continued walking south until she came to Pennsylvania Avenue. Surprised at how many poplar trees lined this wide street, she saw that they nicely filled in the spaces between the buildings. My goodness, how much farther would she need to walk?

By the time she reached Fifteenth Street, she had seen quite a bit of downtown Washington and was no longer surprised at the roughness of the city. Thin cobblestones covered the streets, and other roads were left in total mud with raw sewage streaming through the gutters. Although she was walking along a somewhat stately avenue, soldiers had pitched tents all along the ground.

Then she came face to face with the home of the President of the United States.

She saw that the house sat back from Pennsylvania Avenue, set off by an intricate ornamental iron fence reminiscent of the grillwork in Savannah. A circular drive curved graciously out front, and a prominent statue of Thomas Jefferson anchored the center of the lawn. The house, painted all white, had massive Greek-styled columns supporting the front portico and the residence stretched sideways farther than any house she had ever seen, even in Savannah. Somewhere inside lived President Abraham Lincoln and his family. She couldn't help but feel impressed.

Walking further along the avenue, she finally reached the War Department. The gray stone exterior reminded her of St. Patrick's Hospital back home. Refusing to give into hesitation, she squared her shoulders, held her head up high, and walked up to the entrance. Once inside, she stood puzzled in front of a maze of corridors and doors. She was so close to meeting the Quartermaster that she would allow nothing to intimidate her, not even the immense hush of the empty space. Not sure where to go, she approached a man sitting behind a desk, shuffling papers. He made no move to acknowledge her presence.

"Sir?"

He looked up at her with disdain, as if she were a nuisance. "Yes?"

"Can you direct me to the Quartermaster's Office?"

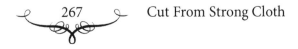

Cut From Strong Cloth

"We don't take petitions in the afternoon. That happens at nine o'clock in the morning."

"I'm not here to make a petition. I am here because I have a business proposition to offer to the government."

"Business proposition is it?" he snickered at her with beady eyes. "Tomorrow morning is when the rest of the lot will be making their petitions for business ideas."

"Is that the only time available?"

"Don't you understand English?"

A flush of indignation spread up through her cheeks. "Of course I understand what you said, but you needn't be so nasty."

"Nasty, am I? Tell me your name, and I'll make sure you never get an appointment."

Ellen looked at the man straight on. "No, thank you. I'll come back tomorrow."

The clerk went back to shuffling his papers, and Ellen marched out of the office. What an eejit, and a rude one at that.

The return walk now stretched to over twelve blocks. She stopped at a large market on the south side of Pennsylvania Avenue. The long rectangular shed-building crowded with peddlers and shoppers had numerous buggies tied out front. She walked past several vendors and then chose some items she and Magdalena could eat for dinner. Worn out by the time she arrived back at the infirmary, she trudged up the steps to the women's ward and passed the other beds, barely acknowledging anyone until she reached Magdalena's.

"Ellen, how was your afternoon?"

"Frustrating, but at least I got a chance to walk part of the city. How are you feeling?"

"Good. I think I've knocked whatever I had, provided of course the fever does not return."

"Magdalena, when did you realize you were pregnant?"

"As soon as I skipped my monthly bleeding."

"Didn't you have any early signs, other than skipping the bleeding?"

"No, not really. I didn't start feeling nausea in the morning, which is what I had been told to expect."

Then I'll have to keep an accurate account of my courses 28 days from now. Any morning nausea should be a warning sign.

"I stopped at the market and bought some slices of ham, bread and cheese, so we should be able to have a small picnic right here on your bed. I'll be spending the night here, too, sleeping on a nurse's cot nearby."

***

Ellen rose the next morning, noting the calendar pointed to Tuesday. Only ten days ago she had been living in Savannah. It seemed like a lifetime ago. Without stopping for breakfast, she left the infirmary and turned west along the same route that she had followed yesterday. She passed the President's house at exactly 8:55 and got on the queue that had already formed at the entrance to the War Department, noting with pleasure the short line.

A clerk stood at the entryway and questioned each person as to the nature of their visit before allowing them to venture inside. When her turn arrived she answered, "procuring a textile contract." She stepped inside to find the same disgruntled clerk from yesterday, barring further entrance into the depths of the building. His shifty eyes narrowed when he saw her; pursing his lips, he fiddled with the ends of his moustache which still contained crumbs from his last meal.

"So, you've returned."

She steeled herself to be as polite as possible, but she did not intend to let him thwart her plans. "Yes. And as I explained yesterday, I have a business idea to discuss with the Quartermaster. One that would involve procuring a textile bid."

"Where are you from?"

"Philadelphia."

"And I guess by your outfit, you're a domestic? You're Irish, too, aren't you?"

"I am a private duty nurse and don't see how my being Irish affects anything."

"Why would an Irish nurse be asking to see the Quartermaster

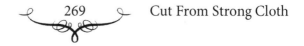

Cut From Strong Cloth

of the Federal Army?"

"My family is in the textile business."

"What kind of family do you come from, where they would send a girl to handle a man's job?"

"First of all, I am a woman, not a girl; and I am a partner in the business."

"Along with who else?"

Ellen could feel her temper rising. She should not have to deal with such an idiot. But she decided to trump him by playing along with his little game.

"My brother."

"Well then, next time send your brother. The U.S. Army don't do business with inexperienced girls posing as nurses."

She tried to hold her composure, having no intention of letting him win; but her anger flared.

"I know more about the inferior textiles the Army is purchasing than you do. Unless, of course, you are one of the unscrupulous dealers in shoddy goods yourself!"

"Your time is over. Next!" he bellowed.

She'd had enough. "I demand to be allowed to see the Quartermaster, and you have no right to keep me out."

"Demand? Well, guess what, girlie? No one's in charge right now. General Quartermaster Johnson resigned yesterday to join the Confederate Army, and a new Quartermaster has not yet been appointed. So you've made this trip for nothing. Nothing, do you hear me? Now leave this building and go back to Swampoodle with the other Irish beggars, or I'll call a constable on you!" The veins bulged in his throat as he yelled and his face turned red.

No Quartermaster? Why in God's name had he not told her that yesterday? She was furious and wanted to slap him in the face. Perhaps she should have offered a bribe after all. She stomped out to the entryway shouting, "There's no Quartermaster here now. A new one needs to be appointed! Don't waste your time!" Several people looked suspicious but stayed on line.

The fools! She was ready to tear out of the building when a new

clerk called out to her.

"Wait, Miss."

She turned on him and forgot all manners. "What do you want? To kick me off the property?"

"No. I heard you shouting that the new Quartermaster has not yet been appointed. That's true, but there are other federal depots whose commanders function as Quartermasters."

Ellen paused and simmered down. "Where would these depots be located?"

"Philadelphia has the closest, and the largest one."

"And the commander there accepts bids and issues contracts?"

"Yes, as far as I know."

"Oh, well then, thank you very much for the information."

The fury of the previous encounter simmered as she began to plan how and when she would seek out the Commander of the Federal Depot in Philadelphia. *Thank God, at least there I'll be on familiar territory.*

***

Clare was working the ward when Ellen returned to the hospital. "Ellen, there's news you need to hear. Several railroad bridges north of Baltimore have been burned, and all train passage north is suspended. In addition, the telegraph lines have been cut, and no communication is getting through. Traveling north is impossible right now."

Ellen bit her lower lip. "But James should be in Philadelphia."

"When did he leave?"

"Early Sunday morning."

"The bridges were burned over the weekend, and the telegraph wires were severed on Sunday."

"How, then, would James have gotten through?"

"That's the point. He couldn't have, unless he found an alternate route. With the telegraph lines down, there would be no way for him to contact you."

Ellen sat down, despair weighing on her shoulders. "Now what?"

Cut From Strong Cloth

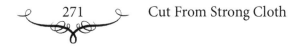

"You'll have to stay here in Washington until rail transportation is available again."

"No. We need to get back to Philadelphia as soon as possible. I need to be with James, and we have business matters to attend to. What other way is there to travel?"

"If you could get to Annapolis, Maryland, you might be able to find passage on a river steamer going north up the Chesapeake Bay. Once you make it to the top of the bay, you should be able to get transportation into Philadelphia."

"Annapolis? There is a family there who might be able to help me." *Damn you, Nash Finch, I never thought I'd have to call on your people for a favor.* "At this point, I'll do whatever it takes to get home."

"It seems like your only option, then."

***

Clare found a reputable wagon driver willing to take Ellen and Magdalena all the way to Annapolis, although the man arrived behind schedule and they got a late start. Unlike Mr. Quigg, this man kept to himself and did not engage either of them in conversation as they headed out along the Annapolis Road. The erratic April weather had turned exceptionally cool, and they pulled their cloaks more securely across their bodies.

Once they had traveled eighteen miles east of Washington, the horse needed to rest. They were obliged to spend the night in a cross-roads called Collington, which hosted only a stable and a cold harbor inn, meaning there would be no warm meal available. The driver paid the liveryman to take care of the horse and asked for two rooms for the night.

Ellen and Magdalena shared a paltry meal of some cold beef slices and thin pieces of cheese served with stale bread. They retired to a barely adequate room, trying not to think of what possible vermin might be crawling in the bed with them. The next day they took the offer of tea and what the proprietor passed off as breakfast rolls, then re-boarded the wagon and continued east.

When they reached Annapolis a few hours later, Ellen asked the

driver to take them directly to the waterfront. Driving past St. Anne's Church, he turned down Church Street toward the city docks. With the water in plain view, he deposited them a block from the harbor. Ellen paid him in federal money, realizing now she had very little left.

The clapboard houses in this town reminded her of Fredericksburg with window boxes filled with blooming phlox and pansy. They picked up their bags and headed straight for the market building, which was considerably smaller than in either Philadelphia or Savannah, but would hopefully have people possessing the information Ellen sought. She began to inquire at each stall about a certain type of business; shipping goods to be exact.

"Who's the family we're looking for?" Magdalena asked.

"Finch. They're supposed to be in a maritime business. Nash mentioned he still had cousins up here."

"You don't mean Nash Finch of Savannah?"

"Yes, he's our shipping agent for the cotton purchases. Didn't Patrick tell you?"

"Patrick and I didn't talk business, and anyway I already know of Nash Finch. Probably every woman in Savannah does. I didn't realize it was his family we were trying to locate."

The tantalizing smells of newly-baked bread and rolls barely concealed the odor of fish waste that hung in the air, but the two women ventured up and down each row hungrily devouring samples of fresh baked goods. Finally, someone pointed out a long, low building about a hundred yards away on Prince George Street, down by the steamboat wharf. Together, Ellen and Magdalena headed straight for it.

The sign read, "Finch," and nothing more, but the weathered boards indicated the business had been in operation for quite some time. Ellen brushed any errant crumbs from her dress and then walked in with Magdalena and peered around. Nautical charts hung on the walls, and cabinets had drawers overflowing with maps and papers. The business looked nothing like the well-ordered cotton factor's office in Savannah, but Ellen only wanted to find owners related to Nash.

A door in the rear of the building opened, and a man with a rugged face, tanned by years on the water, approached her. "May I help

Cut From Strong Cloth

you, Miss? We don't get many women coming in here."

"Yes, I certainly hope so, Mister. . . ?"

"Finch. Reginald Finch."

Ellen's shoulders relaxed. "Well, Mr. Finch, we're looking to book passage up the bay to Wilmington, Delaware, or as close to there as we can get. We need to eventually get on a northern bound train."

"I run a freight shipping business, not a passenger business." His eyes held the hint of humor.

"But your cousin, Nash Finch of Savannah, told me that you shipped all sorts of products on your boats. We would be willing to sit on cargo if needed. We are private duty nurses and desperately need to get to Philadelphia."

"Oh, you know Nash?"

"Oh, indeed we do. I've had several business transactions with him, and he often talked about his cousins in Maryland."

"He does business with nurses?"

"I meant that he does business with my family."

"Well, I wouldn't even know how much to charge you, and anyway, these are troubled times. Women shouldn't be traveling alone on the water, not with all the soldiers being transported through here."

"Well, whoever the captain of the boat might be, he could certainly protect us."

"That would be me," said a voice coming from the back of the building. The rear door opened again.

"Nash!"

"Hello, Ellen. I guess you're as surprised to see me as I am to see you. How fortunate that you remembered I had cousins in Annapolis."

"Nash, I never expected to see you again."

"I'm sure you didn't. Now why don't you introduce me to your friend, and tell me the real reason why you're here."

"Nash, may I present my brother's wife, Magdalena Canavan, recently of Savannah."

"Savannah? How did you escape my notice?" He grinned.

"Probably because I am a married woman." Magdalena smiled back.

"Nash, we really don't have time for pleasant conversations.

We're trying to get back to Philadelphia. My brother's waiting there for Magdalena, and I need to get back for. . . several reasons."

"Ah yes, your cloth. Well it seems the only way we can transport you to a Northern train station is on one of the family's small packet boats with me as captain. I'll be delivering some. . . products, as you so aptly said, to Perryville, Maryland. From there we can get you on a train. As I understand it, the rail bridges south of the Susquehanna River have all been destroyed."

When Ellen did not reply, he quipped, "What's the matter, Ellen? You still find it offensive to be in the company of a gentleman who supports Southern economics?"

"No, Nash. I'm grateful you're here. I wish I had been more cordial to you in Savannah, even with our differences of opinions."

"Oh, I doubt that very much."

***

An hour later, they watched the Annapolis docks recede behind them as the small steamer chugged its way to the mouth of the Severn River and then forged out into the Chesapeake Bay.

Ellen stood out on the open deck beside Nash while Magdalena sat inside, away from the elements. "Nash, you haven't said why you're in Annapolis," Ellen remarked.

"Remember when I told you I had connections up North, and that your precious cotton would be guaranteed of getting through? Well this just happens to be one of those times when I brought a shipment north myself, to Annapolis."

"Do you still have cotton on board?"

"No, I'm carrying a different type of cargo. The final destination will be Perryville."

"Will you head back home then with an empty ship?"

"I never head anywhere with an empty ship."

"Then why are you going to Perryville?"

"To help you."

"To help me? But I thought you had cargo to deliver?"

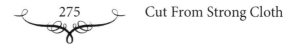

"You don't need to know all the details. Let's just get you there and onto a train."

The April weather had changed to mild, which made the trip up the bay quite enjoyable. Salt breezes teased Ellen's hair while gulls followed the ship, and the lapping of the water made a melody in tune with the tides. The peace of the afternoon refreshed her. She eagerly looked forward to being reunited with James, but she found Nash's presence to be surprisingly soothing.

"We never had the chance to get better acquainted in Savannah," Ellen admitted.

"Oh, I certainly tried." Nash laughed. "But as I remember, you were quite opposed to my company."

"I'm still opposed to slavery, but I realize I cannot condemn all Southerners in the process. Do you own slaves, Nash?"

"No, I don't. But my family does."

"How do you. . . reconcile that with God?"

"With God?" He laughed. "Do you know, Ellen, slavery has existed since the time of the Old Testament?"

"That doesn't make it right."

"Many civilizations have always depended on slave labor. The American South is no different."

"But Nash, it still doesn't make it right for humans to be bought and sold."

Nash took a long look at Ellen. "For all your gumption to succeed in business, I fear you're still naive in the ways of the working world. But I like you that way."

Ellen felt herself blush. "Nash, are you trying to flirt with me? I'm promised to another man."

"I know that. It's just a shame I didn't find you first."

Ellen turned and looked out over the water, wondering what her life as a Southern woman would have been like. "I'm thankful we met each other, Nash, even if we disagree on slavery."

Nash made no reply and then went inside to check on Magdalena.

Ellen peered out over the rail watching the water rush by and thought back to her first voyage, and losing Da. *How much my life has*

changed from being a young girl wanting to honor Da's dream and now a young woman fulfilling my own dream.

***

As they sailed up into the Susquehanna River, Ellen scanned the shoreline for the docks.

"Nash, where do we land?"

"Up beyond the Concord Light House." He pointed. "See, over there? That's the ferry landing, and we'll pull in at that spot."

As the ship reached the shore, Ellen and Magdalena saw hundreds of soldiers waiting in groups to board the ferry. Once on land, Nash nudged them past the gawking men and onto the road, passing an impressive stone tavern along the way.

"The rail station is just a bit further. I'll make sure you get on board a train."

"Then what?"

"Then I'll walk back to Rodgers Tavern for the best shad in all the Chesapeake. You'll go on home to Philadelphia," he admonished.

"Nash, we're both indebted to you. If ever you come to Philadelphia, you will always be welcome in my home."

"Be careful of what you promise, Ellen. You never know where I might turn up." He smiled.

They reached the small rail station, and Nash went inside to buy the tickets. The train was ready to make its return journey. This time, Ellen and Magdalena would be the only passengers. Before the women boarded the train, Nash took Ellen's hand and kissed it, lingering a long moment over the gesture. Her heart began to flutter. *I have already chosen my life to be with James, yet I am drawn to Nash in a way I canna explain.*

Nash turned to Magdalena, giving her hand a quick kiss, and then he picked up their valises and herded them onto the train.

"I'm afraid I haven't enough money right now to repay you for the tickets. Will you let me wire the money later?"

"Not enough money? How clever that you didn't mention that

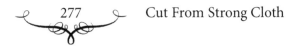

Cut From Strong Cloth

back in Annapolis. Here, you'll need some cash for a carriage once you reach Philadelphia."

"Nash, you're being too generous."

"Remember how much you need to get home. Perhaps I'll collect on this debt at another time." Then gallantly removing his hat and doffing it in the air, he bid them farewell.

As Ellen and Magdalena chose their seats, Ellen peered out the window watching as Nash walked back down the road toward the tavern. She wondered if their lives would ever cross again.

***

When they pulled into the Philadelphia passenger station at Washington and Broad, early evening had already settled. Ellen looked over at Magdalena, delighted to see her peering up at the buildings like an excited child in a candy shop.

"Ellen, Philadelphia is so big!"

"Aye, 'tis. Only a bit further and you'll be reunited with Patrick."

They climbed down the train steps and stepped onto the platform. For once, Ellen knew exactly where they were going and how to get there. Carrying their valises, they walked to the nearest omnibus stop and waited for a coach to pull in. These new modern coaches reminded Ellen of the polished wooden sides of the Southern trains they had ridden. Climbing on board, the two women jockeyed for position with the other four passengers and felt the lurch as the bus pulled out into the street traffic.

By the time they stopped at Broad and Arch, Magdalena's glowing cheeks matched the color of ripe apples, and she sat tall in her seat. They changed to a horse-drawn street car, not nearly as comfortable as the bus had been, and listened to the clip-clop of the horses' hooves as they moved out east and then north on the Fifth Street rails.

Ellen had forgotten how much she loved the hustle and bustle of Philadelphia. Even the smell of steaming horse dung in the street could not dampen her excitement at finally being home. After a short trip Ellen pulled on the rope, alerting the driver that they needed to get off.

"Come on, Magdalena, we're less than a block from home!"

Magdalena smoothed her dress and then excitedly tugged on Ellen's sleeve. "I can't wait to see Patrick."

The two women scooted up the street, past the familiar row houses of Ellen's life, and arrived at number 1225. Ellen bounded up the three steps and opened the unlocked door. "Hallo?"

Cecilia came to the front room, not even taking time to untie her apron. "Oh, Blessed Mother!" she cried, and threw her arms around her only daughter, uncharacteristically letting tears stream down her face. They hugged in such a tight embrace that Ellen began to cry as well.

"Oh, Mam, I thought we would never get back here!"

Cecilia pulled away first, wiping her eyes, and attempting to regain composure.

"Mam, this is Magdalena," Ellen offered haltingly.

"Of course. Welcome to our home, Magdalena. Patrick has told me all about you, but you are even prettier than what he described. He's out with Mr. Nolan, but should be home soon."

"Thank you, Mrs. Canavan. It's wonderful to be here."

"Mam, Magdalena shouldn't have to call you Mrs. Canavan. You're being too formal," Ellen chided.

"We'll let Patrick decide if I'm being too formal or not," Cecilia declared.

Of course. We always let Patrick make the decisions.

"Magdalena, please sit down and I'll brew a pot of tea. Have you eaten?"

"We could do with a bite." Ellen answered for them both.

Just as Cecilia began to busy herself in the kitchen, the front door blew open and in came Patrick and James—surprised to see Magdalena and Ellen seated on the sofa. Patrick ran to Magdalena, picked her up and swung her in his arms. Although James and Ellen had been separated less than a week, they both quickly crossed the room to each other, and stood in a strong embrace. Wrapped in James' arms, Ellen felt home at last.

Cecilia, hearing all the commotion, came back out from the kitchen and stood looking at the tableau in front of her. "Glory be to

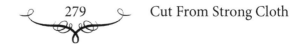

Cut From Strong Cloth

God. Everyone is here, it seems. So sit down, tea is almost ready." Then she headed back to the kitchen to set the tea tray with additional plates.

The two couples sat down as Ellen's words tumbled out.

"James, I was so worried about you when we heard the railroad bridges had been burned. How did you get home?"

"I only got as far as Baltimore and they stopped the train. The streets were crowded with people, and when I saw a group hiring a wagon, I offered to pay to ride along. So, have the bridges been repaired now?"

"Actually, Magdalena and I only got here because of the good graces of Nash Finch."

"Nash Finch, the shipping agent from Savannah?" James queried. "How did you run into him?"

Ellen could hear what she thought might be a touch of jealousy in his voice.

"Well, I remembered that Nash, I mean Mr. Finch, had relatives in Annapolis. So Magdalena and I hired a driver who took us from Washington to the Annapolis port, and we searched for Finch Enterprises. It just so happened that Nash had arrived in Annapolis that same day and offered to sail us to Perryville, Maryland. Somehow he knew that rail station was still functioning."

"How convenient."

"Really, James," she smiled. "Let's just be glad that we're all finally home, safe and sound." She looked over at Magdalena and Patrick, but they only had eyes for each other.

"All right. Everyone help themselves. Mr. Nolan, I, too, am relieved that you are home safe as well as my children, and of course Magdalena." Cecilia was beaming with unbridled joy.

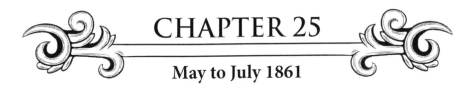

CHAPTER 25

May to July 1861

James wandered over to the factory stables to see Lir. Being with the animal always calmed him. This was his beloved horse, which Ellen had fallen for the first time she stroked the forelocks. The horse turned at the sound of James' footsteps and nudged him with full equine affection when he entered the stall.

"Aye, Lir. I know. I was gone for too long, but at least Ellen is back now, too. She'll be coming 'round to see you soon, bringing some carrots, I suspect." He stroked the horse's neck. "You know, I want to marry her, and I think I should propose soon. What do you think?

The horse whinnied as if in agreement.

"Perhaps I should take her back to where we first went driving. I think she'd like that. I'll plan something special, and I will finally come clean to her about my past. I just hope the truth won't scare her away."

***

April had melted into May, and Ellen decided to pay a visit to the Schuylkill Arsenal, with or without Patrick. She knew they had passed near its perimeter across from Grays Ferry when the train she and Magdalena had been riding pulled up to Washington Street. It would require both riding a streetcar and an omnibus to get there. Once she might have been hesitant about traveling alone even in the North, but the experiences of the past several months had forged her into a stronger woman.

An hour later, when she stepped out of the final omnibus, she saw that the arsenal was larger than she had realized, comprised of multiple buildings with imposing fronts of institutional grayness. She decided to go to the largest building first, hoping to find the Commander there. The memory of the beady-eyed government clerk in Washington made her go on the offense and she looked around for someone she could approach.

"Excuse me, can you direct me to the Commander's office? The one who gives out the textile contracts?"

"We don't usually get pretty girls like you coming here." He smiled. "I think you're looking for Captain Gibson. His office is upstairs on the second floor." He pointed toward the nearby staircase. "Of course, if you need more help than he can give, you can always come back to me."

Egad, another man who thinks that all women can be influenced by flattery. "Thank you. I'm sure I'll be all right on my own."

He nodded and walked away whistling.

She climbed the worn wooden staircase to the next level. Her new rose-striped shirtwaist with one full petticoat helped her feel business-like, but also attractive. No longer relegated to dressing for the private duty nursing sham, she wanted to look her best. She knew men were influenced by the attractiveness of a woman, and she intended to use that for her own advantage.

On the second level, men in federal uniforms were darting in and out of rooms carrying bolts of fabric or piles of paperwork, and Ellen wondered which mill in Philadelphia had produced the cloth these men were wearing. She walked down the hallway and located a sign which read, "Captain W.R. Gibson." She knocked, and when she heard a voice call out, "Come in," she opened the door.

A man far younger than she had expected sat behind the desk. A shock of light brown hair dangled over his forehead and his crisp

blue eyes made her think of Patrick. He looked up from his paperwork.

"Yes, may I help you?"

"Thank you, I'm here to see Captain Gibson about the bidding process for a textile contract. Here, I have my card." *Thank goodness I kept the rest of our calling cards from Savannah.*

He gave her an inquisitive look. "Well, I am Captain Gibson, but what is this you're giving me?"

"'Tis a calling card."

"A calling card? We don't use them for textile contracts. Calling cards are for social occasions. Wherever did you get the idea you needed a calling card for business?"

"Well, sir, I did use calling cards when I transacted my business with the cotton factors in Savannah."

"Savannah? But you're not from the South."

"No, I'm not. I was born in Ireland and have lived these past six years in Philadelphia. I went to Savannah to purchase cotton."

"You went by yourself to Georgia to buy cotton?" His eyebrows shot up in surprise.

"My brother and I are business partners. We made the trip together."

"Well if that doesn't beat all. Is your brother with you now?"

"He's at the mill in Kensington. I came here on my own."

The captain let out a short sigh. "Before we go any further, I'll need to meet him and have him produce a guarantee that he could meet the yardage requirements of a contract."

"Guarantee? Why can't you take my word that we would meet the yardage requirement?"

"Because, you're a. . ."

"A woman? How fortunate for me that you can recognize that. However, I am perfectly capable of guaranteeing the yardage requirement, and I can give my word that our cloth is free of shoddy or any reprocessed wool. I can bring samples to show you, if you like."

"Whoa! Slow down. I was going to say that because you are a . . . new supplier, we would require a yardage guarantee. And we don't bother with samples."

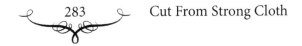

Cut From Strong Cloth

"Oh. I am sorry. Please forgive my bad manners. I am used to having men not treat me as an equal, so I apologize for jumping to conclusions about you. But, if you do not ask for samples, then how do you know that you're dealing with a reputable mill?"

The captain smiled at her honesty. "We need as much kersey as we can purchase, and we need it fast. I tell you what, Miss. . ." He glanced down at her calling card. "Miss Canavan, go home and get your brother. Tell him I would need a surety bond for the yardage guarantee. Then come back with him, and we'll see about a contract."

Ellen looked at him. A sense of deflation crept upon her. She had never considered that a yardage guarantee would be a requirement. Now she realized that she would have to tell Patrick about the surety bonds and yardage requirements, and admit she had come to the arsenal on her own. Not the way she had wanted it to happen, but Patrick needed to know the details if they were to succeed in getting the contracts.

"Thank you, Captain Gibson. I'll come back with my brother." *Just another small setback, Da. It won't stop me.*

***

"Hallo? Anyone home?"

"Stop yelling, Ellen, we're not deaf," Cecilia called out.

Ellen walked back to the kitchen and found Cecilia cooking some canned tomatoes and onions in a savory sauce. "Hmm, smells good. Where's Patrick?"

"Out back in the storage sheds."

"Is Magdalena with him?"

"No, she went shopping."

"For baby clothes?"

"When did you become interested in baby things?"

"Just trying to make conversation, Mam. For your information, I have always been interested in babies. In fact, I plan to have several of my own one day."

"Just get yourself a husband first."

"I have one already picked out."

Leaving Cecilia speechless for once, Ellen walked to the back of the house where three buildings took up most of the backyard. Closest to the house rested the largest one where they stored the raw wool before sending it on to the local factories.

"Patrick?"

"Aye, what do you need?"

"I need to tell you something."

"I hope it's not anything to do with that Quaker woman again."

Ellen ignored his remark. "No, actually it has to do with the protocol for getting a government contract."

"You been reading at that fancy library again?"

"Actually I paid a visit to the Schuylkill Arsenal."

"You did what?" Patrick stopped arranging the wool and glared at her. "I thought we had an understanding you wouldna go behind my back!"

"I dinna go behind your back. I'm planning to manufacture some cloth on my own and sell it for hospital blankets, while you and James sell yours for uniforms. I only went to the arsenal to find out the proper procedure for securing a contract."

"I canna believe you, Ellen. Are you never going to be content? Will you always be wanting to gain the upper hand?" He glowered at her.

"It's not like I'm competing with you, Patrick. I just want to do something that will help people. Decent hospital blankets are needed now, and more will be needed if the war extends."

"So, you're going to try and start your own company after all?" he snickered. "Without me."

"I can use a small room at James' factory to weave, using our wool and cotton for the blankets. It will be my own small part of the larger business."

"So you'll have to buy the wool from me?"

"Patrick, I'm a part of Canavan Wool. Remember?"

"How can I forget?" He turned to restack some bundles.

"Don't you want to hear about the protocol?"

"You go do your own protocol, Ellen. I don't need to take any lessons from you."

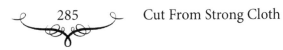

She shrugged. "Suit yourself then, Patrick." Eventually she would have to engage his help, whether he liked it or not.

***

The following week she waited outside the Philadelphia Infirmary until Catherine Biddle emerged.

"Ellen! How wonderful to see thee again. I thought perhaps thee was busy with the new business and not visiting the library anymore."

"I have been busy, Catherine. Can we walk together and talk? I need help with a dilemma and would like your advice."

"Of course. The weather is so much nicer now, than when we walked last winter," Catherine smiled. "What is on thy mind?"

"I have finally decided that I canna give up on my business plan simply because it depends on slave labor for the cotton I need. While James and Patrick produce cloth that will be used for soldiers' uniforms, I will manufacture cloth that will be sold for hospital blankets. That way I will be helping people both North and South, and the poor souls who languish in a hospital bed will at least have some measure of comfort."

"I think that is an excellent idea. Is your dilemma still about slavery, then?"

"Yes and no. While James is in agreement about my manufacturing hospital blankets, my brother Patrick is not supporting me at all."

"Does thee need his support?"

"No, not really. But it would be easier if he were more positive about my ideas."

"No one ever said that success was built on easy endeavors. Just keep him informed, so that he cannot claim you are being deceitful. Now, tell me what your new cloth will look like."

"I'm thinking it should be a lovely cream colored fabric of mixed cotton and wool."

Catherine looked at Ellen a moment then shook her head. "Ellen, I do not agree."

The look of hurt that flashed across Ellen's face prompted Cath-

erine to quickly explain.

"If thee uses a light cream colored fabric, it will show all the blood stains and leaked urine, and any other discolorations as well. The light color may or may not cheer up a sick patient, but the government will not be impressed with cloth of that color because it would require too much laundering. Make it acorn-brown. That way thee stands a better chance of selling it."

Catherine linked her arm with Ellen as they continued their walk. "Think of what is more important: selling the cloth, or insisting on a color you favor."

"But browns are so drab, Catherine!"

The older woman laughed. "Does thee not realize how brown is a color of the earth? It is a color created by God. Did thy father not weave brown yarns in Ireland? If thee feels that acorn-brown is too drab, then add a dark stripe across the bolt of the fabric for contrast."

An image of Da flashed before her eyes, of him handing her a skein of light butternut brown wool and asking her if she would like to see the new pattern he intended to weave.

"Catherine, I don't know how you always find the right combination of words, but I'll try an acorn-brown for the blanket fabric. We'll see how that sells. Thank you."

The older woman patted Ellen's hand. "I think thee will be happy with that choice. As for the issue of slavery, your hospital blankets will be helping unfortunate people. Who knows, Ellen, some of your blankets might even find their way to use on the Underground Railroad." She winked and put a finger to her lips.

***

Summer stretched out the days, humid heat blanketed the air, and longer hours of sunlight illuminated the streets of Kensington. Ellen sweated through her cotton dresses while ordering her own factory equipment and experimenting with different mixes of cotton and wool.

Cecilia did not offer any comments about the lack of income coming from Ellen, but nor did she spew any quips about the new busi-

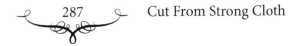

Cut From Strong Cloth

ness that Patrick, Ellen and James seemed to have concocted together. Cecilia's new identity as a mother-in-law and soon-to-be grandmother had softened her around the edges.

June progressed into July. As promised, Dr. Fallon arranged for Ellen to have her own bank account and his loan enabled her to purchase a special loom. In reality, she did not need Patrick's blessing for her business, although she would have liked his support. When the loom arrived from Crompton of Massachusetts, Ellen had it installed in the designated room James set aside for her. Both James and Patrick quizzed her on how she managed to buy the loom when she did not have any money, but she simply smiled and replied, "I have my sources." She went to the factory every day and spent hours working with the loom, finally deciding that a mix of seventy percent wool to thirty percent cotton would produce the exact type of fabric she wanted for her blankets. When several bolts had been finished to her satisfaction, she decided it was time to revisit Captain Gibson.

"Mam, I plan on going downtown shopping today and won't be back till late afternoon."

"Before you go, did you hear that Sean Fitzsimmons is back from Virginia?"

"No. When did you hear that?"

"Couldna help but hear it. Mrs. Fitzsimmons's been braggin' about her son all week, the big soldier coming home from war."

"What was he doing in Virginia?"

"Think he was in that battle called Bull Run. His mother said he volunteered for 90 days, and now his time's up. I'm not sure he wants to re-enlist."

As Ellen started down the block, Sean Fitzsimmons was leaving his house. She waved over to him. "Hallo, Sean! We're all glad you came back safe." He crossed the street to answer her.

"Thanks for the well wishes. But I don't intend to be going off again. 'Tis not how I thought it would be."

"What do you mean?"

"I thought it would be a grand adventure. 'Twasn't. I saw men get shot while standing right next to me and die in the field within

steps of where I was crouching. We thought we'd fight an hour or so and whip those Rebs. But that's not the way it happened. We fought for hours and lost the battle anyway. Never expected that. Then we was ordered to retreat back to Washington and trudged for hours in the pouring rain. Our jackets got so wet they fell apart."

"Were they shoddy then, Sean?"

"Don't know what you mean by shoddy. All I know is that my jacket fell apart and I dropped the whole soggy mess along the side of the road, just like everyone else in my unit."

Ellen listened carefully to his comments about the jacket.

"What a terrible experience, Sean. At least you came back." She gave the younger boy a quick hug.

"Thanks, Ellen. I'll see you around."

Ellen changed course and headed directly to the St. John's Street Factory. By now none of the workers even gave her a second glance when she appeared on the grounds. She walked the halls until she found Jimmy Doyle. "Jimmy, I need a favor."

"Why certainly, Miss Canavan, how can I be helping you?"

"I want you to buy some shoddy from another mill."

"Miss Canavan, you know that Mr. Nolan don't allow shoddy in here."

"Oh, 'tis not for this factory, and Mr. Nolan doesn't need to know. I want a yard piece thirty-six by fifty-four inches. 'Tis an experiment of sorts. I'll reimburse you for the cost involved."

"All right, Miss Canavan. Give me a day or two."

"Thank you, Jimmy. I'm much obliged."

***

A few days later James suggested they take a drive and have a picnic lunch out in the country.

"Should we invite Patrick and Magdalena, too?" she inquired.

"This time, Ellen, I'd rather it be just the three of us."

"Three?"

"Aye. You, me, and Lir." He smiled.

The early August sun had not yet baked the day, and Ellen relished the idea of finally getting away for some alone time with James. Memories of their night together in Washington were never far from her mind. As he drove north of the city, she recognized it as the same route they had taken where she had learned to drive Lir.

"James, I remember this route, I do."

"I thought you might. Let's stop over here. 'Tis near where you first held the reins."

He guided Lir over to a spot near some trees and let Lir nibble the grass while he and Ellen took the picnic basket out to a level area in the shade. They spread out a blanket and began to unpack the basket.

"Ellen, before we start eating, there is something important I need to tell you."

She looked up at him.

"I canna ask you to be my wife until you know something about me."

"I think I know all I need to," she gently replied.

"No, you don't. There's something you need to hear."

Ellen began to feel her stomach churn with the possibility of hearing information that she might not want to know.

"'Twas back during the Famine. My family desperately sought to stay alive, but getting food was near impossible. On a walk one day, I stumbled upon a few coins almost buried in dirt near a graveyard. I pocketed the money and went directly to a place where I knew I could buy some food, though at outrageous prices. While on the road home, a man jumped me and tried to steal the bread I had just bought. He had a knife and sliced open my jaw. In the fight, I broke his neck.

"It wasn't that I meant to kill him, but looking back, I think I did. Mary, the girl I was betrothed to, was sick and starving. I hoped the bread might save her. In the end she died anyway. I've lived with this sin all these years. I should have told you, when you killed the soldier back in Virginia." He waited. "Ellen, please say something."

The voice of the nun in the railroad car came back to her: "You'll be called on yet to serve God by helping others, and your patient will need more than just physical healing for the trials he's gone through." Was she supposed to be a part of James' healing? Could she

now imagine a life without James? No, never. He might always keep a part of himself sheltered from her, but she would have to learn to live with that.

"James, I love you, and I take you as you are. . . if indeed you are proposing."

He lowered himself to a bended knee and looked up at her. "Ellen Canavan, will you do me the honor of agreeing to become my wife?"

"Aye, James, I agree to become your wife, but under one condition."

He stared at her with a quizzical look.

"Can we wait until after the government buys my cloth? I want to be a businesswoman first, in my own right, not simply because I married the factory owner."

He laughed. "I had no idea when I fell in love with you, Ellen, how hard you would be to court, let alone get you to agree to marriage. I'll let you choose the date."

"So, you will take me as I am, with all my hopes and dreams of becoming a businesswoman?"

James smiled. "I doubt I have any other choice." A long and soulful kiss sealed their promise to each other.

Later that night Ellen went up to her room and took out her journal and penned a new entry: In the course of a year's time, I have given my heart away twice. Once to a man who broke it, and today to a man I canna live without. I have no regrets.

Da, I hope you're smiling.

***

A week later Ellen traveled back to the Schuylkill Arsenal carrying a basket with fabric samples and a pair of cutting shears wrapped inside. She hummed the Derry Air as she walked into the main building of the arsenal and walked up to the captain's office.

"Come in," he replied to the knock. "Well, hello again, Miss Canavan. Is your brother with you?"

"Actually no, Captain Gibson. He'll be coming on his own to procure the textile contracts. I came back because I want to show you

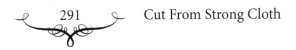

Cut From Strong Cloth

something of interest." Ellen reached into the basket and took out the folded fabric. "Here is a piece of fabric from a local mill. It is the kersey you are looking to buy, is it not?" Then she retrieved a different fabric sample from the basket. "And here is another piece of fabric from a different mill. Now I would like you to indicate which cloth you might be interested in."

He peered at her. "Judging from their colors, I would most likely choose this blue kersey."

Ellen took out the shears and cut off a large piece. "Please watch." She went back out into the hall and retrieved an empty fire bucket from its place hanging on the wall. Then she re-entered the captain's room. "Captain Gibson, would you have water here in your office that I might fill this bucket?"

If he thought her request strange, he did not give any indication. He walked over to the window sill and uncorked two canteens, pouring all the water into the bucket and then handing it to her.

Ellen dunked the piece of blue cloth into the pail, swirled it around hard and then began to pull and stretch the fabric as she yanked it out into the air, with some flourish. To the captain's dismay, he saw sodden strands of wool begin to unravel from the bottom of the fabric.

"That, sir, is shoddy." She twisted the wet wool over the bucket, squeezing out as much water as possible, and then dumped the soggy fabric mess into a nearby waste barrel. Next she took out the shears again and cut off a piece from the other fabric. She lowered this piece into the same water, swirled it around hard, and then pulled it out and stretched it with some force. The cloth remained whole.

"This second sample is from our mill, Captain Gibson." She waited a moment for the effect of her demonstration to set in. "Now, I would like to negotiate with you for the yardage you require. My brother, Patrick, will come here to discuss with you about the surety bonds for the production of the cloth. In the meantime, I want to sell you additional cloth for military hospital blankets."

"Quite impressive, Miss Canavan. Please sit down. I can draw up a contract for hospital blankets today. Can I assume you are aware of the price the government is offering?"

"I know that the government has previously paid $1.55 per yard for cloth that is finished and dyed according to specifications. I also know that the unscrupulous mills have underbid that price in order to gain the contracts. But then, those are the mills passing off shoddy goods. I would be expecting $1.65 per yard because mine is a blended fabric of wool and superior cotton, and it will long outlast any shoddy. Patrick will come to negotiate on his own."

He grinned. "How long have you and your brother been in business?"

"Long enough that we're no longer greenhorns."

"Very well, then. Cloth for soldiers' uniforms and hospital blankets it will be. How soon can I expect to meet your brother?"

"He'll probably come within a week or two. The first bolts of my cloth for the hospital blankets should arrive in about ten days' time." She stood up. "It was a pleasure doing business with you, Captain Gibson." She offered a handshake.

"The pleasure was mine, Miss Canavan. It is always a delight to deal with an intelligent business. . . person."

Now it was Ellen's turn to grin. Life was grand.

CHAPTER 26

August 1861

A few days before her birthday, Ellen emerged from a Saturday noon Mass feeling serene. Then she saw him lounging against a nearby street sign. A flood of memories washed over her and she felt like someone had just stepped on her heart.

"Hello, Ellen. Looking lovely as always, I see. That green dress does justice to your eyes."

"Michael, what are you doing here? I doubt you're going to Mass."

"No, I only did that to try and impress you. Remember?"

She steeled herself. "I remember only too well. But that was a lifetime ago, and we are no longer involved with each other. Not in any way."

"Well, that may not be so. 'Tis why I came to find you."

"What do you mean?"

"I was there."

"Where, Michael? What are you talking about? You sound like you're speaking in riddles."

"Oh, 'tis no riddle, darlin'. You see, I saw what the soldier tried to do to you."

Ellen's face blanched as she strove to keep her composure. "I have no idea what you're babbling about."

He lowered his voice. "A man's dead because of you."

How could Michael possibly know about the soldier? She held herself back from answering and simply stared at him. Other parishioners were coming out of church and several nodded hello to Ellen, curiously eyeing Michael Brady.

"Perhaps we should take a walk?" he asked. "Just like old times."

"I don't need to walk with you anywhere," she snapped.

"Oh, darlin' I think you do. Unless of course, you want your neighbors to hear the word, *murder.*"

"Are you trying to scare me, Michael? Because everything you're saying is pure rubbish."

"I don't think so. Late April? Small camp in Virginia? Federal soldier who tried to rape you? Does that ring a bell?"

She steeled herself not to panic. "All right, let's walk over to the next block. Now, why are you here, telling me this?"

"I saw everything that night. I would have stepped forward to help, but you stabbed the bloke before I could reach you. I saw him fall."

She still did not flinch.

"You see, Ellen, I'm a wee bit short on cash right now, and thought perhaps you could provide me with a small advance? Until things get better."

"You're trying to blackmail me!"

"No, just trying to keep you off the docket and possibly out of prison, darlin', that's all. Why don't you think it over and meet me tomorrow after the nine o'clock Mass? Be smart, Ellen. It would be my word against yours, but I have all the details. 'Tis possible the government might be offering a reward for information like this."

He tipped his cap and winked, then sauntered off down the street.

She watched him for a moment, realizing that a year ago he had held her heart, but now he only held her contempt. His information could lead her to jail.

Swallowing the taste of fear rising in her mouth, she walked in the opposite direction and refused to show any hint of concern until after she turned the corner. Then she choked back the urge to vomit with the memory of the soldier and the idea that she could be arrested.

She couldn't discuss this with anyone but James. Continuing on

Cut From Strong Cloth

home, she tried to calm herself. If she appeared distressed in any way, Mam would be suspicious.

Opening the door, she called out, "Hallo? I'm back. Anyone here?" Her heart was still racing, though she tried to maintain some decor.

Inside the house, the August afternoon heat made even the curtains perspire. From two stories up came the whirl of her mother's sewing machine; Cecilia would be occupied for a while. She went back to the kitchen and drew a cup of water from the crock. The factory shut down by one o'clock on Saturdays, and she wondered if James could possibly still be in the office. The heat felt suffocating, and her anxiety would only multiply if she stayed.

"Going back out, Mam," she shouted, grateful of no reply.

She arrived at the factory and opened the gates, glancing back to make sure that Michael Brady had not followed her. The building was as familiar to her now as her own home. Even with eyes closed, she could find her way through the corridors to Weaving Room Number 4 and her loom.

Pushing open the immense oak door, she did not bother to call out a greeting that James wouldn't be able to hear. Heat from outside pulsated against the windows, making the inside of the factory feel stagnant. She turned left and walked down the center walkway and then to the right to reach James' office but found it empty.

Damn, he's already gone.

She left his office and headed down another corridor where she could at least peek in on her loom. The machine represented more than just a wooden frame; it conveyed Da's old dream and her new prospects for success. Neither James nor Patrick would ever understand her fierce attachment to this loom, but Da would have.

As she entered the room, she noted some small rag piles of cotton and other debris dotting the floorboards. She could tidy this up. She looked around for a broom and dustpan, but found none.

Her gaze turned to the loom. Nearby, stacked boxes of large threaded bobbins sat on a table next to the first few finished bolts of the new fabric. She went over and laid her hand on the cloth with rever-

ence. Then she checked the loom, noting with satisfaction that the yarn had all been properly wound for the next week's production. Soon they would be singing a symphony of woven threads. She smiled to herself with delight.

Then a strange odor began to permeate the air—not the usual smell of sulfur, soap, or lanolin always present in the factory. This was an acrid smell, and it caught in her throat. She couldn't quite place it, but it bothered her.

Inhaling deeply, she detected faint traces of cigar smoke. No one should be smoking inside the factory, and the smell caused her pulse to quicken. She turned around and saw a thin wisp of tobacco smoke lingering by the exit where the back door had been left ajar. A bundle of wet rags lie nearby.

She nervously bent down to investigate, touched one of the rags, then recoiled when she realized it was soaked in kerosene. When she looked over at the other small piles of rags, she saw puddles behind each one.

Dear God in Heaven, why would there be kerosene in the room?

She knew how quickly the kerosene could ignite a fire, so she turned and ran back toward the hallway for water buckets. But the room's front door had quietly shut on itself. She tried to open it, only to discover it was locked. A feeling of panic started in her throat. How had the door swung closed without her hearing it? The only exit now would have to be through the back, cigar smoke or not.

Fear gripped her entire body as she walked over toward the back door. A large shadow blocked the incoming light.

"Who's there?" she called out, her voice trembling.

A figure emerged from the shadows.

"Oh, dear God. You gave me a fright just now. Look out, there's a pile of kerosene soaked rags near your feet."

"Never can stay out of my way, can you?"

"What do you mean? Come help me remove the rags."

As she bent down, he seized her arm and held it tight.

"You weren't supposed to be here, little sister."

"Patrick, stop! You're hurting me. And what are you doing with

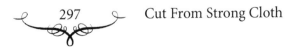

297   Cut From Strong Cloth

a cigar in your mouth? You don't smoke."

"Oh, there's lots about me you don't know. Isn't it obvious? When I drop the cigar into the rags, the kerosene will come to life."

A cold jolt of fear shot through her. Gazing directly at him, she realized she'd never seen him like this before. His eyes were like empty cubes of ice, and the hard line of his mouth held a menacing, twisted grin.

"Patrick, for God's sake, what's wrong? Why would you even be thinking of setting a fire in here?"

"Because Ellen, that's what I do. I set fires for pay and then rush back afterward with my brigade and pretend to help extinguish the blaze. You never knew, did you? Just like you never knew that it was me who sold James' idea for government bids to the McFadden brothers."

"You!" She tried to pull away, but he dug his fingers deeper into her arm muscles.

"Aye, me. I got a tidy sum of cash, and Michael Brady out of your life, both with the same bargain."

"Patrick, I canna believe any of this."

"I've made quite a lot of money through the years with my schemes. 'Twas tough always being the poor Irish immigrant and never getting a break. So I made my own breaks. But this time it's personal, only you weren't supposed to be here to witness it."

"Personal? Dear God, Patrick what are you talking about? You're not a fire setter!"

"But I am. This time, nobody's paying me. I'm doing it to destroy your precious loom. I'm the one in the family who's supposed to succeed! You were to just marry James Nolan, and then I could be rid of you. But you got it into your fancy head that you could take a part of James' factory and use it for your own business. Leaving me only Canavan Wool, a small enterprise."

"Patrick, let's just talk this out, you and I. Brother and sister, one to another. You're acting crazy."

His fingers dug even deeper into her upper arm, causing her to wince with pain. "Half brother," he sneered.

"Half brother? Patrick, nothing you're saying makes any sense."

"We only share the same mother. Da wasn't your father. He

was mine!"

Ellen felt as if her legs would give way. "Don't be ridiculous. Of course Da was my father."

"You know nothing." He spat. "In Dungannon, Mam worked as a hired seamstress for Lord Bedwell, a wealthy Brit who owned an estate in Ulster. One day he came in and raped her. Nine months later you were born. You're a rape child, Ellen. You're a reminder of the Anglo pig who violated her."

"Patrick, I don't believe any of this!"

"Haven't you ever looked in the mirror? We look nothing alike, you with your dark hair and green eyes. You're not a Canavan. You're a bastard! I've had to help take care of you all these years, but I don't intend for you to steal the success and fortune that is my birthright. I'm the only true Canavan."

As the words sank in, Ellen felt a wild panic. *Bedwell? Oh dear God, the same family as Nash Finch's mother?* Of course she didn't need a mirror to know she looked nothing like Patrick, but the idea of Da not being her real father was too painful to even consider.

"What of Magdalena? Does she know this?"

"Leave her out of it. She knows nothing and that's the way it'll stay."

Then without warning, Patrick spit the cigar out of his mouth and onto one of the rag piles. The kerosene ignited. Flames rose from the pile and jumped to the nearest puddle, setting another small fire.

Ellen wrenched her arm away from Patrick's grasp and ran to the rags trying to stamp out the flames, but Patrick grabbed her from behind and dragged her back.

"I'll make you watch your precious loom burn to ashes," he shouted in her ear. "Then you'll see the power of the flames like I do."

"No!" Ellen brought the heel of her shoe down hard in the middle of his foot. Patrick screamed in pain and staggered, but his hand shot out and grabbed her dress. "You and your loom can go to hell!" he roared.

Panicked, Ellen wheeled and tried to pull her dress from his grip. With a terrific yank the material tore, and she managed to break free. But it set Patrick off-balance. Stumbling backwards he fell down on top of some burning rags, and his clothes caught fire. Ellen watched

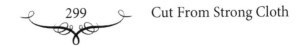 Cut From Strong Cloth

a moment in shock and then rushed at him, beating on his shirt and pants, trying to stop the flames.

My God, Patrick, what have you done?

A nearby bolt of fabric ignited and so did a pile of refuse. Suddenly small fires erupted around the room as Ellen ripped off the bottom portion of her petticoat and tried desperately to smother the flames that were torturing Patrick. In his madness, he grabbed her and pulled her to the floor with him.

Fury combined with her instinct for survival. She bit his arm through his lightweight summer shirt. Patrick screamed in pain and then focused his rage directly on her as she tried to crawl away from him.

"You're not going anywhere!" He bellowed. His eyes were wild with insanity and his mouth contorted in agony.

Flames leapt up a wall, hungry to devour everything in the path, and the wood of the loom cracked as tongues of fire began to ingest it. Patrick grabbed for her throat at the same moment she heard the whinny of terrified horses coming from the stables out back.

"Lir!" she choked on the words.

She turned to see that a heavy bobbin had rolled over toward her. In desperation she reached for it and swung hard toward the intended target. She heard the sickening sound of wood smashing bone but dragged herself away towards the only available escape—the back door of the burning room.

When she reached the hallway, she blacked out.

***

The humming sounded far away, although its strains were familiar. Confused as to her whereabouts, she tried to stay awake. She so desperately wanted to talk, but pain reared up, and once again she slipped away. Dipping in and out of sleep, she tried valiantly to remember what had happened. All the thoughts and images became jumbled together and made little sense.

There'd been cigar smoke and a fire, and a scene in the woods with a dead soldier whose face melted into Patrick's. Michael Brady watched nearby. Patrick told her ridiculous things—he was a fire start-er, he had sold plans to another mill. Michael Brady was trying to tell her something, too. Then the hazy shape of Da appeared, reaching for her hand. They were walking among the sheep back in County Tyrone. She needed to ask him an important question, but he raised a finger to hush her. "Have courage, Ellen, and be bold. Then nothing can stop you."

For quite some time she tried to come back, but the drugs con-tinued to drag her away into the depths of healing and sleep.

**

Voices floated nearby and her eyelids tried to open, but to no avail. She listened.

"Damn lucky you found her in time."

"But she'll have the scars the rest of her life, won't she?"

"She's alive, sir. Clothing can hide scars."

Scars? What were they talking about? Where was she? She thought she heard James' voice, but she couldn't be sure. With great effort, she struggled to open her eyes only to have the light momentari-ly blind her.

"Ellen?"

He had seen her eyelids flutter, and rushed to her side.

"Ellen, can you hear me?"

A slight nod of her head indicated she could.

He reached toward her in the hospital bed, wanting to hold her and stroke her singed hair.

"Sir, we need you to step aside so I can examine her." The doctor lifted one of Ellen's eyelids.

"By God, she's coming back to us," he declared. "Let's keep her resting. She's been through the worst of it, and now needs to regain some strength. Thankfully the burns were mostly superficial and did not damage her leg muscles. She'll walk again."

**

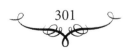 301   Cut From Strong Cloth

Ellen had no concept of time, nor how many days had passed. Finally she could focus and peering up, she saw James at her side.

"Patrick?"

The look of dread in his eyes said everything, but he answered truthfully. "He didn't make it, Ellen. The doctors said too much smoke got in his lungs. I'm so sorry." There was no need to mention the fatal burns.

She nodded her face, devoid of all expression. "Lir?" Her voice was hopeful, but tinged with trepidation.

"Lir's fine. He's the one who alerted me."

She looked confused.

"I was out in the stables that afternoon when Lir reared up and pawed the air and acted like an animal that's seen a demon. Horses only do that for two reasons. One is if they're trapped with a snake, and the other is if they're near fire. I checked his stall, but he continued to whinny with terror in his eyes, and his huge body trembling. I looked towards the factory and saw smoke trailing out from a broken window.

"I knew it was coming from your weaving room. When I got there, the door was locked, so I ran to the back entrance. You were lying in the hallway with your petticoat smoldering. I rolled on top of you to stop the burning and then pulled you outside. Then I ran back inside in case Patrick was there, too. I tried to beat the flames off him as I dragged his body out of the building. Oh God, Ellen. I'm so sorry I couldn't save him as well."

He waited a moment. "Your room and part of the nearby hallway suffered the worst damage. The new loom, however, was completely destroyed. We're lucky the firemen were able to prevent the whole factory from going up in a blaze."

Ellen listened. Patrick gone. The loom gone. But thanks to Lir, she was alive.

"None of us can figure out how the fire started, but Patrick's burns were substantial. Your mam's overcome with staggering grief. Mr. Hookey, the undertaker, has been able to keep Patrick's corpse on ice, until the family's ready for the burial. Your mother wanted you to be a part of the funeral and for his fire brigade to be the pall bearers. Ellen,

you need to know we all believe his body protected you from the worst of the flames. Only your one leg was really burned." In his nervousness and relief that she was alive, he realized he had been babbling.

Ellen did not respond because she knew exactly how the fire had started. Patrick had been a fire starter for years, and no one knew. He had been the informant on the original government contract idea, too. If she ever revealed the truth, the name Canavan would be forever tainted, associated with an arsonist, a criminal. No one in Kensington would forgive her ratting on her own brother. Mam might not even believe Ellen.

I can never tell what I know.

A moment of even deeper clarity began to emerge. Mam. No wonder there had always been tension between them. Bedwell? If it was the same family, then she and Nash were blood kin—another secret she would have to keep. Weariness as heavy as a wet blanket settled on her. She needed to sleep, and time to heal her private heartache.

"I need to rest, James. Can you come back later?"

"Of course. Perhaps I did too much talking just now. Your mother will be here soon, just as she's been every day to check in on you."

But Ellen had already drifted off.

***

Days later, she pulled back the hospital blanket to look at her legs. The damaged one was no longer completely wrapped in gauze, but the flesh felt tight. Looking closer, she saw streaks of ugly puckered skin that ran from her knee to her ankle. She recoiled at the sight.

"Thank God you're awake." Cecilia entered the cubicle and went immediately to Ellen's side. "I've prayed everyday for your healing. Oh God, Ellen, I was so afraid I'd lose you, too." The wall of composure that usually fortified Cecilia broke, and she dissolved into sobs.

"I'll make it, Mam, but I'm so sorry about Patrick."

Cecilia took out a handkerchief and wiped her red rimmed eyes. "They say his body probably shielded you from the worst of the fire. He gave his life to save you."

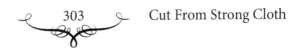

Cut From Strong Cloth

Ellen paused. "Yes, 'tis true," she softly replied.

"Magdalena came for several days to see you, but we decided she needed to stay away from the hospital because of the baby. She's due now in four months."

Ellen nodded.

"Looks like you'll be coming home soon and then we can have Patrick's funeral." Cecilia's voice gave every indication that she was attempting to restore some normalcy back in her life. But Ellen suspected the take-charge demeanor was a feeble attempt to avoid the inevitable chasm of grief engulfing her.

"I'll be glad to get home, but you should go ahead with the funeral, and not wait for me."

"No, Magdalena will need you to be there. She has no family now, except us. For Patrick's sake we must take care of her and the baby. I still need you, too, Ellen."

Ellen looked at her mother, feeling true compassion for why there had always been so much tension between them.

"Before someone else shares the gossip, I want you to hear something from me."

"Hear what?"

"It seems that Weikel Spice was robbed the day after the fire, and a large amount of cash stolen. The word in the neighborhood is that Michael Brady was involved. Apparently he's fled the city, and no one knows his whereabouts."

"He's of no concern to me anymore."

"I know that. But I also know he broke your heart once upon a time."

"I've grown up since then."

"I hope so, Ellen. I do want you to find real happiness in life. Not everyone does."

***

Much later, using a cane to help support herself, Ellen held onto James' arm and riveted her gaze on the coffin lying beside the open grave. Patrick's body lie entombed in the pine box before her. Flowers

were strewn over the casket, but because of the fire, a traditional Irish wake had not been possible.

"*Requiescat in pace.*" Father Reilly continued his burial incantations, but it sounded like a drone of insects buzzing in her ear. Depleted of visible emotion, but keenly aware of Magdalena holding onto Mam and sobbing, Ellen could not force any tears. She fought the urge to cry out that the man they were burying had been a fake. Not a real brother, not a saintly fireman, not even an honest member of the church. But she choked on the words before they could escape from her mouth.

Instead, she took a cue from Mam and tried to think ahead of what would need to be done for the business. If she could concentrate on that, she could almost forget the hurtful shock of Patrick's actions and words. *The weaving room will have to be cleaned of all smoke and fire damages. I'll need to check on the shipments to the Schuylkill Arsenal. Dr. Fallon will have to be notified of Patrick's death and the subsequent destruction from the fire. Thank God James had insurance on the factory. I'll need to order a new loom.*

She felt a squeeze of her hand and turned to look at James.

"Are you all right?"

"Yes, just thinking. That's all." She looked back at Magdalena, who would live with Mam, and give birth to Patrick's child. Then she turned and peered at the empty grave. The priest concluded his part of the service and the pallbearers gathered on each side of the coffin. Using ropes, they gently lowered the pine box into the open ground.

Cecilia stepped forward, weeping. She bent down to scrape up a handful of dirt, then shook it loose and let it fall onto the coffin lid. Crying, Magdalena did the same. James handed Ellen some dirt to scatter as well.

Her father's words came back to her: *Family sticks together. No matter what. Oh, Patrick. How I wish you had never told me.* Then she dribbled the dirt on the coffin.

The ceremony concluded, and the small party left Cathedral Cemetery, the hired omnibus taking them across the Schuylkill River and back into Philadelphia proper. James followed in his buggy. Once home, Cecilia and Magdalena prepared to receive visitors, but Ellen could

not suppress the duplicity of her emotions in front of the neighbors.

"James, could you take me to St. Michael's? I need a bit of solitude and want to say some prayers before I have to greet anyone."

James looked over at Cecilia, who nodded before she walked into the house. He helped Ellen into the carriage and clicked the reins. They arrived at the church in a short amount of time.

"Do you want me to come in with you?"

"No. I need to be alone. But, thank you."

He helped her down and waited till she gained her balance. Then she turned from him and very slowly walked up the steps and into the sanctuary. The church was empty and memories cascaded all around. She remembered fleeing here once before, seeking solace for bruised feelings. Now she was seeking escape from Patrick's words, a freedom she knew would never be granted.

Memories of Patrick floated to the surface: Patrick holding her arm at Da's funeral, Patrick walking with her on the first day of school in Philadelphia, Patrick teasing her about her love of books. Tears slid down her face.

Patrick, I never knew your tortured mind robbed you of the happiness you deserved. How I wish I could have helped you. May God have mercy on your soul.

Ellen wiped away the tears and straightened her shoulders. Two sides to every story is what Mam had said so many months ago. So her life would have two sides. The private side would be hers alone, the keeper of the family secrets. She could never tell anyone the truth about Patrick, not even James. The other side of her life would become a channel where she would focus her energy, her life with James, and the business.

In order to move forward she knew she had to forgive Patrick, no matter how difficult that would be. She sat in the pew and whispered, "Holy Mary, cleanse me of my sins. St. Brigid, give me courage." Then she gazed up at the ceiling. *You will always be my father, Da. No one can rob us of that, not even now.*

Family sticks together, no matter what.

***

Throughout the remainder of the Civil War, thousands of Union soldiers benefited from the blended cloth manufactured by the Nolan Factory. Others lay in hospital tents, resting under Ellen's blankets.

Together, James and Ellen Nolan became a wealthy married couple—and had lace curtains on every window.

To this day, the word "shoddy" still denotes an inferior product.

THE END

AUTHOR'S NOTES

2014

In the dining room of my home, sits an old factory chest that hints of history to anyone who cares to look.

Where long ago it held Ellen Canavan's cotton receipts from the Civil War, it now holds imagined traces of her story. If you bend down and inhale deeply, you can almost envision the far off odor of burnt wood, as if from a fire. Then if you let your fingers trace an invisible line across its top, you would be replicating the demarcation of two families buried in separate cemeteries; Ellen not resting in the same ground as her brother.

The chest is a reminder of Ellen's success—how she produced fabrics of wool blended with Georgia cotton, free from shoddy, and sold them to the federal government. Oh yes, and hospital blankets as well.

The real Ellen Canavan was the inspiration for this novel, and while much of this story was based upon historical facts and family records, I did add embellishments.

The Canavan's did live at 1225 Fifth Street in Philadelphia, and were originally wool merchants, selling to the local textile manufacturers. Mr. Canavan died when Ellen was young, and his widow, Cecilia, never remarried. No birth certificate exists for Ellen, so I invented the idea of her questionable parentage as a basis for the life-long friction that existed with her mother.

My great-grandfather, James Nolan, was the proprietor of the St. John Street Factory in Kensington, the northeast industrial section of Philadelphia. He became wealthy when his factory manufactured a special blended cloth of wool and cotton, and sold it to the federal government for soldiers' uniforms during the Civil War. His original factory was a part of the Globe Mills Complex located on St. John Street, below Girard Avenue. Today that street is called American Street, and as of the summer of 2009, his factory building was still standing.

The factory shown on the cover of this book was the actual Nolan factory.

Mary Ready was James Nolan's sister, and her family lived on Second Street, a few blocks south of St. Michael's Church. Mary and Ed Ready were godparents of James and Ellen's children: two daughters who died in early childhood, and a surviving son, Daniel James Nolan.

Ellen's brother's name was Joseph, although I chose to name him Patrick in my story. Even though he did die in a fire-related event, there is no evidence to suggest that he had ever been an arsonist or mad enough to attempt the destruction of the St. John Street Factory. Joseph Canavan actually became a highly successful factory owner in his own right.

Magdalena Fox was based upon Magdalena Foor, who is listed in the Philadelphia City Directories as Joseph's widow only after he died. She was not buried in the Canavan family plot, suggesting that their union was not recognized by the Catholic Church.

Dr. Fallon's character was based upon Louis A. Fallingant of the Homeopathic Institute in Philadelphia. He did indeed leave Philadelphia to return to Savannah and start a medical practice there; his office stood on State Street and his home was on West Broad. He eventually became the Surgeon General of the Confederacy.

Although James Nolan purchased his cotton directly from Georgia, Ellen's journey to Savannah could not be authenticated.

My mother had always told me the family believed James Nolan's wife gave him the idea of combining the different fibers to produce a superior cloth.

On all public documentations, only James Nolan's name is ever listed. Ellen's part in the business became obliterated with time, especially since she died of consumption (tuberculosis) just prior to her thirtieth birthday. As was the custom of that day, only the husband's name was recorded as the property or business owner.

Later, upon James' death, his son Daniel inherited his father's estate. The bank had called in a loan that existed on the factory, and the property passed out of our family forever; but not before Daniel was able to retrieve Ellen's old factory receipt chest and take it home. That chest was given to me by my mother, as a wedding present.

The tune James often heard Ellen whistle or hum is now known as "Danny Boy," which my mother often hummed in the kitchen when she was cooking. As a child I innocently believed it was written for my great uncle, Daniel James Nolan.

The journey to write this book started when I read the names of those buried in the Nolan vault in New Cathedral Cemetery, Philadelphia. One name jumped out: Mrs. James Nolan. I felt it completely unfair that a woman would be buried with only her husband's name for identification, and what followed was a ten-year journey to find out everything I could about Mrs. James Nolan, nee Ellen Canavan. In the process of the research I unearthed documentation proving that our family stories had been mostly authentic all along regarding the Philadelphia textile industry and how the Nolan's became wealthy, courtesy of the Civil War.

James Nolan, remarried eighteen months after Ellen's death, and his new wife, Sarah Jane Brady, helped to raise Ellen and James' only surviving child, Daniel. Then Sarah Brady Nolan gave birth to James Nolan's last child, Catherine Nolan, who became my grandmother. Even though I descended from James Nolan's second wife, I deemed it a privilege to chronicle Ellen's story, and enhance it to show the strong woman she surely was.

Ellen's fierce determination, courage, and perseverance are all a part of her legacy. Three generations after her, I am the connection that keeps Ellen's story alive—the whispers of bravery and tragedy, triumph and deceit, all sprouting long ago, across a wide ocean, and upon a foreign shore.

Ellen, may you rest in peace.

Every woman deserves to have her story told.

Linda Harris Sittig - Purcellville, Virginia
April 2014

ACKNOWLEDGEMENTS

This book would never have come to fruition without the many people who helped me along the way. With heartfelt thanks, here are most of the people and/or organizations that provided me with invaluable assistance bringing Ellen's story to life.

I would need to start with my parents, Mildred and Bill Harris, who instilled in me a reverence for my ancestors and a life-long passion for history; my incredible husband, Jim Sittig, who accompanied me on every research road trip both stateside and in Ireland and never once complained about having to listen to all of Ellen's stories; and my wonderful writing coach, David Hazard of Ascent Writing Program, who helped me turn the research into a full novel. The unsung hero of my novel was Christine Friend, an extraordinary archivist from the Philadelphia Archdiocese Historical Research Center who read through the old Philadelphia Catholic Diocese records and found that Mrs. James Nolan had indeed once been a young Irish immigrant named Ellen Canavan.

In Ireland, I was assisted by the helpful people at the Public Records Office of Northern Ireland, County Antrim; Dungannon Cultural Center, County Tyrone; Irish Linen Centre and Museum, County Antrim; Moygashel Museum and Linen Center, County Tyrone; Ulster Heritage Museum, County Tyrone; and Ulster-American Folk Park, County Tyrone.

In Pennsylvania, I was helped by the docents at the Philadelphia City Archives; the Philadelphia Historical Society; the Free Library of Philadelphia, Richard Boardman, Map Department who miraculously found the original schematics to James Nolan's two mills and copied them for me; Gerry Burns, historian of St. Michael's Catholic Church, Philadelphia; Ken Milano, historian Philadelphia; the St. Michael's Shamrock Society, Philadelphia; the Philadelphia Cemetery Office; the Catholic Diocese of Philadelphia; Francis Kearns, retired caretaker, Cathedral Cemetery; Sean Feeley, caretaker of New Cathedral Cemetery, Philadelphia; Pennsylvania State Archives, Harrisburg, PA; the Pennsylvania Railroad Museum, Strasburg, PA; and Donna Abraham, owner of *Abraham's Lady*, Gettysburg, whose books aided me with 1860s fashions.

In Georgia, I was aided by the Catholic Diocese of Savannah, and St. John the Baptist Church; the Savannah Visitors Center; Georgia State Historical Society, Savannah; Damon Fowler, cookbook author, Savannah, who helped me authenticate the southern meals; and John Duncan, owner of V. and J. Duncan Bookstore, Savannah, who provided me with an 1861 street map of Savannah.

In Maryland, I was assisted by Back Creek Books, Annapolis where I found an1861 street map of the town; the Librarians at Enoch Pratt Library, Baltimore; Baltimore and Ohio Train Museum, Baltimore; Sister Betty Ann McNeil, Daughters of Charity, Emmitsburg; Civil War Medical Museum, Frederick; Thrasher Carriage Museum, Frostburg; the Transportation Museum, Cumberland; and Gerry Lafemina with the Frostburg University Night-Sun Writing Workshop whose participants gave a valuable critique of my first rough draft.

In Virginia, I was helped by Eugene Scheel, Mapmaker, Waterford, whose incredible maps of Virginia, 1861, helped me to replicate Ellen's journey back north; Chronicle of the Horse Library, Middleburg; Haunts of Civil War Richmond Tours; the Manassas Museum; Liberia Estate, Manassas; Carriage Museum, Morven Park, Leesburg; Museum of the Confederacy, Richmond; Visitors Bureau, Fredericksburg; Civil War Museum at the Exchange Hotel, Gordonsville; Loudoun County Public Library, which arranged interstate library loans with Georgia; and Rich Gillespie's tours with the Mosby Heritage Foundation for the Civil War, Atoka.

Linda Harris Sittig

The members of the Round Hill Writers Group of Loudoun County, VA who still provide me with countless hours of support; my reading group friends who first read through the completed manuscript, including my Quaker buddies who read for accuracy on Catherine Biddle; Cathy Dodds, Leesburg, VA who showed me the entire spinning and weaving process, and shared the Irish traditions of hand weavers; my wonderful publisher, Eric Egger who believed in Ellen's story; Val Muller, my superb editor; and lastly, the trucker on I-95 whose identification was painted on his cab door: Nash Finch. It was the perfect name for a Southern gentleman and I knew I wanted it in my story.

Cut From Strong Cloth

 # GLOSSARY

The following words are a small part of the Irish terminology that could have been used by many of the immigrants in the 1860s. Rather than confuse the reader with a lot of Irish words and different dialects, I have chosen a few to help convey the feel of the conversations. Other terms, hopefully, were explained within the context of the paragraph where they were written.

Acting the goat – behaving like an idiot
Arse – ass
Bangers – sausage
Barque – a ship with three masts
Bashtoon – bastard
Barmbrack – a wheat speckled bread served at many meals
Brass neck – nervy
Boyo – young lad
Bun in the oven – pregnant
Canna – can't
Champ – potatoes mashed with buttermilk and chives
Children of Lir – popular Irish folk tale
Coddle – casserole of sausage and potatoes
Colcannon – meal of potatoes mashed with bacon and cabbage
Con – the "con," or consumption, today called tuberculosis

Cuppa – cup of tea

Da – Dad or father

Dinna – didn't

Eejit – an idiot

Kensington – the industrial section of Philadelphia bounded by
    Girard, N. Sixth, Oxford, and Front Streets

Let the hare sit – leave it alone

Lir – a king in ancient Ireland

Mam – mom or mother

Nativist – an1840s political party opposed to foreigners

Queue – a line of people waiting for service

Shanty Irish – the lowest class of Irish society

Swampoodle – the Irish tenement section of Washington D.C.

Skiver – a ne'er-do-well

Soupers – name given to Irish Catholics who denounced their
    religion in order to gain entry to soup kitchens set up
    for the Protestant Irish during the Famine

Youse – the plural of you

Cut From Strong Cloth

ABOUT THE AUTHOR

Born in Greenwich Village, New York City, and raised in Northern New Jersey, Linda was lured into reading by *Lad, a Dog* and *Nancy Drew, Girl Detective*. Later her attraction to history and a bit of wanderlust led her to study in Switzerland, before returning stateside to earn a B.A. in History and a M.Ed. in Reading.

Combining her passion for history, stories, and the need for literacy, she began publishing commentaries on how parents could encourage the love of reading with their children. That led to a twenty-year weekly newspaper column, "KinderBooks" (*Loudoun Times-Mirror*); a non-fiction text, *New Kid in School* (Teachers College Press); and writing for a nationally syndicated educational newsletter, *The Connection* (PSK Associates). Linda has been recognized twice by the Virginia Press Association with Certificates of Merit for her journalism.

Her articles have appeared in *The Washington Post*, *The Reston Connection*, and *The Purcellville Gazette*, in addition to numerous professional journals and short story anthologies. From 1982 – 1994 she received three separate distinguished educator awards from local, state, and international organizations. Linda teaches at Shenandoah University in Winchester, VA, where she works with educators on how to implement the best practices of literacy instruction.

Currently promoting her novel, *Cut From Strong Cloth*, Linda is paying tribute to an ancestor who in 1860 Philadelphia struggled to become a successful textile merchant as the Civil War exploded around her.

Alimond photography

Linda lives in Loudoun County, Virginia with her husband, and where the Blue Ridge Mountains are the first to greet the dawn. In her spare time she travels with her family and enjoys her grandchildren. Visit Linda's website at www.lindasittig.com, or email her at linda@lindasittig.com. Her monthly blog pays tribute to women of the past who led extraordinary lives but did not necessarily achieve lasting fame: www.strongwomeninhistory.wordpress.com. Find her on Twitter: @lhsittig. Her motto is...*Every woman deserves to have her story told.*

FREEDOM FORGE PRESS

About Us

Freedom Forge Press, LLC, was founded to celebrate freedom and the spirit of the individual. The founders of the press believe that when people are given freedom—of expression, of speech, of thought, of action—creativity and achievement will flourish.

Freedom Forge Press publishes general fiction, historical fiction, nonfiction, and genres like science fiction and fantasy. Freedom Forge Press's two imprints, Bellows Books and Apprentice Books, publish works for younger readers.

Find out more at www.FreedomForgePress.com.

Made in the USA
Middletown, DE
02 December 2014